Awaken Destiny

James Holden-White

New Generation **Publishing**

(For my Girls: Kelly, Sophie and Kate)

Chapter One – The Twins

Jessica Finch was excited. She'd been looking forward to this school trip and today was both her fourteenth birthday and the first day of the school summer holidays. Her twin brother, Max, had forfeited his own seat on the coach through various misdemeanours accumulated during the term, and though Jess was missing him already she still fully intended to enjoy herself during the four day West Country tour.

The coach had rumbled out of Bath that morning and the usual formal school atmosphere had been left behind with the books in the classroom. Both Mr Jarvis, the head of the Geography department and Miss Davies, the History teacher, who was also Jess' and Max's head of year, seemed much more relaxed than usual and it was rubbing off on the thirty children in their care.

Mr Jarvis was a tall, stern-looking, silver-haired man who always insisted on wearing a tweed jacket despite the fact that the staff had no set dress code, and secretly Jess had always been rather frightened of him. Though of course she would never admit this to her fellow students (least of all Max), and she'd been surprised when he'd allowed Gemma Biggs to play her own music over the coach's sound system. Now his usual strict demeanour and stern no-nonsense temperament appeared to have been replaced by a much more relaxed and more approachable figure with a big smile on his face and a large bag of boiled sweets which he kept offering around the coach to stop anyone feeling queasy. Jess was greatly reassured to see this other side to the Geography teacher and said as much to Abi Saunders sitting next to her.

"Well it's the end of term for them too," Abi pointed out. "It's the start of his holiday as well as ours, and he's probably being paid extra for leading this trip."

This all made perfect sense to Jess, and Abi, delighted by Mr Jarvis's abandonment of familiar classroom discipline, took full advantage of the teacher's backs being turned at the front of the coach by flicking the ears of Johnny Norris who sat in front of them, much to her own amusement.

"Pass it on," Abi said quickly as Johnny turned around, but before he could say anything.

Johnny did so, and the girls leant forward to watch the progress of the 'Mexican ear flick' as it worked its way down the coach towards Miss Davies, who sat behind the driver. Somewhat predictably, when Tammy Smith flicked Brendan Johnson's ear the movement came to an

5

end, one seat before the teacher. Brendan - a timid, chubby boy, who had landed the seat behind the teacher by default, having observed the courtesy of queuing quietly whilst the others had all jostled for position on embarkation - clearly couldn't summon the courage to flick the teacher's ear, holiday or no holiday.

Their classmates quickly tuned in to the joke, and passed first pinches and then hair-pulls down the coach, fully conscious that each niggle would end with Brendan Johnson, who all considered too cowardly to pass the chastisement forward, (though truthfully none of them would have done so in his place). The sniggering soon alerted the attention of Mr Jarvis who, looking slightly irritable, kept turning round to try and see what was going on.

Brendan, realising that he had provided his classmates with an opportunity too good to miss, had initially turned round and grinned, but now as they fully exploited it he started looking round with an expression of thorough annoyance on his face that he had to be the butt of the joke that all the others were sharing. He tried to pass things back, but Tammy and Freddie Giles kept sitting right back out of his range and Jess reflected in her own mind what a strange mentality it was that being hurt in this way was fine, so long as you could then inflict it on another. She sympathised with Brendan as he had no such outlet, but in truth she felt really sorry for him; he seemed so often to be the butt of class jokes.

When Toby Barnes sent a head slap down the coach from the back, and Lizzie Taylor slapped Tammy's head a little too loudly, Mr Jarvis obviously decided that a little distraction was necessary to prevent the rowdy bunch of teenagers getting out of hand.

"Right, people," he spoke over the microphone. "Can we... Ah, yes," he continued as the driver switched the music off. "We are now approaching Cheddar Gorge. Now I'm sure you've all heard of Cheddar because that's where the cheese comes from, and we're going to do a bit of cheese-tasting later this morning, but how many of you know about the gorge?" A few hands went up, as well they should; they were not too far from home and many of the kids had been down this road before. "Good. A gorge, as you know, is a steep-sided ravine," Mr Jarvis continued, "but who knows how this gorge was formed?"

Brendan Johnson, clearly delighted by the respite of the torment that was being tweaked repeatedly with your classmate's eyes upon you, unable to respond, put his hand up.

"Yes, Brendan," Mr Jarvis looked down at him, keen to discover how much of his subject the children had grasped.

"A river valley," Brendan ventured with an absence of confidence in his tone.

"Half right," Mr Jarvis responded. "Half right, Brendan, it is a result of water and rivers are often to be found where a gorge has been, but this valley, this steep-sided gorge, was actually caused during the ice age." Mr Jarvis adopted a theatrical tone. "Imagine a huge glacier of ice rolling slowly over thousands of years down this valley." Jessica did her best.

"The glacier literally gouged this gorge out of the earth as it moved," he continued. "It's a staggering phenomenon really, isn't it? I mean, imagine the power of this juggernaut carving its way slowly, ever so slowly, through the earth. Scraping out a deep gorge like this as it went, tearing out earth and rock, changing the landscape for ever."

"Wow," said Abi in a sarcastic voice.

"Yes," Mr Jarvis continued enthusiastically, "unstoppable."

"Until the weather warmed up a bit," Abi chipped in quietly. Jess and several others sniggered.

"Um, yes," Mr Jarvis now appeared a little deflated, but he recovered himself quickly, he was a man with a passion for his subject. "How right you are, and well-observed, Miss Saunders. Admittedly this glacier did melt eventually, and there aren't many glaciers left to see in the world today. Sadly, as world temperatures continue to soar they are all disappearing, global warming will do for them all eventually I fear..." He stood a moment in silent reflection. "Well, we'll be in Cheddar soon, and then on to the caverns at Wookey Hole this afternoon." Mr Jarvis put the microphone down, confident that order had been restored to the coach.

Jessica, much as she enjoyed Abi mocking the teacher's enthusiasm, could not deny that the gorge was impressive. They drove right down it, twisting narrowly through the sheer walls of rock which rose vertically on every side to loom menacingly above them. As she sat back to appreciate the view she could hear Miss Davies, now on her feet, lamenting loudly that Johnny Norris was more interested in playing games on his mobile phone than in looking out at the scenery.

As Jess looked up and behind herself she could see a group of men up on the top of the cliff to her right. She thought they looked like workmen or engineers as they wore florescent jackets and had a tripod with them, like the kind she'd seen the surveyors using when they had measured up before digging up the road outside her house last Easter.

"What do you think they're doing?" Jess pointed them out for Abi's benefit.

"Who cares?" Abi replied. "They're probably a bunch of Geography teachers on a field trip. Fascinating phenomenon, this gorge," she said, in a poor imitation of Mr Jarvis, and as the coach took a hard right hand bend around the rugged cliff the workmen were lost from sight.

"Abi, did you actually want to come on this school trip?" Jess asked her. "After all, it's really a combination of History and Geography, and you hate both those subjects."

"Well maybe," Abi replied. "Actually I hate all subjects. But it's a good chance to get away from my baby brother for a few days, isn't it? And we should have some time on the beach when we get to Cornwall."

"Yeah, looking at sand and seaweed, Abi. I don't think there's going to be much time for sunbathing."

"Well, who knows what you might find on a beach." Abi smiled.

"Crabs?" Jess looked confused. "Shells?"

"And other more interesting creatures." Abi's smile continued to spread across her face into a mischievous grin. "Who knows, there might be some gorgeous surfer hunks out there on the waves in their wet suits."

"Abi," Jess sounded shocked. "It's a school trip."

"You're such a square," Abi teased her in a deliberately loud voice so that several rows in front could hear.

"Oh, well, perhaps we'll be lucky," Jess tried to recover some credibility. "But the nearest thing we'll probably get to that is old Jarvis getting his scuba gear on." Both girls pulled faces of disgust.

"Shame your brother isn't here," Abi mused, "I'd like to see him in a wet suit."

"Ew!" Jess contorted her face further.

"Oh come on, Jess, he so fancies me - how couldn't he?"

"Well, he hasn't said anything."

"Well, he's probably just embarrassed," replied Abi confidently, "most boys are at this age, aren't they?" She spoke as if she were an authority on such matters.

"Well let's hope for some surfers anyway," Jess changed the subject.

"And that old Jarvis keeps his clothes on."

Jess grinned back at her friend and sat back to enjoy the Somerset countryside.

That same day Jessica's mother, Patricia, had decided to take her son up to London for the day to try and make up for his missing the school trip. Max had chosen Madame Tussauds waxwork museum and the Tower of London as the two attractions he wanted to visit and as they sat together on the train his mother, who saw the outing as a good opportunity for some maternal bonding, was vigilantly studying her London tourist map.

"Now Maxie, I've pre-ordered the tickets, but Madame Tussauds is quite a way from the Tower of London, we'll have to take the tube."

"Mum," Max interrupted her, quite adverse to displays of motherly affection.

"What?"

"You know I don't like being called Maxie."

"Oh don't be silly, darling. Whoever's going to think anything of it? I mean, all I want to do is spoil my darling boy on his birthday."

"Mum, that's enough. There are loads of people on this train. Please, try not to embarrass me today."

"But..."

"Please, Mum. You're always embarrassing me in public, I won't want to go anywhere with you if you just keep embarrassing me. It's just plain Max, okay?"

"Of course, Maxwell darling."

Max was infuriated, it was as if his mother was doing this on purpose. "Mum, I'm fourteen now, I'm not a little boy anymore."

His mother looked disappointed and replied abruptly, "Well you'll always be my little boy."

"Argh!" Max grabbed his blonde hair with both hands in frustration, but his mother ignored him.

Patricia Finch handed the map to her son and addressed him formally. "Right, Mr Max, if we go to the Tower of London first, we could hop out at Westminster before we go on to the waxworks and have a quick look at the Houses of Parliament on the way."

Max thought this sounded boring and said so. "Why do we have to go there?"

"Well it is the most famous part of London, darling, that's where Big Ben is and everything."

On principle Max was not keen. If his mother ever expressed an interest in anywhere Max knew from bitter experience that he would soon be getting dragged around a tedious museum or art gallery and into the embrace of mind-numbing boredom. But she did look excited, and he didn't remember ever having heard Big Ben before.

"Okay," he conceded. "We can go there for a bit, just for a quick look, but we aren't going in anywhere." Mrs Finch, sensing a small victory, reached into her bag and retrieved her newspaper. "Is Westminster anywhere near Lords?" Max asked curiously after a pause.

"Oh, no I don't think so darling, hope you're not disappointed." His mother, likewise, regarded the prospect of a full day in the capital watching cricket as a day of high potential utterly wasted.

"Is it anywhere near where Dad works?"

"Well yes, he normally works for the Foreign Office, but he's attached to the European Commissioners at the moment and their office is somewhere near here. I feel sorry for him, having to do this journey every day."

"Who are the European Commissioners anyway? I thought he works in the Civil Service."

"Well he does, Max - you see, all Civil Servants work for the Government in one way or another."

"Well yeah, but you said European." Impatient with his mother and irritated by her vagueness, Max stretched the point.

"Well, you see, the European Commission is a group of very senior politicians who are appointed from each European Union country, darling. They are meant to be the real experts and have lots of very important responsibilities."

"And dad works for them?"

"Well, Britain's Commissioners, yes, Max."

"So what does he actually do?"

"Oh, well I suppose it must be really important, top secret, he can't really talk about it."

"Mum!" Max's patience was being stretched to the limit. It was, he reflected, so hard sometimes to get a straight answer out of his mother. "Do you know what he actually does or not?"

"Well your guess is as good as mine Maxwell. But the Commissioners are really important. I'm sure whatever Daddy does is really important." She began to speculate in ignorance. "I expect he helps draft legislation, make up policies..."

"Mum, got to stop you there," Max put his hands up, "you're boring me now."

"Um, looking forward to seeing the crown jewels?" Patricia Finch changed the subject from her husband's work, though in truth Max's persistence was exhausting her. She found it very frustrating when he cut her off in mid-flow; Jessica never did that.

"Yeah, I s'pose," Max replied unenthusiastically. "But I'm more looking forward to the dungeons, really. Oh, and the chamber of horrors at Madame Tussauds, of course."

"Humph! Boys," Patricia huffed to herself.

The children re-boarded the coach after their stop at the cheese museum, with the taste of many a mature cheddar sample still in the mouth. Jess, who usually enjoyed dairy food, was not so keen on having the strong taste lingering on the tongue halfway through the morning.

"That cheese was minging," exclaimed Abi Saunders as she made for the same seat she had sat in on the initial journey. "I really didn't... Hey, Brendan, what are you doing in my seat?"

"S'not your seat," Brendan defended himself. "Just cause you've had it once doesn't mean you can have it for the rest of the trip."

"I'm sitting there," Abi was unyielding. "Tell him I'm sitting there, Tomo," she appealed to Thomas Lydon, who sat between Nick Bovis and Mark Thompson in the same seats they had themselves previously occupied across the very rear of the bus.

"Shift, Brendan," said Tomo simply; he was one of the biggest boys in the class and his tone did not suggest the issue was open to further argument.

To Jess it really didn't matter who sat where but it was clearly a big deal to Abi, who stood with arms folded and mouth open, feeling unjustly wronged and wanting the whole bus to pressure the usurper out of what she saw as her own rightful seat.

"Well, you might have been sitting here earlier," Brendan fought his corner, "but you weren't sitting here just now when I got on."

"Look, I left my bag there." Abi protested. "Tell him, Jess, tell him I left my bag there."

Jess didn't see the point of arguing and was happy to concede the seats. "Pass my bag Brendan," she said gently.

"No, Jess," Abi wouldn't let it go. "Tell him Tommo, tell him I baggsied that seat," she protested.

"I'm not sitting back up the front so you lot can all keep passing flicks and slaps towards me," Brendan persisted in his defence.

"Brendan," Tommo Lydon spoke even more forcefully this time, "the girls were sitting there. Move."

"No, Tommo, I'll have my say," Brendan continued bravely. "Just because I'm not cool like you three, just because I don't rush to the back of the coach - there's no rules about it, she's not entitled, I'll sit where I want."

Jess could not help but be impressed - though she would never like to admit it if anyone got bullied in her class it was probably tubby, wheezy Brendan Johnson, never far from his inhaler when the class did PE - and it was great to see him standing up for himself. "Come on Abi," she spoke as calmly as she could, "we can sit anywhere."

But Abi was furious. "Now look, Brendan, I'll...."

"What's going on here?" Miss Davies was a large woman in her late twenties, and as she tried to make her way speedily down the coach she bounced off the seats to left and right, waddling with difficulty along the narrow aisle. "Honestly," she huffed as she drew nearer, "I thought we could have a little peace on day one at least."

"He's in my seat Miss," Abi proclaimed the injustice.

"Gosh, am I going to have to seat you at your age?" asked Miss Davies despairingly, but her mind was made up. "Right, there will be no set places on this coach," she announced in a loud voice for the benefit of all aboard. "You will all have to sit in a different place every time you get on, and when you get off you will take all your rubbish and other stuff with you. Might even keep the coach a bit tidier that way," she added under her breath. "Otherwise I'll have to sit you next to people at my own discretion."

"But Miss," Abi continued, "we've got to be able to leave our stuff on the seats."

"No you don't, Abigail, everything should be stored up above in the overhead storage or in your bags under the coach, otherwise it's an accident risk. It's a security risk too to leave your possessions on display."

"Miss…"

"Not another word, Abigail. Any more and you can come and sit up at the front between myself and Mr Jarvis."

The battle won, Brendan smiled to himself as he looked silently out of the window; the empty space beside him might reflect his lack of popularity, but it certainly created a welcome buffer from unwelcome fingers. He would at least be guaranteed a short respite from the flack Abi was inevitably going to throw at him again as soon as the short journey was over.

Miss Davies huffed as she waddled awkwardly back towards the front of the coach, twisting her body half to the side as she passed each set of seats, and straightening up as she passed through each gap like an enormous footballer going through some warm-up drills in slow motion.

Jessica quickly seated herself a few seats forward and on the other side of the aisle, and threw an apologetic look at Becky Stiles and Victoria Todd who had been sitting there. No explanation was needed as they had all heard Miss Davies' judgement on the matter.

"Thanks, Brendan," said Abi sarcastically, and just loud enough for those around her to hear, once Miss Davies had retaken her seat at the front.

"Yeah, thanks Abi," said Victoria and Becky together as they moved further up the coach to find themselves new seats.

"What?" Abi protested to Jess with a gawping mouth once everyone seemed to have settled down.

"Oh let it go, Abi, it's really no big deal."

"That Brendan Johnson," she continued under her breath, "he's always causing trouble, the fat little toe-rag."

"Oh come on now, Abi, that just isn't true... And anyway he's right, isn't he? I mean no one has the right to any particular seat. We wouldn't have been happy if we were stuck at the front behind big Davies and old Jarvis now would we?"

"Eerrough!" Abi had one hand over her nose now and was frantically waving the other in front of her face.

"What?"

"Your breath, eugh... It's all cheesy, errh, ough." She gesticulated as she pretended to gag for fresh air.

"Well I have just been eating cheese," Jess stated the obvious with a little impatience, "we all have. Not to be funny, Abi, but we've just been in a cheese museum... remember?"

Unpleasant though it was to have someone draw attention to it, Jess had to admit that the taste in her mouth was getting a bit stale, and now rather self-conscious that her breath might indeed be rather smelly she decided to waste no time in getting something to take away the taste and freshen her mouth when they next stopped.

"Yeah but, ugh," Abi continued relentlessly. "I didn't have any, I hate cheese."

"Oh yes," Jess remembered. When the sample plates had been passed round Abi had recoiled away as if the plates contained some kind of poisonous and highly toxic substance. "You didn't have any, did you?"

"No, but fat Brendan did didn't he? He was guzzling it down his fat throat, wasn't he? Must have been getting hungry. Must have been at least twenty minutes since he last had a snack."

"Abi," Jess tried again, "you go on at Brendan too much. Come on, let it go... Oh," she changed the subject, "should be some good fudge when we get to Devon, my mum said I should bring her some back."

"Yeah," Abi finally appeared distracted, "like fudge, I do. Hate cheese, like fudge... I Bet Brendan likes..."

"Abi, no!"

The coach continued twisting its way through the patchwork of crops and pasture land.

It was not a long journey to their next destination, but when the coach pulled up in the car park at Wookey Hole caves, the children, whose ears had been relentlessly battered by Mr Jarvis's in-depth briefing on

13

the impressive geographical nature of the huge network of underground caverns, felt as if they had already been through them a hundred times.

Mr Jarvis ordered them off the coach, and Miss Davis organised the children into a line to approach the ticket booth. Once through the barrier they formed a huddle round a big basket of hard hats, and like a group of vultures pecking violently at a carcass, a flurry of hands dipped into it, seeking headgear which they thought would fit and discarding anything they believed would not by dropping them straight back in to the turbulent basket before snatching out another. Jess thought she kept picking the same one out, as each time she put it back someone else would grab it and then throw it back in. She finally chose one and took a few paces away from the basket to join Becky and Abi who stood together, pulling faces of disgust.

"Ugh," Becky announced to anyone who would listen, "this one's got hairs trapped in it."

"Oh," Abi chipped in, "and this one's all greasy."

"What's the matter, girls?" asked Mr Jarvis, his own hard hat, chin-strap and all, already fastened. Jess noticed that he had also taken the precaution of tucking his trousers into his socks to avoid getting them wet in the damp cave, a measure which made him look quite ridiculous.

"Don't know who's been wearing these, Sir," Abi whinged.

"Yeah, could have been someone with lice or something," Becky added.

"Oh, don't be so pathetic," Mr Jarvis, worn down by the bickering on the bus was no longer in such good spirits. "One size fits all for heaven's sake, you just have to adjust them. Now put a hat on each or you won't be allowed in the caverns."

"Suits me," Abi challenged him.

"Now, Abigail, don't be so silly," Mr Jarvis's patience was at breaking point. "We've already come a long way to go into these caves, they are enormously intriguing and it would be terrible if you missed out."

"Why do we have to wear these stupid hats anyway?" Becky would not be easily won over.

"Because," said Mr Jarvis sternly, "if you bang your head on a stalactite you will know about it, especially if one falls on you. Now pick one out and put it on. I know they won't always be the best fit, but as I say, they are adjustable, and we'll just have to make do."

"Right, if you would all just wait here another minute or so," their guide interrupted them. "Sorry to keep you, but we just have to get a VIP visitor out of the caves, and then we can all go in."

"Ohhh!" The group let out a collective sigh; they had already been waiting ten minutes. But Abi wasn't listening. "Wish he'd fall on one of his precious stalactites," she muttered to Jess. "Then he'd know about it!"

"Stalagmites, maybe. They are the ones that grow upwards."

"Er, yes, thank you Brendan.... Ugh..." She tutted at his interruption. "Stalagmites then, whatever. I wish he'd impale himself on one anyway, we'd see if he was still so fascinated by them then."

"Well he might lose a little of his admiration for them," Jess giggled having attempted an impression of the teacher, "but Abi, that's a bit harsh."

"Well he did go on and on during the journey. Water formations this, and mineral deposits that. Precipitation, erosion, underground waterways, build ups of this that and the other, I mean it's just rocks and water, isn't it?"

"Yeah, well I know what you mean," Jess conceded "I feel like I've got stalactites coming out of my ears..."

"Ugh," Abi cut in cruelly. "Your breath still stinks, you know."

"Thank you, Abi." Jess tried to stay calm, but was getting increasingly frustrated with her friend continuously mentioning it at top volume. "Look, if we've got a minute I might just go to that kiosk over there and see if I can get some gum or something."

Jess got permission from Miss Davies, who said it would be fine so long as she was quick, but then refused Tomo Lydon the same privilege. "I don't want you all wandering off," Jess heard her explain, "it'll be hard enough not to lose any of you in the caves."

"So who's the VIP, Sir?" Jess heard Tammy Smith ask Mr Jarvis in an excited voice as she walked away from the group.

"Oh, I haven't the faintest idea," he replied. "Now, who knows how long it takes a stalactite to grow six inches?"

Jess reached the kiosk and bought a packet of mints. She shoved two straight into her mouth and turned quickly to return to her classmates, but a group of men, some in smart suits, now gathered in her way. They stood together in a crude semi-circle of grins posing for a photograph, and to avoid spoiling the picture Jess held back for a moment.

Her attention was caught by the sinister-looking man in the middle. He had dark hair, oiled back, and a put-on, sarcastic-looking smile. His narrow eyes were also really close together, and as he held the fixed expression for the photograph he almost appeared to be sneering at the camera. It didn't look quite right to Jess; the smart suit and shiny black shoes didn't go with the white hard hat he wore on his head, but the expression on his face didn't seem to fit either. He smiled with none of the sincerity of the others in the picture and in truth, he looked bored.

The other suited males had all pandered around him, jostling for positions around his personage, and unlike himself they seemed to be filled with genuine enthusiasm. These, she assumed, had to be the management team for the caverns, and no doubt the snap was to be a keepsake for the office wall, or perhaps they were hoping to get in the paper.

Even the guides in their caving gear seemed to have been able to make themselves available for the photo. Jess spotted their own guide, who far from 'getting the VIP out of the caves,' was grinning like a monkey on the fringes. He was one of the lucky ones - most of the track-suited workplace staff had been forced to take up positions at the back where they could barely be seen behind their office-bound colleagues - but nonetheless they still looked proud to be in moderate proximity to the sneering personage in the middle.

The picture taken, the silence was broken, and the man in the middle, though he relaxed his face, still appeared to Jess to be sneering sarcastically. The assembled group broke up quickly, and the two men who had been most central to the picture began to talk.

"Well, it has been an honour to have you with us today, Mr Dredmor," said a smart, suited man who Jess though had to be a senior manager. "I hope you enjoyed your visit."

The VIP led the man aside, but they remained in Jessica's earshot as the rest of the group continued to disperse.

"Oh please," the sneering one responded. Jess could see that he was thin with a very thin face, and he wasted no time in removing his hard hat. "Just call me Commissioner, or Sir Morgan, I mean it's really up to you."

"Oh of course, Sir Morgan," the other continued in a grovelling tone, "and excellent that you have been able to see for yourself the fine work that we do here. I mean, I know sustainable tourism has been high on the national agenda for some time and we really need to encourage our European neighbours to come to Britain, and especially the West Country, and I hope we can encourage a little investment..." His face contorted into an enquiring and hopeful smile which made him closely resemble a dog hoping for a tasty morsel to be dropped from the table. The VIP just blanked him. "An investment to make our little project sustainable..." he begged again with imploring eyes, having gleaned no reaction from the personage.

"Yes well, the thing is Mr, umm..."

"Twistle."

"Mr Twistle," the VIP looked ever so slightly twitchy, "as

Commissioner with the environmental directorate I am really more concerned with environmentally friendly policies, you see. Tourism, well, it really isn't my bag."

"But..."

"Now, now, just hold on," he waved the Manager to silence. "In Europe our cousins are much more alerted to the dangers of pollution. All businesses, all industry, all tourist and leisure attractions must also share in that concern, must take steps to..."

"Oh, but we have," the other interrupted desperately. "We've got our own wind turbine, we've installed solar panels, we've never been so green. But we need to encourage more visitors so as to boost the coffers and plough it back into the infrastructure, the main aim..."

"Mr Twistle, please." The VIP raised a finger to demand silence once more. "Spare me the management speak, I am no stranger to it. More visitors you say, yet can you handle what you have at the moment?"

"Well, of course we..."

"Mr Twistle, please stop interrupting," and it seemed to Jess most unfair, for he had after all just asked the site manager a question and now seemed opposed to letting him answer it. Instead the VIP turned dramatically and pointed at an overflowing litter bin. "The waste your visitors are already creating here, for example." He let this hang in the air a moment. "It's staggering, and the more people who come here the worse it will become. Where there are people, Mr Twistle, rubbish will be generated. The cities, well..." He left it unsaid.

"But we have plans to cater for..."

"The cities overflow with rubbish, Mr Twistle." The VIP seemed to have acquired a new energy. "We must clear these up, but at what cost to the country...." His voice had adopted a cold tone as he spoke, and again he left his last words hanging in the air.

"But surely you must agree we need to encourage eco-tourism, Sir Morgan?" The manager was desperate. "Surely there is some grant, some availability in the budget?"

"We must clean up Europe, Mr Twistle; it's a tall order, and in any case I thought I had made it clear, tourism budgets are most certainly not my mandate." Jess saw the manger's face fall, his hopes were clearly dashed and he had now to be fully aware that he wasn't going to get any help out of the influential visitor. "Now then," the personage enquired, "what capacity of tunnels do you have down there? What's the extent of the network, I mean?"

"I fail to see what relevance that has to Europe's environmental policy," Twistle went on the defensive. Childishly, it seemed the manager, having not got what he hoped for, was going to refuse to satisfy the visitor's curiosity in turn.

Jess saw a change come over the visitor as he rose to the challenge; his eyes seemed to narrow yet further into vicious slits and ice cold aggression came into his voice. "Need I remind you, Mr Twistle, that under regulation seventeen/sixty two as a member of the European Commission I have an investigative power to demand information from any Member State, let alone an individual such as yourself?"

Twistle made no attempt at a reply, he appeared dumbfounded by the forcefulness of the others approach, and the speaker once again just let the question hang in the air a moment before continuing. When he did it was in a much warmer and reassuring tone, as if Twistle, a naughty child who had been sternly told off, was now to be offered comforting.

"However, in this case I am merely asking a civil question. I have been impressed with what I have seen today," - his cold tone had become a sincere and flattering one - "and I ask as would any interested visitor."

"Oh, I see." The change of approach ensured co-operation and the manager swelled with pride, as he had in the photo, as he boasted of the attraction in his care. "There are hundreds of miles of caverns down there, a huge volume of subterranean space. I mean some are flooded of course, and there are still several miles undiscovered or so the estimates...."

"Excellent," the VIP interrupted, again appearing satisfied.

"But you see, Commissioner, we encourage all sorts - look." He pointed to Jess, who having seen her tour guide making his way back towards her group was keen to rejoin them so she wouldn't get left behind. "We even get school groups, it's very educational, got to bring up the youngsters to respect the environment haven't we?" He was desperately trying to recover something. "Couldn't you at least talk to whoever it is who does hold the tourism purse strings?"

"Mr Twistle, I really..."

But Twistle had taken Jess by the arm and wasn't about to let the Commissioner silence him again whilst there was a publicity opportunity presenting itself. "You, girl," he virtually ordered her, "come and be in a quick photo, just you, me and the Commissioner."

"Oh, I don't know," Jess felt uncertain, "I've got to get back..."

"Ah, just a quick photo, it won't take a second, come on - I insist. This is the European Commissioner, Sir Morgan Dredmor, you know, he's very important, and he's come to visit us today. Come on, we need you in it, you're the future my dear."

As the manager gestured frantically at the photographer, a glance over her shoulder told Jess that her group was about to be led into the caverns, and with reluctance she posed quickly for the photo. As she did so she felt a cold shudder down her spine as the thin sneering man stood behind her put both hands on her shoulders. She felt incredibly uncomfortable, sensed a great feeling of mistrust, but in a passing moment, and with a quick flash of teeth the photo was taken and she stepped away from him.

"Have you enjoyed the caverns, young lady?" Twistle asked her, keen that the Commissioner would hear her response.

"Look, I haven't been down yet," she replied quickly. "I really don't want to be rude but my group are about to go in and I don't want to be left behind."

"Of course, of course my dear, and what a treat awaits you," Twistle apologised. "You mustn't let us keep you." He turned his back on Jess dismissively; she had served her purpose. "Now, Commissioner…"

"Thank you, Mr Twistle," the reply was blunt, "but I really have to go too."

"But you haven't seen the cafeteria, the gift shop…"

"No time," he said firmly, "I've seen what I came for," and as the manager once again looked completely dejected, Jess couldn't help but feel sorry for him.

"Rindburn." Sir Morgan Dredmor beckoned to another dark-suited male, with prominent teeth, who Jess assumed must be one of the entourage who accompanied the Commissioner on such visits.

"Sir," the suited man responded immediately. He almost snapped to attention when his name was called, and as he approached his master he removed his own hard hat to reveal a bald head.

"Do we have the result of the gorge survey?"

"Not yet, Sir Morgan, but I think you will be impressed with the capacity." Rindburn grinned smugly, his teeth sticking out yet further from his mouth.

"Good." Sir Morgan turned and walked towards his shiny black chauffeured vehicle, Rindburn trotting at his heels like an obedient dog. As he passed Mr Twistle the manager of the caverns offered his hand in the hopes he could bid the VIP a good journey, but Sir Morgan totally ignored the attempt and thwarted it further by thrusting his hard hat into the outstretched hand of his host as he passed him.

Jess returned to her group just in time to avoid the guide's predictable lecture on safety and the importance of keeping together, and joined the tail end of the group as they entered the caves. She had no intention of getting left alone in the dark wet caverns deep below the ground in any case, and she made sure that she kept a steady footing as she moved through the impressive cavern network. Inside she was impressed by the size of some of the chambers, and even Abi stopped chunttering when they entered the witches cavern.

Max had been right, he'd enjoyed the dungeons best, just as he'd expected. His mother had said how perverse it was that boys seemed to enjoy torture chambers so much, and had then bored Max for what seemed like hours staring with a similar awe at the crown jewels. After a lengthy wait, which Max considered totally unjustified, they had finally got into the Tower of London's most secure attraction. Max had given them a quick look, and had walked back out, which he had thought sufficient. But Patricia Finch, who had also bought the guide book while they were in the queue, and clearly knew exactly what they were going to see long before they actually saw it, was now irritating her son by going on about the jewels and how beautiful and special they were.

In frustration, Max seated himself on a bench in the Tower Courtyard; he'd been on his feet in the queue long enough. "They're just silly rocks mum, shiny rocks on a bit of gold, I don't see how it's such a big deal."

"Gemstones, Maxwell, beautifully polished and mounted." She looked down at the tiny diamond stud in her own engagement ring. Mounted as it was on a delicate twist of silver and positioned next to her golden wedding ring on her finger, it just looked minuscule in comparison.

Her son caught her glimpsing at it. "How much would that've cost?"

"I have no idea, Maxwell Finch," she replied, quite taken aback by her son's impertinence. "It's the thought that counts, and anyway, your father bought me this ring eighteen years ago, prices were all very different then."

"Well, if it's the thought that counts I'm surprised you can't remember."

"I wish you'd stop being so grumpy, darling, I really do. Now I know jewels are girly, but just think about what you just saw, I mean those jewels are priceless. Just think about how much they might cost - now, that has to make you impressed, surely?"

"Yeah, I s'pose," he reflected, but a mischievous glint flashed in his eye. "But if they are priceless, how can I think how much they cost?"

"Alright, clever-clogs," his mother sighed. "Have it your way. Honestly," She shook her head in mock despair and tutted to herself. Oh well, she thought, he's a grumpy teenager, a grumpy teenage boy, what's more. It had to be inevitable that he would clash with his mother from time to time. It just upset her a bit that her son so often came across as ungrateful, and that he'd begun to snap at her whenever she expressed an interest in what he was up to, or where he was going, simple matters she still believed she had every right to be fully informed about. She sighed again. She had to put it down to all being a part of growing up, 'the teenage rebellion' one of her friends had called it, as much a battle for the parents as the children, and she seated herself next to him and wondered how her daughter was getting on at the other end of the country.

Max for his part knew he wasn't making things very easy, but he just found his mother so interfering, so nosy. She seemed to be constantly pestering him, and when he did spend time with her he always felt she was molly-codling him, treating him like the little boy he just wasn't anymore. In truth he knew he carried a bit of a chip on his shoulder about how much better his mother and his sister seemed to get on and it frustrated him that his hard-working father was so rarely available to spend time with him uniquely, in order that he could enjoy a similar relationship with his dad.

He wasn't jealous of Jess, and he knew any slight resentment was entirely unfair as Jess always made a big effort with him, and chose to spend more of her available time in their mother's company than he did. His sister's closeness to his mother was not born out of favouritism, but out of the simple fact that Jess chose to spend more time helping her round the house and less time shut in her bedroom playing video games than he did. Right now he knew he had the chance to mend a few bridges with his mum, a chance to bond with her, but it was so hard; he had to question himself, did he have the willingness to really put in the effort? He knew that the opportunity was there, but it was so hard not to get grumpy when she managed to embarrass him so easily and so frequently. He knew she meant well and didn't do it deliberately, but he just wished she would think things through a bit more before she said them.

"Come on Maxie-well, er, Max, darling," his mother quickly corrected her mistake in front of a small horde of paddle-footed Japanese tourists who were pit pattering slowly along behind their tour guide, who carried an open umbrella over her head even though it wasn't raining. "What about a picture of you in front of that Beefeater."

The Yeoman Warder, one of the guardians of the Tower and an ex-soldier, who in the world of the civilian would be addressed as Mr Joseph Banks, stood tall in his full regalia, with his tunic, tights and long pole-axe like weapon in hand, and Patricia Finch thought it would make a good photo opportunity. "Go on, it'll be a good one, I'll send a copy to granny."

Max wasn't listening; instead he was watching intently as a big, black, bird hopped along the ground towards the bench he was sitting on. "What's that big crow doing?"

"Oh, that's a raven," replied his mother, quickly taking a picture of the bird and her son together before he could object.

"Mum," he responded in annoyance, "you know I hate being photographed."

"Oh but that was a nice one, darling, granny will love that one."

"I think he's after the rubbish in that bin there," Max was transfixed.

"Yes it's quite possible, they are scavenging birds ravens, though I'm sure they get properly fed here."

"Why would they bother feeding them?" Max asked, though it was clear they obviously did. There were several old ravens hopping about in the castle courtyards and if pickings were thin, he thought, they would have quickly moved on.

"Well, they feed them in order to keep them here, I suppose," his mother attempted a considered reply.

"But why would they want to keep them here?"

"I really don't know, darling. It's a tradition - there have always been ravens here at the Tower of London, they're part of its heritage. I guess the Beefeaters just don't want them to leave."

Max studied the strange animal. It was an odd-looking bird, much bigger than a crow, and with a chunky, powerful-looking black beak too. It seemed to cock its head to one side as it looked at him, and it didn't seem so much scared of him as curious. "I think he just wants to get close to that bit of sandwich that someone has dropped on the floor by that bin over there. He's just trying to work out if I'm going to go for it too, or whether I'm going to chase him off it."

The raven swept forward in one great bound and a mighty flap of its wings and seized the bread in one movement. Max, taken by surprise, leapt back, and as the raven flapped and hopped away his mother couldn't help teasing him.

"Looks like he chased you off," she chortled insensitively.

"Yeah well you'd jump," he defended himself, "if you'd just had that great beak coming at you." He felt embarrassed. A number of Japanese in the group huddled around their tour guide seemed to be sharing a joke, and Max just hoped it wasn't at his expense.

"Right, well let's go and look at Traitor's Gate," his mother spoke quickly - sensing her son's mood, she for once seemed to be displaying some tact by changing the subject and sparing him any further embarrassment. "It's where the prisoners were brought in from the Thames."

"Yeah okay," Max rose to his feet, "as long as we can have a look at that tower where Raleigh's ghost is supposed to be before we go."

"Sir Walter Raleigh, was he locked up here?"

"Oh yes, Mum," Max nodded as he shared his knowledge.

"But I thought he was an explorer. Didn't he bring back loads of stuff from America? I thought he was popular with Queen Elizabeth the first."

"Well he was, but when she died and James the first became King he pissed him off and James locked him up here. His ghost is still supposed to be seen in one of the towers."

Patricia winced at her son's choice of language but consulted her guide book for clarification. "You're right, the Bloody Tower, that one over there," she pointed. "Oh, you are clever, Max," she said proudly.

"Well, we did just do the Tudors and Stuarts in history, Mum, Queen Elizabeth, the Spanish Armada and all that. That's half the point of the school trip Jess has gone on, remember?"

"Well yes, I suppose it is. Well, I'm glad you do sometimes listen at school after all."

They left the bench and made their way to the Traitor's gate first. Mrs Finch deliberately hung back, and as her son passed the smiling Yeoman Warder with his silver whiskers protruding from under his black bonnet she quickly snapped them with her camera. She knew it wouldn't be a great photo as she was walking when she took it, and Max would only be in profile, but her son hadn't noticed and she was delighted to snap the image whilst avoiding further confrontation.

Max noticed a big green information board on the grass by the path which bore a picture of one of the mysterious black ravens on it, and he paused to read the English script underneath. The information was of course repeated in French, Italian, German, Japanese and Hindi for the benefit of other tourists, so there wasn't actually as much to read as it had first appeared.

Just like his mother had said, the information board confirmed that the ravens had intentionally been kept at the Tower for hundreds of years, and that part of the Warder's responsibilities was to feed and look after them. It even informed him that there is a specialist 'Raven-Master' amongst the warders, that the birds were bred at the tower and that the current feathered residents had their wings clipped to prevent them flying off. 'Legend has it,' it declared, 'that if the ravens ever leave the tower both the castle and the kingdom would fall. England should be secure so long as they remain.' The board could not confirm how long the ravens had been in residence, but there was an account cited of King Charles the second being told of the legend, which suggested there had clearly been a tradition in place long before his reign.

"Well, this explains why the raven sort of flapped and hopped away," Max turned to his mother, "they can't actually fly properly. Oops, too late for that," he added, pointing to the writing at the bottom of the information board. 'Please do not feed the ravens' was written in bold characters. "Had that sandwich, didn't he."

"Well I told you they are scavenging birds, if there is food on the ground they will take it. It just shows the importance of putting litter in the bins provided," Patricia Finch reflected. "People generate such a mess these days."

Fast food was not something that Patricia Finch really approved of, but it was her son's birthday, so with the Tower of London behind them, and Madame Tussauds yet to come, they had a burger and chips each before taking the tube to Westminster.

She had of course initially suggested they take a picnic with them on the trip, but Max had made his views on eating a picnic with his mother on a London park bench quite clear. He'd said he wouldn't be seen dead unwrapping his mother's sandwiches in public, and that packed lunches were for primary school kids. "Oh sure, Mum," he'd mocked sarcastically, "I'll just take a lunchbox around London with me, shall I? That'd look good, wouldn't it? Getting out two thick-cut sandwiches, a biscuit bar, a carton drink and a piece of fruit - wouldn't we look like the cool ones?" He'd reasoned that there is no shortage of fast food outlets in the Capital, and that they should get something hot on the run.

His mother, (who deep down had anticipated greasy chips from the outset) had reluctantly agreed, and so it was that with the taste of ketchup and gherkin victory still on the tongue, Max had hopped off the tube at Westminster furious that his mother had taken full advantage of an opportunity to embarrass him by requesting a knife and fork of the spotty youth at the burger service counter in front of everyone. "I mean, who has ever heard of anything so stupid?" he ranted to himself unreasonably as he emerged from the tube station. His mother, still oblivious as to how or why the request had been anything other than perfectly reasonable, had kept quiet on the short journey, hoping Max would finally calm down.

Max soon forgot his annoyance as he emerged into the centre of

London, with the London Eye and all the towering buildings around him he really felt like he was in the middle of it; he had to agree this was spectacular, and he lapped it up. As they passed a statue of Boudicca on the banks of the river by Westminster Bridge, Max noted how the Celtic Queen was depicted standing proudly in defiance within her chariot, and no amount of pigeon poo on her head and shoulders could take the expression of determination off her face. It summed up his mood and made him feel proud to be British.

As they walked a little away from the Houses of Parliament and left the throng of seemingly aimless, camera-toting tourists behind them, they found themselves outside an oppressively large if not beautiful building, and looked back to enjoy the bigger scene.

A side door to the building behind them opened and a group of pompous-looking, smart-suited men spilled out and started moving quickly towards a waiting car with blacked out windows.

A huge, grey-haired, fat man in a pinstriped suit and carrying a shiny briefcase emerged behind them and proceeded towards the car at a much more leisurely pace. Max noted a red and white spotted bow-tie at his throat and in his slow rolling movement he looked incredibly self-important. For someone who to the intents and purposes of the others was supposed to be sneaking out quickly and inconspicuously he appeared to be doing his level best to draw attention to himself, but wrack his brains though he did Max did not recall ever having seen the figure before.

When he finally reached the vehicle, far from leaping in to be whisked away, the fat man totally ignored the waiting chauffeur who held the door open for him, paused, and instead, with aplomb, handed his briefcase to one of those who accompanied him. It was taken by a tall thin man with ginger hair, a huge nose and protruding Adam's apple, who took the case with a flourish and placed it with apparent reverence in the boot of the open vehicle. The fat man stopped and reached into the inside pocket of his suit, from which he pulled out a huge cigar.

"That's one of daddy's bosses, Maxie." His mother sounded excited. "Yes, that's Denis Hitoadie, one of the Commissioners, one of Daddy's bosses, I wonder where he's going."

"I wonder where he's come from." Max was curious. "What is that building? Is this where he works? Is this where Dad works? Do you think Dad might be in there?"

"Honestly, Max, so many questions."

As Max watched, the big fat man, cigar in hand, clicked his fingers impatiently for a light, and the tall, ginger, big-nose aide stepped

25

forward immediately brandishing a silver plated lighter. The tall one flicked his fingers over it several times but the lighter only sparked and failed to ignite, it must have been out of fuel.

"Come on Sludboil, come on," snapped the obese figure impatiently. "See to it quickly man, I haven't all day, eh, what!"

The tall man desperately laboured with the lighter, shook it, and finally it produced the required short burst of flame for the big man to get his huge roll of Cuban tobacco smouldering. Sir Denis Hitoadie glanced at the end, saw the faintest edge of the cigar tip smoking and took two or three mighty puffs on it which soon had the whole tip glowing an angry red. He inhaled greedily as the lanky aide stood by as if ready to satisfy his every whim, but rather than give thanks for his trouble the aide received a huge cloud of blue smoke straight in the face.

With a broad smile of yellow teeth the big man finally, and laboriously, clambered into the open car. The aide looked on with adoring eyes and a grin on his face like the cat that had just got the cream. He shut his master safely inside, beating the chauffeur to it, and scurried round the vehicle to scoot in through the other rear door at great speed, so keen was he not to be left behind. The chauffeur, with a sigh, clambered into the driver's seat, and with a screech of tyres the car sped away. As Max looked on the remaining group of suited aides all seemed to relax rather, and, happy that the big man had finally made his exit, they all turned and walked briskly back indoors.

"Dad works for him?" Max repeated his mother's words, but not with her enthusiasm.

"Oh yes, that's Sir Dennis Hitoadie, the Duke of Man, he's really important, a real Duke. He's one of the Commissioners I told you about, one of the European Commissioners whom Daddy works for."

"Well I can't see Dad wanting to work for him, did you see the way he treated that bloke who lit his cigar?"

"Yes, well. Your father does often say that Sir Morgan and the Duke are both extremely hard to work for, but I don't think he has to follow them around like that, I think he spends most of his time in the office."

"My dad wouldn't stand for that," Max spoke defiantly. "He just looked so rude."

"Well he is a Duke, Max, his seat is the Isle of Man, and he's a knight as well. I suppose he's used to people waiting on him like that, calling him your Grace, acting all formally..."

"Well, I don't like him," Max cut across his mother's almost awestruck tone. "I can't see why he deserves respect just because of who he is."

"Well I suppose you have a point, my little revolutionary," Patricia reflected, "and come to that I don't think your father is overly fond of him, in fact I don't think any of them are. Dad says the Duke always comes back from lunch smelling of gravy and red wine - he says his nickname in the office is the toad."

"Well he certainly looks like a toad, a big fat, lazy, greedy... How did he get to be European Commissioner anyway?" Max was baffled.

"Well, he was a very important Tory politician at one time darling, very influential, I suppose he still is. Dennis Hitoadie was a conservative and Sir Morgan Dredmor, he's the other one, he was a senior Labour politician, and the two of them..."

"Right okay, enough, Mum," Max put his hand up to halt the explanation, "if I wanted to have a lecture on politics I'd take an exam in it. Oh sorry," he added, sensing his mother's annoyance at being cut across once again, "I shouldn't have asked, I'm just not interested."

Max thoroughly enjoyed the waxwork museum and the rest of his trip to London, and no more was said about the fat aristocrat they had sighted in Westminster. But that evening when his father, Julian, finally returned from work to the family home in the little village of Weston-Bissett just outside Bath, his curious son approached him with the question of how he could work for a man like Sir Dennis Hitoadie, Duke of Man.

"Well," Julian Finch responded through mouthfuls of searing hot microwaved supper, for he had been too late to eat with his wife and son. "I don't really have any choice in the matter. The Commissioners are appointed by the Government, and I work for the Commissioner's office at the moment so I just have to work for whoever the Government appoints, it's my job."

"But he just seemed horrible," Max protested, "a big fat bully."

"Well the toad certainly won't let himself starve, you're right there," his father laughed. "But he's not so bad. The other one, Sir Morgan Dredmor, now he is a nasty piece of work. Hitoadie will approach me when it suits him and he likes the occasional laugh and a joke, especially around the lunch table, but Sir Morgan is just so cold with everyone, so intense. If I didn't know better I'd just keep wondering what I've done wrong, wondering if he had it in for me. He was the young Labour whizz kid in his day, he got sacked by the government over some scandal, worked his way back into favour and got dismissed again. He seems to keep bouncing back, but he's just as icy with everyone else. The Toad may be a port-swilling glutton and he's out for himself, but Sir Morgan is a bit more menacing. He's always been ambitious and there is something I don't trust about him."

"So what is it you actually do for them?" Max tried to sound interested, tried to make that effort he had wanted to put in with his dad.

"Well, Max," his father sounded tired, "it's mostly pretty boring really. We've all been working pretty hard on the final draft of the European Environmental Act, it's all about enacting an environmental policy which will best benefit all the countries in Europe. You see every European country, every member state I should say, has senior politicians appointed as members of the Commission. Their job is really to come up with the ideas for new European laws."

"So what sort of rules, what sort of ideas do they come up with?"

"Well, all sorts of things really, you see different Commissioners are given different Directorates, areas of responsibility," he explained more simply. "My bosses, the Duke and Sir Morgan, head up the Directorate on Europe's environment policy, that's their portfolio. So their office, where I work, is chiefly concerned with making environmental laws which will benefit Europe.

"Right now we are all working on an Act to address environmental challenges, and to be fair on Dredmor and the Toad they have been working fairly tirelessly on it. In fact it's most odd to see a Labour politician and a Tory getting on so well." Julian crossed his knife and fork across his empty plate. "They didn't get on too well at first, but just lately they've spent hours locked away in their office, and they keep having meetings with Commissioners from other countries, they had the Danish and Portuguese Commissioners in there with them this afternoon. I don't know the details going into the planning of the Act, I only proofread it, but I think it could be pretty major. I suppose it will all become clear in time."

Max yawned widely, he couldn't help himself. He appreciated that his father spoke with him frankly and treated him like an adult, but he really hadn't taken much of it in.

"I did warn you it was pretty boring," his father smiled, "we shouldn't be talking about boring work stuff on your fourteenth birthday anyway. Now," he changed the subject, "before I give your sister a ring to find out what sort of a birthday she had, what presents did you get?"

Chapter Two – The Admiral's Drum

The previous day the group had enjoyed a full day in Cornwall, including the whole afternoon by the sea. However, just as Jess had predicted, the section of coastline selected by Mr Jarvis for this part of his Geography field trip had been chosen more with the taking of sand samples and the investigating of rock pools in mind than in trying to get a suntan. In any case it had continuously drizzled on an over-clouded day not ideal for sunbathing, and Abigail Saunders' hopes of being happily distracted by surfers were also dashed as a lack of waves had encouraged them to try somewhere else. Jess could certainly see why, she wouldn't have fancied falling off a board in the rocky shallows or being washed up on the jagged rocks, good waves or no waves. She'd made sure she paired up with Gemma Biggs to count and record the crustaceans and plant life in her grid square of rock pool, safely out of range of Abi's whinging.

The evening in an amusement arcade had helped the group relax a little, and whilst the girls had eaten a vast amount of sweets before making themselves feel sick on the dance stepper machines, Tommo Lydon had beaten all comers, including Mr Jarvis, soundly, on the car-racing simulator. Toby Barnes had caused a few moments of panic amongst the staff members and a few tears from Lizzie Taylor, by wandering off and getting himself lost, but now all accounted for the whole group were back aboard the coach as it wound through the fair county of Devon, and along the south coast towards Plymouth.

Miss Davies was in her element; she had patiently endured the Geography part of the trip, doing her best to get involved and help the children even though she had only a limited interest in the subject. But now that the focus of the trip had turned to History, her own subject, she happily emerged from Mr Jarvis's shadow and took charge of the itinerary.

Maxwell Finch may not have listened quite as attentively in lessons as his sister Jessica, but he'd informed his mother correctly that their class had indeed been studying the Tudor and Stuart periods during the previous term. They had read and researched and taken exams on the reign of Queen Elizabeth the first, and of course the Spanish Armada, the huge fleet of ships which were to be filled with soldiers assembled by the King of Spain in an attempt to invade England and seize her crown. Therefore, as the bus stopped at Plymouth Hoe, where Sir Francis Drake had famously been playing bowls when news of the Armada's sighting in the channel was brought to him, Jess couldn't help feeling that perhaps the trip was a little late to be of any real benefit to the class.

"Miss, shouldn't we have had this trip before the exam?" she asked Miss Davies as she disembarked the coach. "Anything we learn now will be too late to get us any extra marks."

"Don't be a smart arse, Miss Finch," the teacher replied, "you aren't supposed to just forget things as soon as you've taken an exam, you know. There simply wasn't time to squeeze this trip in during the term, and it's always worth learning a bit more about things anyway."

"The whole point about education is that it's supposed to be continuous,," Mr Jarvis chipped in. "We teachers are supposed to open your minds and plant the seed, to let a little knowledge in. If you are interested, Jessica, motivated, you are supposed to thirst for more. And that goes for all you lot," he added in a loud voice which addressed the whole group.

Jess heard Tammy Smith respond to this by stating openly that rocks were far from interesting, and that Geography sucked. Mr Jarvis, looking rather hurt, took her aside in an attempt to raise the profile of his subject.

"It's not that I don't want to learn, Miss, not that I'm not interested," Jess tried to explain, "it's just that if we'd been on the trip before the exam we could have referred to it."

"I know, Jess," Miss Davies spoke to her quietly. "I had hoped that you were going to take History for GCSE, remember what I said at parent's evening, you are quite strong in this subject."

"Yeah, well, I'm thinking about it, Miss."

"And you see, the syllabus is constantly being moved around so year groups end up having to repeat things. There's a good chance that what we did this year could end up in the exam in two years time, so learn all you can. If we do end up going over it again I would expect you to get really good marks when it really matters."

"Um, okay," replied Jess uncertainly. She wasn't sure she fancied repeating work they had done before and knew the very thought of it would bore the life out of her brother who found lessons tedious enough without going over the same work again. But she knew the importance of getting good marks; she had done very well in the end of year History exam and she found the Tudor period especially interesting.

The morning, as Miss Davies had explained on the coach, was orientated towards Sir Francis Drake, the great sailor and explorer who used to live near Plymouth and had close ties with the area. "England had a small army," she had reminded the group, "and if the Spanish had landed they might well have succeeded in capturing the Kingdom. However the English Navy was superb, and as The Armada was defeated at sea they never actually got as far as landing. The Spanish King, Philip, had paid for an Army that never embarked, and lost a Navy in the process."

Drake, as Jess knew, had played a major part in defeating The Armada. He had engaged the Spanish Admiral's own flagship off Gravelines, had sent fire-ships amongst the Armada at anchor which caused them to panic, and took much credit for the victory. But she also knew that he had been somewhat of an opportunistic adventurer, and that even when he was supposed to be keeping in formation with the fleet with the aim of destroying the enemy in mind, he had instead slunk off to recover the damaged Spanish galleon Rosario in dead of night in order to claim the prize money for capturing the ship himself.

The Armada had rallied out of several Spanish ports and massed in the channel heading for the Netherlands where the Spanish Army were ready to board for the short crossing. The English ships were a lot smaller and more manoeuvrable than the imposing Spanish galleons, and Drake and the other English captains had harried them, their attack breaking up the Spanish formation.

When The Armada had stopped to fill up with soldiers off the Dutch coast they had anchored all the ships close together and near the shore. That's when the fire ships had been brought into play. Old vessels filled with anything that would burn were towed up close to the Armada under cover of darkness, were set alight and sent into the midst of the Spanish fleet.

The Spanish, whose ships were built of wood and were full of men and supplies, were heavy in the water and didn't see the flaming hulks until they were almost upon them. They panicked, fearing that if the fire ships got amongst them they would catch fire one by one and that the fire ships themselves could be full of gunpowder, ready to explode at any minute. The Spanish captains, desperate to escape, ordered their anchor cables to be cut as they didn't have time to haul the heavy anchors in.

In disarray there was more intense fighting back on the open sea, and then a violent storm blew up. The ragged remains of The Armada, almost completely out of ammunition and unable to defend itself, tried to escape up into the North Sea, hoping to sail round Scotland and back southward towards Spain. The English pursued them initially, then left them to the winds. The Spanish ships which had escaped being captured or sunk in the fighting were unable to stop because they had no anchors to lower, and were eventually wrecked as the storms blew them onto the jagged rocks of Scotland's coast. The English people had breathed a collective sigh of relief, and Drake, already probably the most famous of the English Captains, had secured his own place in legend.

"Right, so standing here we are at the point of Plymouth Hoe," Miss Davies swung her arm in a wide arch. "We can see the city of Plymouth over there, and of course we have a fine view of the English Channel. So Johnny, Johnny Norris, I'm only picking on you because you are at the back. Drake was about here playing a game of bowls when a messenger came and told him that the Armada had been sighted off the coast. What did he say? What was his famous quotation?"

"Um," Johnny Norris looked blank. "Up and at em," he said hopefully, though with a total absence of confidence.

"No. Tammy Smith, tell us." Miss Davies had seen Tammy with her hand high in the air.

"We have time enough to finish the game and to beat the Spaniards too, Miss."

"That's right." Miss Davies looked relieved. "I'm glad some of you were listening in class, but why couldn't you remember that in your exam Tammy?" Tammy Smith made no reply and Miss Davies shook her head in mock despair. "Too little too late, but at least you can remember it now Tammy. So, this gives us an idea of just what a cool customer Drake must have been. Having waited all year for the enemy to come, and knowing that he is properly prepared he's told that the enemy are coming, and while everyone is starting to panic he keeps his head. He takes his time, he has confidence in his ability and he won't be rushed." She paused. "We on the other hand are on a tight schedule and are heading for the exhibition at the great man's house, so back on the coach, we've got plenty more to do before lunch."

It was not far to Buckland Abbey, the house which Drake had bought when he came back from sailing around the world, and there was plenty for the children to do there. Miss Davies handed out the activity packs for them to work through as they went round the sea-faring exhibition, the Elizabethan garden and the museum, and she made sure she paired the children up to avoid any squabbling, the even numbers ensuring that no one got left on their own.

Jess found herself paired with Brendan, who seemed relieved to be put with her, and she didn't mind in the slightest that she had to work with him even though Abi Saunders had pulled a face of disgust at her when the teacher had announced who she was with. Brendan was a quiet boy, but he certainly wasn't stupid, and Jess was happy to hang around at the back of the group as the rest of their classmates rushed to get through the questions as quickly as possible. Abi, who had sat with Jess again on the coach that morning and was becoming hard work, had let her know that she also fancied Tommo Lydon, and was now taking full advantage of being paired with him by flirting outrageously, and leading him by the arm around the exhibition she giggled almost every time he spoke. In fact Abi was now beginning to annoy Jess so much that she happily encouraged Brendan to hang back and let the others zoom ahead just to put a little distance between herself and Abi, as the pairs gathered round each information point to find the answers to their list of questions.

It was the house itself which impressed Jess most. It had originally been a Cistercian Abbey, which no doubt gave the house its name, and when the monasteries had been sold off by Henry the eighth, Queen Elizabeth's father, to raise himself some money, the Abbey had been converted into a country house. The building had been extended in all directions, but the tower from the original church still remained in the middle.

"Oh, Cistercian is spelt with a C, Brendan, not an S," she corrected him as he answered the question about which order of monks had originally built the Abbey. "How old was Drake at the time of the Spanish Armada?" she read off the next question.

"Says here he was born in about 1540," said Brendan.

"And the Armada was in 1588."

"So he was about forty-eight," Brendan reasoned.

"Yeah, forty eight will do. It's a bit easy really, isn't it? Oh, the word for sailing around the world is circumnavigation," she answered the next question. "To circumnavigate, he circumnavigated it."

"And he did it between 1577 and 1580," Brendan read the next answer off the information notice in front of them and jotted it down on the sheet. "Blimey, three years to sail round the world, but the writing's on the wall, Jess," he joked in agreement that the quiz was far from challenging. "And he sailed around the world in a ship called... The Pelican."

"The Golden Hind," Jess corrected him. She could remember the answer from class and she knew that on his return he had been knighted on the deck of the ship itself.

"Ah, no, you're right," Brendan conceded, "it says here that he changed the ship's name to the Golden Hind halfway through the voyage."

"Well we'd better put both down, it could be a trick question. It must have been pretty scary to sail all the way around the world," she reflected. "I mean, to be one of the very first people ever to do it, it must have taken some guts."

"Yeah, especially when most people were convinced the earth was flat. He must have half-expected to just fall off the edge on the way round. You're right, he must have been pretty fearless. Pretty smelly as well, imagine, three years sailing a little ship around the world, he probably didn't even have a bath in all that time."

"Well in an age where men wore jewellery and tights," said Toby Banes, who with his partner, Gemma Biggs, was finished and off into the next room, "I would have thought that'd be the least of his worries."

'The Spanish were very afraid of Drake,' the next information board explained, 'and they called him El Draque, because he kept attacking them in South America and taking huge amounts of gold and jewels back to England.'

"El Draque comes from the Spanish word Draco, and means The Dragon," Brendan scribbled down the next answer. "Clever play on words that."

'Openly Queen Elizabeth was disapproving,' the board went on, 'but he presented most of the wealth he took from the Spanish to his Queen, and she was secretly delighted with it. Whilst Drake became one of her favourites, the Spanish King, Philip, called him a pirate, and his anger at Drake and other English sailors would only have contributed towards his desire to invade protestant England and bring men like Drake to heel.'

"I suppose King Philip of Spain thought he was entitled to be King of England really," said Jess. "I mean, he was married to Elizabeth's sister, Mary, when she was Queen, and she was Queen before Elizabeth, so he probably thought that made him King or something."

"I think he wanted Elizabeth to turn England into a Catholic country again," Brendan reasoned, as Nick Bovis entered the room followed by Lizzie Taylor and Mr Jarvis. "It was Catholic under Mary, but Elizabeth was a Protestant, wasn't she?"

"True, but Philip would probably have just started burning Protestants again, that was the way they settled arguments in those days."

"The Protestants were burning Catholics too, Jess. It didn't seem to matter who you were or what you thought back then - someone wanted to kill you for something."

"Well, speaking for myself," Nick Bovis interrupted, "I'm glad things didn't turn out differently. Everyone goes on about the Germans and World War Two and everything, but if The Armada had actually landed, well, we could all be speaking Spanish now."

"Nothing wrong with that, Bovis," Mr Jarvis imposed himself on the conversation. "I like a good paella myself." He chuckled at his own feeble joke.

Lizzie and Nick were struggling with their worksheet and Lizzie was glad to pursue any distraction. "But Spanish is a silly language Sir," she said provocatively. "Female this and male that, the table's a girl, the chair's a boy, I mean, what the heck are they on?"

"Languages not your strong point, Miss Taylor?" asked Mr Jarvis with a smile.

"French is stupid too, Sir, don't see the point of learning it."

"Well that's where you're wrong, Lizzie. Why should everyone else make the effort to learn our language if we can't be bothered to learn theirs?"

"What's the point of learning theirs when they all speak ours anyway?" Lizzie was sticking to her guns on this one.

"Funny that you should say that, Lizzie, because actually most of the English language comes directly from other European languages, you know; it's a complete mix. Every time a nation invaded they brought words with them, the Romans, the Normans, the Vikings... If we'd never had those influences we'd probably all still be running around in loincloths and grunting at each other." He adopted an authoritative tone. "Oh yes we need those outside influences, one culture rubbing off on another, that's how societies develop."

"Rubbing off on each other," Jess looked amused. "I thought invaders usually just moved in and killed the people who lived there so they could take over."

"I thought Anglo-Saxon words were all rude, Sir," Lizzie sought to lower the tone. "Least ways, Mrs York keeps saying they are."

"I think perhaps only the short ones are rude, Miss Taylor," mused Mr Jarvis. "I'm sure your English teacher is only trying to ensure you express yourself with an absence of expletives, swearing only shows a limited vocabulary."

"Depends on how many swear words you know, Sir. I know..."

"No, Lizzie, not now," he shook his head hastily, urging her to silence.

"Well I wouldn't want to be Spanish," Nick Bovis interrupted again. "I went to Spain last holiday and none of the women shave their armpits. They're all greasy and smelly and..."

"That is entirely the problem," Mr Jarvis cut across him before he could say any more. "Us British are always stereotyping other people, grouping them together and making sweeping judgements about them."

"But this bloke really smelt, Sir." Nick was enjoying both the attention and the annoyance he was causing his Geography teacher.

"Well maybe, maybe you did meet one smelly Spanish man, I'll concede that to you. But you can't make a sweeping statement like that Nick, you simply can't generalise with any authority and say that all Spanish people smell."

"Well, I think…"

"No, Nick. Look, have you smelt all Spanish people? Have you been up to every Spanish person in the whole world, every single individual Spanish person on every continent of the globe and smelt them?"

"Well no," Bovis replied sheepishly.

"Then you simply can't say things like that, can you? Not only is it entirely empirically unsound, it will only get you in trouble."

Mr Jarvis had wagged his finger with each syllable as if the authoritative gesture made his point all the more valid, but as he considered the argument won a cheeky grin spread over Nick Bovis's mischievous face.

"Well I can make it my mission to find out, Sir. Running up to Spanish people, having a quick sniff and running away."

"Well good luck with it, Bovis, it'll take you a lifetime. I never thought you would be one to dedicate your life to research."

"Why don't they shave their armpits then Sir?" Lizzie Taylor could see that the teacher was irritated and seized the opportunity to wind him up some more.

"I don't know," Mr Jarvis was flustered and frustrated now. "Perhaps some people think it's more natural not to shave their armpits. It's nice to be natural sometimes. Sometimes you girls put on far too much makeup, spend far too much on cosmetics. Some of you girls," he added quickly with a defensive glance at Nick Bovis, "not all you girls, I don't want to be accused of generalising."

"So Sir," Lizzie replied provocatively, "does that mean you like the natural look?"

"Yeah," Nick Bovis couldn't resist it, but as soon as he spoke he regretted it.

"Does that mean your wife, Mrs Jarvis, doesn't shave her armpits?"

"Don't be so damned cheeky, Bovis." The flustered tone had given way to anger and it was clear to all the children in the room that the subject was open to joking no more. "I am serious, you know, I really am. It's all very well having a laugh but xenophobia is a serious problem."

Lizzie looked blank. "Zen…"

"Xenophobia, not liking foreigners," Mr Jarvis explained. "It's a fine line between that and full out and out racism, and we all know how unpleasant that can be."

"You're right Sir," Jess agreed, "look what happened in the war."

"Yes, stirring up racial hatred only leads to violence." The teacher seemed to calm down a bit now that he knew he was being taken seriously. "Forgive me one sweeping generalisation, but the problem with the British is that although we are a nation made up of lots of different peoples we have formed our own little identity on this island and we still don't like foreigners. We still seem to have it ingrained in our psyche, still think ourselves superior, the empire has long gone; when will people finally accept it? The British are incredibly arrogant, behave like louts when we go abroad - I mean look at the football fans, for example. It may only be a few setting a bad example, but it gives us all an awful reputation and the other nations hate us when we behave like that."

"Well if they hate us... why can't we hate them back?"

"Bovis they don't hate us, they hate our behaviour and our attitude. Learn from this boy, learn from it. We live in a new Europe now, there's no reason why anyone should have to put up with xenophobic opinions anymore. The British have to take it on board, the world does not revolve around this country, Greenwich mean time or no Greenwich mean time."

"Yeah, I s'pose," Nick Bovis reluctantly conceded.

"We are still an island though," Brendan spoke carefully, wanting to add something to the mini debate. "I mean we are still out on our own, aren't we?"

"Part of Europe, we are all part of Europe, Brendan." The teacher shook his head mournfully. "Honestly, you're all such a bunch of Euro-sceptics, you really are."

"Euro-septics?" Lizzie looked confused.

"Yes, no, Euro-sceptic as in sceptical. "If you are sceptic about something it means you disagree with it or you think it's a bad idea."

"Yeah, septic is when you've got germs," Nick added unhelpfully. "I had a septic finger once and it was all full of puss and..."

"Yes thank you Nicholas," Mr Jarvis interrupted, "we really don't want to hear about that now."

"Oh I do," Lizzie looked wide eyed, "sounds gross."

"Look, stop trying to avoid the issue in hand," Mr Jarvis spoke firmly and in a voice which demanded their full attention. "A lot of British people are Euro-sceptic, they don't like the idea of being part of Europe, they don't like being part of the European political entity, and that's fine, but making racist jokes about other nations, making sweeping statements and generalisations really isn't on. It really won't make us popular with our neighbours and it just isn't constructive... Right, you two," he beckoned to Lizzie and Nick, "come with me - we are disrupting Brendan and Jessica's learning."

"But Sir, we'll end up missing some questions out," said Lizzie, trying to be difficult.

"Oh I don't think you're too bothered about that now, are you," he replied, following the other two out of the room. "Don't try to be obstructive, Miss Taylor."

"He's got a point," Jess reflected when the others had gone.

"Yeah, not much has changed really, has it," Brendan agreed, "I mean back then the Spanish didn't like us because we kept picking on them, and Nick still picks on them now."

"I think Nick would pick on anyone," Jess spoke carelessly. "He and Tommo would pick on anyone for being short, or having big ears, or being fat... Oh, sorry Brendan." She hoped she hadn't upset him by drawing attention to his own size.

"Don't worry about it."

"I mean, you're not fat as such, are you? Just a bit chubby."

"Jess, you're really not making it any better."

"Sorry, I'll stop." She felt embarrassed and made one more attempt to make up for her mistake. "I don't like bullying, Brendan, of any kind, and I don't like name-calling or any other meanness. I know Abi says some pretty horrible things sometimes, but well, I'm sure she doesn't really mean them." Brendan looked uncomfortable, but said nothing in response. "I guess what I'm trying to say is... Well," Jess felt awkward now, "I thought that was great the way you stood up to her on the bus, the way you stood up to Abi and Tommo and the others."

"Yeah well," Brendan sighed. "I just don't let them bother me anymore, it's just not worth the hassle is it? And I mean you've got to stand up for yourself haven't you? That's supposed to be what us British are meant to be good at," he joked.

"Don't let old Jarvis hear you say that," Jess smiled back at him. "You know, you're all right, Brendan Johnson. You're all right, you are."

"I'm not sure your brother would agree with you."

"Max hasn't given you a hard time, has he?" Jess looked shocked, she'd never taken her brother for a bully.

"No, no of course he hasn't," Brendan replied quickly, but he hung his head and studied his toes mournfully. "It's just, well you know, I'm not exactly considered cool am I?"

"Well Max likes his sport and all that Brendan, and he's good at it too, but he's not exactly scoring centuries in the classroom is he? School's going to get serious soon, it'll be all about exams and results and Max will get a shock if he doesn't put some effort in. He won't be able to take his cricket bat into his GCSEs. You're much brighter than he is, Brendan, and you may not be an athlete but you're no wimp, you proved that today." Jess was blushing now and quickly changed the subject. "I'd be surprised if Nick or Lizzie take History next year."

"Yeah well, I'll be careful to avoid any class taught by Mr Jarvis I think. He's just so serious all the time."

"Old Jarvis isn't too bad. I used to find him pretty scary, but, well boring as he is, I've seen a different side to him on this trip."

"Yeah, that was funny when Nick asked him if his wife didn't shave her armpits." The two of them had a giggle and both felt much better. "Right - where were we, Jess, before we were interrupted?"

"We were just saying about the Spanish seeing Drake as a pirate. I mean that's a bit rich isn't it? They were stealing it all off the South American Indians in the first place, they took a huge amount of gold off the Incas, slaughtered thousands of people, and when Drake pitched up and swiped a bit of stolen treasure off them they called him a pirate."

"Yeah, well I suppose he got the better of them more than a few times, what with his part in defeating the Armada as well. He must have been pretty unpopular with the Spanish."

"Yeah, with his fire ships and everything, I bet that's where his nickname 'The Dragon' came from."

"Because dragons breathe fire," Brendan ventured.

"Exactly, and dragons like to hoard gold too."

They caught up Lizzie Taylor and Nick Bovis as they moved into the Great Hall, a large room on the first floor of the building built inside the old church. The décor was just as Jess had imagined the inside of a Tudor mansion to look. The ceiling was low and beamed, the walls whitewashed, and dark stained wood panelling dominated the room. There were stands of candles and a chandelier which would provide a dim lighting during the night, and a dark wooded table stood in the middle of the room in front of a large open fireplace with a huge hearth which was exactly halfway along the back wall. There was still a faint smell of soot, which created an atmosphere, but the overpowering aroma was that of wood polish, which Jess assumed was splattered on in buckets by those who lovingly ensured that the public would see the house at its best.

"You can just imagine a whole pig roasting on a spit in there." Brendan too was very impressed.

"Hungry, are you?" Lizzie Taylor asked unkindly.

"Yes, it is pretty cool." Jess deliberately ignored her.

"Oh, there are loads of questions on this stupid old drum," said Nick Bovis from the corner of the room. In front of him was an old wooden cylindrical drum which hung on the wall. "There's so much to read," he complained as he worked his way through a large sign next to it covered in extensive script.

"Well shut up and stop talking and you'll get through it quicker," Jess spoke under her breath, but Brendan could hear her clearly.

"What?" Nick demanded, turning around.

"I said, um... We'll just wait until you've finished then." She'd be glad to have the peace, and the room to themselves. She grinned at Brendan, who smiled back at her - he was clearly thinking the same thing.

Jess waited patiently, quite happy to soak up the Old World atmosphere of the room. She imagined Drake hosting a gathering after the defeat of the Armada, sitting around the big fireplace with the other victorious sea Captains, all smoking their pipes and sharing stories of the great battle they had just won. She walked over to the intricate metal-framed window, which had shards of lead-work in a pattern breaking the window into a hundred little diamonds of glass, and looked out over the recreated Tudor garden at the rose beds and an old peacock, who was strutting his stuff on the lawn below. Something, suddenly came to her.

"Brendan, what number question was it that we hadn't got?"

"Six," Brendan replied, and after a quick consultation of the question paper, he read it out to her. "Which Spanish aristocrat was the Admiral commanding the Armada?"

"Oh yes, well I've remembered now. It was the Duke of Medina Sidonia," she spoke confidently, "not sure how you spell it...."

"I, T."

"Yes, thank you Nick," Jess again let the interruption go. "I'm not sure how you spell Medina Sidonia, Brendan, but he was definitely the Spanish Admiral, I remember from class."

"Nice one Jess," Brendan jotted down the answer. "I've no idea what the prize is for this quiz but I think Miss Davies will be giving it to us at this rate."

"You really are a pair of little swots." Lizzie turned from the drum to face them with disgust.

Jess could see Nick Bovis, who had clearly benefited from eavesdropping her and Brendan's conversation, scribbling 'The Duke of Medina Sidonia' down on their own answer sheet and struggling even to spell the Spaniard's title correctly. "Not at all," she replied, "the answers are all on the info boards, Lizzie."

"Well that one wasn't, you said yourself, you just remembered it from class."

"Well, well done for listening then," said Jess, irritated that she should be spurned by her classmates for having actually managed to learn something. "You should try listening in class sometime, it's sort of what school is all about, really."

"Oh you really are a pair of swots." Lizzie repeated her earlier accusation.

"Yeah, far too keen," Nick Bovis chipped in.

"Well seeing as how you two clearly couldn't care less, I take it you've finished answering questions on that drum."

"Yeah, stupid old drum," Nick replied scornfully. "Come on Lizzie, the sun's shining outside, and the kiosk probably does ice creams. See you, losers," he added as the two of them left the room.

With the rest of the class ahead of them, and there being very few other visitors to the house that day, Jessica and Brendan found themselves alone in the Great Hall.

The drum did look old and fragile, but it also had a mystery and beauty to it, or so Jess thought. She approached it with curiosity, eager to find out more about whose it was and what it was doing here hanging in the Great Hall. To one side of it was a sign saying 'don't touch,' and to the other, screwed to the wall, was the lengthy information board which Nick Bovis had been complaining about, and which announced that the tall cylindrical instrument was of course Drake's drum; it had belonged to the Admiral and had accompanied him on his many voyages.

From a distance it looked yellow, but up close Jess could see that it was really coloured with a faded gold and was edged with a tired-looking red band around the rim to top and bottom. The taut skin, which would actually be struck to make the noise, looked very worn and faded too, and Jess could see Drake's own crest painted on the side. The crest was the hero's own heraldic badge and consisted of a helmet with drapes coming off it and a globe on the top. Beneath the helmet was a shield in sable black displaying a white squiggly wave which ran across the middle of it, and a star above and below it.

"Pretty cool," said Jess. She thought it beautiful, a real link to the past.

"Well that wiggly line is probably supposed to represent the sea, and that globe on top is probably there because of his circun... certum... Because of his having sailed round the world and everything. Yeah, look, there's a question on it." Brendan filled the answer in.

Jess busied herself reading the information board and Brendan on completing the answer paper. The drum, so the board stated, had been taken with Drake on his last voyage, and when he had died of dysentery in the Caribbean and been buried at sea the drum had been brought back to England by his crew.

There was, it claimed, a legend that in times of victory and in times when England was in danger, the drum had been heard to sound, though no drummer was ever seen, and the board cited several examples. It had been heard when Oliver Cromwell and Lord Fairfax had come to thank the people of Plymouth for defending the town against the King's army during the English civil war. It had been heard when Nelson had been made a freeman of Plymouth, and when the Duke of Wellington had left Plymouth for his day with destiny on the fields near Waterloo. The danger averted, the drum had again been heard when Wellington's victory was complete and his captured enemy Napoleon was brought by ship back into the port after the battle. Many years later the drum had been heard to sound a victory roll in triumph when the Kaiser's German Navy had surrendered to the British in 1918. And most recently, in the early days of the Second World War when the overwhelmed British expeditionary force fled France from the beaches of Dunkirk in the face of the powerful German onslaught, the drum had sounded once again. Though whether this was in relief that a large proportion of the Army had been spared or in warning of a potential and looming invasion of Britain by the enemy, it was unclear.

Legend had it, the board continued, that whilst the drum had been heard to signal both danger and glory on its own, it was also believed that if England was ever in danger and the drum was deliberately played, Drake himself, the drum's owner, would come back to save the English people from disaster. There was an extract from a poem by Sir Henry Newbolt under the script:

'Take my drum to England,
hang et by the shore,
 strike et when your powder's runnin low.
If the Don's sight Devon I'll quit the port o' heaven,
an drum them up the channel as we drummed them long ago.'

"Wow," Jess exclaimed, and she felt a cold shiver run through her body, "I don't much like ghost stories. Do you think it's true, Brendan?"

"What, that he'd come back? That people have heard it but haven't seen anyone playing it? Who knows? It's probably just a legend, Jess," he replied, trying to reassure her, "probably just a myth. Come on, we've finished in here now, we've got all the answers we need, let's catch the others up."

Jessica followed Brendan, but she felt really uncomfortable, perhaps even a bit scared. That cold shiver she'd felt, she had felt the same thing just recently, perhaps even in the last few days, but she couldn't remember exactly when and it bothered her. She tried putting it to the back of her mind as they caught the others up, grouped on the lawn of the Tudor garden and seated in the picnic area by the kiosk, eating ice-cream and sipping cold drinks in the sunshine. But the thought just kept nagging at her and so she bypassed the kiosk and went straight up to Miss Davies to see if she could find out more.

"Oh you two, you took your time," said the teacher, her mouth full of ice-cream. "Answer sheet, please." Brendan, who had followed Jess with a sorrowful glance at the kiosk as he passed it, handed the answer sheet over and the teacher grabbed it with her podgy fingers and slid it with some difficulty, so as not to drop her melting ice cream, into her folder along with the others. "I was just telling the others, I'll mark them up later and announce the winner on the bus," she added, before taking a huge noisy lick of the dripping combo she had in her giant size cone.

"Um, Miss Davies," Jess felt a bit silly, "you know that drum?"

"Drake's drum, what about it?"

"Well that legend, Miss, is it really true?"

"Who knows." She licked up a drip which was running down her fat fingers. "Different people all say they've heard it, and over different centuries."

"So who actually plays it, Miss?" Jess implored her. "I mean, if it was heard to sound someone must have played it, right?"

"Well we don't know, do we?" the teacher replied. "I guess it wouldn't be a legend if we did. No one has been seen to play it but numerous witnesses have claimed to have heard it. Perhaps it plays itself, perhaps the ghost of Drake plays it, we just don't know."

"But if someone was standing next to it when it sounded they would have seen someone playing it, wouldn't they? If there was actually someone there, I mean... if they were there with it when it sounded they would have seen whether or not a person, someone was actually playing it, or whether it played itself, or whatever."

"Well, I suppose they would," Miss Davies agreed, making a start on the cone. "But according to the legend it doesn't always get heard by people standing right next to it. For example, when the German Navy surrendered in 1918 a victory drum roll was heard on HMS Royal Oak several miles out at sea." Jess nodded. "Well, the Captain did a search of the ship but there was no drum on board and certainly no-one found drumming."

Jess felt a cold shiver go through her once again. Ghost stories were unsettling at the best of times but this one made her feel especially uncomfortable; she could feel the hairs on the back of her neck bristling up and a lump in her throat.

"Well, how did they know it was Drake's drum then?" asked Mark Thompson, who had been listening in. "If they didn't find anyone drumming and his own drum was miles away, how did they know it was his drum they could hear?"

"Oh I don't know, Mark," the teacher replied; the last remnants of cone had disappeared and she dabbed at her fingers and mouth with a crumpled tissue. "Perhaps they just assumed it was Drake's drum, perhaps they assumed it because of the legend."

"But if they were miles away how did they hear it at all?"

"It's a myth, Mark, isn't it, who knows if it's true. Who knows if it really sounded or not, strange things happen, people hear things. Anyway, sailors are notoriously superstitious, they're always making things up, aren't they. Mermaids, giant squid..."

But Jessica wasn't listening; she'd just remembered when it was that she'd felt that cold shiver before. It had been just two days previously at Wookey Hole when the sneering man, the thin man with the narrow eyes, had put his hand on her shoulder for that photograph. She racked her brains, what was his name? Oh yes, Dredmor, Sir Morgan Dredmor, that was it. That's what the manager called him, 'Commissioner'. Jess just wanted to be on her own for a minute, just wanted to get away from the group. "I'm just going to the toilet Miss," she said faintly.

"Alright Jess, but don't be long, we have to get back on the coach in a minute."

Jess didn't know what it was that made her go back. Maybe something was leading her, maybe it was just curiosity, but she walked herself back up the stairs and into the Great Hall for another look at the drum. The room was empty and there it was, silently hanging in the corner on the wall. She walked over and read the poem extract again:

'If the Don's sight Devon I'll quit the port o' heaven,
an drum them up the channel as we drummed them long ago.'

She felt cold, clammy, she couldn't get the sneering face of the narrow-eyed Morgan Dredmor out of her head, she could even hear the chill of his tone of voice in the back of her mind: 'The cities overflow with rubbish, Mr Twistle, we must clear these up, but at what cost to the country...'

The room was quiet, so still, and outside the sun was beating down. Despite the warmth of the day Jess could feel goosebumps coming up on her fore-arms and that cold shiver once again running down her spine. She just wanted to go, to leave, to forget the sneering face. She tried desperately to put the Commissioner out of her mind. That moment was over, she reasoned, she would never see him again, and if she didn't hurry up she might get left behind. She walked to the door, and just as she passed through it she heard, or she thought she heard, a faint but distinct noise; a drum roll, short but clear.

She stopped. She stood dead still, barely daring to breathe. She was so sure she'd heard it but it had been so faint, so quiet, could she have imagined it? Jess turned really slowly on her heels to look back at the drum, half-expecting to see a ghost, but there was no one there.

She breathed deep, she tutted to herself and turned again to leave, she must have imagined it... But there it was again, another faint drum roll, just loud enough for her to hear. Jess paused again, she stood dead still, she held her breath and didn't flinch a muscle, but this time it didn't stop; this time it kept going very quietly, very gently. 'Rrrrr rrrrr, rrrrr rrrrr, rat tat tat, rrrrr rrrrr.'

Jess turned again just as before in reverend silence, but the drum roll continued. 'Rrrrr rrrrr, rrrrr rrrrr, rat tat tat, rrrrr rrrrr.' She walked cautiously over to the drum, though she had no idea what actually led her to do it. Her instinct was to run out of the room and tell Miss Davies, but she just felt drawn to the painted cylindrical object which beckoned her with every tat, tat, tat, and the feeling became stronger, more consuming the closer she got to it. Jess took tiny soundless steps and it seemed to be taking an age, but suddenly there she was, now standing straight in front of the drum, and no other sounds but that of her own heavy breathing and the gentle drumming could be heard.

Jess could feel her heart beating uncontrollably as she peered cautiously at the worn skin on the top of the drum. It was moving, vibrating ever so slightly as if it was being patted incredibly delicately and with great precision and care. She raised her right hand silently and in what seemed to her like slow motion, and reached out towards it. She just couldn't resist the draw of it, the all-powerful hold the drum seemed to have over her.

She felt transfixed, mesmerised, as if trapped in a compelling daydream, and whilst the compulsion led her on almost completely against her will, she also sensed the importance of avoiding any sudden movement incredibly keenly. It was as if although she didn't will to be here she really felt there was nothing she could do, that she had to see it through, had to find out what would happen next, but that one jerky flinch could break the spell and shatter the sensation, and just at that moment the prospect of being anywhere else was just unbearable. Then, just as she held her outstretched hand over it, the drumming stopped. The room seemed to Jess to be spinning all around her now and she could hear an uncontrollable buzzing in the back of her head, but as she focussed on the drum and her hand outstretched above it she could hear the rat, tat, tatting no more and the skin on the top of the drum was still.

The compulsion remained. As Jess spread out her fingers it became almost more consuming, more unbearable in the silence, more intense, even more impossibly overwhelming than it had already been, and though she had no desire to do it, Jess felt so drawn, so compelled to act as if the drum itself was willing her on, and she touched it.

Jess only tapped it twice, so, so gently with the tips of her fingers, and the drum only made the tiniest of thudding noises, like but quite unlike the drum-roll she had just heard.

She had no idea what would happen next, but she half expected something to. A ghost to jump out and grab her, or to find herself transported back to the Tudor period. But nothing did, the room was completely silent, eerily still, and in a second a wave of relief seemed to break all over her. No sooner had she felt it though, she suddenly felt weak at the knees, sick and faint, and the room was spinning again even more violently as she gasped for breath. She felt compelled again but this time it was her own body commanding her, she had to get outside in case she passed out.

As she left the room and started walking unsteadily back downstairs she felt a bit better. The fresh air as she got outside was flowing oxygen into her lungs and though her heartbeat was slowing a bit she still felt a bit dazed, and could feel a cold sweat down her back and on her forehead.

"Oh my goodness Jess," said Abi as she emerged into the sunshine, "are you okay? You look so pale."

"Yes I'm, I'm fine," Jess replied feebly.

"Well come and sit over here," Gemma Biggs suggested, "I'll get you a coke, you need the sugar."

"Thanks Gemma," she mumbled.

Abi was wide-eyed and right up close to her. "You, you look like you've just seen a ghost. What happened to you?"

"I'm fine," Jess mumbled unconvincingly, "honestly I am." She seated herself in the shade, all her classmates grouping around her with concerned expressions on their faces.

"Alright, give her some space," said Miss Davies breaking up the crowd. Gemma handed Jess a cold can of fizzy drink with urgency, and Jess gratefully sipped at it and felt much better. "Are you alright, Jessica?" Miss Davies towered over her.

"Yes, oh." Jess wanted to tell her, wanted to tell Miss Davies everything, but she knew she couldn't. She knew all her classmates would laugh at her, clearly no one else had heard the drum and she didn't want to get in trouble for touching it either. "I, um, went to the toilet and I suddenly felt a bit faint. I don't know what came over me, but I feel a bit better now," she smiled back.

"Alright, you rest here a minute, drink the rest of that and come and join us on the coach in a little while. Right, you lot," she raised her voice as she addressed the group, "back on the coach, come on give Jessica some space."

"Is she really alright, Miss?" Jess heard Brendan ask the teacher as the others filed past, and she felt much better knowing he was concerned.

"Yes, she's just fine. Now come on, back on the coach we have to be going shortly, Jess just needs a few moments - she'll join us when she's ready."

Chapter Three – The Office

Julian Finch was frustrated. He worked incredibly hard in this office, he travelled long distances every day and never seemed to get home until late, the commuting made him feel so tired all the time and he felt as if he just didn't get any quality time with his family anymore. Now that his children Jessica and Maxwell were growing up they seemed to be out whenever he was in, and he really missed spending proper time with them and doing the things a family man ought to be doing, but to cap it all Julian just wasn't enjoying the work.

He laboured for long hours only for jumped-up politicians and more senior Civil Servants to take the credit for his efforts, and the pressures on him were only increasing. Julian was under tremendous pressure today, but rather than leaving him to finish his work in peace and within the time limit, all his senior colleagues seemed intent on constantly ringing him up for an update on his progress, or walking into his little office themselves to remind him that it was crucially important that he got his part of the document in on time.

Julian wasn't lazy, far from it, he was meticulous, but to be meticulous took time and care and most of all it took concentration. Try as he might he couldn't concentrate through the endless interruptions, and as a result he was becoming increasingly frustrated. By mid-morning as the phone calls and the endless stream of unwelcome visitors continued he was totally fed up with schedule two of the European Environmental Act.

He wanted to tell them all that it would have been finished hours ago if it wasn't for the constant interruptions, but he always had to be respectful when dealing with some of the big wigs, and having finished his brunch, one of the biggest wigs of all, Sir Dennis Hitoadie, the Duke of Man himself, had even come to interrupt him. The Duke, similarly, further harassed him, before waddling off to shut himself in his own palatial office at the end of the corridor with his fellow Commissioner, Sir Morgan Dredmor, and their Greek and Spanish colleagues for a secret meeting.

"Finch, old boy, when will that damned paper be ready?" the Duke had asked rudely. The lift was out of order and Hitoadie had been sweating heavily due to the effort of shifting his vast bulk up the office stairs in the summer heat. He had coffee stains down his shirt just below his bow tie where drops had dripped from his jowls as he'd previously consumed one of his several cups of morning refreshment, and Julian Finch had quietly wondered if his boss had even noticed.

"Nearly there, nearly done, your Grace," he'd replied as calmly as he could.

"Blast you man, I gave you the rough draft weeks ago," the huge aristocrat had grunted back impatiently, "surely you should have finished finalising it by now, eh, what!"

"Getting a finalised draft to a Legislative Act properly written up takes time, your Grace, it requires complete and utter concentration," Julian had replied defensively, hinting as tactfully as possible that he could do without this new distraction.

"It's virtually copying though, isn't it?" The cold voice of Sir Morgan Dredmor had seemed to come from out of nowhere. "It's given to you Finch, you simply proofread it and return it to us, my five year old nephew could read faster than you."

Sir Morgan had entered the small office, which Julian shared with his secretary Jennifer Stone, behind the Duke, but with the fat figure of Hitoadie standing in front of his desk Julian's view of the doorway had been totally blocked.

"Oh I didn't see you there Sir Morgan," he'd apologised.

The narrow face had peered at him round the Duke and contorted into the familiar sneer. "Now listen to me Finch. It's very important that this Act goes through at this reading, understood? We don't want it coming back for any other alterations. The final draft must be on my desk by this afternoon. We have to take the whole thing with us to the Commissioners conference in Belgium tomorrow - once they have passed it, I mean approved it, the document needs to be ready for the European Council meeting on Monday. Woe betide you if we don't have it shortly - now hurry up with it, Finch."

"Yes, get on with it man," Hitoadie had added, "this document is extremely important to Sir Morgan and me, could be career changing. Onwards and upwards eh, Dredmor, eh, eh, what!"

"Indeed your Grace," Sir Morgan agreed, "so hurry it up, Finch. Come on, Dennis, we have visitors."

"Ah yes," Hitoadie had exclaimed, remembering he was keeping his guests waiting. He paused as he turned to leave the room and let off a massive meat and gravy fart, the release of which triggered a huge beaming grin of satisfaction. "'Twill lighten the load," he'd remarked before squeezing himself out of the room and away after Sir Morgan down the corridor.

"Oh Commissioners," Julian had called after them, trying not to inhale as his Grace's flatulence filled the room. "There seems to be something missing from this paper. I've looked all through it and there seems to be a protocol missing."

"Ah, the old elusive Protocol Fifteen eh!" Hitoadie had stopped in his tracks and turned to speak to him. "Don't worry about that, Sir Morgan and I have written that up personally. Don't concern yourself Finch, there's a good fellow, we'll make sure it's not left out." As a broad smile had spread across the fat face Julian had thought he saw the huge man wink quickly at Sir Morgan.

The other however had not been quite so hospitable in his own frosty response. "Now look here Finch, Protocol Fifteen is no business of yours, understand? You just get your work done and don't meddle in things which don't concern you. I want the finished copy on my desk by lunch."

"That's what I love about working here, Jen," Julian spoke sarcastically as he returned to his office, "it's such a happy working atmosphere."

"I've not known them be as rude as that for ages, Mr Finch."

"Well you saved yourself from a broadside there Jen, I don't think they even noticed you there in the corner."

"Yeah," she conceded, "I think I'm safest behind the door." She paused thoughtfully. "But I've never seen them so driven before. I mean they really are working hard at the moment, so many meetings in their office, so many other foreign Commissioners coming to see them, I've never seen them so focused. Sir Morgan always appears pretty dedicated but his Grace, he seems so keen to just get the paper finished and approved."

"Yes, it's not like him at all, the toad is normally so lazy, he normally likes to drag even the smallest issue out over as many drinks parties as possible."

"It's not like his Grace really, not like his Grace at all... His Grace," she continued in a mocking tone as she opened the window, "not exactly graceful, is he?"

"No, I'll give you that."

"He blooming well stinks, and I've never seen so many coffee stains down his shirt, I think he's getting clumsier as his fingers get fatter."

"Yes well, I noticed the stains, but don't worry, I'm sure he'll cover then up with wine and sauce dribbles over his well-earned luncheon." Julian seated himself and got ready to try and continue.

"Mr Finch," his secretary asked carefully, "Julian."

"Um."

"How can they really expect to get this European Environmental Act of theirs made law so quickly? I just don't understand it, these things normally take ages. I mean, I know the European Parliament have had their reading and they raised objections..."

"That's right, they did. They didn't like the original proposals for the placement of wind farms."

"Yeah I know, but they would make some objection about something, wouldn't they? It makes it look as if they are doing something after all."

"Well I suppose, but it also means that the Parliament have had their reading now, it won't have to go through them again."

"Exactly, Mr Finch, that's my point. It's like they've rushed it passed the Parliament in its early stages so they won't get another chance to discuss it, and come to that it's a pretty quick turnaround, isn't it - the Commission meet to approve it on Friday and the Council meet on Monday. How can the Council arrange a meeting to sign up to it if the Commission haven't even approved it yet?"

"Well I think we both know the Commission are going to approve it, all these private meetings the Toad and Sir Morgan have been having with the other countries' Commissioners would be wasted if that weren't the case. But I agree with you, it does seem to be rather rushed; it's hardly a comprehensive document, is it? I mean the principles are there: reducing Pollution, Carbon emissions and Greenhouse gasses. Committing to deal more effectively with waste, rubbish, and sewage in a way which avoids causing Environmental damage. Recycling after all sounds great but it has many environmentally unfriendly by-products and it's very expensive, in some cases it causes more pollution and guzzles more energy than just throwing the old away and making the new from scratch. But then again, landfill as we know is far from ideal and they want to scrap that in Europe too. And of course, importantly, let's not forget, the Act proposes committing Europe as a whole to sourcing a considerable amount of its energy from renewable means. But I agree with you, Jen, it's hardly specific on how they will achieve these aims."

"You mean it doesn't go into any great detail."

"Well, hardly."

"So how are they going to achieve those objectives? It all sounds so sketchy, so rough. I mean in principle it sounds great, but in practice..." She shrugged. "Do you really expect the European Council to sign up to it so quickly, to make it law so soon?"

"Absolutely. You see, rightly or wrongly, Jen, the Council members are all politicians, and all politicians want is popularity, popularity after all keeps them in power. They get votes when they promise to make things better and the environment is a huge issue, a real vote winner, everyone is in agreement that steps have to be taken to address all these environmental issues, the voting public Europe-wide are passionate about it. I reckon the Council members will be biting their hands off to sign up to it, to be seen by their own voting public to endorse the EEA will boost their own popularity, I doubt there's been a more popular piece of legislation in years. And besides that, the Council take their recommendations from the Commission, don't they? If the Commission with all the research at their fingertips advise them to sign up to it that's exactly what they'll do."

"So how will it work in practice then?" Jennifer was insistent. "I can see it's desirable, desirable to everyone to improve environmental policy, but how do you think they will actually enact those aims?"

"Well, you're asking me," it was Julian's turn to shrug, "I've no idea, I suppose it'll be back to our Lords and masters won't it, back to the Commissioners to put their heads together and come up with some workable secondary legislation. That's why Sir Morgan and his Grace have such an important job after all."

"Powerful men."

"Yes, Jen, with powerful salaries," he joked. "Oh, did I say salaries, I meant responsibilities. Now I'm sorry, Jen, but I really can't cope with any more interruptions, you heard the Commissioners I'm going to have to just shut the door, unplug the phone and get this proofreading finished."

Julian settled himself down to work again, but the obvious lack of any solution being posed in the document began to worry him. Just as Jennifer had pointed out it was a bit odd to try and force an Act through in its apparent infancy, and the inclusive absence of the curious Protocol Fifteen intrigued him. If it was the answer to all the questions why was it not included for him to proofread? And stranger still was the Commissioners own all-embracing personal interest in the document, it was true they were normally somewhat distant from their work force, and there was no doubt much they wouldn't normally share with the lowly likes of himself. But to be on his back, so desperate to have their document finished, was indeed most odd, they wouldn't normally be seeking its endorsement so quickly, and they certainly didn't normally write protocols themselves let alone uphold such efforts of protective secrecy.

Julian put the mysterious protocol out of his mind, and with most of the staff out of the office on their lunch breaks and the telephones quiet he was at last able to concentrate. Having waded through the remnants of the papers for about an hour he was just printing off the finished document when Nigel Sludboil and Trevor Rindburn, Hitoadie and Dredmor's Private Secretaries, took it upon themselves to enter his office and remind him that his part of the document was required.

"Morning, Finch," the lanky, big nosed Sludboil greeted him scathingly, "have you got that schedule finished yet? His Grace the Duke and Sir Morgan are very keen to get their hands on it."

"Yes I am aware of that, thank you Nigel, I think the whole office has done its best to remind me of that this morning."

"Supposed to have it in by lunchtime," the bald headed, bucktoothed Rindburn announced himself. "Lunchtime now," he spoke through an impish grin, "or could it be sack time?"

"Yes, well I gather it is lunchtime, so how lucky I am that the document is ready and finished. Sorry to disappoint you, Trevor, but I think the sacking will have to be put on hold, at least until the next unreasonable deadline is imposed upon me. You two at a loose end?" Julian asked provocatively.

The two Senior Civil Servants who had come to torment him were always going round the office making themselves unpopular by slavedriving on behalf of their Masters the Commissioners, and gave them a valuable ear on the office floor. Julian was in a bad enough mood already without Rindburn and Sludboil throwing their own tuppenceworth at him, and, refusing to be intimidated, he seized the opportunity to wind them up.

"I suppose the Commissioners are in a meeting and kicked you two out so they could discuss their precious Protocol Fifteen with the Spanish and Greek Commissioners in private."

"How do you know about Protocol Fifteen?" Sludboil asked after a sharp intake of breath. Julian could see his Adams apple bounce up and down in his throat.

"Oh come off it, Nigel, I'm supposed to proofread the document, I wouldn't be doing my job properly if I didn't realise a whole section was missing, would I?"

"What do you know about it anyway?" Rindburn asked quickly.

"Well a great deal less than you, Trevor, I don't doubt. Bet you two stand up against the door with a glass pressed to your ear whenever your Lords and Masters are in private, secret meetings don't you? Honestly, you're like a couple of schoolboys."

"Don't get smart, Finch," Rindburn snapped like a petulant school bully. "I can break you."

"Don't be such a fool, Finch," Sludboil patted his colleague on the shoulder to calm him down, "the Commissioners take us into their confidence occasionally, they know how to reward loyalty."

"Yeah," Rindburn grinned wider to reveal black bits at the top of his yellowing teeth, "they do that."

"Good for you," Julian responded sarcastically. "Now if you'll excuse me I have to hand this paper in without delay." He gathered the document off the printer and straightened his tie in preparation to stride along the rest of the office floor to the corridor which led to the Commissioner's own private room. "Shouldn't you two be sucking up to someone?" He put in a final dig as he turned to leave the room.

As Julian approached the Commissioner's office he saw their Spanish and Greek counterparts taking their leave of their hosts with much hand-shaking and big smiles all round. With a final goodbye to Hitoadie and Dredmor the Spaniard pushed their heavy oak door to (but not completely shut) behind him, and the foreigners bustled past Julian amid a chatter of excited babble.

Julian paced up to the Commissioner's door silently, and as he approached he could hear his bosses talking.

"Cheers," Hitoadie boomed, and Julian could hear the distinctive clink of glasses.

"Well that's it, Dennis," Sir Morgan announced, "an excellent job well done."

"Here's to Protocol Fifteen, eh - drink to it Morgan old boy, come on, see it off there's plenty more."

Julian had reached the door, but intrigued as to what he might hear he stopped for a moment before entering.

"Protocol Fifteen," said Sir Morgan's voice again, and he paused as if drinking a toast. "Well they've all assented to it now, it'll be a mere formality getting it through tomorrow now they've all seen it."

"Indeed yes, it's just a small matter of batting off the infernal journalists. No doubt we'll have to endure a wretched press conference, eh!"

"Well it'll be expected Dennis, but don't worry I know how to handle the media. We'll just take pains to draft a little statement on the way over."

"Good man, then it's just the little matter of getting our humble paper signed up by the Council. I dinned with the PM yesterday, he's simply gagging to get pen to paper. I've told him what the main Act is about and he's already said he's in agreement with the whole thing, though no mention of our little protocol of course. He's just pleased the proposed wind farms are to be re-sited."

"Well it was very clever of you to suggest putting that in initially, Dennis, it was clear they would never agree to them on mainland Europe in such numbers. It's been the perfect distraction."

"Indeed it has, but no, no, fairs fair and credit where its due," Hitoadie played the tribute down, "we both know the Politicians like to dispute things, gives em a chance to debate something eh, a chance to put their mark upon it, to do their bit. Why I bet they all think they came up with the whole Act themselves in the first place, what!"

"Well we're certainly lucky that all parties are taking the environment issue so seriously," Sir Morgan spoke with his usual coldness. "It gives us the bargaining tool, the solution itself will win our colleague's support once the EEA is passed, and it's the prospect of a very different New Environmental Solution Act, or NESA as I like to call it, in the here and now which will ensure the Council endorse our very own European Environmental Act, Protocol Fifteen and all."

"Well here's to the future of Europe," Hitoadie proposed another toast. "Protocol Fifteen to the EEA." The glasses clinked again.

"NESA," Sir Morgan proposed a further toast of his own, and the gulping of liquor was audible to Julian on the other side of the ajar door.

"Ah!" Hitoadie let out a contented breath, the liquor had obviously hit its mark. "Just one thing left to do, Morgan, old bean - got to get those damned birds bagged, what!"

"Honestly Dennis, you're so superstitious, are you on about the birds again?"

"The plan won't succeed unless every avenue is covered, Morgan, old boy," and the Duke sounded serious.

"Oh very well Dennis, but that's a job for the last minute."

"Last minute, good Lord no, anything can go wrong at the last minute. That idiot Finch has nearly botched everything already by being so damned thorough, we're pushing the deadline as it is. No, I insist we get the rollers moving on that one, I'm not leaving anything to chance."

"Oh very well, we'll make our move in good time," Sir Morgan conceded. "Oh," he sounded alarmed, "Dennis, we really must make sure we keep the door..." With a thud the heavy wooden door was slammed in Julian's face and he could only hear the end of Sir Morgan Dredmor's sentence in an almost completely inaudible mumble.

Julian decided to wait a second or two before knocking so they wouldn't think he might have heard anything. He had no idea what they had been talking about exactly, but they certainly seemed pleased with themselves and confident that the EEA was going to go through smoothly. Julian glanced around; there was no sign of Rindburn or Sludboil spying on him and everyone else was on lunch, the main office floor was deserted. He paused, counted to three, and knocked loudly.

"Come," came the booming voice of the Duke of Man through the thick door.

Julian entered to see the two Commissioners sitting opposite each other in their big leather arm chairs, each with a large tumbler of whisky cradled in hand and Hitoadie with one of his enormous cigars tucked in the corner of his mouth. On a low table between them he glimpsed a thin document with 'Protocol 15' written on it in black type, and a half empty cut-glass whisky decanter.

"Ah, Finch." The Duke rose to his feet, carelessly dropping a folded copy of the Financial Times over the document in an attempt to cover it up. "I trust you have completed your paperwork."

"Yes Commissioner, here it is, your Grace..."

But as Julian stretched the document out towards Hitoadie, Sir Morgan Dredmor snatched it from his hand.

"Not before time," he snapped rudely. "Now get out, Finch, the Duke of Man and I have private business to discuss."

"Certainly, Commissioner." Julian backed to the door.

"Oh Finch, old boy," Hitoadie called after him amid tobacco puffs.

"Yes, your Grace."

"Track Rindburn and Sludboil down for us will you, tell 'em to report to me office. Got a little job for 'em, what!"

"Yes, Commissioner, I'll tell them just as soon as I can."

Julian went in search of the Commissioners lap-dogs as bid, but his curiosity was now fully awakened. What was the NESA, that hadn't been mentioned before? And what the heck was actually in this secretive Protocol Fifteen?

Chapter Four – Homeward Bound

The coach drove on through the Somerset countryside, but Jess, staring silently out of the window, did not notice the view. Her ears were deaf to the endless background tittering of her classmates too. She was lost in a world of her own, trapped in a nightmare; she just couldn't stop thinking about the old drum and the spooky noise it had made.

As she went over and over it again in her mind she was in no doubt she'd heard it, she knew she had, she'd even seen the drum skin shaking as the invisible drummer had beat out the tune. The drum had been struck so gently, so quietly, over and over again, but why had it been so quiet, so deliberate? It was as if the noise had been made only for her to hear.

Jess remembered how frightened she'd felt, how terrified that something supernatural was happening, and yet how curious she'd been to find out more. Try as she might to forget all about it she just couldn't get the image out of her head, and she relived it again in her mind just as she had a hundred times since she left the drum in the silent Great Hall the day before.

She'd felt so faint, the room had been spinning, there had been no ghost to be seen but a chill had run down her spine, and she could feel again the sweat prickling at her forehead as the hairs stood up on the back of her neck while the drum rolled menacingly on in her mind. As she focused on the drum skin again in her memory the room began to spin around it, faster and faster and then suddenly it went still and the silence was deafening.

She remembered stretching out her fingers, why had she done that? She just didn't know, but very slowly in her mind, in her memory she was reaching out again. In her daydream she lived through it all again, the fear, the tension, she reached out her fingers and so gently, so delicately she tapped the drum skin.

Why had she tapped it? What had made her do it? It was so unlike her to be fearless and yet she had been so frightened. She knew she shouldn't have done it and quite apart from the sign saying 'don't touch' she hoped she hadn't annoyed the invisible drummer or annoyed the drum itself, if indeed it was playing on its own as Miss Davies had suggested. Could it have been? Jess just didn't know and a hundred questions flashed through her mind, every one chased by doubts and insecurity. Could she have imagined it all? Was she ill?

She reflected in glum silence just how drawn to the drum she had felt, so compelled, it had been as if some invisible force; perhaps even the old drum itself had been willing her on, urging her to tap it, she knew it had been real. For the hundredth time she reassured herself, it had happened, she knew it had, she just had to find out what it all meant.

Jess hoped she hadn't done wrong, hoped she hadn't called Drake back, that might get her in real trouble. But she just couldn't help thinking, believing, that something, or someone, had wanted her to tap the stretched leather skin.

She tried to convince herself that everything would be alright. After all, she reasoned, she'd only tapped the drum with her fingers, she hadn't beaten it properly and she'd made no real tune, she didn't even know any. And anyway, Drake was only supposed to come back if England was in grave danger and so far as Jess was aware there was no enemy army poised to invade her country.

This thought cheered her, if the country was in trouble she'd have done the right thing in calling the hero back, but if it wasn't he wouldn't return, so what harm had she done either way? But try as she might to dismiss these thoughts she just became more bothered. If there was about to be an invasion, what good would Drake do? How could he handle a modern-day Navy, let alone helicopter gun ships and nuclear submarines? The very idea was ridiculous. She shut her eyes, tried to will it away, but the wretched image of the painted drum just wouldn't leave her mind. There is no imminent invasion force looming, she told herself again, there's no need for Drake to return, but if there is no danger and no famous victory to celebrate why had the drum been beating at all? Her head thumped; in frustration Jess screwed her eyes tight shut and hid her face in her hands.

"You alright Jess?" Abi nudged her. "You've gone all quiet again."

"Yeah, no I'm okay, just thinking."

"Tommo just bet Toby he could beat him in an arm wrestle left-handed. What do you think?"

"Oh, I'm not sure, I'm not really interested."

"Come on," Abi insisted, "even if you don't want to bet on it you might as well watch."

"Whose, what? You mean both left-handed?" She asked distractedly.

"No you nonce, Tommo'd hammer him with his right hand on right hand and left on left, it's Tommo's left against Toby's right."

"But how will they grip?" Jess asked carelessly, "they can't go palm to palm can they?"

"Oh yeah, you're right. Guys," Abi frantically addressed the assembled rear of the coach, "how can they get a grip…?"

Jess just wasn't interested in the background noise, she hadn't even welcomed the distraction. The drum sailed yet again into the forefront of her mind and she was numbing again to the background banter.

"Jess," Abi nudged her again in the ribs.

"What?"

"Tommo's going to hold on to the back of..." She stopped. "You know, you really don't look too good."

"I'm okay."

"Are you feeling sick again? Coz if you are tell me before you hurl, I don't want any vom on me."

"I'm alright Abi, honest."

"You're just being so quiet though - something's wrong, Jess, I know it is."

"I'm allowed to be quiet if I want to be," she replied gently, "I think I'm just overtired, that's all."

"Better mind out you don't get boring," said Abi cruelly, "you've been spending too much time with Mr boring Brendan Johnson." She turned her back on Jess to concentrate fully on her judicial role of umpiring the arm wrestling contest.

"You sure you're okay?" Brendan turned round from the seat in front of Jess. "You don't seem yourself."

"Yeah I'm okay, I just, I can't help thinking about that drum," she replied carelessly. "I mean I don't know why," she added quickly, "it's just got me thinking that's all."

"Ghost stories eh."

"Yeah, I s'pose."

"Ghosts are just legends Jess," he spoke comfortingly, "they're just silly old myths, they aren't real. Don't let it bother you." He smiled and his warmth was reassuring. "You can't come back from the dead," he said with finality.

"Yeah, yeah you're probably right, I must have imagined it."

"Imagined what?"

"Oh um, just imagined the ghost story," she said quickly. "Bad dream, Brendan, I just had a bad dream last night."

"Well I hope you feel better." He turned back to face his front.

"Yeah, thanks Brendan."

A massive shout and a crash finally brought Jess out of her private thoughts. Toby Barnes had been flung out of his seat by Tommo Lydon to whoops of delight from Abi and the other girls, and was sprawling in the aisle.

"Not fair," he protested. "You were supporting yourself by holding the seat in front."

"Referee?" The gum-chewing Tommo coolly referred the appeal to Abi's judgement.

"Nothing wrong with that, you're allowed to steady yourself."

"Yeah but come on…"

"No arguing with the ref," said Abi firmly, her ruling having been somewhat predictable. "Tommo left-hand Lydon is coach champion again."

"Come on then, Lydon," Mark Thompson challenged, "left on left."

"I demand a re-match," said a blushing Toby retaking his seat.

"Well you can't have one," Abi berated him, "you weren't good enough, Toby, you've been beaten fair and square, you should wrestle someone weaker like Brendan. Not that he's your size of course," she added, laughing at her own cruel joke. Brendan ignored the jibe, and Toby reluctantly made way for Mark Thompson to take the place opposite Tommo.

Mr Jarvis, clearly now aware that the behaviour at the rear of the coach was becoming disorderly, made his way down the aisle to put a stop to the children's fun.

"Sit quietly now," he said firmly, "Miss Davies is about to announce the winners of yesterday's quiz."

"Ooh, boring," came a collective moan from the girls on the back seats.

"Quiet, Norris, or I'll move you."

"Me, quiet!" said Johnny Norris looking hurt. "I didn't say anything."

"Norris," said Mr Jarvis again sternly, "I won't tell you again. And that goes for all of you," he added quickly. "Now, we've had a great trip so far and we all get home this afternoon, so don't spoil it now." He left his words hang in the air and turned to make his way back to the front, but as soon as the babble of voices begun again Miss Davies' shrill voice blasted out of the loud speakers.

"Right, the prize for the quiz as you know is twenty quid's worth of record tokens to be shared between the pair, so that's ten pounds worth each - it may not be the world cup but I'm sure it's worth winning." She coughed loudly, ensuring a pause in which to build tension. "Here we go, then: in last place with a miserable seven out of twenty five in the Francis Drake quiz we have Tammy Smith and Mark Thompson."

"Seven!" came the disbelieving voice of Mark Thompson.

"Seven, only seven," jeered Abi scornfully.

"Quiet. Fourteenth, with eleven out of twenty five: Gemma Biggs and Johnny Norris. Just twelfth with eleven, that's twelfth equal: Nicholas Bovis and Lizzie Taylor and Lisa Scott and Michael James."

Miss Davies worked her way up through the places, and third place having been announced, Jess and Brendan still hadn't heard their names called. "In second place, with twenty-four out of twenty-five, an excellent effort: Brendan Johnson and Jessica Finch. Just one wrong answer, well done."

Oh blow it, thought Jess. She had hoped she had won and now Abi was sitting beside her looking very pleased with herself.

"Which leaves, in first place with a whopping twenty-five out of twenty-five: Miss Abigail Saunders and Mr Thomas Lydon," Miss Davis announced the winners to a round of applause, but Jess couldn't understand it. Abi was not remotely interested in History and there was no way it could ever be counted as one of her stronger subjects, and come to that, Tommo's result in the end of year History exam had been far from exceptional.

"However," Miss Davies continued in dramatic tones, "it has come to my attention that there may have been an element of foul play." She was on her feet now and waddling awkwardly up the aisle.

"Oooh," the kids were hooked by the scandal and started throwing intrigued glances around the coach. It was unlike Miss Davies to expose a cheat so publicly and Jess presumed Mr Jarvis must have put her up to it.

"A National Trust tour guide took it upon herself to inform me that she had been approached by a couple from the class, and that she had given them all the answers not realising this was a competitive quiz. Therefore, Tommo and Abi are disqualified and the prize goes to Jess and Brendan." Squeezing her bulk around the seats in front of them she handed the vouchers to the winners. "So well done you two, and may that be a lesson to Miss Saunders and Mr Lydon," she said light-heartedly. "Nice try."

"Whatever happened to initiative?" Tommo asked jokingly. "It was only research."

"Out-swotted by the swots," said Abi more sourly.

But Jess just laughed it off, "You didn't expect to get away with that did you?" she giggled.

"Humph, you're such a teacher's pet. Don't want music vouchers anyway, humph, record tokens, so square," Abi sulked under her breath.

"Right," Miss Davies restored order, "we have a quick stop this morning in Glastonbury, and then, as you have mostly all behaved well on this trip, we will head on to Longleat Animal Park before we get home to Bath."

This news was welcomed with whoops of joy and shouts of "yes," and "get in there," from the back of the coach.

"Okay," Miss Davies imposed herself again over the loud speaker, "do you all know the legend of King Arthur?" There were noises affirming recognition from her students. "King Arthur and his knights of the round table, Merlin, Sir Lancelot, Queen Guinevere and all that."

"Yeah," came the children's voices again.

"Right, then let me tell you a little about the real King Arthur." This news was met predictably by a few moans from certain children. Jess glanced to her side to see Abi pulling faces of boredom and gloom. "The real King Arthur was no medieval knight in shining armour who lived in enormous castles and held splendid tournaments on romantic tented paddocks; he was a Romano-British chieftain, a warlord who would have lived about five hundred AD.

"The Romano-British period is basically just after the Romans have left and the Saxons and other invaders are starting to arrive on these shores. Picture it: the country would have been in sharp decline, Roman infrastructure falling apart, Roman management, administration and of course protection all gone, the people vulnerable, their future uncertain - and then a new threat, raiders and migrating peoples invading in force on every side. The Saxons landed in the south east, and to the natives they were heathens, barbarians. They quickly settled and took over that area of the country, killing the British and moving west.

"Arthur becomes the great British hope. It is believed that he had lands in the south west of England, Wales and probably Cornwall too, but there are also legends which associate him with northern France, Brittany in particular, so it's hard to say where exactly his territorial boundaries were, and where he actually campaigned, but we do know that his kingdom was under huge threat and that the native peoples rallied to him. He fought many battles and secured many victories over his enemies, but in the end there were just too many of them.

"Of course there are many ancient legends, and many more much more recent stories. There has been much talk and debate about where his last great battle, Camlan, was actually fought, but many agree that somewhere around here close to Glastonbury he was struck down with a grievous and potentially mortal wound. He is supposed to have been taken to the mystical Isle of Avalon to seek healing, and to be buried in a chamber deep in the earth where he sleeps, still nursing his wounds, whether to die or recover. Look out of the windows."

Jess did so, and could see that the landscape had dramatically changed, they were no longer amongst rolling hills, a great flat plain spread out before them. "The Somerset levels," Miss Davies announced. "Over there in the distance is Glastonbury Tor. That hill over there," she pointed, "you can't miss it." Jess couldn't, in the middle of the vast flat plain was a hillock with a tower on top of it. It looked like a cake with a single candle standing alone on a smooth tabletop.

"Now I'm sure Mr Jarvis could be more specific, but years ago all this flat land, all this plain would once have been underwater and that Tor, that hill, would have been an island." Jess did her best to imagine it; it would have been properly cut off and too small to have sustained any population.

"This is Avalon," Miss Davies announced with as much drama as she could muster through the microphone. "Of course, as with anything to do with Arthur there is much debate as to where Avalon is supposed to be, but most experts agree that this is the most likely spot and Arthur could be somewhere around here sleeping, maybe even under the Tor itself.

"Any of you who know anything about the Arthurian legends will know that Arthur is of course known as the Once and Future King. Legends have it that if ever Britain is in terrible danger Arthur will return to save his people and lead them to victory... Now we are going to have a quick stop in the town, but this is Arthur country, so keep that in mind." She replaced the microphone noisily, and the children, seeing this as a signal to talk again, started tittering amongst themselves once more.

Jess sat in contemplative silence. Arthur, she thought, that's all I need. Just as she was trying to get one legend out of her mind Miss Davies was throwing another one at her. She secretly decided to ensure she stuck with the main group on this visit, and above all not to touch anything.

Max went in the car with his mother to pick his sister up from school, and much to his irritation he had to kick his heels in the car park for thirty minutes waiting for the coach (which was, he thought, predictably behind schedule) to arrive.

The car park was packed with other parents all parked up waiting to ferry their children home. Some looked anxious, as Patricia Finch did, worrying as to why the coach was delayed and hoping all was well, while others shared Max's annoyance at being inconvenienced by having to wait for them at all. Others still looked apprehensive that the trip was soon to be finally over and that their children would now be home for the duration of the long summer holiday.

"It's been so nice and quiet at home, Patricia," Abi Saunders' mother reflected sadly, "so peaceful."

"But it'll be a nice relief to have them home won't it?" Patricia Finch replied. "Maxwell, Julian and I have all missed Jessica terribly. You'll be glad to have your sister back, won't you, Maxie? I know I will."

"Mum," he snapped angrily, "its only been three nights." Fond as he was of his sister he could do without being made to look a total wimp, especially as Tommo Lydon's mum was walking over to join the small throng of parents gathered around his mother's car.

"Max," Tommo's mother greeted him warmly. "Are you coming over this week? I know Thomas is very excited about trying to get his new cricket net up in the garden and I'm sure he'll need someone to pitch a few balls at him. We got it for his birthday," she added for the benefit of the assembled mothers, "Dewer's in the town, they're awfully good."

"Bowl I believe is the term," Toby Barnes' mother chipped in, noting the irritation on Max's face.

"Oh yes of course, sorry Max, bowl. Thomas will need you to bowl at him," she corrected herself. "You'll have to bring your cricket bat too, are you a bowler or a batter?"

"I'm an all-rounder really, like Flintoff. I'm a good batsman and I notch up the runs but I take a few wickets as well." Max tried to humour the ignorance of the feminine onslaught, but it persisted, Tommo's mother thinking herself friendly by taking the trouble to engage Max in conversation.

"It's awfully rough, you know, terribly dangerous," she addressed her peers once more, "that ball seems to go at a hundred miles an hour - it's a wonder there aren't more casualties. Do you wear padding, Max?"

"Well I've got some old ones somewhere... if they still fit."

"Wants some new ones this summer," Patricia Finch explained. "Keeps saying his old ones are too small, I've heard nothing else all spring," she adopted a patronising tone, "but they grow so fast, don't they?"

"Mum!" Max protested. But his mother wouldn't spare his embarrassment, and continued to talk about him as if he wasn't even there.

"That's very kind of you, Celia, I'm sure Maxwell will be delighted to come and roll a few balls at your Tom. I mean, its nice for them to have something to do, isn't it? Maxie just didn't know what to do with himself last summer and its such a long holiday isn't it?"

"Oh yes it is," Mrs Saunders agreed wholeheartedly, and Max could sense a tone of deep regret in her voice.

When the coach did finally arrive he was relieved that the gaggle of mothers abandoned their interrogation and left him alone to swamp the coach instead as their smiling children descended the steps to retrieve their luggage from the storage lockers under the vehicle. Max noticed that Mr Jarvis and Miss Davies looked more relieved than anyone to be back as the children chattered excitedly to their parents of all their adventures, and as he spotted his own friends exiting the coach he went forward to greet them.

"Alright Tommo, Nick."

"Alright mate," Tommo Lydon replied. "Don't worry, Max, you didn't miss much."

"Boring," he heard Abi Saunders grumble as her long-suffering mother lugged her enormous suit case back to their waiting car. "The animal park was okay but the rest of the trip was just sooo boring."

"That's nice dear," he heard Mrs Saunders reply, though she clearly wasn't listening.

"Hi Sis," he greeted Jessica after their mother had finished hugging and kissing her. "How did you cope with such a small bag?"

"Small!" Jess looked back at him in surprise, struggling under the weight of her own perfectly conventionally sized case.

"Well yeah, I know you girls don't travel light, but compared to Abi Saunders…"

"Yeah I think she had her whole wardrobe with her," Jess shared the joke. "She fancies you, you know."

"Ugh don't," Max shuddered.

With her own case safely transferred to the boot of her mother's car and Max and her mother strapped in and ready to go, Jess asked them to wait a moment and quickly walked back to the group of children gathered around the coach, still saying their goodbyes or waiting for their parents to arrive.

"Where's she going now?" Max demanded of his mother impatiently.

"Oh she'll only be a second darling," Patricia Finch started the engine, "now what do you want for your tea?"

Max didn't answer but looked on in amazement as his sister, having said a quick goodbye to her female friends, approached the portly figure of Brendan Johnson, who sat alone on his suitcase to the rear of the bus and away from the rest of the group, still waiting for his lift, and kissed him goodbye on the cheek.

Patricia Finch saw it too and quickly advised her son. "Don't you say anything Maxwell." But when Jess got in and the car pulled away Max couldn't resist but wind her up.

"Ooh Brendan," he mocked sarcastically, "will you be my

boyfriend?"

"Shut up, Max," she defended herself.

"Yes Maxwell, leave it out," their mother spoke firmly. "If your sister has a boyfriend be nice to her, be happy for her."

"But Brendan Johnson!" Max persisted. "Brendan Johnson!" He repeated the name in disbelief. "He's the biggest un-co in the class!"

"Look, Max, he's not my boyfriend, okay..."

"Don't worry, Jessie darling," Patricia defended her daughter from the driver's seat, "Maxie's just jealous. Don't be jealous Maxwell."

"Jealous," he protested, "I'm not jealous, not of Jess anyway. Eurgh, it'd be like me getting a crush on that minging Tamara Joyce in Five F."

"He's not jealous, Mum," Jess agreed. "Look, Max I told you, Brendan isn't my boyfriend, okay?"

"Der," Max replied quickly, "then what were you kissing the fat little podger for?"

"He's a nice guy, okay. He gets so much stick off everyone. I guess I just feel a bit sorry for him that's all."

"Feel sorry for Brendan bloomin' Johnson?" Max still couldn't get his head around it.

"So anyhow, Jessie, how was the trip?" Patricia Finch swiftly changed the subject.

Anxious and exhausted, Jessica Finch sat quietly with her brother, Max, in the comfy lounge at Weston-Bissett. Their dog, Benji, a soppy brown and white springer spaniel, rested his head on her lap and in an attempt to distract herself from the ever-present image of the drum in her mind she gently massaged the dog behind his ears as he flickered his eyelids in pleasure. She was tired and had barely been able to sleep as every time she'd shut her eyes she had pictured the drum skin vibrating, and every time she'd put her head on the pillow she'd heard the beating of the drum in her ears; she just couldn't get it out of her head.

The safari park had been a welcome distraction but finally being home, safe and sound, made Jess feel a little more secure. To have her parents and Max close by, to have the prospect of her own bed tonight and being free of Abi's endless whinging all made a difference, but even in the peace and quiet of the room she couldn't take her mind from the beating drum.

Max dropped the TV remote on the floor in defeat. He'd been flicking through with the telly on mute and hadn't been able to find anything he wanted to watch, and whilst Benji yawned as he enjoyed Jess's attention Max wasn't finding his sister such entertaining company. He glanced over at her as she caressed the dog; her fingers worked but she stared blankly ahead and looked completely lost in thought. Max frowned, this wasn't like Jess, she wasn't normally one to bottle things up.

"You alright, Sis?"

"Yeah, just thinking."

"About Brendan?" he probed mischievously, but Jess wouldn't take the bait.

"No, as it happens, but if you're bored you can always go and help mum with the washing up."

"Urgh," Max winced at the thought of it. "Mum's been doing my head in lately."

"Well Dad'll be home soon, perhaps you can play computer games with him."

"He's never got time for that," Max replied bitterly. "So what were you thinking about then?"

"Oh it doesn't matter, it's not important." Jess looked down at Benji evasively.

"Course it matters, anything that's bothering my little sister is important to me."

"Max we're twins, you're not older than me. Mum's never told us who was born first, so until she does we'll never know."

"Well yeah," he conceded, "but you're still littler than me, aren't you?"

"Yeah, okay, I'll give you that, fat boy," she smiled.

"That's better. So what is it that's bothering you?"

"Well, if I tell you will you promise you won't tell?" Desperate as she was to get the drum off her chest she tested the water gently, she didn't want Max to hold it up as a big joke.

"Oh no, it's not one of those girly secrets is it? You've snogged Brendan haven't you?"

"No Max," Jess was annoyed but let it go. "It's got nothing to do with Brendan, its... kind of spooky," she said mysteriously. She half expected her brother to go 'woooh' and run around the house shouting 'Jessica's scared of ghosties,' but Max just sat in silence, intrigued as to what she would say next. "I can trust you, can't I Max?" she asked again. "I mean, you really can't tell anyone."

"Yeah," Max tried to sound important, "course you can trust me, Sis, what happened?"

"Well, it's Francis Drake," she began awkwardly. She felt so silly telling her brother what had happened but it was reassuring to finally be able to tell someone about it. A problem shared is a problem halved, or so the theory went. "You know we went to his old home in Devon, Buckland Abbey?"

Max nodded, though in truth he had no clue as to where the Elizabethan explorer had lived and little interest in the itinerary of a trip he had not participated in. He frowned and a twinkle of excitement came into his eyes. "You didn't see his ghost, did you? Mum and I went to the Tower of London, you know where Walter Raleigh's ghost is supposed to be, but we didn't see anything."

"Calm down, it's not as exciting as that, though I wish I had seen his ghost - it would have explained everything."

"Explained what?" Max was full of interest now, but Jess was clearly frightened and he could see that it wasn't going to be easy for her to talk about it. He knew he shouldn't be pushy, that he should offer support, but he just couldn't help himself. Ghosts fascinated him.

"Well," Jess paused as if to take care what to say next. "Someone was playing his drum."

"So?" Max's face fell, this didn't sound too exciting at all.

"Well that's just it, I heard the drum, Drake's own drum, but I didn't see anyone playing it."

"Well what's so spooky about that? You can hear drums miles away...."

"Max," she interrupted him, "I was there, I was right by it, standing next to the drum. I heard it, I saw the skin move, it was being tapped but there was no one else in the room... I didn't imagine it, it's true, I swear."

"Well there must be some reason why, drums don't play themselves... A poltergeist," he considered. "Was it loud?"

"No, really faint, I don't think anyone else would have heard it... I don't know if anyone else was meant to hear it... I think it might have been beating for me."

Max frowned in confusion. "Well um, what does that mean?"

"Well it means, I'm not sure, but the drum is supposed to be heard when the country is in danger, or when we've just had a great victory... We're not in danger, are we?"

"No," Max was certain of this, "no war going on, Sis."

"So we've not won a victory either?"

"No, course not, the Ashes proper don't start for weeks."

"Cricket doesn't count Max, come on I'm serious. I know you think I'm just a wet girly, but I was really scared Max, and I did hear it, I know I did."

"Course, Sis, sorry." He didn't really know what to say. "So, um... What did you do, turn and run?"

"No, not exactly."

"But you did get a proper look round, didn't see anyone playing a joke or anything?"

"Yeah I, um, I did look properly round the room, there was no one there, but the drumming went on for a while, Max." Jess was leaning forward and was almost whispering now. "Like I said... I went right up to the drum, and the skin was moving."

"So what did you do?"

"I, um... I tapped it."

"You played it!" Max was amazed at his sister's bravery. "But you could have been talking to a ghost."

"Max, please don't scare me, okay. Do you know what's meant to happen if you play Drake's drum?"

"No, what's meant to happen?"

"He's meant to come back, I mean, if the country is in trouble that is."

"And did he?" Max looked anxiously at his sister, but Jess had her eyes fixed downwards at Benji as she still ruffled him with her fingertips.

"No... I don't know... Look, I told you I hadn't seen any ghosts... I wish I hadn't told you now, I feel so stupid."

"Sis," Max tried to comfort her, "don't be scared, you're home now... But what did happen?"

"Nothing," Jess replied simply, and she looked up at her brother briefly. "The drumming stopped and I just left the room." Max remained silent, and after a pause Jess went on, dropping her eyes away from her brother and back to the dog's head in her lap. "It was just so weird, I felt so cold, so scared. It was like there was some kind of presence there. It was like I was being willed to do it, like some force really wanted me to be playing the drum... I know I shouldn't have touched it and everything, but I just couldn't help myself."

"Well, um, I shouldn't worry, there's no harm done, is there... The country isn't in trouble and he won't come unless it is, right?"

"Right."

"And if it is in trouble he'll sort it out... So you've done the right thing I suppose."

"Thanks Max, that's what I needed to hear, that's what I've been trying to tell myself." Jess looked up at her brother again appreciatively. "But it doesn't explain it though does it? It doesn't explain why the drum was playing itself."

"No," Max conceded, there seemed no need nor reason for it to play. "Oh, was the window open? Wind might have played it."

"No Max it didn't, I swear - the drum was being played for my benefit, I'm sure it was."

"Um," Max wracked his brains, deep in thought.

"Do you believe in ghosts?" Jess asked him.

"You know I do."

"But no one can actually prove them, can they?"

"Well no, not usually, but so many people have said they've seen them, I mean throughout history...."

"History, yes.... And do you believe in myths Max, old stories, legends and stuff?"

"Well monsters don't exist do they? Dragons, sea-monsters and stuff."

"Well no, they haven't found any evidence, but what I mean is, well, all these legends from history, they all must be based in some truth mustn't they? Otherwise they never would have grown into a legend over time. Robin Hood, Jason and the Golden Fleece, Helen of Troy. After all, there was a Trojan war wasn't there, Trojan horse or no Trojan horse?"

"Yeah, yeah I think so. So what are you getting at?"

"I'm just, I'm just wondering if it could be true, if that drum really does have the power to bring Drake back.... And if I was being pressured into doing it..."

"Now, anyone want a drink?" Patricia Finch burst into the room. "I'm about to put the kettle on."

They heard the sound of a key turning in the front door lock and Benji instantly sprung from Jess's lap and ran to the hall barking in greeting. "Oh good," their mother voiced her approval, "and your father's home at last."

Chapter Five – The return of the King

Julius Caesar first came to Britain in 54 BC. He came in search of wealth and raw materials: tin, copper, gold, and people. People, a valuable commodity, could be returned to Rome as slaves. His own personal wealth and power he sought to enhance, but the material gain to Rome would serve to strengthen the expanding Roman Empire.

He was to find Britain a land of tribes, divided under their own chieftains they fought each other as much as the new invader, and divided they were no match for the disciplined Roman legions on the battlefield. The strongest adversary; the British chieftain of the Catuvellauni tribe, Caswallaun, whom the Romans called Cassivelaunus, was taken to Rome a prisoner, to be paraded in victory. Yet he was not himself to see the eternal city, as in his humiliation his captors had put out his eyes.

Britain was a wild country, cold and wet. There were drover's routes, but nothing of a like to the roads, bridges and aqueducts of Rome. The Britons had no written language and used no currency but that of trade and barter, it was to take the Romans a long time to bring the land and its people slowly under their yoke.

After Caesar a new Emperor, Augustus, sent a further invasion. The Romans founded cities, built roads to link them and slowly advanced northwards through Britain, ever expanding the frontier of the mighty Roman Empire. They crushed the resistance of Caradoc, the latest British hero, and sent him back to Rome as they had Caswallaun before. But given his chance to address the Senate, Caradoc, known to his vanquishers as Caractacus, was able to bowl them over with a speech of eloquence and noble passion which granted him their pardon.

They called it 'civilisation,' for a Roman it was everything: education, technology, engineering, architecture and entertainment. For the British it was a life of misery and slavery. It was British slaves who cut the stones and mined the metal, it was British slaves who dug the fields and built the Roman villas, temples and bath houses, laying each block under the direction of their Roman masters, and it was British slaves who died in the arenas for their oppressors' entertainment. In the early years they were not citizens of the empire but prisoners of it. It broke their bodies and it hurt their pride, and the Romans pushed them and pushed them until they could take no more.

A mighty warrior Queen of the Iceni tribe, who lived in what is now called East Anglia, was to lead a rebellion. Boudicca burnt Roman cities and threatened to drive the invaders back out of her country and into the sea. The Empire could not stand for such a threat, as other enslaved nations might rise up too, and so, with clinical discipline they crushed it; first with tactics on the battlefield, and later with a terrible oppression even more brutal and humiliating for this proud warrior people than anything they had suffered before.

The British were a pagan nation whose religious and spiritual leaders were the Druids, and the Romans blamed the rebellion on these tree worshiping shaman. The 'pax Romana' was broken. No longer would the British be allowed to keep their Gods and their customs, the Druids were hunted down and slaughtered, and their sacred sites and strongholds as far away as Ynys Mon, now called Anglesey, were burnt to the ground. Boudicca, fearing the capture of herself and her daughters, had committed suicide to avoid falling victim to the Roman's revenge, and the people of Britain, with their warrior Queen and the Druids destroyed, were leaderless.

The Britons had always carried weapons as a sign of status, as well as to defend themselves and make war on their neighbours, but the Romans now prohibited them from owning weapons and to prevent them ever rising up again they banned them from learning how to fight, thus ensuring their humiliation was complete and their traditional way of life was forgotten. In a stroke the Britons' very culture and ancient religion had been dragged from under their feet. The very things that defined this people and made them who they were had been taken from them, and they were now even more enslaved and at the mercy of Rome than they had been before, an underling class of slaves ripe for deserved exploitation by their all-powerful and merciless masters.

As an outpost of Empire Britain was an unhappy place where the garrison of men from the Mediterranean shivered in the rain and missed the warm sun of home. They guarded the 'North Wall,' built on the orders of the Emperor Hadrian to mark and protect the frontier from the wild Picti tribesmen who threatened raids from the mountainous north, but whom the Senate did not believe it was in the interests of the Empire to subdue.

With the baptism of an Emperor, things were to change slightly. In the eternal city they no longer cheered as wild beasts tore the saints apart in the Coliseum. The Emperor, for so long worshiped by the Roman people as a God, denied his divinity and became a Christian himself, and with the Emperor a believer in the new religion his subjects too began to convert. Once the Christians had been burnt as candles to light the Emperor Nero's garden, but with the Emperor a believer the faith spread via the roads and trade routes of the Roman Empire, until eventually it reached the rugged shores of Britain.

The gap between Roman and Briton narrowed slightly, the tyranny lessened and Roman and Briton began to live more harmoniously, began to integrate together. Time had played its part too; it was the best part of five hundred years since the Legions had landed at Pevensey and a new generation had been born, a more educated more enlightened nation which embraced Rome as it's protector and knew no other system, a nation richly mixed between Roman and ancient British ancestors, a people now referred to as the 'Romano British,' cultured citizens of the Empire living in an island province and under the protection of the Roman Governor and the soldiers garrisoned there.

Then suddenly it all began to go wrong, and hordes of marauding Barbarians began to attack the frontiers of the Empire on all sides. Even Rome itself was threatened by enemies from the east and the north, and the Empire just didn't have enough soldiers to defend itself on all fronts.

The decision was made. Britain was abandoned and the legions defending the island frontier were taken away to fight in defence of the provinces nearer to Rome. The inhabitants of Britain, this new generation no longer used to war, were left defenceless, unprotected, to fend for themselves.

The invaders needed no invitation; they came like wolves to the sheep fold and began to raid. Saxons, so called because of the huge battle-axes they carried, arrived in their long ships packed with warriors. At first they raided the coast, but soon they realised that by sailing inland up rivers from the sea they could strike deep into the country with deathly silent surprise, stealing food, gold and animals, killing any who didn't run from them, and burning houses to the ground before returning to the sea. These were a people untouched by the influence of Rome. Pagan and brutal they raided with a merciless intensity and slaughtered wantonly.

In the absence of a Roman Governor the Romano British chieftains tried to resist the new danger and put an end to the panic. A chieftain from the south east marshes named Vortigern declared himself 'King,' and realising that his people were no match for the furious foe he hired two Saxon chieftains, Hengist and Horsa, to fight for him against the raiders, granting them lands in the east of the country.

The plan backfired. The mercenaries found the land to be fertile and the natives to be easy prey. They settled, invited more of their fellow Saxons to join them, and finally turned on Vortigern. They were raiders no longer, but invaders who drove the British off the land and settled in their place. It signalled the beginning of a dark age of struggle. Other migrating peoples soon learned of Britain's vulnerability and hastily made landings of their own in the hopes of carving out a homeland. The Angles, Jutes, Scots from modern Ireland and Vikings from Scandinavia all began to invade in time, and it seemed that disaster threatened from every side.

Vortigern was besieged in his tower on the marshes, a tower he had begun to build when the Saxons first arrived for his own protection. By day the labourers had built up the tower, but each night the foundations had crumbled. Vortigern knew not why, and in a throwback to the old religions and traditions of the Druids he decided to sacrifice a boy to the gods of the marshes, intending to use his little body as the foundation stone so the building would stand firm. The boy Merlin, considered blameless and suitable for such sacrifice, was brought to the King, but in his wisdom he explained to Vortigern why it was that the tower's foundations kept crumbling and his life was spared.

For Merlin had seen, deep beneath the earth, in a great cavernous chamber, two dragons fighting. By day they were still, but by night they tore and thrashed against each other with ferocious violence, crashing and smashing each other against the walls of the chamber and causing the very ground to shake and the foundations of the King's tower above to crumple and fall.

When he heard this, Vortigern moved his tower to firmer ground and his wooden fortress was finished, but it was not to save him. The Saxons surrounded it, and when the British King refused to come down or surrender they simply burnt it to the ground with Vortigern and his entourage inside.

The other British chieftains fared little better against their enemies, though most notably Uthyr Pendragon, a Lord of the west, held them back for a time. As the Saxons settled they multiplied, and as they multiplied they became stronger but outgrew their new living space. They began to spread ever westward, pushing the British who tried to resist them ever backward, penning them into the West Country and what is now Wales. They knew that if they could stamp out the resistance the whole country would be theirs, and they slowly gathered and accumulated armies ready for a decisive push into the heart of the British defence.

Uthyr grew ill, and Merlin, now an old man, was both advisor to the Chieftain and tutor to his son and heir Arthur. Arthur was Artos to most of his followers, the simple men who spoke the British tongue, but

Arturias to the older generation of more educated nobles who surrounded his father. These were the Latin speaking descendants of Roman society who had remained in the island when the legions deserted them. In time, Arthur's mixed ancestry and influence would serve him well.

Merlin worked the young Arthur hard, for it was clear that his father's time was passing and it was he who would have to carry the banner of resistance against the destructive force of the Saxon horde, and he was to benefit from Merlin's enthusiastic tutorship. Brought up in a Roman villa and educated in Latin he was a follower of the new religion, but Merlin now taught him much of the old ways too. He lectured him in the ways of the ancient Britons, seeking to rekindle the warrior spirit, and in the lore and customs of the Druids, if not the pagan rituals long forgotten by the modern Romano British. For Merlin knew Arthur would have as much use for traditional healing as he would for weapons and tactics in the struggle ahead. He nurtured Arthur, he encouraged and strengthened him, and he set out to inspire him by telling him what it was that he had seen in the cavern below Vortigern's tower on the marshes, years before when he himself had been a youth with his life in front of him.

Each night the dragons had fought - one a huge white dragon, powerful and terrifying, the other much smaller, but no less ferocious, and red in colour. "The white dragon represented the Saxons," the aged Merlin counselled Arthur, "and most nights it would win because it was so much bigger and stronger than the other. But the red dragon fought bravely and hard, breathing fire and tearing at the white dragon's flesh with its claws. Just occasionally," Merlin told Arthur, "the red dragon would win. He will always have his day."

"You must become the dragon, Arthur, son of Uthyr," Merlin pressed him. "This is your destiny. Your enemy may be stronger, but you are wiser, and with cunning and endurance, and with tenacious determination and bravery, you too will have your day."

Uthyr Pendragon made sure that his son was trained for war, and Arthur cut his teeth leading raiding parties against their Saxon foes. He became experienced, battle-hardened and successful, and his fame spread. Merlin's influence had made Arthur the unifier; his Roman education twinned with his understanding of the old ways meant that all Britons came to see him as their leader and great hope against the Saxons and their other enemies. His call was for unity, for he realised that together the Britons were stronger, but divided they were no match for the foe, and petty power struggles had to be put aside. When Uthyr died Arthur set up a red dragon as his standard and the other minor chieftains of Britain flocked to him. By popular consent they crowned him king, for they knew that whilst they had Arthur they had hope.

The King set up fortresses at Chester and Caerleon, converting old Roman forts to be seats of power where he held his Court and counsel of war. As history became legend and legend myth, the mystical Camelot would later find its inspiration in the ruins of his two 'Caerlleons,' his two 'cities of legions,' one on the Usk and one on the Dee. Here Arthur gave the other chieftains the title of Knights. He was desperate that there should be unity amongst them, that none should seek to be more powerful than another, so he built a circular table at which he and his Knights could meet, all on an equal footing. 'The Saxon is the enemy,' he repeatedly drummed into them, 'divided we fail,' and with such wisdom and the sound advice of Merlin, Arthur moulded his people.

He led them in battle boldly, defeating Saxon armies in the field with a mixture of Roman and more modern tactics. He looked to rekindle the traditions of the warrior amongst his people, and realising that they fought not just for their homes, their religion and culture against the pagan invaders but for their very lives, they fought all the harder. He gave them a great victory at Badon and another at Dyrham. The Saxon advance was faltered, they would need time to re-group, and as they did so Arthur and his generals harried and raided them; any delay forced upon the Saxons bought his own people a freedom prolonged.

Arthur married the lady Gwenhwyfar, first daughter of the chieftain of Gwynedd in the mountainous north of modern Wales, and so strengthened ties with those whose ancestry was most closely linked to the ancient Britons, the old people of the past. Legend would distort her to the Guinevere of poem and song, and Arthur was proud to have her as his Queen.

In winter they held on to the latter day cultures of Rome; they read, took baths and wore clean clothes. They ate feasts and banquets where wine, music and song entertained their guests. In summer the people gathered the harvest, all the strong men were needed and the warriors could not be spared. It was life or death to all of them, and it was the same for their settled enemies, for even raiding could not guarantee a fruitful crop would be secured, and raiding would wait until the autumn. Spring time was when the King campaigned with purpose, seeking to meet the enemy in full and open battle, and advancing out of his strongholds to find them. Attack he believed was the best form of defence, for when they got to him it would be too late, he had to hold them in the east.

For many years the boarders quivered and quaked, like two strong men arm wrestling each other the advantage seemed to totter one way and then be held with the other, but try as they might the Saxon numbers were too many, their irrepressible tide was all too strong and it was slowly turning against them, forcing the Britons ever backwards, ever west. Eventually, time ran out for Arthur son of Uthyr Pendragon. Merlin, his trusted advisor, was gone and his nephew, Mordred, son of his own half-sister, Morgan Le Fay, so long a Knight at his table, became his enemy and treacherously sided with the Saxons against him. Hoping that the Saxons would likewise spare them if they collaborated, a number of desperate Romano British flocked to Mordred's ranks to turn against their own kinsmen, and take up arms with the Saxons. And so, massively outnumbered, Arthur, his army and his loyal remaining Knights were struck down in one last great battle at Camlan.

Believed mortally wounded, Arthur was taken to Avalon, the isle of healing and rest by a handful of loyal comrades. They took him by boat to the island, and there, weary, they collapsed, less than a dozen exhausted men and their writhing, semi-conscious and injured Lord. They hid in a cavern beneath the ground to guard him, to regain their strength or to die... With one great yawn, Arthur woke.

It didn't seem to matter how much he blinked, he couldn't see anything. All was in darkness, perhaps it was night. But then again he couldn't hear anything either, and used as he was to camping under the stars his ears should pick up the faintest noise, the fall of a leaf or the tread of a beast far off, but he heard nothing, all was silence. The King lay on his back with his thick red sagum woollen cloak draped over him as covering, his grimy clothing and dirty bandages still clinging to his body.

His checked himself over in the darkness and made a quick assessment; he wasn't bleeding, and though stiff, nothing seemed to be broken. His lamcllor breast plate, made from strips of reinforced leather, had been taken from him, presumably to aid his breathing, but he still wore his chain mail singlet, a valued item indeed. Under the mail he wore his coptic dalmic, a kind of long T-shirt of wool which hung down to just above the knee. The mail coat and coptic dalmic were fastened tight at the waist with his belt, and he was reassured when his hand closed over the hilt of his dagger, Carnwennau, still tucked into it. His woollen leggings were strapped tight around his legs with leather thongs, and he still wore his leather shoes, just as he had when he took to the field at Camlan. But his helmet was gone, his head was firmly bandaged and his beard had grown thick and long.

His heart raced as he felt to his ring finger and at his neck, but calm seemed to envelop him like a warm blanket when his clutching fingers closed over his most prized tokens and badges of rank. The cold torc of twisted gold at his neck was the crown of the ancient Britons, Boudica herself had once worn it. The signet ring which bore the face of Caesar had once been the seal of the Roman Governors of this isle, and with both he held the regalia to unite his Romano British peoples.

He felt no pain but was incredibly groggy and wondered how long he had been asleep. There was a horrible smell all around him, a festering stale smell of foul air. He had a revolting taste in his dry mouth and felt desperately thirsty.

He sat up slowly and with great care, the thick cloak fell off him and he stretched out his legs. There was a sudden clatter and clinking and Arthur realised that he'd kicked something over. He felt around himself and his hand closed on something - a sword hilt? A spear shaft? No, it was too light. He felt along it, his coarse stumpy fingers warming up gradually. A bone, it was a bone unmistakably, the thigh bone of a man he guessed from its size, but what was he doing lying next to a pile of bones? He felt around some more, touching one bone then another, then a shield, a helmet. He scratched his head and yawned again. He wasn't comfortable, knew he needed a drink, needed to warm up and desperately needed to relieve himself. Now he was properly awake it felt like he hadn't urinated in centuries.

Like a bear easing himself out of winter hibernation, he wrapped his cloak around himself and slowly got to his feet. Having fumbled around in the darkness a few moments longer he was sure he was in some kind of a chamber, and after a few more minutes feeling his way blindly around the walls, he thought he'd found a narrow passageway. He decided to crawl along it in the hope that it would lead to a way out, that it would lead to daylight, and as he crawled and fumbled his limbs began to warm up and loosen, and so too as his strength returned his fuddled memory slowly began to return to him....

The battle, the enemy, thousands of Saxons. The noise of the fight, the clinking of sword on sword, the thumping of axe on shield, the baying of horses, the battle chants of Saxons advancing in a tight shield wall, packed so deep, so tight that there was not a chink of light to be seen between them. The war cries of his own men 'Artos Rex...' The end. They had closed in. Arthur could remember seeing Gwalchmai fighting over the limp body of another of his trusted Knights, Sir Galahad, desperately trying to protect his friend before Saxon axes hacked Gwalchmai also to his knees and then to the ground. Cai, his own step-brother and most loyal of friends, fell to his right, and Derfel fought back their enemies to Arthur's left, slashing and hacking at them.

The enemy had come on so thick, and Arthur could remember thrusting at their tight ranks and pinning three men together on the haft of his mighty war spear, Rhongomyniad, as he drove it home through the solid wall of flesh and bone. He remembered leading a charge, cutting through the Saxon ranks, trying desperately to get to their leader's standard.

Mordred had got in his way, had tried to stand against him, he could remember the fear in his eyes. As he fought off enemies on all sides his nephew, his own flesh and blood, had slashed at him, cleaving open his leg and stabbing at his body. Mordred's blade had cut his arm and side, a wound which would have been fatal but for his chain-mail, as he tried desperately to get his sword up under Arthur's shield arm and through his unprotected armpit into his body.   In his fury he had swung his own long-bladed spatha sword, Caledfwlch, at Mordred, and struck the traitor down... That's when it had hit him. As he watched Mordred fall he had sustained a huge blow to the head from behind, probably with an axe, because he could remember feeling his helmet splinter and his knees buckle, and as his great shield, Wynebgwrthucher, adorned with the red dragon, slipped from his arm, he fell to the ground.

He remembered coming round with a terrible headache, Sir Bedwyr carrying him from the field and telling him the battle was lost. With a few others he could remember being taken in the boat over the lake to the Isle of Avalon. Slipping in and out of consciousness, the groaning of the bleeding Sir Bors beside him in his ears, he'd felt so close to death. Merlin had often told him that on Avalon he would find rest, and he'd felt so tired, so exhausted and weak, he'd just wanted to sleep, to drift off and join his ancestors... Yes he could just about recall it now, being laid down with just a few others, Bedwyr laying the cloak over him, his eyes shutting...

Arthur panicked. With his army defeated the Saxons were free to move west, and with him at rest there would have been no one to stop them - why, even now they could be at Caerlleon. He could see a chink of light ahead of him now, and burrowing forward as the passageway narrowed he started to tear at the earth with his fingers, pulling out roots, stones and earth clods as he slowly made the opening bigger.

He was sure he would have to fight - why, there could even be Saxons outside waiting for him, they could have scoured the countryside looking for him, they could even be standing over the opening right now with axes raised, waiting for him to stick his head out.

He paused. He would need Caledfwlch, the flashing blade given him by the Lady of the lake, whose outstretched arm had handed it to him from the waters of Avalon when he was a younger man and in his prime, it had to be somewhere in the chamber. He was about to return to search for it when he flashed back again to his arrival in the chamber. Believing he was surely to die of his wounds he'd asked Bedwyr to return his blade to the Lady lest it fall into the enemies hands.

'Throw it back into the lake from whence it came,' he'd asked, and he could picture Bedwyr's own grimy, blood-smeared face leaning over him.

"Are you sure, my Lord?" He'd questioned anxiously.

"It's over," his own voice had come in an exhausted whisper.

"Very well." Bedwyr had taken the sword and he had collapsed, but he could remember being shaken awake by his friend shortly afterwards, who told him that the deed was done.

"What happened?" he had asked, and Bedwyr assured him that when he threw the sword as far as he could into the lake it had hit the water and quickly sunk. He'd known that Bedwyr, loyal as he was, had been reluctant to dispose of Caledfwlch. The sword itself was a talisman of Saxon resistance, legend would re-name it Excalibur, and Arthur had known that Bedwyr hadn't been able to bring himself to do it, and was speaking untruthfully as the Lady had not shown herself. He'd told him again to throw the sword into the lake, and when Bedwyr came back a little later looking as pale as if he'd seen a ghost, Arthur knew the deed was done for real. Yes, that was the last thing he could remember, Bedwyr telling him that Caledfwlch was returned to the Lady.

Well then, if the sword was even now in the lake there would be no point going back into the chamber. The beginnings of a plan was forming in Arthur's head. He'd get out of here, go down to the water, retrieve Caledfwlch (as surely the Lady would return it to him), and then, when he'd viewed the lay of the land and made a torch he'd return to the chamber and wake the others. They would seek out some horses, ride to Caerlleon, and once he'd taken stock of all those available to him and learned of the enemies' strength, he would lead out whoever was left against any Saxons he might find. He couldn't be too hasty for there would be little time before the harvest needed reaping in.

He felt strengthened, and his pain lapsed a bit as his limbs warmed up and lost a little of their stiffness. His head no longer hurt, and though he couldn't examine himself properly in the darkness he could feel that his cuts had healed. The plan seemed good, he just had to get out of this cavern first, and he burrowed all the faster, if the Saxons were waiting for him outside then so be it.

With one great push light flooded into the passageway. It filled his eyes, which had been in the darkness so long he was nearly blinded. But as they slowly adjusted he listened carefully to the sounds from outside and sucked in the clean air, he could hear no voices and thought it would be safe to slowly edge his head and shoulders out into the sunlight. The warm sun and fresh breeze were heavenly; the stale air in the chamber had made him feel nauseous and now as he breathed deep he felt more awake, more alive.

He looked out, and what he saw he could scarcely believe. The lake was gone, totally dry, and all the forest around it was felled, the landscape was totally levelled, all was fields, a vast patchwork plain as far as he could see. What desolation of mystical Avalon was this? Was this the Saxons doing? Was it magic? He looked more carefully, and trying to calm his beating heart, he tried to take it all in a little more calmly.

It was all changed, it was true, but it wasn't all destruction and death. The fields were fruitful, he could see huge expanses of ripening wheat, he'd never seen so much corn, and plenty of lush green pasture land well stocked with sheep and cattle. It must have taken years to fell the trees and establish crops like these, and on this scale, why he could feed his army on crops like these for years to come. This could be heaven and not the hell he had first thought it.

As he looked more intensely still he could see that the fields were broken up by a series of hedges, and that whilst these for the most part followed straight lines they occasionally meandered, curving like snakes either side of what looked like streams through the plain stretched out before him. But strangely the streams did not follow the gradients of the land and at times seemed to intersect each other, neither one flowing into the other but crossing and flowing with a similar strength seemingly through the flow of the other, and out the other side. This was most odd - he would have to get a closer look.

He pulled himself quickly out of the ground and lay flat on his sagum cloak on the grassy slope. The grass of Avalon's mound flattened beneath his prone shape as he kept himself as close to the ground as he could lest a Saxon patrol sight him, and to cover his cloak lest its red colour give his position away. With care not to make any sudden movements he turned his head up the hill to survey the top of the Tor.

There appeared to be a tower at the top. Well that hadn't been there, it must be a new Saxon fort.

He breathed silently, fearing to make even the slightest sound. He just couldn't believe it, a Saxon fort built right on top of his resting chamber! They'd be kicking themselves if they knew how close they had come to finding him. It was strange though, this tower was of stone and the Saxons built mostly in wood, it must have taken time to construct such a tower... Well he didn't have time to consider it, he told himself, he had to get away from here, and quickly, before he was seen and taken prisoner.

Arthur glanced down the hill again, and his eyes rested on a clump of bushes about twenty yards from him. He crawled slightly to bring his legs up into a more favourable position, glanced around once more, and believing there was no one watching he quickly brought himself to his feet, and bent double sprinted for the cover. It was more of a lope than anything else, for his legs were still quite stiff and the King felt clumsy as he crashed along on them, almost tripping and losing his balance on the steep gradient.

When he reached the bushes he dived behind them and pulled his legs in so that he squatted, panting, and hid himself amongst them. He peered through the cover anxiously but there was no sign of any movement, no sign that he'd been seen, and his exit from the chamber was hardly obvious either. He rubbed life back into his limbs all the more and got the blood circulating. His heart pounded following his short burst, and this helped.

He checked himself over more thoroughly in the daylight, removing the bandages from his head and touching his hands to where he had been cut on his head and arm, and under his clothing to his side. When he examined the hand there was no fresh blood, and to the touch he couldn't even feel any scarring, his wounds seemed completely healed and he thought he'd be able to manage a longer series of sprints if he had to run - but run where? He checked his equipment too, his dagger. The trusty Carnwennau showed no sign of rust and the face of Caesar gleamed back off the smooth, polished, round surface of the Governor's signet ring. The torc felt good, and reassuring himself that he was still King and he would find a way out of this mess, he tried a re-think. He wouldn't be able to retrieve Caledfwlch as the lake was dry, he could only mourn the fate of the Lady, but he couldn't let himself dwell on it now. He could always go back into the chamber to try and find another sword, breast plate and helmet, but...

'WOOSH.' A huge shiver went through Arthur's body and he hugged the ground - he'd never heard a noise like it, it seemed to quiver through his whole body, it had to be like the horn to signal the end of the world that Merlin had said the Druids spoke of long ago. Then he saw it, and was filled with fear. A huge monster in the sky with wings like a bird but held out straight at the sides and not beating, it shot across the sky in a straight line like an arrow but at great speed, and in just a few seconds it was gone over the horizon. Had it seen him? He didn't know, he was filled with panic, totally startled, he didn't know what to do and in fear that the monster was going to return imminently he wrapped his red cloak into a ball, and carrying it at his waist he bolted down the hill and into the nearest wheat field, plunging down amongst the standing corn hoping to conceal himself. He'd never seen such dense corn, nor such strong and healthy-looking wheat. The ears were fat and the stalks stood at an almost uniform height in neat rows.

He looked up, breathing heavily, and surveyed the Tor from its foot on the plain. There was no one chasing him, no one shouting the alarm, this at least was good, but he had to get well away from here and fast. Hunching as he jogged he made his way to the far end of the field, crouching at all times so as to hide as much of himself as possible amongst the crops. He suddenly startled a strange-looking bird which took off in front of him flapping and squawking. It was the size of a chicken with a great long tail, and Arthur hoped it wouldn't give his position away, for there had to be lookouts in the tower. Raising his head slightly to make it easier, he ran all the faster.

He burst through the hedge which divided the wheat field from some open pasture, which was being grazed by some strange-looking black and white cows, and noted a trough in the corner which one of the beasts was drinking from. Desperately thirsty, Arthur made quickly towards the trough, but he knew he had to keep his eyes open and moved cautiously, for where there were cattle there would be cow herds nearby, probably only boys more likely to run and alert their men than try to attack him themselves. But if they chose to he had only Carnwennau for protection and it would be an embarrassment indeed for the King of Britain to be captured by children. He was so parched that he had to endure an element of risk, and as the cow moved slowly and obligingly away he took cover down the side of the trough, and having first relieved himself he drank his fill.

After a glance around, and when he was sure that it was safe, he ran along the hedge line to the far end of the pasture field and ducked down into some bushes to again see if anyone was following him. The hedges were good, he thought; they might be hiding bandits on another day, but right now he was a fugitive and they served well to conceal him. He thought again about the monster he had seen and the terrible noise it had made.

Many times had he heard tell of dragons in the bard's songs, but he'd never actually seen one, and from what he understood they were meant to flap their wings and breathe fire from their mouths. This one had appeared to have its bottom on fire, for it had trailed vaporous smoke behind it, and though it had certainly roared it hadn't flapped its wings once. Arthur knew that to take another's word on something as a universal rule was far from wise in most circumstances, for the bards who sang in the halls of Caerlleon, if pressed, would mostly admit that they had never actually seen a dragon either. Yet he was in little doubt that it had to have been a dragon that he'd just seen, for he couldn't think of any other beast it could be. Perhaps it was flying backwards he thought - that might explain the smoke trail.

He feared the monster would sight him easily on the open plain and would swoop on him like an eagle. For all he knew it might work for the Saxons, who knew what Devilry they had developed while he had rested at Avalon.

Arthur wracked his brains: he needed a plan. He had to get to Caerlleon, had to be sure that Gwenhwyfar was alright, he would never forgive himself if the enemy got hold of her. He could not now go back to the chamber, he just couldn't risk being seen. He'd been lucky so far and perhaps he stood a better chance alone, though he rued the loss of the chance of a sword, a helmet and his lamcllor breast plate, for while he still had his mail, any other protection was a bonus and even lamcllor had been scarce in the last days.

He decided to take a closer look at one of the strange streams he had seen from the Tor, and moving down the hedge line he found a position of cover from which he could investigate. What he saw intrigued him greatly. The surface was black and appeared completely still, there was no sign of a current whatsoever and no flotsam being carried by it. Perhaps it was some kind of enchanted water. He dug in the hedge with his toe and flicked out a stone; he launched it in the air, judging it perfectly to land in the middle of the brook, but when it did it simply landed with a dull thud and rolled a little before coming to a stop. He ducked down at first in case the noise brought enemies or broke some kind of spell, and looked up to see the stone quiet, still and un-sinking on the hard and solid surface. Well that would make it safe to cross he thought, like a road... Well that was it, it was a road, that's exactly what it was, he cursed his own cautiousness. But they were like no other roads he had ever seen, quite apart from the surface roads were meant to be straight, a legacy of Rome, roads to get you from where you are to where you need to get as quickly as possible. He was puzzled, he couldn't remember any roads near Avalon, just swine herds tracks through the forest, and roads like these would have taken ages to build. The number of them was also extraordinary. It made sense to him now that roads could intersect each other where streams could not, but why so many? And why so meandering? And why the hedges? Everybody knew that a windy road was gifting the enemy a means of ambush, and that undergrowth should be cleared back at least a hundred yards on each side so a travelling army could sight any surprise attack, but these hedges almost hugged the roads in places as if they were trying to conceal them. It really was most strange.

Arthur decided to try and cross, for there were more crops for concealment on the other side which would give better cover, and he was picking his way over some spiky metal string, which presumably was there to keep the cattle penned in, when he heard a zooming, roaring noise approaching. Another great shining monster seemed to glide suddenly around the corner towards him with no warning and at great speed. The King was startled once more, his trews got caught on the barbed wire and he fell off, spiking his leg as he did so and landing flat on his face on the road side of the hedge.

He had no time to react but it didn't matter - the monster sped on passed him blue and shining as if he hadn't even been there, he just couldn't believe it hadn't seen him. In a few seconds it was gone and its roars faded into the distance. Arthur was terrified, he'd never dreamt of such frightening creatures, not even in his most troubled sleep.

He longed that Merlin could be here with him, Merlin was wise in such things, he could open a window to the past, or see a mirror of the future in his fire, or so he said. Gwalchmai had always teased him saying that if he ever drank just half as much mead as the old man he too would be blessed with visions of things to come, but Gwalchmai, like so many others, was dead, and even memories of his smiling face could scarcely cheer Arthur now.

Merlin had always seen the end. He'd always said that the Saxons would eventually triumph and lay waste the land; that's why he'd instructed Arthur that he should keep on fighting, that he should hold them back as long as possible, and that when his wounds took him he should head to Avalon for healing as he might be needed again. Poor Merlin, but perhaps it was best that he hadn't lived to see this transformation, that he hadn't lived to see what had become of his beloved Avalon, that he hadn't lived to see this future.

Arthur slapped his forehead. For that was it, this was the future, it was all so clear to him now. The lake would have taken years to dry up, the forests decades to fell and the land generations to cultivate. This was Avalon, there was no doubt about it. The Tor had once been an island but he knew it well enough, and he realised now that he must have been asleep much, much longer than he first realised. How long, he could not tell.

The more he thought about it, the more it hit home. The bones in the chamber had to be those of his comrades from the field of Camlan, they had rested with him and had long since rotted away. No wonder the air had been so stale in there. Bors, Bedwyr, gone. Cai, Gwalchmai, Galahad, he could name a thousand more who had fallen in glory in the field and he was here now, alone. There wasn't even one of his army left, and perhaps even his beloved Gwenhwyfar was no more. A tear rolled down his grimy check at the thought of it and dripped into his beard; he felt so deserted, so completely and utterly abandoned. He breathed deep, tried to gather himself. He couldn't let himself grieve, not yet anyway, there still had to be some hope, there could yet be some loyal to him, and if he had to fight the Saxons alone he would do so willingly, even if the only motivation left to him could be revenge.

He rose and quickly began to cross the road, firm beneath his leather-sandaled feet. But as he did so another zooming, gliding monster, this time a red one, sped round the corner towards him from the other direction. It headed straight for him as if to run him down and beeped at him loudly, a piercing noise to add to the roaring and whooshing it made. He tried to jump aside, to reach out his dagger, Carnwennau, desperate not to turn his back on the monster and to face it down as bravely as he could. But it just swerved violently around him, beeped again and glided off round the next corner just as before.

Arthur recovered himself and ducked under the wire and into the field opposite. He was most perplexed by what he'd just seen. The monster had definitely challenged him, why else would it have sounded its menacing, if strangely-pitched, battle horn? But it didn't take him when it had the opportunity, it had actively swerved away from him, he just couldn't understand it. Most oddly of all he had seen a man within it, a person actually sitting within the very bowels of the monster. What was this magic at work? Had it eaten him? The man within hadn't seemed frightened, hadn't even seemed in pain. Was he in some way controlling the monster? Arthur thought this unlikely, for no horses or oxen drew it, and it sped faster than any mount he had ever known.

He was over the field now and across country. The sky was clear of dragons and he had now to keep his distance from the roads - he had been lucky at least three times already and couldn't risk pushing his luck. Looking back he was miles from the Saxon tower now, but the plain spread out many miles more in front of him, and reaching the shelter of a copse of trees he sat to rest and think once more.

He had to take stock, had to find someone loyal to him, and fast. He had never felt so dirty, so grimy, greasy and filthy. Muck and dust were caked into his skin, his beard and hair were long and dishevelled and his clothes were absolutely stinking, perhaps that's why the monsters had passed him by. His coptic dalmic was discoloured by dirt and his woollen leggings were torn, dirty and faded. His sagum cloak had not grown threadbare or his mail singlet rusty, but he still felt dirty and was desperate to freshen up and get clean. Yet he had to concede that his very appearance was not a bad disguise, for how many of his foes would recognise him like this?

He thought carefully. From Avalon it would take several nights to reach Caerlleon, but he could reach the small garrison fort on the hill at Little Solsbury in half the time, it had still been in tact not long before Camlan and there he might find food, fresh clothing, perhaps even a horse and some warriors with whom he could plan a campaign. He could get a full update on Saxon movements, of all that had been and gone, maybe even news of Gwenhwyfar. And as the fort was not far from the old Roman town of Aquae Sulis at Caer Afon, he might even be able to bathe in the hot springs of the Roman bath house as he had done of old in more peaceful times. There would be razors there for sure.

His mind was made up, he would make for Little Solsbury, but he would take a direct route across country, keeping away from the roads and giving a wide berth to any homesteads he might come across. He was a past master of covering ground with stealth and at speed, and having sighted the position of the sun and found north with a competence which would have made his old tutor Merlin proud, he set off at a trot.

Chapter Six – Embrace the Present, it is the Future

Arthur had walked for the remains of the afternoon, and continued into the night. He had no need of sleep and told himself that anyone who had been at rest as long as he had shouldn't feel remotely tired, whatever the hour. The moon was high in the sky and was almost full, and this gave him comfort as he picked his way along the unfamiliar hedgerows and over fields of crop and pasture by its light.

He was overwhelmed by the changes, the huge sprawling ancient forests which had covered this part of the island since the dawn of time were gone. They had taken root long before the old peoples had built their first barrow and Arthur knew the Druids would shift uncomfortably in their graves if they could see what had become of their sacred oak woods.

The beasts which in his time had sheltered in these forests were nowhere to be seen either. He'd sighted a lone buck in the dusk on a ridge, and the call of an owl had told him something was hunting, but there was no evidence of bear or boar, and whilst he heard the unmistakable bark of a vixen calling her cubs on the wind, the howl of wolves was absent in the night air.

Years before, when he'd pulled the sword of Kingship from the stone under Merlin's gaze, so young and lacking in confidence, he'd confided in the old sage that he knew little of leadership and destiny. Merlin had told him then that whilst destiny was preordained and need only be fulfilled by the willing, and that whilst leadership could be learned, he already had a gift of wisdom which would go a long way to seeing him through. His old perceptions had not forsaken him, for the further he went from the Tor the more sure he became that a significant period of time had passed him by while he had lain in his tomb. It was not just mystical Avalon which was changed but this whole part of his kingdom; perhaps even the whole of the country had been so altered. He knew not how long he'd slept, but he now, with every step, knew in his heart that his chances of ever finding his Queen alive or the fort at Little Solsbury intact were increasingly remote, and as the temperature had fallen slightly he'd resolved to simply wrap his cloak around himself and stride on, for there was little else he could do.

The shining monsters he'd seen and heard in the afternoon had continued to hunt up and down the roads at night, and they passed along with great roars, their lamp-like eyes searching the ground in front of them, flooding it with a light far more powerful than the brightest torch. He had tried to avoid the perilous roads but he found them so numerous that he had to keep crossing them as he moved north, and always with an eye at the sky, for the vapour-trails of dragons showed that several were in the air at once, criss-crossing as they flew close to the moon. It was so dangerous that he felt continually on edge.

He was hungry and had thought to try and catch a rabbit to eat, but knowing that a cooking fire might bring enemies to him he'd decided against it, and as his belly became rebellious and the urge to eat overtook him he'd decided there was nothing for it but to approach some homesteads and try to steal some food.

The houses too, like everything else he found, were so very different from anything he'd ever seen or heard of before. His own people had progressed from the huts of weave, roofed with reed thatch, that their ancestors had lived in, and mostly dwelt in one-level huts of wattle and daub. The animal dung and mud mixed with straw had bonded and hardened well when plastered over a thinner inner weave structure, though it had to be constantly added to and patched up when the heavy rains fell. Of course the Romans had left forums and villas of stone as their legacy to Britain, but the average family group crowded in together around a smoky fireplace, and in winter their animals had to be accommodated too.

The dwellings he saw now intrigued him greatly. Each looked different from the next in shape and size, and the styles also varied considerably. Some were coloured whitewash or pink, others were built in the sandy coloured limestone found in the nearby hills, while still others were built of a red-coloured brick of fired clay which Arthur had never seen before. They were roofed with many different materials too - some with slate, some tiled, some thatched - and most were built with at least two levels, some, higher still, comprised of three or four, and all had windows of glass.

He was struck by the variety, the size, and the funny little walls and fences which seemed to divide each house from its neighbour. One dwelling had a house of glass outside it full of vegetation, while another had a hut of wood, and most had the shiny monsters outside shimmering in the light of slow burning lamps held on high posts and guarding, he supposed, the entrances to the homesteads. They looked as if they must be hungry, for Arthur could see no people trapped within them, and he believed that their sitting in silence was probably some kind of trick to coax their unsuspecting prey, believing them to be asleep, to venture within pouncing range.

These were most unlike the long wooden halls the Saxons built, for he knew their ways well. They dwelt together in one long room of timber, laying together at night on the floor of what was by day their living and eating area. They burnt well, he reflected, for he had raised many to the ground, especially with the dawn after their pagan feast days when frequently the inhabitants had been so full of mead they hadn't even woken as the flaming timber roofs had fallen in on them.

He just didn't know what to make of these strange buildings or the oddly-dressed people he could see moving about within the brightly lit dwellings, but he didn't want to get too close and squatted in the bushes, watching quietly and trying his best not to wake the monsters. The settlement was huge, it must number at least fifty buildings, and Arthur was trying desperately to place it, reasoning that he couldn't be lost and that this must just be an expanded village known well to him and not a completely new town, when he heard a door open. From his hiding place he watched a woman struggle out and throw a big black bag into a large green container at the end of her path.

He watched in silence as she walked back inside, and curious to see what she had put in the container he crept slowly forward when he saw her light go out, lifted the lid and peered inside. The opportunity was too good to miss - there was no monster outside this house and no one else seemed to have noticed. As he lifted the bin lid a warm smell of cooked food filled his nostrils, and with a quick cut of his dagger the bin bag was open and he was making off, a thief in the night, with a greasy paper box in his hands.

Back in the bushes the King dinned ravenously on chicken, ripping every last piece from the sticky carcass and bolting down the burnt crusts of the strange white bread with its powerful garlicky taste as if his very life depended on it.

Feeling as if at last the edge had been taken off his hunger the King relaxed a little, but as soon as he did so he was alerted by one of the noisy monsters pulling up outside a house opposite, its eyes shutting suddenly and going dark. The innards of the creature immediately lit up and a man stepped out, pushing open the monster's side to enable himself to exit. He emerged unharmed and strolled easily to his front door, pausing for a moment and fiddling with it briefly before he went in. The man had worn the most odd looking clothes: a coptic dalmic which was open at the front, an undershirt and trews with no thongs to hold them, and an odd strip of fabric dangled like a snake skin from his neck. Arthur wondered what plausible purpose the item fulfilled.

He walked on passing one settlement after another, but always skirting round them, trying his best to stick to the fields. But when his route took him close he could not help but stare in fascination at what he saw. With the dawn the houses came to life, people flooded out of them, and, wide-eyed, he saw a woman climb into a monster by her own free will. He saw her seat herself and then the monster roar into life, opening its bright eyes. It glided purposefully away on its wheels as if completely under her command, and realising now that these monsters worked for the people and didn't after all hunt them, he wondered what powerful magic it was which made such fearsome creatures obey the commands of men. The people he had seen did not dress or look like his Saxon enemies, but they would be a force to be reckoned with indeed if they could subdue these noisy beasts, and he didn't want to approach them nor make himself known until he had a better idea of how to deal with them.

He trotted on, resting briefly mid-morning in the shade of an orchard, and having drunk at the brook and eaten the fruit heartily he set off again, keeping a low profile and ensuring that he stayed in the low contours of the land to prevent himself giving his location away by breaching the horizon. A short rest again in the afternoon, and then on through the night with a sense of urgency, for strangely he felt increasingly drawn, compelled to continue. The moon was even fuller than the night before and he flitted through the twilight with expectant dread as he neared his target. It felt so odd to him; he found it hard to believe his destination too would not be changed beyond all measure, and yet, though he could think of nowhere else to go. It also seemed right in his heart that this was where he should head, even though in his mind he expected to be disappointed, and didn't want to have to face the reality of what he might find.

Arthur reached Little Solsbury at dawn the next morning; his fears were realised and what he saw destroyed all the hope he had left. On the grass-covered hill no sign of his old fortification was left, not so much as a timber foundation remained, and the view from the site confirmed once again, and beyond all doubt, that times had truly changed. He'd taken a wide route in order to avoid the settlements as best he could, and from the top of his old hill fort he could see why the way he'd come had been such an awkward one. He'd chosen this very sight for its view as it commanded a good lookout over the valley, but the valley itself was now full of houses and buildings creeping up the hills on every side. He'd never seen such an urban sprawl, and all in the local stone from which the bath-houses were hewn. He'd heard that Rome looked like this in its prime, huge and rolling, but the Aquae Sulis or Caer Afon he'd known had been nothing more than a fortified town on the river nestling in the valley of the surrounding hills, which, heavily-forested, had then seemed to pen it in on all sides.

He knew this was no dream, for the lay of the land was known well to him and this was the very same place he had chosen many ages ago for its position on the hill. He'd known the town was too low in the valley to defend appropriately and on this very spot he had hoped to stop those who might have planned to destroy the town below him. But now he sat in awe and wonder. The Saxons he'd fought were destroyers, not builders, and far from destroying this town, far from raising it with fire, they seemed to have expanded it beyond measure, and not with timber or clay but with stone, cut and dressed. What was he to do, one man against all this?

There was no doubting it now: an age had passed, maybe even several ages, as such a city would have taken very many years to construct, and while he sat in lonely wonder he considered carefully the possibility that indeed the Saxon age too might have passed away while he slept at Avalon.

He saw a long snake-like monster making its windy way through the valley below him and into the city. It disappeared briefly into the thicket of buildings, and later he saw it again moving away in the opposite direction. Yet far from leaving destruction behind it, the creature glided steadily away and hid itself amongst the far away hills.

What did it all mean? What was it all about? This strange world was so far-removed from the country he remembered. He knew nothing of this age, nothing of its dangers and nothing of its comforts. He was filled with sorrow, and now that his quest seemed beyond hope perhaps it was indeed time to grieve. He just kept asking himself the same questions. What was he doing here? And why had he come back? Unsure of what to do next, and suddenly feeling weary and emotionally drained, he stretched himself out in the shelter of some bushes. It was becoming incredibly humid, but he declined to take off his chain mail, and lying down on his cloak he fought back the choking tears and tried to sleep.

"Maxwell and Jessica Finch, you've been sitting in front of that TV all morning, it's time to get up, come on you two."

"Oh come on, Mum, it's the summer holidays," they'd protested, and Max had gone a step further with "I'm bored, and there's no point getting up anyway, there's nothing to do."

"I thought you were going to play cricket at the Lydon's," his mother had urged him, but Max had assured her that he wouldn't be doing so until much later in the afternoon and voiced his intentions to remain in his pyjamas until after lunch.

"There's loads of telly on," he'd persisted.

"Well that's just silly, Maxie darling, it really is, it's a lovely day out there and Benji needs a walk. You two could go and take him out before lunch, it'd save me a job," Patricia had called back, more in hope than expectation, as she'd walked through into the kitchen.

"What else needs doing, Mum?" Jess had asked.

Max had pulled a face at his sister and mouthed the word 'creep,' before whispering to her "You always play the goody-goody, don't you?"

"Thank you, but nothing else Jessica darling," their mother had called back from the kitchen, "all under control."

"Ah." Max looked delighted to see his sister's offer of help declined.

"But you can take Benji out, as I said," Patricia Finch continued, "while I make the lunch. I do wish you'd get dressed, your cousin Rhys will be dropping in later and you don't want him to see you in your PJs."

"Disappointed?" Max asked Jess sarcastically.

"No, lazy arse, and I don't mind walking Benji anyway. You might as well come along for the exercise," she teased him, "you'll get all out of shape if you lounge on that sofa all holiday."

"Oh alright," he reluctantly agreed, and having pulled his clothes on, Max joined his sister and their expectant, bouncy pet, on a quick trek of the fields behind their home in Weston-Bissett village. As they walked their friendly banter continued and Benji dashed about in circles, sniffing trees and hedges and bouncing through the long grass with his ears flapping, repeatedly stopping to relieve himself. The humidity was rising and Jess tugged at her sticky clothing uncomfortably.

"Well you won't get changed without a shower, Sis, that's for sure."

"Why's that?"

"Because you so fancy Rhys and you don't want him to see you as the smelly grease-ball you are first thing in the morning," Max teased her.

"Max, he's our cousin!" Jess tried to look shocked but started to blush and turned away, hoping that her brother wouldn't notice.

"You do fancy him though."

"Do not, it's you that idolises him." Jess was not to be outdone and put on her own adoring impression of her brother in a high-pitched mocking tone. "Oh Rhys, do you want to play cricket? Rhys, come and play football. Rhys, do you want to play on the Playstation with me?"

Max, whose voice was breaking and was very sensitive about people drawing attention to it, defended himself with a deliberately deep reply. "He's a boy, Jessica, I think he likes a bit of a kick around in the garden."

"Max he's nearly five years older than us, do you really think he wants to spend his time playing silly games with you?"

Max was hurt by this belittling comment and tried to argue his point. "Like I said…"

But Jess interrupted him in a stern voice. "He's only coming down because his girlfriend lives here now, you do realise that, don't you Max? He's not coming all the way from South Wales just to kick a football with you."

"Yeah that's right," Max replied angrily, "he's got a girlfriend - jealous, Jess? Oh look you're blushing… Still, never mind, you've still always got podgy Brendan Johnson."

But his sister wasn't rising to it - instead she was watching the dog who had found something in the bushes about halfway up Little Solsbury hill. Benji was barking and bouncing up and down as if keeping another animal at bay. He backed off, barked, then leapt forward and barked again.

"What's he found?"

"Don't know, Sis," Max walked briskly forwards to catch up with the spaniel. "Could be a fox, a badger, probably just a rabbit - let's find out." Jess looked apprehensive and Max thought he would press this advantage, he might be able to give his sister a scare. "Could be a body or something," he said in a serious voice, "you'd best stay back."

The King couldn't believe his poor fortune. His keen warriors ears had picked up the dog some minutes ago crashing about in the undergrowth, and he'd quickly shaken himself awake. He'd seen the dog run this way and that, and twice it had passed him without picking up his scent, but now it was bearing down on him, bounding up and down and barking in a way which would surely give him away. Arthur had never seen a dog like it before and wondered if it was some kind of special Saxon hunting hound which called its masters to it when it had found game.

A boy was making towards him now, tall and slight and blonde-haired like a Saxon, but the clothes he wore, like those on the people he had seen the nights before, were most strange and unfamiliar. He wore long straight blue trousers and a short sleeveless top, he wore no cloak and carried no shield or weapons of any kind. Arthur took him for a shepherd boy and, quietly reaching for his knife, he thought it best to take this Saxon child prisoner, for as a hostage he might prove useful, and as his captive Arthur would be able to interrogate him and find out more about this mystical age he found himself in.

"What you found, Benji boy?" Max approached the bushes and could see a crouching figure in the undergrowth. "Who's there?" he called. He walked nearer a little more cautiously, and as he did so a wild-looking man, short, dark and stocky with a long wiry beard and a tangle of knotted, greying hair sprang out of the bushes towards him. Max had never seen anything like it - in chain mail and with his cloak trailing out behind him the man more resembled a character from a fantasy film than anyone else he had ever seen, and at first he jumped in surprise, letting out a shout of "What the...?" But then realising that the man was coming straight at him he turned to flee and let out a shout in his terrified panic of "Run, Jess, run!"

Arthur was in full stride when he saw the girl, she was some fifteen yards behind the boy, and knowing that he could never catch and hold both of them he was for a moment unsure of what to do, for even if he did take the boy hostage the girl could still run off and tell her kinsmen that Arthur was at large. They could be out in force and tracking him within half an hour, and whilst the boy as a hostage could give him something to bargain with, taking a prisoner with him would only slow him down as he tried to escape. He'd just be hunted down like a lone wolf heavy in pup by the town's men-folk and their dogs, and couldn't hope to elude them for long.

He resolved in a fraction of a second that as he had shown himself he would have to do something or they would just run to their homesteads and raise the alarm anyway, so he decided he'd seize the boy and at least try to stop the girl from making off with a quick piece of hostage negotiation right from the very start. If nothing else he might be able to question them as to the Saxon strength and positions.

Maxwell Finch was quick, but not as fast as the sinewy warrior King, and Arthur quickly caught him, jumping on him from behind and knocking him to the ground. In a single jerking movement he had the teenager back on his feet and held him tight to his body, one hand over his mouth and the other holding his dagger, Carnwennau, to the boy's throat.

Max tried to struggle but Arthur held him steady in a powerful hold. Max bit the hand that gagged his mouth, and Arthur, wincing in pain, released his grip just enough for Max to shout "Jess," before once more Arthur held him firmly and still, the point of the dagger pressed in against his flesh.

Jess, having heard her brother shout, stopped running and turned to see the strange-looking man holding Max so tightly around the neck and mouth that it looked as if he'd never be able to breathe. Benji jumped up and down in excitement at the stranger's side, but Jess could see a look of terror in Max's eyes as he tried to edge away from the sharp triangular blade of the dagger, which looked uncomfortably close to quickly ending his young life.

"Arhosa bachgennes, gwisga t bagla."(i)

Jess panicked, the man was shouting something, giving her commands, but she didn't know what they were, she couldn't understand a word he said.

"Bagla a fi ll ysglisia eiddo 'n arswydns hychydig gwddf,"(ii) Arthur shouted again.

Jess didn't know what to do, she stood dead still and it all suddenly seemed to go so quiet. The sky suddenly darkened over, and like two Wild West gun-slingers both waiting for the other to make their move, they weighed each other up in silent stalemate. As Arthur and Jess stood eyeballing each other, all Max could do was fight for breath, and Benji, assuming the fun was over, calmed down and lay panting at Max's feet.

"Awron jyst gostega, gwisga t chwimia cadw arafa."(iii) Arthur spoke after a brief pause.

"Don't hurt him," Jess pleaded.

"Arafa,"(iv) Arthur made a shushing noise, and with a gentle movement of one finger he beckoned Jess forward.

"Ummh, nmmhn," Max's muffled protests to his sister fell on deaf ears as she ponderously stepped forward, just as his captor instructed. Max struggled with all his might but the incredible strength of the wild man held him steady in a vice-like grip. "Urummh," Max grated again at his gag, and with wide eyes implored his sister to keep her distance.

Jess stopped. She had to be careful; get too close and the stranger might kill them both. She tried to get the measure of him and looked him carefully in the eyes. They were fixed, hard and determined, sunken in a mournful and grimy, weather-beaten face. This man could be desperate, could be completely mad, but there was a compassion she could see in there somewhere, a suffering, and maybe even a sense of vulnerability. For the second time that week a strange sense of calm in a crisis came over her, just as it had when she'd been drawn to the drum and her mind had likewise resisted the urge to run. She felt a similar intensity now. This man was hard, rugged, wild, but she just had to do as he bid her. It was a gut feeling but looking at him she didn't believe he would harm Max, she felt she just had to trust him, but more than that she felt the same captivating sense of curiosity that she'd experienced when she'd heard the summoning drum roll in the Great Hall those few days before. Who was this man and what was he doing here?

Arthur felt uncomfortable. The girl had stopped but here they stood, out in the open for any passer-by to see. He'd hoped when first she stepped towards him that she'd get close enough for him to grab her too, but she just stood there staring at him, studying him intensely. He knew they had to get out of sight, and hoping to interrogate the boy, he slowly, very carefully, took a few steps backwards into the bushes from whence he'd sprung. He kept his eyes on the girl, beckoned her again, and was relieved to see that whilst the boy burbled noisily in protest she slowly edged her way after them.

Jess felt compelled to follow. This man held all the aces; he held Max, and she knew that if she could do no more for her brother she could at least offer him some comfort through this ordeal and get the best look at the man she could in case he took Max away and she had to pass on a detailed description later. She was scared, terrified, but she kept calm, and whilst for a moment she feared that in the bushes there could be other such men ready to grab her, she knew she had no choice but to follow. Keeping her distance, and on her guard, she had no idea how long the stranger's shuffling, backward walk would go on, and the storm clouds were moving in fast.

She was relieved to discover that this was no wild goose chase, for once concealed between some bushes the stranger stopped, and carefully spoke in Max's ear.

"Dde Sais, ddwend wrth'm. Bloeddia achos chyfnertha a agora 'ch fwnwgl at'r spine, namyn ddwend wrth'm sy'ch? Abeth faint ydy'ch cheiftans gwersylla?"(v) The accent was hard, the tone harsh and imperative, urging Max to obey. But as to what he actually said neither child had a clue. The man very carefully, slowly and deliberately released his left hand grip on Max's mouth, and Max, gasping for air, just wanted to break free.

"Let go of me, you freak," he snarled back at him.

"Gwisga t gwinga bachgen. Arafa. awron ddeud'm sy'ch."(vi)

"Let me go," Max pleaded quietly, almost in desperation, "please let me go, please."

"Ateb'm,"(vii) the man demanded.

"Max," Jess spoke earnestly, "don't struggle, he looks serious."

"Looks serious, that's not all he is, he darned well feels serious too. That knife is really sharp, and believe me Jess he smells serious, like a porta-loo at the end of a festival. When's the last time you had a wash, dung-breath?"

"Max," Jess spoke through clenched teeth, "don't antagonise him."

"Antagonise him, that's rich."

"Ateb'm bachgen, ddwend wrth'm. Ca'r Saeson cymeredig Caerllion?"(viii) Arthur was insistent but getting frustrated.

"Well, answer him, Max," Jess sounded desperate.

"How can I answer him? I don't know what the hell he's on about. Nor do you for that matter... Honestly, Jess, he's got breath like a fishmonger's bin."

Arthur was annoyed, it was clear the boy didn't understand him, and he had so little Saxon himself he didn't think there was much chance of him being understood if he were to attempt the few coarse sounding, guttural, words he could remember. Anyhow, the language these two children spoke to each other was quite unlike any tongue he had ever heard before, Angle, Jute or Saxon. As they spoke to each other they were clearly arguing, yet their voices were soft and expressive. These children did not look like barbarians. Their clothing might be unfamiliar but their complexions were clear and their hair and appearance was so clean, they wore no charms, and didn't carry as much as a knife between them.

"Es vos a Saeson? Qua es vos ex?"(a) he asked them, switching to Latin, for it was possible these were educated children, perhaps the son and daughter of a privileged or noble family.

"What are you on about, weirdo?" Max defied him.

"Don't wind him up."

"Me, wind him up..."

"Have vos a chieftain? Qua es suus proeliator castra?"(b)

"Eh, a chieftain, I don't know what you mean. Jess, what is he blabbering about?"

"I don't know, Max, I really..."

"Quis of Caerllion? Have Saesons captus is?"(c) It was no use, the children just looked back at him blankly, and in wide-eyed frustration he desperately implored them for news. "Est Regina Gwenhwyfar alive?"(d)

Jess picked up her eyebrows at this last question and mouthed the name Gwenhwyfar back to her brother who frowned in response, Max didn't follow. Arthur noticed nothing of this exchange, for he had given up hope. He sighed deeply and looked at the ground. There was no point interrogating the boy if he didn't understand his questions, and there would be no point trying to bargain and use him as a hostage either, for if he couldn't communicate with this strange people how could he negotiate with them?

This left him with two choices: to take the children with him so they wouldn't run and alert their kinsmen to his return, or to kill them both, conceal the bodies in these bushes, and make his way to Caerlleon unhindered.

He chose neither. Killing children had never been his style, and he wasn't about to start slaughtering defenceless ones now just to save his own hide. He was no Saxon but a civilised, cultured Romano Briton, and a Christian King, what's more. Then there was the question of who they actually were? For if they weren't Saxon, and he was now sure they were not, then what was his quarrel with them? Invaders they might be, it was true, but he'd never met a people like them, and this people had never done him any harm. The Saxons were his enemy, they burnt and destroyed everything in their path. Perhaps this people had made enemies of them too, perhaps he shouldn't be too hasty in making enemies of them himself.

Besides, he knew the truth anyway, there could be only one answer and it was foolish to hold any hope that it could be otherwise. He'd seen such transformations and wonders, such changes to his island already that he knew for a certainty that the old order had passed completely away. Whilst life went on, and the expanded town of Caer Afon proved that it had, his fort was gone, and he was sure that just as the grass covered it as if it had never been there, so too time would have altered Caerlleon. The awful realisation which had tormented him as he'd gone to sleep flooded back to him again. Deep down he knew his own inner mental battle was over, he'd feared the worst but he'd held on to some slim hope on his journey, and now in his heart of hearts he knew for sure that Gwenhwyfar was no more, and that she and his citadel, like everything else he'd failed to find, had faded with time.

A tear rolled slowly down his cheek, and tenderly, almost apologetically, he released his grip on the boy, and as he pulled away Arthur tapped him gently on the shoulder. He didn't understand this age, it was all alien to him, and the draw of a new world did not excite him in that moment. It was time to mourn for his Queen, time to let the dream go. Once again he felt so alone, so deserted. Why had he come back? What was he doing here?

Max, relieved to be free, ran straight over to his sister, desperate to distance himself from the maniac who'd seemed so intent on harming him, and Benji, who thought it was time to play once more, bounded after him and yapped in excitement. Max, on reaching Jess, rubbed his neck with both hands to reassure himself that he wasn't cut, and once sure that he wasn't bleeding he suddenly felt full of anger towards the sorrowful figure who'd given him such a fright.

"You terrified me, you freak," he shouted. "I thought you were going to kill me. I've never been so scared. I'm going to call the police. Come on, Jess," he grabbed his sister's arm ready to move off, "lets go."

But Jess stood her ground. She was enthralled and stood staring at the strange figure who now sat on a tree stump looking totally beside himself, his head in his hands.

"Come on, Sis," Max urged her.

"Wait," she replied quietly.

"Oh I'm not waiting, not going through that again. Besides it's going to rain, look at those thunder clouds."

"Look at him," Jess insisted, and turned her brother to watch the stranger who was now speaking to himself in a tone of deep distress though muffled sobs and choking tears.

"Gwenhwyfar mortus... Caerllion hand magis.... Oh Sarcalogos quare ego non sileo per lemma?"(e)

"Um, are you ok?" Jess asked cautiously.

But the man just kept talking to himself. "Quare cun ego non exisisto mortuns? Meus absentis est super. Quare can ego non exisisto mortuus iungo Gwenhwyfar quod meus miles militis?(f) Paham wi'ma?"(ix)

"Don't cry, please don't cry," Jess spoke in comforting tones, and with an anxious glance at her brother she edged towards the stranger.

"Jess, are you mad?" Max, maintaining a safe distance, could scarcely believe what he was seeing. "He's a jibbering madman."

"Max, please," Jess turned to her brother. "Gwenhwyfar. He keeps saying that, who do you think he's talking about?"

"I don't know. Jess, I don't care, he almost killed me. Please," he persisted, "leave him, lets go."

Jess didn't answer, and full of curiosity she edged closer, totally engrossed by the strange, oddly-dressed figure who sat before her. He didn't appear to be drunk, and though she had to agree he could be both mad and dangerous, she could see that he was upset. His head rocked up and down between his knees in anguish and she pitied the old tramp.

"Jess," Max urged her again impatiently - he desperately wanted to go, but couldn't leave his sister alone with this man.

But Jess felt drawn to the stranger, full of sympathy, and she called out to him once more. "Mister don't cry. It's alright, we won't hurt you."

"Hurt you!" Max was furious. "He nearly killed me! Jess..."

"Who are you?" Jess asked again, but the man didn't seem to hear her, he made no response.

"He can't understand you, Jess... Come on, won't you, its going to tip it down in a minute."

"What's your name?"

This time the man, who seemed surprised that the children were still with him in the bushes, slowly looked up towards Jessica. What was she still doing here? Was she trying to offer help?

"Who are you?" she asked slowly. "Where are you from? Why are you here?" The dirty, fraught-looking man held her gaze steadily.

"He can't understand you, Sis. We couldn't understand him, he won't be able to understand us."

"Beatus vos puella,"(g) he said gently, "Namyn ach na chyfnertha ata neb newyddion."(x)

"I want to help you," said Jess quietly. The words had just slipped out but Max was incensed.

"You are, you're mad, stark raving bonkers."

"Quiet, Max," she waved an arm to calm him. "He does need our help, can't you see that? He's lost." The man looked up at her and wiped his eyes with the back of a grimy hand. "Um, er, I'm Jessica," she said uncertainly. "Jessica Finch." The man held her eyes with the same blank expression. Jess pointed to her chest and tried again. "Jessica Finch," she repeated slowly. "Um, Maxwell Finch," she pointed to her brother. "Benji," she pointed to the spaniel who was relieving himself again at the base of a tree.

"Have you any idea how stupid you look?"

"Give it a chance, Max." Jess tried again. "His name is Maxwell Finch. Max," she pointed to her brother. "Jess," she said pointing to herself, thinking it best to simplify the introductions. She pointed at the stranger and nodded as if urging him to speak.

"Um..." Arthur shuffled his feet, but to Jess it was a breakthrough.

"Jess," she said again pointing to herself. "Jessica."

"Jessica," Arthur repeated slowly, trying the odd sounding name on the tongue. "Jessica, Jess."

"Yeah," she smiled and pointed to her brother. "Max," she instructed the stranger.

"Max," Arthur spoke up a little. "Jess, Max."

"Very good, now you," she pointed at him.

Arthur was unsure; he was not keen to reveal himself, but perhaps fate was handing him an opportunity through these children to realise his destiny or at least the route towards it. When he replied he spoke quietly, uncertainly, not of who he was, but of the reaction his name might bring.

"Ergo sum Arturias Rex Britanicus."(h) The Latin introduction caused little more than a confused frown from the girl so he tried again in his native tongue, and as he spoke he raised his voice, a little pride returning to his tone. "Dwi Brenin Artos, Arglwydd a Brenin ar hyn hynysoedd."(xi)

"Long name," said Max sarcastically.

"Jess, Max..." Jessica hoped to persuade the stranger to simplify his own name and went round again pointing to herself and her brother before pointing to the stranger and nodding to urge a response.

"Artos," he said simply. "Artos Rex Britanicus..." Then again, seeing that they still looked confused. "Artos."

"Right, well that's the introductions over," said Max as the first drizzle began to fall, "can we go now?"

"Artos Britanicus?" Jess tried to clarify the man's identity.

"Artos Pendragon," he said getting to his feet. "Artos ap Uthyr Pendragon."

Jess felt stunned, like a brick had just hit her between the eyes. "Arthur Pendragon," she said slowly, "Gwenhwyfar... Guinevere," she almost whispered to herself as she made the connection.

"So the freak has an odd-ball name," said Max irreverently "what a surprise, and by the by, how appropriate."

"M-Max," Jess was still in shock, a stutter coming into her quaking voice, "d-don't you realise who this is?"

"Try me. Conan the barbarian? The Dungeon master? Artos the intergalactic space explorer?"

"No, Max." Jess couldn't take her eyes off the man. "This is Arthur, son of Uthur Pendragon. He just said so, didn't he? He's King Arthur."

"Oh pull the other one, Sis." Max would not be won over so easily.

"He just said he's Artos Pendragon. He's King Arthur. He's come back, he was always meant to return."

"What, and you believe him?"

"King Arthur," Jess repeated in stunned amazement, she was untouched by her brother's scepticism and tried to take the enormity of all this in.

"So you believe he's King Arthur just because he tells you he is? Come on Jess, madmen often think they're famous people don't they. Atilla the Hun, Napoleon... I mean, I could go on. Come on, Sis, he's just a mad old tramp. A mad old tramp who tried to kill me."

"If he'd wanted to kill you he would have, Max. Now listen, you couldn't dress up like that if you tried now, could you?"

"I wouldn't want to."

"I mean you can't get clothes like that stupid... The language he speaks, he's not making it up, its consistent... The dagger he's got, it's authentic..."

"It most certainly is, I'll vouch for that anyway."

"He mentioned Guinevere, didn't you hear him?"

"No."

"He did, Gwenhwyfar... Guinevere, he means Guinevere."

"Well if he meant Guinevere, why didn't he say Guinevere?"

"But he did, his language is just a bit different that's all. Artos, Arthur. Gwenhwyfar, Guinevere." She tried to explain to Max, but on hearing his queen's name spoken so readily, Arthur's face lit up. "You see, Max, it is Arthur, the once and future King. He's come back."

"But if he's a king, where's his crown?"

"Oh don't be so foolish, Max, kings don't wear crowns all the time. Besides, look, look at that."

"At what?"

"That bangle round his neck, it's a torc isn't it. Don't you remember from when we did the Celts in history? The ancient Britons, their chiefs wore torcs like that."

Max didn't remember, but he studied the twisted band of gold all the same with a critical eye. "Must be worth a few quid."

"It's a Celtic crown. He is King Arthur, Max, I know he is."

Looking attentive, and believing himself recognised at last, Arthur held out his left hand to Jess, offering the signet ring on his finger for her to kiss as his Knights used to do as a sign of submission to their overlord.

But Jess, seeing the outstretched hand walked forward, and taking it in her own she shook it warmly.

Confused by this gesture Arthur frowned, but taking no offence he smiled back at the kindly girl, flashing her a gappy grin of dirty yellow teeth.

"Did you see...?" Max was repulsed. "That's disgusting."

"That just proves it," said Jess firmly, "and this ring," she slowly turned the grubby hand over in her own and examined the motif on the round, flat surface. "An emperor?" she wondered. "Could be Roman, it's solid gold."

"Is est Romanorum,"(i) Arthur confirmed her suspicions. "Is est Caesars orbis. Is est Romanorum governors orbis of auctorita. Permaneo rectum left is secundum ut signum fortuna Brittanicum ita is has obduco volo."(j)

"What?" Max didn't understand.

"No idea."

"Come on, Jess, its raining properly now." It was, the wind was

103

rising, the temperature had dropped and in the distance thunder rumbled, a summer downpour was almost upon them and all around them the rain drops made a showering noise as they fell on the foliage. "Come on, Jess, we'll be caught in the storm."

"Well, we can't just leave him."

"You're damned right we can."

"Max, we can't leave King Arthur out in a storm," Jess persisted.

"Well, he's done alright so far."

"Come," Jess beckoned to Arthur. "Artos, come back home with us."

"Jess, Mum'll kill us if we take this bloke home. Look at the state of him, you know she doesn't like us talking to strangers."

"Well Mum won't find out then will she? Honestly Max, who's the goody,-goody now, eh?"

"Well, where are you going to hide him?"

"Garage," she replied simply.

"Urgh," Max looked up at the sky in desperation and shook his head. "Oh sure," he spoke sarcastically, "lets take the freak home with us. Looks like cricket's off for the afternoon, so we might as well harbour a lunatic instead."

"Come," said Jess again, but Arthur didn't seem to understand her. "Food," she said and mimed putting food to her mouth and chewing it slowly. Arthur pointed to his mouth eagerly and nodded his head, and Jess rubbed her tummy as if digesting a nice meal and beckoned again. Max smirked at the miming, but it was enough urging for the ravenous King, and he followed with caution but no great hesitation.

He knew this could be a trap to lead him to his enemies but he had to trust these children now, he was a stranger in an alien world and had no choice. Even if he was heading for a prison and death, it might just re-unite him with Gwenhwyfar and his Knights all the faster, and perhaps these children were the God-send he required just to show him his purpose for return. The tables had certainly turned, it was them leading him now; but he couldn't refuse food and shelter nor the chance to befriend some of these people and discover more about them.

The short walk in the ever heavier rain was an eye-opener for Arthur. The fields gave way to streets and they were fast amongst houses. He'd been curious to see inside such a dwelling and his excitement mounted with anticipation as he prepared for his curiosity to be satisfied.

The rain got heavier and heavier, and though they'd hunched their shoulders against it initially, the children were now so soaked that they just gave in to it, relaxed their limbs and walked on at a steadier pace. The rain hammered it down, throwing up a spray as it bounced off the pavement and road, and to Jess's relief the weather seemed to have emptied the village of all signs of life. All were sheltering and no one would see them making for home in the company of such a strange companion.

Arriving at their house, which Arthur noted had a small red monster sitting quietly outside it, Jess paused briefly to confer with her brother. "I'll go and grab mum's attention, you rush Arthur through to the garage," she suggested.

The garage no longer had an outside door to give access, as this had been bricked up when two years previously it had been converted into a kid's room to give the twins more living space. Access was now gained from a doorway knocked through from the lounge, and the garage, as the family still called it, was really to all intents and purposes just another downstairs reception room. The beauty of it however, so far as Jess was concerned, was that this room functioned almost solely as a recreation area for herself and Max and their mother, Patricia, rarely ever went in there.

"Why me?" Max objected "You can't leave me alone with him, he's almost killed me once already."

"Well, take Benji with you," Jess suggested.

"Oh sure. Fat lot of good he was last time, didn't exactly bite the guy when he had a knife at my throat, did he? The big soft coward."

"Don't be so wet, look I'll only be a minute. Ready?" Jess braced herself.

"Ready as I'll ever be to welcome a madman into our house."

"Max."

"Yes, yes, okay, let's get out of this rain." There was a huge clap of thunder almost exactly overhead and this seemed to decide things.

Jess opened the door and, kicking off her shoes, ran through to the kitchen.

"There you are darling, and wet through, I was getting worried. I've put the radiators on so you can dry your clothes." Max could hear his mother's voice as he quickly pulled his wet shoes off in the hall. He placed them on the mat and beckoned to Arthur to do the same. He chivvied the visitor, who seemed to take an age undoing his sandal straps while the two of them dripped all over the carpet. Max was relieved to see that the leather throngs which ran in a criss cross up the leg to the knee over the soaking woollen trews were not part of the footwear, and when the shoes were finally off he led Arthur quickly by the wrist through the lounge to the garage room, and pointed to a chair.

Arthur looked baffled, and Max too, suddenly felt some sympathy towards the forlorn, anxious-looking figure. He gestured at the King to stay with an open hand, and then, shutting the door behind him, he led the dripping dog back through the lounge towards the kitchen and his warm basket next to the cooker.

"Argh - shoes!" Max suddenly realised that the extra pair of footwear by the door would rouse his house-proud mother's suspicions that she had a visitor, and he could only imagine the line of questioning which a pair of unusual muddy leather sandals might bring. He ran quickly back to the front door, retrieved Arthur's shoes and rushed them back to the garage where he put them down on the floor, protecting the carpet with an old magazine.

"Maxie, where are you?" he heard his mother's voice. "Lunch is waiting for you."

"Coming, Mum," he called back.

Arthur, who had jumped when Max rushed back into the room, now stood and held out his hand to him. Thinking it best to make peace with the young man, the King offered the signet ring for the boy to kiss just as he had to the girl in the undergrowth earlier.

"Ah, okay," Max grudgingly shook the outstretched hand. "Now wait here," he instructed slowly. "Ah, what's the point? You don't know what I'm saying anyway." He raised his hand to Arthur with the palm up and the fingers splayed. "Five minutes," he said in accompaniment to the gesture, then pointing to the floor, "You wait here, five minutes." Having reached the door Max put his finger to his lips in a massively over-acted movement. "Shhhh, don't make any noise," he said in a whisper, and with that he shut the king in the room and went to find his lunch.

"Simply ghastly weather," his mother greeted him, "not much chance of cricket this afternoon."

"Um, no Mum, it doesn't look like it, does it." He glanced across at his sister, who raised her eyebrows behind her mother's back to check with him that their visitor was safely out of the way. Max nodded in silent response. "What's for lunch?" he asked casually.

"Pork chops, peas and scrummy new potatoes," Patricia Finch replied with a flourish as she placed the plateful in front of her son. "I know it's one of your favourites, Maxie."

Max resisted the urge to grumble about his mother's use of the irritating nickname and glanced again at Jess with open eyes, questioning her next move so far as feeding their guest was concerned.

Jess took up the challenge. "Can I eat mine next door, Mum?"

"No you cannot, Jessica. Honestly I'm most unimpressed, you can eat at the table like anyone else."

"But there's a.... programme I want to watch."

"Well you can have the telly on in here if you must," their mother shook her head in despair, "honestly, when I was a girl we were never allowed the goggle-box on when we were eating, but if you must," she flicked on the small screen on the sideboard.

"Problem is, Mum... Max doesn't like the programme I want to see, do you Max?"

"Er, no," Max responded to her prompting most awkwardly. "No I don't like that programme," he frowned across the table at his sister and mouthed "what programme don't I like?"

"Right, no bickering please," Patricia spoke quickly. "Now I've got to go out to catch the library, then I'm going shopping. I'll see you in about an hour and a half, perhaps a bit longer." She folded her apron, grabbed her handbag and coat from the hall, and having zipped it right to the chin and opened an umbrella ready to face the elements on the short trip to the car, she shouted a quick "Bye," and was gone, shutting the door behind her.

"Well that's a result," Max looked up at Jess, his mouth full of pork. "He can have your chop," he added quickly. "After the morning I've had, I'm going to need mine."

"Well you go and get him, I'll pour him some squash or something."

Arthur had sat quietly in the garage room and taken in his surroundings. The furniture was comfortable, padded chairs and a Roman-style recliner which had a side at each end and looked like it could be a seat for two people at a time. There was a thick padded rug which fitted the whole floor snugly, and having seen a similar rug in the hall he wondered if the whole house was covered in such a way. He presumed the presence of the unfamiliar carpet meant that under-floor hypocaust heating was not in operation; the absence of slaves in his own time had certainly put most of them out of use in the old Roman villas too.

The walls were a world away from the dung-covered huts of his own people, and they weren't decorated with the frescos and mosaics of his palace in the old Roman villa at Caerlleon either. They were smooth, and painted uniformly in bold colours, with a border halfway up and pictures spaced around providing decoration. A rain-spattered window gave a view out to the soaking wet enclosed garden behind the house.

Arthur decided to look at the pictures a little closer, each was encased in glass and one showed the most incredible likeness of the children stood on a beach with a man who looked to the king as if he could be their father. They stood together in the foreground with the man behind them and the sea and other people beyond splashing in the surf, and Arthur had never seen a painting like it. The artist had captured a three-dimensional style and perspective he didn't think could even be possible, their features were shown in almost perfect detail, though Arthur hadn't noticed the boy Max's eyes to be so strikingly red.

His eye was drawn to a daubing of a vase full of flowers in the most amazing colours he had ever seen, it was not such a perfect resemblance and had 'Jessica Finch, Class 5A,' scrawled underneath it. Next to this masterpiece was another portrait, this time of a group of men lined up in ranks: the front rank kneeling, the next sitting and the row behind all standing. They carried no weapons or shields, though they looked like warriors and all wore the same clothing. The smiling man in the middle had a spherical ball in his hands and there was writing all around it. He could read 'To Max' at the top, but none of the other strange squiggles which surrounded the ranks of men.

On the far wall was what looked like a big white shield with pipes running from it and these seemed to disappear into the ceiling. There was so much more to take in, and he was just examining a big white box which had what appeared to be a dark mirror on the front of it, when the boy came back into the room.

"Oh, you found the computer then. It's no good unless you turn it on." Max mimed eating as Jess had done earlier. "Food time," he said, and led the curious King into the kitchen.

Patricia Finch had turned on the kitchen lights to combat the darkness of the thundery, overcast day outside, and Arthur was fascinated by the bright lamps that hung from the ceiling, illuminating the room but casting no flame.

Max, noticing the King almost transfixed by the lights, allowed himself a mischievous grin before flicking the switch to darken the room. When the King jumped, suspecting magic, Max flicked the switch again to illuminate the room once more.

"And off," he said flicking it again, "and on, and off."

"Max," Jess told him off, "you'll scare him."

But Arthur understood now, and in wonderment he too took a turn at the switch, filling the room with light and plunging it into comparative darkness at the touch of a finger. So mesmerised was he that Jess had to physically pull him away from it to take his place at the table in one of the strange high-backed chairs.

He was delighted to discover that the homestead's table was round, and as he cast his eye around this room he couldn't help but think it stranger still than the last. The floor was tiled in black and white, and all around the room hung pots and pans and cupboard after cupboard. There were surfaces all around the room which seemed to be covered in food: some in jars, tins and boxes, and all sorts of other strange contraptions which flashed occasionally and made strange noises.

Arthur was given a plate of food by the girl, and ravenous, he wasted little time in setting about it.

He noticed the boy ate in a most curious manner, holding his meat steady with a strange little tool with points on it, and cutting slices off it with an almost blunt knife before bringing the food to his mouth with the little pointed shovel. Arthur didn't fully understand the point of this, and cutting big chunks off his own chop with his knife, he ignored the fork, and took the food to his mouth with his fingers where he tore at it with his teeth. The pork tasted good, though less flavoursome than boar, and he was grateful to the girl for all her kindness.

"Nice manners," Max observed, "I wonder if his dentist taught them to him."

"Max."

"Or his tailor."

"Max," Jess spoke in a disapproving tone.

"Or his barber."

Arthur picked up a small yellow vegetable from the plate and examined it carefully. It was about the size of an egg and soft to the touch; he'd never seen one before and wondered if they were some kind of soft root. He watched as the boy ate one, and deciding they couldn't be poisonous he popped one into his mouth. The flavour of the potato was good and the fluffy substance filling.

As he sat in the room he was exposed to one great wonder after another, it was so much to take in. When he'd drunk the odd-tasting water from the clear glass, the girl filled up his cup with the twist of a pipe, and the boy handed him slice after slice of strange white bread and produced one topping after another to spread over it which all seemed to come from a great white cabinet full of meats sliced very thin, milk, cheeses, vegetables and all sorts of other foods, all of which were kept cool. When he was fully satisfied and felt totally stuffed he belched heartily and threw his chop-bone to the sleeping dog.

The girl walked around the room trying to explain each object and making strange sounds by way of explanation as she pointed to them. Here was a jug which could boil water on its own, here a box with a window in it. When she turned a dial a lamp came on inside and a plate within the box spun round; after a few seconds it made a loud pinging noise and the girl opened the door, though Arthur couldn't understand why.

Here was a smooth block made of a light shiny substance he'd never encountered before. The girl held it to his ear and he could hear a buzzing noise. Believing there might be a bee trapped inside Arthur shook it violently, but the girl pressed some numbered bumps on it and all of a sudden he could hear a ringing noise coming from the boy. The boy pulled out a similar little block from a pouch in his trousers, and though he left the room briefly, giggling to himself, Arthur could hear the boy's voice through the block he held to his ear

"Artos, hello Artos," the voice kept saying. It really was a fascinating device, and Arthur paid huge attention to each new mystery object, feeling each artefact with great interest, smelling it, running his eye over each new thing with a cautious yet intrigued air.

The girl showed him another white cabinet. This one was full of foods again, but all the contents were frozen solid, and to the touch the inside of the cabinet was as cold as a bitter winter's night, there was even ice held at the top. What magic was this that could freeze ice in mid-summer? And the sorcery continued, for here was a large black-coloured cupboard in front of which the dog slept comfortably. Exploring, Arthur opened the drop down door to discover in amazement that this 'oven,' as the girl called it, could quickly be made very hot, and that though there was no flame within it and he could see no embers of a fire to explain how it could be used for cooking, he could see from the metal tray within that the pork he had just consumed had been prepared inside.

Above the oven was a surface covered in pots and pans, and the boy showed him how to summon a flame with the flick of a switch, hot and blue and seemingly from nowhere. No wonder he hadn't noticed a hearth in this dwelling, there was clearly no need for one if cooking could be done without the need of laying a fire, and this development intrigued him more than anything else.

The boy took his dirty plate and put it inside another white, smooth-fronted cupboard, opening the door and slotting it into a shelf he pulled out from within it. The boy shut the door and with the press of a button the cupboard turned into a noisy monster roaring away in the corner of the room. The children didn't appear concerned and the dog slept on undisturbed, so Arthur too attempted to give off the impression that he was ignoring it.

The boy handed him a squidgy, brightly-coloured pot from the cold cupboard, and following the boy's lead he pulled off the top to discover it was filled with what appeared to be very cold, dark mud. He tasted it, as the boy demonstrated with a tiny shovel, and although the consistency made him want to throw up, he couldn't deny the rich taste and slight burning sensation was strangely pleasant.

"Mousse," the boy explained.

"Ah," Arthur nodded, it could be some kind of animal dung for all he knew, but it didn't seem to be killing him and it tasted good so he finished it off happily.

Max was enjoying his guest's fascination with all things electrical, and seeing Arthur turn his attention to the small black box on the sideboard, he slowly reached for the remote, and just as the King recognised his own reflection in the dark screen, Max turned the television on.

The King jumped back in surprise - more magic. The front of the box now showed a picture, a woman, brightly-coloured beyond reality, stood on a flat surface. Sound was coming from the box now, more of this fascinating new language. Could this box be a vortex? Or a window to the future? Merlin had once spoken of such wonders after a particularly heavy night on the ale at Caerlleon. Arthur was unsure, this was the future and this strange box could be capable of all sorts of mysteries. As he looked he could see that the woman was singing. The tune was extraordinary and the instruments backing her were loud and intimidating, she was jumping around and couldn't keep still. Arthur wondered if she was trapped in the box and trying to escape.

With care he tried to reach into the box to pull her out, but his hand touched the glass and he couldn't get to her. Max, timing the moment perfectly, and grinning from ear to ear, flicked the buttons on the remote to change the channel and the woman was gone.

A man now sat behind a table, speaking as if straight at him, and Arthur leant forward in amazement, pushing his nose right up to the screen as he tried to see where the woman had gone. With the press of a button Max changed the channel again, snorting as he tried to hold back his giggles, and now the man was gone and there were men on galloping horses. The beasts were charging as if vying to be the first to the enemy shield wall, but the riders wore light garments of bright colours and none carried any swords or spears.

"Ydy hon 'r gweithia 'r andras?"(xii) Arthur demanded in frustration, but the boy was laughing, laughing at him. Arthur turned round, and Max waved the remote at him in explanation. He again flicked the channel, and this time a romantic movie came onto the screen, all in black and white. A dapper young man in a dinner suit was embracing a beautiful woman in an eloquent ball dress. Max, pulling a face of disgust, reverted to the original channel and the woman who had

111

just finished her song was joined on stage by the host as the camera panned round the audience, clapping and cheering.

The King scratched his head, it made no sense. All these people, tiny men and horses, huge crowds all trapped within this little box. Was the boy a wizard? How could the people grow so small? How did they all fit in this box in the first place? And could they see him as he could see them?

"Max, please don't wind him up." Jess used her most authoritative tone.

"Yes, Mother," he replied sarcastically. "But he has to learn, doesn't he? It doesn't even look like he's ever seen a TV before, or a light switch even."

"Well he wouldn't have, would he?... Max stop him, quick."

Jess had sighted Arthur, knife in hand, about to try and cut the window out of the television to release its little prisoners, and Max had to react at great speed to prevent him damaging it. He showed Arthur the remote and demonstrated how to use it, flicking from the horse racing to the news reader and back to the entertainment show again. Arthur soon got the idea and started pressing the buttons himself, watching in awe as the screen changed at his every command. He sniffed the remote, held it to his ear and shook it, he tested it with his teeth...

"Here," Max snatched it back off him, "don't bite it."

"That's enough," said Jess, and taking the remote from her brother she flicked the telly off. Both males, boy and king, looked at her as if she was a total spoilsport, but she wasn't going to let herself be manipulated. "So do you believe me now, Max? Do you agree this is King Arthur?"

"I don't see how I've got any choice, have I, Sis?" But Arthur smiled sheepishly back at him, and with a nod of his head Max had to agree. "Don't see how he can be anyone else really, I mean how many freaks do you know who nearly wet themselves with excitement just because you open a fridge?"

"Well then. We have to decide what we're going to do with him," she said firmly.

"What?"

"Exactly, what are we going to do with him?" The rain was still falling, but less furiously, and Arthur had walked over to the patio door and now tapped on the glass like a dog who wanted to go outside. Absent-mindedly, Jess opened it for him, safe in the knowledge that he couldn't wander out of the enclosed rear garden. "Don't get wet," she said gently.

"Fi must arllwys 'm ymysgaroedd,"(xiii) Arthur murmured back.

"Oh, he wants to explore, let him explore." Max looked after him with newfound affection, it was like having a new puppy, just watching Arthur was endless entertainment.

"Yeah okay, Max," Jess turned back to her brother, "but what are we going to do with him?"

"Well he could do with a bath."

"Yeah, after that."

"Don't know. Show him to our friends."

"Max, we can't let Mum find out he's here, we can't have people know about him."

"Why not?"

"Because mum'll freak, for one thing, and because no one else is likely to believe us."

"Well, I'm starting to think he's quite fun."

"Well that's certainly a turnaround from this morning, but he's not just come here for you to play with, he's here for a reason, don't you realise that?"

"What reason?" Max didn't follow.

"I don't know, that's what we have to find out. I think we're going to have to keep him here in secret until we can work out why he's returned."

"But that could be ages, and anyway, how can you be so sure he's come back for any particular reason? He might just have suddenly woken up and thought, I know... Hang on, Jess, what's he doing?" Max pointed outside to where Arthur, in the corner of the garden, was digging a shallow hole in the flowerbed with their mother's best gardening trowel.

"I don't know," Jess replied, looking out... "Oh no, stop him Max, stop him quick." Their guest, having finished digging, had discarded the trowel and was lowering his trousers to squat over the hole he'd just dug.

"Errrogh! No, no," Max waved his arms at Arthur as he ran out into the garden in his socks. The King swung round quickly. Was the boy about to attack him right now at his most vulnerable, quite literally with his trousers down? Max beckoned him to follow, and the King, in confusion, and leaving his business unfinished, followed the boy back inside, the two of them trailing soggy footprints across the tiles.

"Come on," Max led him upstairs and showed him another room, small but again packed with curious new experiences.

He showed him to a white throne with water in the base of it, and gestured to him that he could sit down on it. The boy dropped some thin parchment down it and depressed a lever on the side. As the King watched, water gushed from around the bowl and carried the loo roll away.

"Okay?" Max asked him, and Arthur nodded in understanding.

There was a mirror on the wall, a big one which confirmed in great clarity just what a state he had become, soap with a sweet fragrance and a big lidless tub with metal handles at one end.

As he watched, the boy twisted one of the handles and to Arthur's amazement water gushed out of the pipe just as it had done in the kitchen downstairs. Here was a spring you could simply summon with a twist of your wrist, and even more amazingly the other handle let hot water out. The boy plugged the hole in the bottom of it and began to fill the bath for him, pouring in a thick blue liquid which caused bubbles to rise like surf.

Max gestured to Arthur to leave his clothes outside the room and handed him a towel before leaving him to it and returning to his sister, who was busily wiping up muddy footprints from the stair carpets.

"He's um, in the bathroom at last," Max announced. "There," he smiled as he heard the distinctive flush of the toilet over the background running of the bath taps, "now that is progress."

"He's going to have to stay, Max. I've been thinking about it and he's going to have to stay with us until we've worked out what he's doing here."

"Fine, but he's your guest when Mum finds out. I don't want anything to do with it, not when she gets on the warpath."

"Fair enough, but will you help me in the mean time?"

"S'pose I haven't anything better to do at the moment," Max smiled.

"Then grab his stinking clothes will you, I'll give them a wash."

"Well that would certainly make him a more welcome guest, he blooming reeks." Max turned to go back upstairs.

"Thanks, Max."

"Oh, Sis?" He stopped halfway up the stairs with a frown on his face.

"Yeah."

"Well, what's he going to wear in the meantime? While they dry I mean."

"Don't know. Oh, grab something of Dad's."

"Formal or casual?"

"Max it really doesn't matter, jeans and a t-shirt should do just fine."

"But they won't fit him, he's far shorter and stockier than dad."

"It's the best we can do, your stuff will never fit."

"Right-ho," Max trotted off cheerfully, "I'm sure he'll be much more comfy in dad's underpants anyway," he smiled, and returned to the landing to find a pile of soggy clothing, though he noticed Arthur had retained his ring, torc and dagger. Max made off with the rest back downstairs to the washing machine. The chain mail was predictably heavy, but Max was surprised by the weight of the sodden woollen garments, and once they were entrusted to Jess's care he washed his hands thoroughly in the sink to try and neutralise the smell. "Make it a hot wash," he urged his sister.

"Like you know how to operate this machine," she teased. "Hadn't you better go and check on him?"

"He'll be fine."

"Max..."

"Jess I don't really want to walk in on a naked man, okay. A naked king," he protested.

"Well its better you do than I do." It was a simple argument.

"Well, what's the rush?"

"He's just left the taps running by the sound of it," Jess replied casually, "it'll be overflowing any minute."

"Oh heck!" Max left his protestations aside and bolted back upstairs two at a time, leaving Jess to examine the elaborate needle work of the decorative calvi strips on the hems of Arthur's coptic dalmic around the neck and cuffs. With an appreciative sigh she threw the soggy clothing into the machine along with the leggings and sagum cloak, hoping the hot water wouldn't damage the needlework or make the colours run out of the cloak. She looked at the clock - there couldn't be too long until her mother returned - and taking a dry cloth she set to work shining up the King's chain mail singlet.

Arthur was enjoying himself. Though the bath was very different from the great bath at Aquae Sulis where he had hoped to bathe, it being too small for swimming, and there being no plunge pools, masseurs or steam rooms, the water was warm and with the twist of a tap he could adjust the temperature. Above all, in solitude he could relax. He scrubbed himself with the soap and as he lay back the thick covering of bubbles spilled gently over the side. He wondered quietly to himself if the hot springs which had once fed the Roman bath house had been simply piped from the surrounding hills so that each homestead could have a private bath house like this. He tasted the hot water quickly and was delighted to discover that if this was the case they had disguised the foul flavour very convincingly.

The door burst open to shatter his peace, and Max, pleased to see the

King's body hidden beneath the bubble bath, burbled words at him which he couldn't comprehend. "It'll spill over," as he frantically turned the taps off. "Honestly, it's like looking after a child."

Arthur closed his eyes and considered his good fortune, these children were a God-send and he thought it best to stay with them; he hoped to try and understand their world and that his own reasons for returning might become clear to him.

'Splosh!' Something fell into the bath beside him. It rose to the surface where it floated and he examined it closely.

"Beth ydy ho nachos?"(xiv) He asked after its purpose.

"It's a rubber duck," Max answered in amusement, "don't ask me what it's for I haven't the faintest idea, I don't think anyone really knows."

Max disappeared and returned a few moments later with some odd looking clothes, similar to those which he wore himself, and indicated to Arthur that he should put them on when he got out. The king tugged at his beard and hair and gestured, scraping at his face with his fingernails. "Here," Max passed him some scissors, a shaving mirror and his father's razor and shaving soap. "This is ridiculous," he shook his head as he left the King to his ablutions. "I'm the child, you're supposed to be the adult."

A little later a transformed King Arthur made his way rather gingerly back downstairs and uncomfortably stood with his arms outstretched, as if presenting himself for his host's approval. On the third attempt he'd managed to get the jeans on the right way around and he found the coarse material was a most peculiar feeling on his legs. His unkempt grey-streaked hair was washed and cut back to a slightly less scraggly shoulder length, and his beard was trimmed and shaved into a neat goatee. He looked altogether a completely different person.

"Hey hey," Jess greeted him.

"Now that's what I call an extreme makeover," Max added with a hearty clap. "King Arthur in the twenty first century, snazzy jeans and a natty T-shirt, all he needs is a pair of shades, man. I like it."

"You certainly look a lot better," Jess assumed a patronising tone, "much cleaner and more comfortable."

But Arthur felt ridiculous; the jeans were far too long in the leg and the material was all bunched up around his feet, nice though it was to be washed and shaved, and light-weight though the loose fitting T-shirt was, he felt defenceless and vulnerable without his chain mail singlet.

"M ddillad ydy hyd yn oed hychwaney gwlych na anad,"(xv) he exclaimed when he saw his clothes on the radiator, and to the touch they were soaking.

"They're dripping Arthur, you'll have to let them dry," Jess explained, "you can have them back as soon as they're dry."

"Volo induviae ut induvine es siccus,"(k)

"Now come on, mum'll be back soon, we have to get you and these clothes back out of the way."

"So where?" Max shrugged.

"He'll just have to stay in the garage during the day, and you can make up the spare bed in your room for tonight."

Max saw no point in arguing, Arthur couldn't be left to sleep with Jess, and anyway he was turning out to be rather more fun since he'd taken the knife away from his throat.

"Come on Artos," he called him. And then to Jess. "I rather like ordering a king around, it's almost better than cricket," and he led his new roommate upstairs.

As Max made the bed Arthur occupied himself, as normal studying all the curiosities of a new room, and Max, when his work was done, had to draw his attention from the Playstation by urgently beckoning him back downstairs.

"Come on, Artos, its back to the garage for us."

Arthur turned to follow but almost tripped over his dragging trouser-legs, and in frustration sat himself quickly on the freshly-made bed, drew Carnwennau, and wasted no time in slicing the excess material from the jeans with the dagger's sharp edge.

"Well that's one way to take up a trouser leg," Max grinned, and the King, catching his eye, grinned back.

"Come on Max," said Arthur awkwardly, rising from the bed and hoping that he'd got the words right, and from the beaming smile the boy gave him in return he could see that he had.

(i)   Stop girl, don't run.

(ii)   Run away and I'll slice his horrible little throat.

(iii)   Now just stay still, don't move, keep quiet.

(iv)   Quiet

(v)   Right Saxon, speak to me. Shout for help and I will open your neck to the spine, but speak to me. Who are you? And what size is your chieftain's camp?

(vi)   Don't struggle boy. Quiet. Now tell me who you are.

(vii)   Answer me.

(viii)   Answer me boy, speak to me. Have the Saxons taken Caerleon?

117

(ix)   Why am I here?

(x)   But you are no help to me without news.

(xi)   I am King Arthur, Lord and King over these Islands.

(xii)   Is this the work of the Devil?

(xiii)   I must empty my bowels.

(xiv)   What's this for?

(xv)   My clothes are even wetter than before

(a)   Are you Saxon? Where are you from?

(b)   Have you a chieftain? Where are his warriors encamped?

(c)   What of Caerleon? Have the Saxons taken it?

(d)   Is the queen Gwenhwyfar alive?

(e)   Gwenhwyfar dead... Caerleon no more... Oh Christ why can't I rest with them?

(f)   Why can't I be dead? My mission is over, can't I be dead to join Gwenhwyfar and my knights?

(g)   Bless you girl

(h)   I am Arthur, King of Britain

(i)   It is Roman.

(j)   This is Caesar's ring. It is the Roman governor's ring of authority. The last Governor left this behind to seal the fate of Britain and so it has passed to me.

(k)   I want the clothes when the clothes are dry.

Chapter Seven – All washed up

As the storm winds rose to gale force and the rain fell, a lone and bedraggled mariner out on the churning, choppy sea in a tiny sailing boat weighed up his options. The little vessel was being tossed and turned by the angry waves, and he feared it might not hold together in the face of the onslaught.

He took in the sail and tried to row against the waves, but the force was too great and he couldn't even hold her steady, so he raised the sail again, thinking it best to let the wind and current take him where it willed, and though he was blown off course, the wrong side of Cornwall, he knew better than to fight it and concentrated instead on keeping his craft from being dashed against the jagged rocks.

The wind dropped a little as the boat was carried up the Bristol Channel towards the Severn Estuary; it was a little more sheltered, and though the rain kept coming, progress was good with the tide in his favour. The little boat had taken a lot of water on the open sea, and given a respite from holding the tiller and sail for dear life, he now bailed it out vigorously and resolved in his mind to make to Plymouth over land. There would be plenty of coaches from Bristol, and with a couple of stops on the way to change horses he didn't think it could take more than three days.

With the tiny deck clear, he studied the familiar coast. He prided himself that there were few who knew it better, and yet it was strange to him. Clusters of lights, some large, some stretched, had been visible since first he had passed the Pembroke peninsular, and though he had initially thought them warning beacons, he was now bemused and intrigued by their brightness and number.

He was cold, tired, and totally wet through. It had been a long voyage and he had done it all without compasses or any other navigational instruments. This last stretch battling the weather had drained him, and now as darkness had fallen and his wet toes scrunched in soaking stockings, he felt the strange sensation of longing for shore. How strange it was he told himself, that when he was at sea, hungry and made nauseous by the claustrophobic smell of unwashed bodies, he longed for land, yet when he was ashore he yearned for the tide, the open swell, the salt on the wind and adventure.

As he had floated on towards Avonmouth with the wind behind him, he'd half expected to dock to the sound of the Port's cannon and a hearty three cheers from the townsfolk, but now uncertainty gripped him as he floated past some huge steel vessels at anchor with enormous metal cranes towering over them. He surveyed these seafaring monsters in open-mouthed wonder. What tonnage could they carry? And how could they put to sea at all? For bearing such weight and some having no sail or mast to be seen, he saw not how they could catch the wind. They were defenceless too, he noted disapprovingly. Not a single cannon could be seen on deck and he feared they would be easy prey for pirates and enemy alike on the ocean waves.

He floated up the Avon thinking to put ashore in the heart of Bristol, curiosity leading him on up the river. He was keen to take in more and more, yet weary of the political climate he might find, he was also keen to keep his head on his shoulders and knew he would have to be careful in how he announced his return.

But as he sailed into the city, the lights of the Bristol were so numerous and the buildings so plentiful that the whole place looked entirely different. Gone were the timbered houses and whitewashed dwellings of the Bristol he'd known, and he floated passed the sprawling stone and brick metropolis in confusion.

Feeling dispirited he sat back down and drifted in solitude, taking it all in from his sodden seat, and the flow carried his small craft through and into the outskirts of the City. How long had he been away? How long at sea? He wondered if the Spanish had invaded in his absence. He could picture the Dons routing the noble English Yeomen mercilessly, and he wondered if he now beheld the work of their hands, the towering Papist buildings on his beloved English soil.

It was now almost completely dark, (as though the moon was full the cloud cover was heavy,) and very late in the day. He cursed aloud, for water was once again slopping over his buckled shoes in the bottom of the boat, and though he was sure the tiny vessel must have sprung a slow leak in the storm he could barely see to bail out, let alone to plug a hole. As his craft sat lower and lower in the water and rounding a bend he could once again see the bridge behind him, he decided enough was enough - he was losing the battle to stay on the water. The sailor took in the sail with a sigh and reached for the oars. He rowed to shore in the gloom, pulling hard to propel the water heavy prow towards a piece of unlit land in the hopes of finding unpopulated country where he would be safe from the potentially inhospitable local constable, at least until morning.

The prow hit the bank and the mariner squelched ashore. In great relief to be back on home soil he fell to his knees to kiss his beloved green English grass, but ugh! Cow pat! With a cough and a spit he tried again and took hold of the grass with two firm hands and gave thanks. It had been a long journey, he was home at last. But the rain kept falling.

Rhys Jenkins was eighteen, and although he'd been driving for a year already he was still no master of safe motorway travel and swerved daringly from lane to lane of the M4 while the base-box in the back of the car blasted out his favourite tunes.

He'd finished his exams two weeks ago and had enjoyed the freedom of giving his school a heartfelt two fingered salute before embarking on a fortnight of partying with his mates in Newport. His father, a mechanic and reluctant co-fitter of the chunky body kit which made his son's beloved first car look rather lower to the ground than it actually was, had been on at him about getting a job since he walked out of his last exam, but Rhys had managed to persuade his mother that he needed a long summer off to release some steam and consider his career aspirations.

She'd suggested a change of scene would do him good, and desperate for a break herself from Rhys' loud parties, she had fully supported the idea of his going to stay with her sister Patricia in Bath for a few days. 'She'll be happy to put you up,' she'd urged him, 'and I know your cousins Max and Jess are always pleased to see you.'

But Rhys's reason for heading east was not to see his cousins but to spend some time with his girlfriend, Rhiannon. He needed no urging and had missed her badly over the exam period, which had interrupted the frustratingly infrequent catching-up they'd been doing by train since a year ago when Rhiannon's father had got a new job and the family had moved to Bath so he would be closer to work.

It had been hard on Rhiannon to move away from home in the middle of her own studies, but it had been really hard on what had, at the time, been her fledgling relationship with Rhys. They had known each other since primary school, but had only been boyfriend and girlfriend a few months when her family had moved, and Rhys, as he sang along to another thumping track, was really looking forward to some proper catching-up. He'd agreed with his mum that he would stay with his Aunt Patricia, but he wasn't anticipating spending too much time with Max and Jessica.

He cruised over the Severn bridge, perhaps a little too fast, and on past the sign welcoming him to England. A mile or so onwards he had slowed a little and was dangerously fiddling with his CD player, as he tried to find a particular track, when he looked up ahead to see a figure standing in the road.

Rhys may have failed to ingest the whole of the Highway Code, but he knew that pedestrians were not supposed to be on motorways, and initially suspected there might be an accident ahead. Scanning the road, however, he could see no evidence of a collision or other obstruction to the carriageway, and would simply have swerved around the figure with an instructive blast of his horn had a Lorry not taken advantage of his having slowed to fiddle with his sound system and boxed him in as it tried to overtake.

Rhys was bearing down on the figure fast, he could see now it was a man who stood directly in the road ahead of him, legs apart and waving his arms in the air. He had no idea what he was doing - playing chicken perhaps, and intending to run out of the way at the last second? Or perhaps he was trying to commit suicide, perhaps he wanted Rhys to run him down? He'd heard of such things happening, people throwing themselves under trains or off motorway bridges - but why wave at him as if he wanted him to stop?

Rhys really had no option anyway. It was either stop or run the madman down, for it was clear he had no intention of getting out of the road, and boxed in as he was by the lorry he couldn't avoid hitting him. He slammed on his brakes and swerved onto the hard shoulder, bringing his car to a screeching halt. It had been close, and with only a few seconds in which to react he'd only missed the pedestrian by a couple of metres at best. He flicked his sound system off, and as he sat panting in his car and trying to calm his heart, which was beating like never before, he saw the man running up to his car in the rear view mirror.

The teenager had never seen such a man. He had buckled shoes on his feet, white tights to his knees and a pair of baggy pantaloons from his knees to his waist. He wore an elaborate puffy yellow and gold top, and had a small yellow cape hanging off his right shoulder which trailed behind him as he ran. Had he been wearing a mask he would have looked like a poor imitation of a superhero, but his attire ended with a flappy piece of material at the neck. In his right hand he carried a black bonnet with a huge white feather sticking out of the top of it, and he held a long sword with an elaborate hilt and scabbard to his left hip. He pulled up at the passenger door with a delighted: "A-har!"

"You total idiot," Rhys greeted him angrily.

"Ahem…" The man tried to interrupt, but Rhys was determined to have his say.

"You scared the life out of me, I thought I was going to run you over,"

"Urm…"

"No 'Urms', I tell you. You know you're not supposed to hitchhike on the motorway... But in the middle of the carriageway... What were you doing? Trying to get yourself killed?"

"Um, hitchhike?" The man looked confused. "I wouldst be held to thee, good Sir, if thou wouldst furnish me wi' transport."

"Oh well, you might as well get in - I suppose I'll have to give you a lift now won't I? Where to?"

"Where?"

"Yes, where are you going?" asked Rhys impatiently.

"Prithee, I be bound for Plymouth Hoe, aye, 'pon my troth be it so."

Rhys couldn't help but think the man a total eccentric as he climbed scruffily into the seat beside him. His shoes and tights were filthy and spattered with mud, his top, which Rhys could see was intricately patterned in gold thread, was sodden wet, as was the ruff at his neck, and his curly, reddish-brown hair and scraggly beard - which oddly, Rhys noted, was longer at the chin - were both streaked with grey and were a tangled unkempt mess. All in all he looked like a bedraggled old hippie.

"Well, I'm going to Bath," Rhys replied in annoyance as his passenger dirtied his clean floor with his muddy feet. He took pride in his little run-around and frowned as his passenger lounged back in the seat next to him and expressed a contented sigh.

"Aye, well an ale house and hot tub wouldst be a welcome sight t' behold indeed, for my garms bring much discomfort. 'Twas a most inclement storm I hath endured all o'er yon wretched night past."

"Well it rained a lot, I'll give you that." This man didn't just dress weird, thought Rhys, he spoke like a freak too.

"In troth hadst I thought mine next wallow in the hot tub to be several months hence, for 'tis rotten on the health to wash more frequent. But 'tis of import to scrub up when preparing to home, an' I fear I must endure't and suffer't presently."

The man unbuttoned his top and removed his ruff to reveal a soaking wet, frilly white undershirt which clung to his skin.

"Mine doublet an' hose hath taken in half an ocean I fear, an' be they in need o' a cosy parlour yonder where canst they, perchance, be laundered aright."

"Right, well get the door shut," Rhys replied "and we can get moving. I might be able to dry you out a bit and all."

The passenger pulled the door to with a great sense of urgency, and turned to Rhys with imploring eyes.

"A thousand pardons, young Master, for mine good manners hath deserted me." He removed a teardrop-shaped pearl earring from his own lobe and held it out to the driver. "For carriage," he gestured, but

Rhys didn't understand. "Payment," he waggled the earring all the faster, "for hath I a want o' sovereigns, nor neither hath I even a purse."

"Oh, don't worry yourself about that," Rhys was embarrassed. He wore an earring himself, a single gold hoop, though he knew his Aunt Patricia didn't like jewellery on men and he would make a point of removing it before he arrived at her house. Through politeness he declined, for he never would have worn anything which looked so girly, but Rhys couldn't deny the traveller's earring had to be worth a small fortune, a real pearl mounted on a solid gold hoop, and it looked like an antique.

He pulled gently away and turned the car's hot air blowers on the passenger who let out a contented purr.

"Thou hast a furnace herein, young master?"

"Um, something like that. What are you doing here anyway?"

"Meanst thou, wherefore hath I come hence?"

"I mean, what are you doing here on this motorway?"

"Thou speakst in riddles, Master Mariner, yet shalt I give mine answer plainly - 'tis a mysterious tale, but true.

"The last occurrence in mine memory 'twas but the grip o' nausea most queer, didst grab at the bowel an' twist an' clutch it most cruel, a troublous pain an' weakness which hadst I feared wouldst overcome even I. Then didst I open again mine eyes and 'pon my troth 'twas I alone, adrift o' the open sea in a craft I hath not known. Mine crew, mine ship, hadst taken flight, or be she sunk wi' all hands I know not.

"I hadst set course for the Indies whence camest a storm o' such violence unknown but for the Horn, an' blew mine wretched craft a merrie way. Set I then mine heart on fair Plymouth an' set sail for home, yet so raged the storm that were I blown up yon channel to the Port o' Bristol yonder. Any lesser a sailor wouldst even now be dancing a jig o' death i' the depths, yet didst I moor her safe."

"Okay..." Rhys wished he'd never picked this oddball up, let alone ever actually asked him a question.

"Hadst I a mind to moor at Bristol, yet be the town so altered didst I pass her by, rest a while till dawn broke, an' made afoot unhindered by light o' welcome day to yon turnpike whence didst we tarry a while yonder."

"Right, so you walked did you?"

"Aye, young Master, afoot hast I met thee hence, and canst I tell thee what a joy 'tis t' behold thy speech, for hast I thought, the Don's overrun fair England."

"Eh?"

"Didst I think yon fortress o' the bank I passed to be a Don

124

stronghold, for it didst billow smoke like t' the singeing o' the Don King's beard, an' methought a battle raged. Yet hath I found no army o' this turnpike but carriages o' a like t' this, an all so move at speed unrivalled."

"Look, that's a power station back there and it smokes because... well, everyone knows why it smokes, it's cooling towers anyway, and why are you talking in that strange way? Where are you from?"

"Hold thy peace, Sir, I prey you. Must I speak o' mine undertaking."

"Um, go ahead."

"Never hast I beheld a carriage the like o' this afore, an' so be mine adventure awakened. 'Tis true, canst man travel even now at speeds hitherto undreamt of, an' so canst I contain mineself no longer. Prithee, Sirrah, let me take a turn at driving the cart."

"You want to drive!" Rhys could hardly believe his ears.

"Well aye," his passenger sounded hurt, "for hast I as deft a hand for the tiller as to any pilot who hath rounded the Good Hope Cape, for circumnavigation heldst no fear for me."

Rhys assumed he was talking about steering and not an uncomfortable form of mutilation, but he couldn't help but laugh at this comment.

"Look here, mate, this is my car and I want to keep it in one piece, okay? Whether you're in one piece or not. You might have sailed round the 'Good Hope Cape,' as you call it, but you've been walking the wrong way for Plymouth, that's for sure, good pilot or not! You can have a lift alright, but I'm driving."

"Ah, but thou speakst fair." But the passenger couldn't help but look disappointed. "Be it that I must serve mine apprenticeship then must I serve't wi' patience. Prithee, pardon mine forthright manner."

"It's okay." But Rhys was finding his passenger's raw energy somewhat exhausting already.

"These be troubleous times and much change hast there been since last didst I set foot upon these shores. Speak Sir, who is't thy monarch? Who sits upon the throne o' fair England?"

"Um, Queen Elizabeth, everyone knows that."

"Ah, good Queen Bess, sweet Mistress, noble Lady Regina. Thou canst but guess what joy 'tis t' behold such news. O' such bounteous fate, such gracious fortune, I must t' Court an' seek her favour," he spoke quietly to himself. "But what o' these times, young Master? For 'tis strange indeed that her realm be so altered while still she sits o'er it. What be the year o' her reign?"

"Not sure, no idea. She's in her eighties I know that, she'll be ninety or thereabouts soon, certainly getting on."

"Aye, but there be such change as I thought couldst be but in a dream o' Master Shakespeare's devising, these horseless carts an carriages, the sprawl o' Bristol, yon bridges, an galleons afloat in yon harbour - be all the land so altered?"

"Look, who are you anyway? And why are you talking like that?"

His passenger breathed deep and his chest seemed to swell with pride. When he spoke it was with pompous arrogance.

"I, Sirrah, be Sir Francis, El Draque the scourge o' the Dons, Admiral Drake to the stout Yeomanry o' England, favourite o' the Queen an latterly Mayor o' Plymouth."

"Oh so you're from Plymouth are you? That might explain a few things," Rhys teased him.

"Aye it be so, Devon boy born an' bred."

"You reckon you're Sir Francis Drake?"

"Aye, yet tremble not whilst thou art in the presence o' greatness."

"You're a grade-A loony."

"Holdst thou thy tongue, thou churl, for thou charge wi' lunacy a Knight o' this realm an none bolder."

"Well clearly you rate modesty highly. If you're Sir Francis Drake I'm Micky mouse."

"Jest ye not, Master Mariner for thou art no rodent. Furnish me now wi' thy name an forthwith."

"Very well," Rhys laughed. "My name is Rhys Jenkins, I'm a Newport boy born and bred, well my Mum's from this side of the bridge like, but... Gor, you're a state man you really are, you really should see yourself."

Drake was nothing if not vain, and having his appearance criticised hit him hard.

"An' canst thou, I fear, magic up a looking glass?" he asked sarcastically.

Rhys could not contain his laughter. "Is there someone who looks after you? Are you missing from some special hospital?"

"Ah but 'tis good fortune indeed, hath I chanced upon one." A delighted Drake plucked a loose CD from the side pocket of the passenger door and began admiring his reflection in the shiny disk, immediately setting himself to re-styling his ragged beard by pulling the longest bit on his chin into a firm, neat point, and ruffling his eyebrows.

"Give that back here," Rhys snatched it off him, "you'll mess it up with grubby fingers and it won't play."

"I beg'st thy pardon, Rhys, but what meanst thou?"

"Oh good Lord!" Rhys was despairing, and thinking action would save a thousand words he flicked the CD into the sound system and turned it on.

As the music flooded out into the car, thumping drum beats and bass guitar from every speaker, Drake leapt in his seat and twisted round.

"We be under fire, from whence comes it?"

"We are not." Rhys turned the CD down and switched it to a calmer track. "See, relax, its only music." He flicked down the sun shield to reveal a small vanity mirror, and the passenger, delighted to see that he could indeed 'magic one up,' calmed immediately and set himself to preening once more.

"Thou hast minstrels up front, do they also tend unto your fire?" Drake looked uncomfortably confused, for this technology was a step ahead of him.

"No, look the music's all recorded on here," Rhys tried to explain, but he was finding the situation frustrating, and choosing action again he flicked the CD on and off a few times.

"Tis a wonder," Drake started switching it on and off himself, "that a group o' minstrels canst be put unto their art wi' the touch o' a finger."

"Yeah, well, technology, isn't it."

"Aye, but what to the sounds o' their art? Canst I make out no lyre, no lute nor harpsichord, methinks this the very sounds o' hell, or be it Don babble Master Rhys?"

"Look, if you don't like my choice of music..."

"Ah yet meant I no offence, thou mayst bend they ear to what thou wilt."

"Yeah, that I wilt, I mean will, in my own car. And stop fiddling, will you." Rhys took Drake's hand and placed it firmly back in his passenger's lap. "That sword real?"

"Verily, young Master," Drake replied. He held the sword between his legs as it wouldn't fit beside him, and he lovingly massaged the intricate hilt. "Yet fearst I the rains o' last night wilt hath done her ill."

"I bet you're sensible sometimes... You're an actor obviously, got to be. I tell you it's a damned good act, I don't know how you keep a straight face, I mean you come across as really authentic."

Drake responded to this accusation with theatrical horror.

"Thou cur," he snarled through clenched teeth, "how darest thou accuse thy servant - I, who hath navigated single-handed the spice routes, I who hath put to fire the Don King's Armada an' raided his galleons o' the open sea - how dare'st thou, Sirrah, accuse I o' being a lowly, nancy boy player? Neither the Horn nor the Good Hope Cape couldst stand afore mine skill in fair winds nor foul, yet thou wouldst charge I, thy noble Knight o' England, o' fancy so flippant an moral so base as t' play the part o' women! I be all out o' patience wi' thee - a pox o' thy throat, you bawling, uncharitable dog."

"Alright, calm down, I didn't mean to upset you. Here," he offered his passenger a cigarette, "have a smoke and chill out." Rhys couldn't believe his bad luck, this madman clearly did believe he was really Sir Francis Drake and didn't like to be told otherwise. He couldn't deny he looked the part, but what was he supposed to do with him? He decided the best bet was just to get him to Bath and then drop him out. He daren't antagonise him as the bloke was armed, and although he just wanted to laugh at him he couldn't deny the oddball could be dangerous.

Sir Francis, hoping to have restored the deserving respect of the youth beside him, had retrieved a slender cigarette from the packet and was sniffing it cautiously.

"Well, what's wrong now?" Rhys asked in irritation.

"Tis tobacco aright, wilt thou not bring forth thy pipe an tinder box?"

"No, look," Rhys, ever the rebellious teenager, flipped a cigarette into his mouth and with a flick of his lighter was puffing smoke out of his mouth.

"Well bless me," Drake was amazed. "Thou canst make fire wi' thy fingers."

"You really are a nutter you are, look," Rhys handed him the lighter. "Put the fag in your mouth - no, the other way up, that's it - now you flick that little wheel, hold the button down and light the other end."

After some fumbling, Drake had the lighter burning a flame and lit his cigarette with much coughing. Rhys took the lighter back from him before he could do any damage with it, but Drake didn't want to let it go.

"Prithee, Master Rhys, I'll make no mischief. Let me keep't, I pray thee. T'would be but a revelation unto a Master Gunner at sea."

"Oh well, all yours," Rhys handed it back, "they're only disposables anyway, I've got a load more in the car somewhere. Just don't play with it now, it's dangerous in the car."

"Shalt I remain forever indebted unto thee." A delighted Drake pocketed his new toy like a contented child. "Yet methinks it strange indeed to take into thy mouth tobacco smoke wi' no pipe for filling."

"Well, pre-rolled aren't they."

"Aye, yet spoke I unto Raleigh, t'would never catch on."

"Eh?"

"Sir Walter Raleigh, a sailor o' skill second unto only mineself.

Hither carried Raleigh tobacco plants from the Indies, an' breathed he the smoke as if t'were fresh air. Spake I unto Raleigh t'would never catch on, for 'tis most abhorrent on thy good health."

"You told Sir Walter Raleigh smoking would never catch on," Rhys uttered sceptically, almost bored by the act his passenger was putting on.

"Aye, 'pon mine honest troth."

"Well it is bad for you that's for sure. They've certainly proved that now."

"An' a socking didst Sir Walter endure for his pains," Drake laughed at the memory. "I recall't well, so was the tale told me. Seated was Raleigh betwixt table an hearth for to digest his meal, and took he unto himself his pipe from the new world. He puffed out such smoke as his servant feared he be afire, an' tipped he o'er Sir Walter, a pail o' water most frigid, for to extinguish all combustion."

Drake rocked with laughter, and Rhys, finding it infectious, chuckled too, not just at the ridiculous tale but even more so at his own unlikely predicament. Here he was in his car with a total madman in period dress laughing at sixteenth-century clowning. Were the tale true it certainly suggested the modern custard pie routine was hardly a significant comic development, but who tomorrow would believe him when he told them about the eccentric old lunatic he had given a lift to?

"Ah, thou hast a good heart," Drake thumped him warmly on the thigh, he was pleased to see the driver laughing. "Beg'st I thy pardon for spurning thee so just now."

"It's okay, I guess no one wants to be accused of acting when they are just living a life they enjoy, I mean everyone's different, aren't they?"

"Indeed it be so - here play I at liking Sir Walter's fireworks." Drake coughed again as he attempted to smoke the cigarette, and on Rhys' lead he stubbed it out in the car's ashtray.

Rhys turned off the motorway, and having negotiated the roundabout, proceeded south towards the city of Bath.

Drake had sat for a few moments in contemplative silence, but now sought to change the subject. "Tell me Master Rhys, wherefore ist thou bound for Bath?"

"Where? Oh why?"

"Aye."

"Oh, well my girlfriend lives there you see."

"Ah, thou hast a Lady." Drake looked intrigued. "Hast she a name?"

"Well yeah, Rhiannon, she's called Rhiannon."

"Ah-ha! A bony name an true, an I'll wager she be a buxom wench full o' japes an merrie sport?"

"Um, well I haven't seen her for ages," Rhys replied awkwardly; this was embarrassing. "I was gonna ask her if she wants to come travelling with me, I wanna go off and do the travelling thing, you know, don't really feel up to the world of work yet - I mean, we've only just finished our exams."

"Ah but thou speaks't sense indeed, exploring, adventuring - canst I tell thee once or thrice o' the joys o'such endeavours."

"Yeah, well, I want to see the world, you know. Thailand's meant to be pretty awesome."

"Then mark me must thou seekst an apprenticeship pon a seafaring venture. Thou wilt see all continents o' the globe if thou wilt brave the spice routes, and so too wilt thou acquaint thyself wi' the ways o' the sea. So shalt I count thee then Rhys on mine next voyage amongst mine crew," Drake offered generously. "Thou mayst be captain 'pon this cart, and so thou shouldst for I be but a novice o' such transport. Yet canst I show thee the seven seas an how thou canst navigate them by the stars, how to take unto thyself a top sail in a storm, an' when we chance upon a Don galleon, how thou canst board her an make off wi' all the gold o' the Indies.

"I tell thee, Master Jenkins, when thou doest sight a Don ship on the open sea wi' Admiral Drake in thy company 'tis said; 'don thee thy deepest purse all hands, for shalt there be plunder undreamt of therein.' There be no better tutor, Master Rhys, for be I Captain unrivalled o' the waves. Wouldst I blow off the very head o' Leviathan if t'would dare to face me, an prithee, here I offer thee a voyage in mine service for fortune an adventure. Mark me, young Rhys, t'would be no adventure were't not for endeavour. Wilt thou come?"

"Um, well it's very kind of you to offer," Rhys felt awkward and most ungrateful knocking back such a heartfelt offer, but the bloke was mad. "But we'll fly of course... Yeah, I get seasick actually, and um, well, we'll only be going for a year or so, I mean all that time on a sailing boat, it'll sort of cut into the time I want to spend backpacking in Asia."

"Asia, pray you, didst thou say Asia? For 'tis a land much uncharted where the ague blights an' natives mayst cut thee down as hay in a meadow. Why t'would take a hero such as I to... Hold young Master, did'st thou spake o' flight?"

Rhys was starting to think twice about his passenger now, he did seem genuinely out of his depth and amazed at such a notion. If this was an act he was incredibly consistent and deserved credit for it - but what if it was not?

"Um, yes, of course we'll fly, its miles away."

"But how canst thou take flight, thou knave? Thou hast no feathers nor plumage - thou takest thy servant for a fool to jest so."

"No, no, you just get on a plane and away you go, it's about ten, maybe twelve hours and bingo, you're in Thailand."

"Thou art mad, I beseech thee, how canst it be that thou can fly?"

"Me mad - that's rich, that is. Look, up there," Rhys pointed impatiently to a vapour trail high in the sky, "right up there Sir Francis or whatever your name is, up there, that's a plane and its carrying people and its flying, what's so weird about that?"

"It canst be but the work o' Beelzebub," Drake replied in shock.

"Nope."

"The Papist Catholics?"

"Nope, look, it's just like this 'horseless cart' you're sitting in, you were playing up about the car a few minutes ago. There's nothing amazing about it, you just fill it up with fuel, fill it up with people and take off - look, there's another one. Come on, mate, air travel is hardly new - it's got to have been going a hundred years at least."

"Thou jest again, Rhys, for I hath not heard tell o' such a wonder this side o' Doomsday, yet 'tis a sight indeed to behold. Speak thee now, Master, how couldst it be that I, Francis Drake, couldst be numbered aboard such a craft, for t' fly above the world couldst be subject o' mine dreams no more."

"Um, well, just like everyone else I guess, you just have to um, buy a ticket." Rhys didn't know quite what to make of his passenger anymore; he'd humoured the freak at first, for he hadn't known how best to take him, and he'd been a little unnerved by his unpredictability, yet eccentric actor or madman he was beginning to feel more real, more authentic the longer he stayed in his company, and as they entered the outskirts of Bath he was beginning to wonder what best to do with him.

"Look, do you want the bus station, the train station or what?"

"Train station, bus station, I know not o' these places o' which thou speakst. I implore thee, Rhys, speak plainly, for fair England be so changed that I find her unfamiliar."

"Perhaps the nuthouse should be your first port of call."

"Oast houses I hath seen, an' malt houses sighted, yet never, Master, hath I heard tell o' a 'nut house' - for what purpose be they erected?"

Rhys gave Drake a sideways glance. He was much drier than he'd been when first he had picked him up, the hot air blowers had done their work well. But he was still every bit the eccentric and he'd kept up the act for the whole journey.

Rhys was more amused now than threatened by his odd behaviour, and he made a decision quickly in his mind. He thought it was probably rash, but opportunities to share such experiences were after all very few and far between, and he wanted to see how the passenger would react to further company.

"Look, I'm going to take you to my Aunt's house for a cup of tea, okay? I think my cousins have to meet you."

"Thy cousins must meet wi' me?"

"Yeah, they'll just never believe me when I tell them about you otherwise."

"What mean'st thou?" Drake looked suspicious.

"I mean they'll never believe me when I tell them I've met the great Sir Francis Drake," he replied carefully.

"Ah, then shalt we be well-met indeed. T'will be an honour to takest refreshment at they Aunt's home... Tea, thou spake of?"

"Yes, um, don't worry, you'll see for yourself soon enough." As Rhys brought his car to a stop outside the Finch's house in Weston-Bissett he turned to Drake and addressed him in a slightly more serious tone. "Look, Sir Francis, go along with it as far as you like, just promise me one thing."

"Aye."

"Well, two things actually."

"Name thou thy terms."

"No swearing - my Aunt Patricia is quite formal and proper, she's really house-proud too and she really doesn't like it."

"Thou hast mine honest word, I shalt not curse."

"Good, and no mention of the smokes, okay?" Rhys quickly removed his earring before he forgot and left it in his glove compartment. "My aunt doesn't know I smoke either and she'll only freak out if she thinks I'm going to give them to Max, my cousin Max, that is."

"Thou hast mine word upon't."

Patricia Finch was delighted to see her nephew and welcomed him with great enthusiasm.

"Rhys darling how wonderful to see you," she kissed him on both cheeks without pausing for breath. "Now I know you'll be keen to get on and see your girlfriend but Maxwell and Jessica are simply dying to see you and I hope you've got time to see them before you go off, you know how they look up to their older cousin... But who's this?" She asked curiously having only just noticed Drake, who stood behind her nephew, and with his hat on resembled a slightly damp peacock.

"Oh, um, Auntie Pat, this is um," he paused. "This is Sir Francis Drake," then, leaning forward so only she could hear: "Barking mad but he seems harmless, I picked him up on the motorway, I hope I wasn't being rude but I've invited him in for a cup of tea, honestly, you've got to see him to believe him."

Patricia Finch was somewhat taken aback but tried to respond tactfully.

"No, no, not at all," she replied, but then similarly she whispered to Rhys, "Um, now you see, Rhys darling, it is a little difficult, I mean if he's a total stranger and..."

"Good Madam," Drake interrupted, "I pray thee be not angry wi' Master Jenkins, he meant no ill in his invitation. Regard me solely as a weary traveller made parched by a long journey. I meanst not to impose, yet if thou hast a surplus o' warming refreshment herein, t'would be a fine act o' a gentlewoman to bid a man to take his ease an' break a fast which t'were it t' tarry wi' him longer, couldst prove his most misfortunate undoing."

"Um, er, yes Mr Drake, um, of course, do please come in." She could always take Rhys to one side later for a lesson in etiquette when the unexpected guest had gone.

"Ah, a thousand blessings be rained upon thee madam, and never a fairer maiden hath I set mine eyes upon in many a long year."

"Oh, you flatterer." Patricia Finch could not resist any appeal to demonstrate her qualities of hostessing, and though the eloquent tongue of the eccentric tramp had won her over, she suddenly realised she was still standing in the doorway trying not to look too shocked at his appearance. "Oh excuse me, we are dithering aren't we - come in, Mr Drake, come in do, and have a cup of tea."

"He's larger than life, Aunt Pat, he really is. I just thought Max and Jess had to meet him," Rhys followed her through into the house with Drake a little further behind, and both dropped their voices hoping he wouldn't hear.

"Where has he come from?"

"I've no idea, he won't say. Escaped from the circus I reckon, he's totally convinced he's Sir Francis Drake, I just don't really know what to do with him. Got any ideas?"

"Well yes, um," - she spoke a little louder so as not to give the visitor the idea that he was being talked about, "You're welcome to stay as long as you like Rhys, just use us as you will, come and go as you please," - and then more quietly, "Perhaps we should ring the police, he might be reported missing or something."

"Um, maybe, but I don't want to get him in any trouble." Rhys also

raised his voice. "Thank you, Auntie, it's nice to be made to feel so welcome. Now, where are Max and Jess? I'm sure they would like to meet Sir Francis."

"Oh, yes indeed, I'm sure they will." Patricia sounded a little uneasy, and ran her eyes over her nephew's companion, taking in his whole appearance. "Er, um, your clothing is most unusual, Mr Drake - where did you come by it?"

"These be tailored by the finest craftsmen o' Putney, Madam - though in troth they be but sea-faring garms, mine finest clothes be held at mine estate o' Plymouth. 'Tis true, I wouldst do well t' endure a change o' clothes, an wouldst be beheld t' the trouble o' a reputable barber-surgeon, for mine beard alike is most dishevelled."

Benji came bounding out of the back room and jumped up to Rhys in greeting. "Hello boy," Rhys patted him, but the dog began to sniff Drake with no shortage of inquisitive energy.

"A fine hound, my Lady, doest thou take him to the hunt?"

"Er no, I haven't done."

"Ah, but forgive me Madam, for wi' as slight a hand as yours, an' fair, 'tis like as not thou wilt favour the falcon."

"No, I've never done any falconry." Patricia and Rhys exchanged strange looks, she raising her eyebrows as if to question who is this strange man you have brought into my house? and he raising his own in return as if to say I told you he was a weirdo.

"So where are my cousins then?"

"Well they are in, I'm sure, but they keep shutting themselves in the garage. They must be up to something in there because they won't let me in, they've even shut Benji out." She led her visitors briskly to the doorway which led to the converted garage and knocked impatiently at the door. "Jessica, Maxwell, come to the door please and let us in."

"Later," came Max's voice through the door.

"What are you up to in there?"

There was a brief hesitation. "We're busy, um, we'll tell you later."

"We're not up to anything, Mum," came Jess's voice, "we'll be out in a minute."

"Rhys is here to see you, darlings, and a friend of his."

Slowly Max opened the door just enough to poke his head out, he smiled widely at his cousin. "Hi Rhys." Max looked a bit shaken, but his eyes widened further when he caught a glimpse of Rhys' companion. "No, it can't be..." Max stepped back in surprise.

"Ah yes, but I be recognised at last." Drake sounded full of enthusiasm, "Sir Francis Drake at your service, young Master."

Benji suddenly lurched forward and hurled the door open to reveal

134

Jessica Finch looking rather nervous, and in the corner a strange, stocky, little man in a shiny chain mail singlet and freshly laundered woollen trews, who was holding the radio to his ear.

Patricia Finch screamed to see the rugged stranger sheltering with her children.

"Mum, please don't be cross..." Max tried to explain, but his mother cut across him.

"Who, who... who is he?" she demanded in disbelief.

"Um, well we think he's King Arthur," Max replied guiltily, "but we can't understand a word he says."

"Ave." Arthur raised the palm of his hand to his hostess in formal Roman greeting.

"Oh," Patricia did the same uncertainly, but twiddled her fingers at him in a feminine wave, "Oh, hi, oh..."

"Bloomin' heck," Rhys exclaimed trying not to swear in front of his Aunt, "another one!"

But Jessica Finch had gone as white as a sheet and was staring at Drake with her hand to her mouth. Suddenly she passed out, and fell to the floor.

Chapter Eight – On Lunch

As he sat at his desk over what was supposed to be his Friday afternoon lunch break, eating his sandwiches with a paper on over fishing laid out in front of him, Julian Finch couldn't concentrate. He found himself, instead, chewing over the comments he'd over heard from the Commissioner's office two days before. What was Protocol Fifteen to the European Environmental Act? And what on earth was the New Environmental Solution Act which they had been toasting so heartily?

Jennifer, his secretary, was out on her lunch break, and as Julian sat alone in their small office, pondering in thoughtful solitude, his peace and quiet was suddenly, and rudely broken as the ginger head of Nigel Sludboil followed its owner's large nose round the door and into the room. Somewhat predictably, the bald and bucktoothed visage of Trevor Rindburn followed in his wake.

"On lunch?" asked Sludboil scathingly.

"So it would appear," Julian gestured to his half-eaten sandwich. He hoped this would be a brief visit and intended to give as good as he got. "You two lap-dogs not dining at your Master's table today?"

"As you well know," Rindburn responded, "both his Grace and Sir Morgan have another engagement today."

"Off to Brussels, aren't they?" Sludboil chipped in. "For their official (he emphasised the word) meeting with their European counterparts. The Commissioners meeting to officially, (again he emphasised the word) approve the European Environmental Act. Then on Monday it's off to the Council and... Swish, swish, swish, it's made law." He theatrically mimed the signing of a document with the swirling of his wrist.

"But I trust his Grace has not foregone his lunch."

"Oh rest assured, Finch," Rindburn answered with reverence, "they travel on a direct train as we speak."

"First class," Sludboil added.

"And with their own private dining car."

"But of course," Julian smiled, and he could picture the Duke of Man sat even now at a spacious table in an elegant dining carriage with a fine spread of rich foods laid out in front of him, a huge white, but stained, napkin tucked into his collar. It was a world away from the modest dusting of crumbs on his own desk.

"Only the best for those two most noble of men, real heroes."

"Too right, Rindburn, they are geniuses," Sludboil agreed.

"Great servants of the nation," Julian joined in, but in a voice of clearest sarcasm.

"Now look here, Finch," said Rindburn, "you should watch your attitude. There are going to be some changes around here shortly."

"Yes, very shortly," his companion added.

"Yes, hopefully you two will move on and let me finish my lunch in peace."

"No, real changes," Sludboil continued in a serious voice, "personnel changes. It won't be worth your job to get cheeky with us."

"Yes, we'll have some very new responsibilities in the near future," added Rindburn patronisingly, "so it wouldn't pay to get on the wrong side of your potential new employers now, would it?"

"You wouldn't want to get yourself in the poo now, would you, Finch?" snorted Sludboil, and he and Rindburn both whooped with laughter as they shared a private joke.

"No indeed," Julian replied calmly. It was clear that as usual these two trusted aides of the Commissioners were in receipt of confidential information long in advance of the rest of the office, and that as usual they couldn't help themselves but do a tour of the building gloating this fact, and dropping clumsy great hints about whatever it was that they were supposed to be keeping quiet.

Much as he didn't want to spend any more time than was necessary in their company, Julian decided that, with their guard down, the best way to find out more about the hush-hush Protocol Fifteen and the even more private New Environmental Solution Act, which he'd overheard the Commissioners toasting, was to keep the conversation going to see what cats they might let slip from the bag.

He couldn't ask them directly, nor could he show any great enquiring interest or the two gloaters would simply close up and move on, but if he could just persuade them to talk, perhaps even loosen them up with a bit of shameless flattery, he might get lucky.

"But our glorious leaders haven't taken you two gentlemen with them on their little business trip this time," Julian spoke carefully. "No doubt they must have something important they have entrusted you to do."

"Oh indeed," Sludboil replied pompously, "we are entrusted with a most important task."

"Uh-hum," Rindburn coughed, as if to warn his friend not to give too much away.

"Well it must be most important, I mean they normally need their valets, don't they? I can't remember the last time they went off to a really important Commissioner's meeting and didn't take you two with them to ensure them a smooth and efficient ride."

Sludboil couldn't resist the bait, and took it greedily. "Let's just say we have a task they couldn't entrust to any but their most loyal…"

"Employees," Julian interjected.

"And dependable Private Secretaries," Rindburn corrected. "Oh how we senior Civil Servants suffer and toil for the greater good of this great nation."

"This greater Europe."

"Indeed, Finch, indeed," Rindburn slapped Julian on the back warmly. "I had always taken you for a sceptic, but I see you have a mind to share in the Commissioner's great vision."

"Finchy," Sludboil hailed him, "comrade Finchy. We march together into this new Europe, eh?"

"Well, of course," Julian assured him, "if comrade Finchy it must be, and anyway, what makes the Commissioners so sure that their European Environmental Act will be passed without any problems?" He tested the water carefully. "You two have been around long enough to know what its like - I mean, what's to say all the other countries' Commissioners will be happy with it? These are all senior politicians in their own countries, aren't they, and it's so hard to get them all to agree on anything."

"True, true," Rindburn agreed, "and that is the depth of our leader's great genius."

"Already decided, isn't it," Sludboil couldn't help himself and let slip excitedly, confirming Julian's own suspicions. "They've already all agreed to it, what do you think all these private meetings have been about? The actual signing up will be a formality, they'll just be going through the motions."

"Oh, well that explains why they won't need you two academics to brief them on the intricacies of the process, I'm sure they can manage that on their own. But they've been busy, very single-minded. No doubt it's their hard work which has led to the mutual understanding, all the foundations laid in that office."

"There is no end to their commitment to forge a better Europe, Finch," Rindburn explained, "an environmentally-friendly Europe, no less."

"Already agreed, eh," said Julian in put-on wonderment.

"Ah, pure genius," Sludboil shook his head in appreciation. "Ever since his Grace and Sir Morgan were handed the Directorate on European environmental policy they have worked tirelessly for a solution to the current environmental crisis."

"Natural resources," uttered Rindburn.

"Global warming," echoed Sludboil.

"Sustainable and renewable energy." Rindburn bounced it back to his colleague.

"What to do with waste, the cost of recycling, the by-products of European industry, European life. We have a huge population in Europe now, Finch, and the single most important portfolio, that which determines the future of us all, the environment, handed to our own two Commissioners." Sludboil was almost bursting with pride. "The European Environmental Act," he continued dramatically, "is their vision, their plan for a better world, their gift to us all. There will be sacrifices, of course, but we are all part of Europe now and must assent to the common good."

"The general will," Rindburn grinned toothily.

"Oh, so it's a utilitarian theory?" Julian asked carefully, though he wondered what sacrifices the two idiots were talking about.

"Exactly, exactly comrade Finchy," Sludboil welcomed his understanding as if it were blind acceptance, "and the EEA and what follows is all for the greatest good of the greatest number. Ours is not to question the judgment of the Commissioners, for who is better placed than such raw geniuses to instruct us mere groundlings of what our best interests are?"

Julian wanted to suggest that he would like to make his own decisions in life and was the best judge of what was best for himself, but held his tongue as Rindburn then took up the torch.

"Great men both, and wise, truly blessed with a vision for the future." Rindburn snorted with purpose as if this made his point more valid.

Julian was full of curiosity now; he had to move in for the kill, he had to get as much out of these two cretins as he could. He knew there had to be some sort of mini conspiracy afoot. All the private meetings behind closed doors certainly suggested so, and this confirmed what he'd already suspected anyway; the other countries' Commissioners had already agreed to endorse their plan, and he would expect the Council to endorse it too on the advice and recommendation of the Commission.

He'd seen the EEA, he'd proofread it, all but for Protocol Fifteen. It had seemed buffed out with theory, empty of substance, devoid of method and explanation about how the desired environmental changes and policy would be brought about. There was nothing in it to explain how the waste issues or the power issues were to be resolved - just that it needed to be sorted out and that they intended to do so. And when Sludboil spoke of 'what follows', Julian could only presume they meant secondary legislation, new laws to be brought in by the Commission once the European Council, the heads of each Member State, had approved the EEA, passed it and made it law. New laws to actually enable their objectives as set out in the EEA to actually work.

"Yes, I wonder what secondary legislation will follow the act," he mused delicately as if to himself, but it was all an act for the benefit of his unassuming audience.

"Oh, don't worry about that." Sludboil snapped onto his hook once more with jubilant aplomb. "That's already drafted too, drafted and agreed on."

"Ho ho, yes," Rindburn grinned. "You could say it's in the pipeline, eh, Sludboil."

"Pipeline," laughed Sludboil in appreciation of another shared joke. "Good one, Rindburn."

"You mean to say that's already written as well?" Julian, unable to contain his surprise, interrupted their laughter.

"Of course," Sludboil confirmed it.

"It's a bit early though, isn't it? I mean, the Council haven't even signed the EEA yet."

"Such is the brilliance of our leaders," Sludboil puffed his chest out proudly.

"And um, will the Council know the details of this pre-drafted secondary legislation?" Julian chose his words carefully but wondered why such solutions hadn't been put in the EEA in the first place.

"Well I'm sure they will know that there is a framework in place, a skeletal plan," Sludboil spoke carelessly.

"But they won't actually see it?" Julian hoped his persistence would pay off; this was most irregular, and he wanted to know more.

"See it? Lord no, have you ever actually known of a Politician to read legislation properly?"

Rindburn coughed loudly to halt his colleague in his tracks, and Sludboil, perhaps realising that he had said too much, shuffled his feet awkwardly and picked nervously at his long nose.

"And I suppose the Council will sign anything the Commissioners in their informed wisdom recommend?" Julian spoke quickly, hoping to probe more deeply, expecting to have his concerns confirmed. But he could sense from Sludboil's body language that he realised he'd jut let slip, and the Private Secretaries' collective guard was up.

"Maybe, maybe," Rindburn waved his hand as if to dismiss Julian's last question as unimportant, "but we mustn't stand here talking all day."

"No, you really mustn't," Julian replied, tongue-in-cheek.

140

"We, um, we have work to do."

"Important work," Sludboil added.

"Yes, you'd better go and do your Master's bidding," Julian urged them. They clearly weren't going to throw him any other scraps of information, and he needed time to think.

"Yes, back to the grindstone for us, it seems our work is never done." Rindburn exited Julian's small office at last, but as he did so he couldn't resist one last authoritative dig. "Now, get back to it Finch."

"Back to what?" Julian asked innocently.

"Oh, whatever it was you were doing," he replied distractedly, and walked off.

"Right, so back to my lunch then, that's what I was doing before I was interrupted... And by the way your work is never done because you never do any work."

But Julian's mumbled reply was not heard by the Commissioner's Private Secretaries; they were halfway down the corridor already and he could hear their voices gradually drifting away.

"Got your costume, good Yeoman Sludboil?" he heard Rindburn ask jovially.

"Just short of a pair of shoes, old boy, but it's nothing to get in a flap about."

"Ha, ha," the other laughed, his voice ever fainter, "nothing to get in a flap about, good one, Sludboil." Their laughter drifted down the corridor just a few moments longer, and they were gone.

Julian Finch let out a long sigh. "Idiots, utter morons," he said under his breath. He often wondered just to what extent the Commissioners really did bring their sidekicks into their confidence, and how much of their master's business they really knew. Both, after all, made such a show of self importance, and neither, Sludboil especially, could be trusted with items of secrecy.

It wasn't for disloyalty - both idolised the Commissioners, and that was clear - but Sludboil, Julian reflected, was so clumsy he could trip over his own shadow in the dark. It amazed him sometimes that they had risen to such senior Civil Service posts, when both were such blatant liabilities.

He thanked them both for their carelessness. It had given him much to think about, and as he sat chewing slowly on his sandwich he reasoned that their rise was evidence indeed, and a perfect illustration of the unfortunate fact that politicians - especially pompous, egotistical ones like Sir Morgan Dredmor and the Toad - found it much to their liking to be surrounded by such slimy, creeping little 'yes' men.

In any case, they both had access to their Master's mail and all

141

their private dispatches and documents. Perhaps they hadn't been confided in at all but had instead abused their position to read things they were never meant to see in an attempt to boost their own sense of self-importance. But either way, it didn't matter. They'd made it clear through their own foolishness that something was up, and though of course Rindburn and Sludboil could be exaggerating the importance of it to flatter their own egos, it was all a bit suspicious, the Commissioners making deals on the quiet and the like.

Julian sighed again, cleared away his lunch and returned to the over-fishing dossier. As Rindburn and Sludboil had themselves explained, it could all be law in a very short time; no doubt he would find out very soon just what the Commissioners were up to.

Chapter Nine – A lot of sorting out

"Jess, Jess." The words seemed to come from out of the fog, far, far distant from her. "Jessica, wake up." That was her mother's voice.

"Come on, Sis, you're alright," - and that was Max. He shook her gently and lifted her head. "Jess," she opened her eyes to see his worried face crouched over her. "You're okay, Jess," he spoke gently, but he looked scared. "It's like you said Jess, he's come back. But you'll be okay, it's just a bit of a shock."

"Jessica Finch," her mother placed a warm hand on her clammy brow and held it for a few seconds on her forehead. "I don't know what's going on but you've got a temperature. Come on, upstairs and lie down."

Jess protested, but her mother chivvied her upstairs, and Max supported her as she climbed them.

Patricia Finch was rattled, but relieved to see her daughter on her feet, and after all the stress of seeing her collapse in front of her she now needed a moment to gather her thoughts while her child rested and recovered. The children were making it up, of course, but Jess had seemed so genuinely frightened when the rather odd but polite stranger had arrived with Rhys, and she needed to know why. She would also make the most of the chance to speak to her daughter alone to discover exactly what the other rough looking figure had been doing squatting like a fugitive with her children in the garage, and right under her very nose.

"It, it's him," Jess spoke in bewilderment. She was over the initial shock now. Drake was no ghost, Rhys had brought him into the house large as life, but what was he doing here, what was he doing in her home?

"Who are these people," her mother asked her, trying to keep calm, "and what are they doing in our house?"

"I don't know, Mum," she replied weakly and in a voice of mystique. "They're here... But why?"

"Yes, Jessica, why? And who are they young lady?" Her mother persisted. "I want answers, and fast."

"They are who they say they are, Mum," Jess spoke firmly and tried to sound convincing.

"What rot. I've never, never heard such total... Such utter..."

"They are, look at them. Their clothes, the way they talk - it's them, Mum, King Arthur and Sir Francis Drake." Jess paused, and then repeated in a murmur to herself, "but why?"

"You're sick, Jessica darling," and as Max left the room Patricia Finch, her own head spinning, ushered her daughter to bed and closed the curtains. "You need to rest, I need to think."

"They have to stay, Mum," said Jess feebly, "and I have to think too."

"Right." It was her mother's turn to adopt a stern tone; she had to go downstairs and get to the bottom of this. She certainly wasn't getting anything out of Jessica, and made to leave the room. "I'm really disappointed in the pair of you, Maxwell has to learn that he can't just bring people round like this, not to our home, not without asking, without telling me, he has to..."

"It wasn't Max's fault, Mum," Jess interrupted her, "it was mine." Her mother paused in the doorway. "I really did it, Mum," she said quietly.

"Did what?" Patricia was confused.

"I brought him back, I really brought him back."

"Who?"

"Drake."

"Why?"

"I don't know," Jess spoke in tearful frustration. She let her head fall back on the pillow and shut her eyes.

Patricia Finch stopped on the stairs to compose herself; she was the hostess, this was her house, she had to retain her dignity, she would be polite and civil to her guests, for guests they were, and if she acted properly the answers would come.

Arthur studied the new arrivals with suspicion. The younger male was in clothing similar to the children and appeared to be a kinsman, for the boy certainly seemed pleased to see him and it was clear as they spoke that they knew each other well; but the other man, draped in his fine clothes, was more of a cause for concern.

To Arthur he seemed to combine the cocky carefree attitude of a stable boy with the kind of inbuilt arrogance that Arthur had himself been so keen to exclude from his own Court.

As he ran his eyes over the man in front of him, the new arrival looked down his own nose at him as if he were a leper loose from the colony who'd just stumbled into a threshing barn unannounced. Arthur noted his sword with interest. He reasoned that he had to be a warrior for he carried a weapon, but what a strange blade it was: long, thin and pointed, quite unlike the chunkier sharp bladed weapons he was used to handling himself. He noticed too its delicate, intricate hilt and hand-guard, and it clearly belonged to a man of rank, for such a blade might be no match for Caledfwlch in combat but it clearly indicated status... Oh how he longed to hold Caledfwlch again in his hand.

The boy was questioning the stranger, talking excitedly, and the boy's kinsman too. Arthur wondered if the stranger could be the Master of the house, perhaps the local warlord, but it couldn't be, this couldn't be the boy's father, it was obvious they'd never met before. The boy, Max, continued to speak quickly in words he couldn't understand, he indicated Arthur to the two strangers, pointed towards him and said "This is King Arthur."

"So I see," the boy's kinsman replied. "Today is really getting stranger."

"King Arthur." Drake ran his own critical eye over his new acquaintance. "If this be King Arthur I be Lambert Simnal," he laughed. "Folk like to King Arthur doest not re-appear young mariner, why bless me 'tis like to a ditty o' Master Marlowe's, yet thou canst find reason in poetry if thou wilt," he chortled to himself rudely.

Arthur, who had taken an instant dislike to the flippant warrior, re-took his seat in mock indifference.

"It is," Max continued as his mother re-entered the room. "Francis Drake, King Arthur. King Arthur, Francis Drake," he introduced them formally.

"As simple as that," Rhys added, as if it really was that simple, but Patricia Finch just shook her head in disbelief. This charade was still clearly far from over.

"We found him yesterday," Max tried to explain, but to his mother's annoyance he spoke to the other stranger and not to her. "Out in the woods."

"Oh, did you?" Patricia sought the explanation which had alluded her so far.

"Yeah, sorry Mum, we just didn't know what to do with him. He looked like he hadn't eaten for thousands of years."

"Sounds feasible," she replied sarcastically.

"Well he can't have can he?" said Rhys in wonderment. "Not if he's really come back, like."

"Oh Rhys, not you as well."

"He has, Mum. I didn't believe it at first either, but he really doesn't know where he is: lights, hot water, the TV, it's all new to him. It's doing my head in really it is, why this? Why that? He just doesn't get it, it's a right struggle to get through to him sometimes."

"Him too," Rhys pointed to Drake, "all fidgety in the car, the stereo, the heaters, you'd think he'd never been in one before. I mean I didn't believe him at first, but now..."

"Really." Patricia didn't seem too amused. "Will you two stop making it up, it's not April the first."

"I'm really not, Aunt Pat," Rhys persisted.

"'Tis most strange," Drake interrupted. "As Master Rhys spake, wi' the touch o' a finger camest to mine ears the sound o' a dozen bards, at the flick o' a switch hast he conjured lanterns alight, and spake he, wi' the press o' his foot... Motion itself."

"Compact disk, electricity, petrol engine," Rhys spoke impatiently, "we've been over all this."

"Aye, yet still it be a wonder indeed. Thou speakst o' electinkery, yet thou canst not smell o' it. Thou canst not have sight o' it, taste o' it nor touch o' it... 'Tis o' a power like unto the spirit o' a ghost, I know not how..."

Rhys sighed loudly as if he had just about had enough of such talk. "At first I just thought he must have escaped from the theatre, but then..."

"Ah, theatre," Drake spat. "Hast I set thee clear Master Rhys that thou shouldst not belittle a tamer o' the foulest seas such as I by denouncing me a lowly player. Flippant fancy doest blow gaily on the breeze, but what knowst the playwright o' the true fire o' battle? Wherefore canst he call upon his own experience an' terror to re-create the violence an malice o' a biting storm? Nor can he fitly pass comment on the poor soul who be driven to madness all-consuming by the supping o' brine t' cure a gripping thirst anon under the scorching pacific sun?

"I call a pox 'pon the theatre an upon that oaf Shakespeare, for doest the playwright an player alike disown the valiant Kings who fell in conflicts past. As like to a child wi' a corn poppet they play at war, yet know they nought o' it.

Madam, 'tis as Master Jenkins first announced me, I stand before thee Sir Francis Drake, Admiral o' her Majesty's fleet an scourge o' the Spanish Main. Be I honoured to enter thy fine kept house as thy guest, an' prithee Madam, I pray thee, be not angry wi' they charges, for it is as Master Jenkins spake unto thee just now, t'was this day mine first venture in a motor-cart."

"Car," Rhys corrected, "motor-car."

"Aye, motor-car if thou wilt. Yet t'was mine first voyage and t'was much sport in't."

Patricia Finch was a practiced hostess and was not about to react rashly, let alone rudely. Yet few people could be expected to remain calm when two such crackpot strangers were suddenly thrust upon them, and under her formal exterior she was flapping like the best of them. She didn't really know what to say so she just said the first thing that came into her head.

"I'll put the kettle on," and with that she headed to the kitchen.

She needed time to think how best to deal with them, for this would take a lot of sorting out, and as her head spun she had to disagree with the charming Mr Drake. She rather liked Shakespeare plays herself, and keen not to compromise tact she whispered as much to Benji as he followed her in to the kitchen hoping for a snack - he could always be trusted to keep a confidence - and she resolved to hold the fort until Julian came home, he might know what to do.

"Well, this is going to take a lot of sorting out," said Max. "Sir Francis, I know this seems far-fetched, but this really is King Arthur. Like you he's come back."

"Why?" Rhys interjected.

"I don't know, but Jess said he's always been meant to come back. He doesn't even seem to know why himself."

"Methinks thou wouldst jest wi' me Master Max, couldst not the rogue be but an undressed fool practiced well in merrie japes?"

"I don't see him laughing," Max replied, and indicated towards the sullen-looking king, who sat alone in silent frustration.

Arthur knew they were all talking about him, but not what they said, and left to his own thoughts he pondered again why it was that he was here. Why had he come back?

"Adwaen mo paham Dwi'ma, eto ni must bath I maes hon chybola."(i)

"He doest not speak like to a fool, yet wi' what tongue spake he thus?"

"Welsh, Sir Francis," said Rhys excitedly, "he speaks Welsh or something like it. I speak a little myself, I recognise it. Areithi Cymraeg 'na?"(ii) Rhys addressed Arthur.

"Areithia,"(iii) Arthur replied. "Namyn beth feddyli Cymraeg? Areithia 'r balog chan 'm boblogi. Dwi Artos, Brenin chan 'r Prydains, a dydy aruthr at chlyw hun 'm gwladwyr areithia."(iv)

"Wow," Rhys didn't know what to say, but translated as best he could for Max and Drake's benefit. "He is King Arthur, you're right, he says he doesn't know what Welsh is, he just says it's the language of his people, but that figures doesn't it? I mean there weren't borders then like there are today, no separate..."

"Beth newydd chan Caerllian? Gwenhwyfar? Ydy fel 'r blant ddend? Ydy hon 'n sylweddol 'r ddyfodol?"(v) Arthur seized the younger man by his forearms and implored him desperately.

147

Max was impatient. "What's he saying?"

"This is just too weird," Rhys looked confused. "This is all some weird dream, right? Like in a minute your Mum'll come in dancing with a giant fruit bat or something?"

"I don't think so, Rhys," Max shook his head.

"Well then he's asking where Gwenhwyfar is, whoever she is, and about Caerleon near Newport. He's got it though, realises he's come back, realises he's in the future."

"Yeah, well, the evidence is fairly overwhelming," Max gestured around the room. "Oh, Jess says Gwenhwefur or whatever her name is, is Guinevere, you know, his Queen... Ask him why he's here, Rhys."

Rhys did so, having first confirmed to Arthur that this was indeed the twenty-first Century and having then explained as sympathetically as he could that to the best of his knowledge Queen Guinevere had not survived from the age of long-gone Camelot to the present day. The King looked sad, he had already accepted the truth, but to hear it confirmed in words he could understand brought it all painfully home to him. He was stranded, marooned in the future, and as he spoke to the newcomer tears pricked at his eyes.

"Well he doesn't have a clue why he's come back," Rhys translated, "think it's all a bit of a shock to him really. He says he needs some time to think... But don't we all? Says he felt a sort of pull, and the closer he got to here the more certain he was that this is where he needed to be, though he didn't really expect to find anything as he left it."

"Ah, and so be it wi' mineself," Drake explained. "A yearning hast I like to a salmon homing t' sporn, though I know not from whence have I come by this jerking in mine gut. Thou shouldst have us acquainted, Master Rhys," he urged, though in truth he looked sceptical and eyed Arthur with like suspicion.

"He understands me, Max, I understand him, this is just so weird. Arthur, this is Sir Francis Drake," Rhys explained in Welsh, but Arthur looked baffled. "The sea Captain..." Still no response. "Oh but he was born hundreds of years after you," Rhys reverted to English again, "how can he even begin to understand, Max? There must be the best part of a thousand years between them, and it's the twenty-first century now."

"Woooh. Doest thou speak true?" Drake whistled. "Twenty-first Century spake thee."

"Been away a bit longer than you thought too?" Max laughed. "Well welcome to the future, both of you. You really may find it an improvement."

Drake had to pause a moment, for this was all rather a lot to take in.

He looked over at Arthur, who sat in the corner; his mail coat and woollen trews certainly set him apart from anything he'd seen before. Could this really be the King of legend? What strange twist of fate had brought them both together?

"King Arthur," he said in a puzzled tone. "'Twas said of old he would return when Albion had need."

"Well now he's here, and so are you," Max beamed.

Drake eyed the King with curiosity, yet looked down at him with an air of patronising superiority and pompously exclaimed: "Reason not the need for his return, for Drake is here and I be ready to embark on any new venture."

"Yeah, but what new adventure?" Max smirked at him, "You don't know why you're here either."

"Ah 'tis true, I know not. 'Twill take some sorting, to be sure."

Jessica Finch sat up in bed, her own head also spinning. The whole situation was going to take some sorting out, that much was clear. They had to have returned for a reason, that much was also clear, but what was it?

She'd banged the drum to bring Drake back, but only because she'd felt drawn in to do it, and he was only meant to return if the country was in danger. She hadn't been aware of any danger when she'd struck the drum and nor was she any the wiser now.

Jess turned the argument over in her mind again. She'd also heard the drum, which was only meant to be heard when the country was in danger or in times of great victory - so again, what had caused the drum to beat?

Arthur was meant to return in the country's darkest hour of need, that's what Miss Davies had said, so there had to be some peril looming, and no one seemed aware of it. Great Britain was not at war, she was unaware of any great political crisis, and acts of terrorism never seemed to amount to more than petulant little strikes, nothing which threatened the security of the whole nation at once.

She was scared, and she considered this perfectly reasonable as there had to be something to be scared of; Drake and Arthur wouldn't be in her house if it were otherwise. But what scared her most of all was that she was so unsure of what it was that she was meant to be scared of, and the uncertainty was terrifying.

She had to think, had to talk it over and get to the bottom of it; there might not be much time. Her mother knew now, though she hardly appeared pleased about it, and her father had to be told when he got home. He would find out anyway so there was no harm in that.

Arthur didn't seem to know why he was here, there could be no guarantee that Drake would, and Max, totally won over since his first meeting with Arthur in the woods, was far too busy enjoying the novelty of having him in the house to realise the seriousness of the situation.

Jess knew she had to speak to someone, had to talk it through with someone who might also understand, but who?... Brendan, Brendan Johnson might be able to help. He might not believe in myths but there was no denying that the two visitors were real, and he was the only person she could think of whom like herself might really understand the significance of the two heroes' return. Brendan might even know more about them than she did, and he'd been her partner that day at Buckland Abbey when she'd first seen the drum. In the back of her mind she just wondered if that could be significant.

Her concentration was broken by the sound of the telephone ringing, and Jess got up quickly to answer it. She didn't feel queasy anymore and decided there was nothing to be gained from staying in bed. There was a phone in her parent's bedroom and she rushed to answer it before anyone else could. "Hello," she said quickly.

"Hey Jess, it's Abi." Abi Saunders' piercing voice came down the line in a welcome wash of normality.

"Oh, Abi," said Jess in surprise.

"Well, who'd you think it was? Mahatma Ghandi?" Abi was abrupt and sounded vaguely hurt.

"Well it's funny you should say that, Abigail." Patricia Finch's voice came over the line. Jess hated it when other people picked up the other phone when she was talking, she was often sure that Max had been listening into her private conversations, and although her mother had clearly picked up the downstairs handset at the same time as herself to innocently answer the call, she didn't want her mentioning their strange visitors to gossip-spreaders like Abi Saunders.

"Mum, put the phone down," she said rudely. "How are you, Abi?"

"Yeah cool, listen. My mum's going out tonight so I thought I'd have a sleepover at mine. Tammy and Lizzie are coming and maybe some of the boys, you up for it?"

"Look, Abi, I'm really sorry, but I've got something else on tonight..."

"Yes, it seems we have visitors," her mother's voice came over the line again in an authoritative tone, "and Jessica isn't well I'm afraid, Abigail, she needs to rest. Does your mother know you are having this party?"

"Mum," Jess snapped again.

"Okay, okay, phone going down."

Jess waited to hear the rattle of the other handset being replaced before she started talking again. "Sorry Abi, but it's like my Mum said, we've got visitors, friends of the family, you know how it is," she said vaguely, the excuse forming as she made it. "Mum won't let me out of it, we haven't seen them for ages... They haven't seen anyone for ages, really."

"Oh come on, Jess, I'm your best friend," Abi persisted.

"You heard my Mum."

"Does that mean Max can't come either?"

"I'm afraid so, Mum wants them to see both of us, you know how it is."

"Oh, but it won't be the same without you there." Abi sounded disappointed.

"Abi, we've only been back from the trip a couple of days."

"Yeah I know, but Max didn't come on the trip."

So that was it thought Jess, she only really wanted Max to come. "Look I don't think it's really Max's scene anyway, Abi - I mean, painting toe nails and gossiping..."

"No it won't be like that," Abi protested. "Loads of the boys are coming, it's going to be a real party."

"I don't fancy being in your shoes when your Mum finds out."

"Why would she?"

"Look, I'm sorry Abi but you heard my Mum, I can't make it tonight. Maybe in a few days time... Oh, you don't happen to have Brendan's number do you?" Jess immediately regretted asking the question.

"Erhh, Brendan Johnson. Why would I have fatty Johnson's number? Of course I haven't got it, if I wanted to talk to a tadpole I'd go down the pond."

"Just asking."

"Why? Why are you asking? What do you want Brendan's number for?" She teased. "You fancy him, don't you? You sooo fancy him."

"I don't," Jess snapped defensively. "I just need to talk to him about..."

"About kissing," Abi was enjoying this and mocked Jess in a put-on voice. "Oh Brendy-wendon, I fancy-wancy you sooo much."

"No, actually." Jess was really regretting ever having mentioned Brendan, Abi was sure to spread rumours in no time, "about homework, he's good at History, you know."

"Jess, that's boring schoolwork, it's the holidays now if you hadn't noticed... You do, you want to kiss the fat slug."

151

"Look, have you got the number or haven't you?"

"Of course I haven't. Why don't you try the phonebook if you really want to talk to him?"

That was it, of course, the phone book might have Brendan's number. "Yes thanks Abi I'll try that," she said, but Abi was just laughing down the phone.

"Brendan and Jess in a tree. K.I.S.S.I..."

"Bye Abi," said Jess quickly, "see you soon." She hung up, cross with herself that she had gifted Abi such a meaty piece of gossip, but relieved that the conversation had at least been of some use. She ran downstairs to retrieve the phonebook, keen to run the circumstances of Drake and Arthur's return past Brendan as fast as she could.

When Jess got back downstairs her mother was carrying a tray of tea and biscuits through to the waiting guests.

"You're..."

"I'm... not going to Abi's," they both said simultaneously.

"Oh," Patricia looked relieved, she had anticipated an argument. "Are you feeling better, darling?"

"Yes, it was just a bit of a shock. Look Mum, they have to stay until we find out why they're here," Jess spoke quickly.

"Jessica...."

"I'll explain later, I need to speak to someone." Jess bounded back upstairs, brandishing the phone book.

"Oh..."

"I've got to go, Aunt Pat," her nephew greeted her as she brought the tea tray through into the living-room.

"Oh, but I've brought you a cup, Rhys, are you running off too?"

"I've got to go and pick up Rhiannon."

"Oh, right, but will we be seeing you...?"

"I'll be right back, Aunt Pat," he replied excitedly. "I'm going to bring her over to see the..."

"Circus."

"Freak show," he corrected her, "she can't miss this." He closed the door behind himself.

Patricia Finch, finding herself all but abandoned to the two unexpected guests, sighed deeply, and having composed herself entered the living-room with a forced smile. "Well, here's your tea, Mr..."

"Artos," Arthur took the delicate cup and saucer from her.

"King Arthur," Max explained; he noticed his mother was using her second best china.

"Teee." Arthur tested the odd sounding, unfamiliar word on the

152

tongue.

"Tea," Max corrected him.

"Tea."

"Very good."

"Yes, um, and here's your tea, Mr..."

"Admiral," Drake corrected her in a pompous voice which added to her confusion.

"Mr Admiral," Patricia Finch, flustered, handed a cup to her second guest.

"No, no, dear lady," Drake interjected. "Sir Francis, prithee, Sir Francis."

"Oh, okay, Sir Francis it will be... And I am Mrs Finch," she introduced herself formally, for she had been so thrown by the discovery of Arthur that she had all but forgotten her manners. "Call me Patricia."

Arthur nodded in understanding and again sampled the new word out loud. "Pat-rish-er." He sipped his tea and then sat back in the comfort of the soft furniture to enjoy the warming sensation of the curious drink.

Drake sipped his own and winced. "Goodwife Finch," he exclaimed, "'tis a strange brew, where camest thou by it?"

"The supermarket," she replied quickly, but registered the lack of understanding displayed in her visitor's heavy frown. "But it's from India I think, or maybe China, I'm not sure, somewhere round there."

"Ah, hast I travelled the spice routes mineself," he looked excitable, "untold treasures o' the orient didst I carry unto mine Queen."

"Mum didn't go there to get it," Max sniggered, "she only went to the shop on the way into town."

"Oh, well so be it, yet 'tis as strange a brew as have I supped, Goody Finch. I wonder, hast thou a drop o' grog t' dash in't?" he asked wistfully.

"Grog?" Patricia didn't understand.

"Um, rum," he suggested hopefully.

"Oh, I see, booze. Well I'm sorry Mr Admiral, Sir Francis, but my husband doesn't drink rum," she thought a moment, desperately trying to be hospitable. "But we do have some sherry, I think."

"Argh, sherry," Drake nearly choked on his tea. "The Don-Dago slop. Come fine lady, t'were the Queen's navy fuelled on the Don sherry her seamen wouldst be all clad in frilly lace. Wouldst they handle the tiller like to a boy player an fall from the rigging like to tumblers at court."

"They'd tickle the enemy rather than fight 'em," Max added in jest.

"Aye it be so, well spake thee, Master Mariner," Drake patted Max on the back, and having seized a biscuit from the plate he proceeded to tap it on the top of the coffee table. "Shouldst I wager one English sailor t' ten Dons couldst hold a ship steady in a storm. The English be born unto the sea, my boy, but 'tis rum which furnishes 'em sea legs."

"Well we have no rum, I'm terribly sorry," Patricia Finch apologised again, though in truth she thought it rather rude that her guest, having been given tea, had then asked for alcohol. "Um....?"

"Weevils, madam," Drake explained his odd behaviour, but continued tapping the biscuit, which was now spreading little crumbs all over the table, "thou must have a care t' tap em out."

Jess had re-entered the room and eyed Drake critically. "I don't think you're going to find weevils in a bourbon biscuit, and there won't be much left either if you keep breaking it up."

"Aye, yet t'will it be well softened. 'Tis a pity thou hast no grog," he stroked the long goatee tip to his beard between his thumb and forefinger.

"It's a pity you underestimate your enemies," Jess responded; she was already finding his arrogance annoying. "Things could have gone very differently with the Armada you know, you shouldn't just make out the Spaniards to be a bunch of muppets, and if anything it devalues the victory."

"Muppets...?"

"Oh by the way, Mum, I've got a friend coming over."

"Oh, fine," Patricia looked dumbfounded. "Don't bother asking me, Jessica, just keep them coming," she said sarcastically.

"Sorry Mum, it's just, well, I think he might be able to help..."

"Muppets?" Drake demanded again, "What meanst thou?"

"Oh, idiots, fools. But they weren't, circumstances just..."

"T'was in the hands o' the most capable o' seamen Miss, charged wi' their duty by God an' the Queen. 'Twere ne'r in doubt they wouldst be scattered, yet t'was but for endeavour unrivalled that they be defeated."

"And can you be defeated?" Max asked mischievously.

"Thou makest unto me a challenge, young Master?" Drake was wide eyed and full of competitiveness, and he scanned the room for a suitable outlet.

"Um, Playstation, let's see how you do at ultimate football."

"Max, you can't play computer games with him, he'll never get the idea."

"Er, I suppose you're right Sis, how about..."

"Try a board game, something he might know."

"Buckaroo."

"No Max, something proper."

"Then how about chess?" Max retrieved an old set from a cupboard and opened it up, positioning the board on the coffee table between them.

"Ah, thou playst the game o' Court," Drake rubbed his hands in glee and anticipation. "Mayst I proffer a small wager, young..."

"No." Patricia Finch replied firmly. "There will be no gambling under this roof. Play by all means, but no betting, I'll not have it."

"Max, you're crap at chess," Jess added unhelpfully, and Arthur cut her an uneasy glance.

"The young man's experience mattereth not, for had he the countenance t' be Lord Chamberlain would he pose no threat to such as I."

"Oh, come on, Max." Jess couldn't hold it in, Drake was so arrogant and dismissive of his opponent and she was desperate to see him brought down a peg or two.

Patricia Finch left the room to do the washing up, and Arthur watched with interest as Max set the board up and he and Drake began to move the strange-shaped pieces in varying directions around it. He wasn't sure exactly how the game was played or what was going on, but as one after another of Max's pieces found their way onto an ever increasing pile at Drake's feet it became clear that Max was losing.

"Wilt thou yield, young Master?" The sea captain taunted the schoolboy as he pursued him into 'check' with the third move in a row.

Max's face was full of disappointment. His sister's comment had been entirely correct, he was rubbish at chess and when they played together she always drubbed him, but he'd hoped he wouldn't capitulate quite so quickly.

"Don't listen to him, Max," Jess gave encouragement, and as Drake moved in for the kill she slipped into position next to her brother behind his fleeting pieces. She'd sat in near-silence watching a badly-played game unfold before her. Max was poor, but Drake was not much better, and the truth of the matter was that far from trapping her brother's pieces through clever manipulation, Drake had really picked off each piece as Max had walked without thinking into one obvious ambush after another.

"Thou wouldst join the fray too, Miss? Yet thy position be hopeless," Drake smiled in amusement.

"Yeah, well, look, I'm going to withdraw anyway," said Max in frustration, "Jess can take over my pieces, she's much better than I am,

I resign."

Drake smirked but Jess smiled politely back at him, and then mounted a recovery with such skill that within just a few minutes the balance had swung against the odds in her favour. Arthur, enjoying the show, smiled broadest of all to see the proud peacock looking crestfallen as he scratched his head and frowned in frustration, and Drake, sensing that he was in trouble, started to question the rules and imply foul play. He disputed in earnest the variations of moves which could be made by Jessica's pieces despite the fact that they reflected those of his own earlier in the game, and as his King was eventually surrounded and boxed in a corner he conceded defeat ungraciously.

"T'was mayhap a fix, yet t'was well done Miss, thou playst a shrewd game indeed."

"Well there you have it then, Sir Francis, you shouldn't underestimate anyone."

"And Mum should have let us bet him after all," Max joked. "Do you want to play again, or shall we try something else?"

"Um, another game, I fancy." Drake would not be humiliated again on the chess board.

"Okay, well, how about draughts?" Max had dug out the pieces from another bag kept with the chess set. "It's the same board anyway."

"Rhufeiniad herwhela, adwaen hon!"(vi) Arthur leapt forward, "Dyma camp alla chwarae."(vii) Full of excitement, he seemed more full of life and enthusiasm than he had up until now.

Arthur set up the pieces quickly, and beat all comers with speed and decisive skill. Having shaken off his sulky, thoughtful manner with successive victories over Max and then Jess, he beamed with triumph and invited Drake to the table.

The Elizabethan sailor was a much better draughts player than he had been a chess master and he posed by far the greatest challenge to Arthur's domination of the board. Jess could sense the competition in the air as the intensity built and each struggled to out-do the other.

She also thought she sensed for the first time a glimmer of respect being shared between the two heroes as each tried to anticipate the other's next move, though it could of course have just been contemptuous competitiveness and a desperation not to loose.

It was Arthur who won in the end, systematically clearing Drake's pieces once his defensive line was broken, whilst the adventurer once again made excuse after excuse and questioned the legality of the other's manoeuvres.

"Fel dydy,"(viii) Arthur smiled. "Barthu a anrheithia, 'r chymynrodd chan Caesar."(ix)

156

There was a knock at the door, and Jess, with relief, went to let Brendan in. She had explained briefly over the phone what was going on, felt she could trust Brendan, and still hoped that his second head would assist her one in deciding what was next for the two visitors.

Brendan himself had thought Jess was jibbering nonsense, and had turned up with the single aim of making sure she was alright, and hadn't gone completely mad since the episode at Buckland Abbey.

"Hi Max," he announced himself awkwardly as he entered the room. "Wow," he exclaimed as he took in the two visitors either side of the drafts board.

"Oh hi, Brendan," Max said in surprise, "what brings you over here?"

"I did," said Jess quickly. "Well, they did really. Look Max, I don't think you realise. We're in danger, we have to be or these two wouldn't be here."

"Yeah, well, you did say something, Sis, but well, I didn't really get it," Max conceded.

"Well that's just it, Brendan might," Jess explained, but Brendan shuffled his feet uncomfortably. "It's like I told you, Max, King Arthur is meant to come back when Britain is in danger. Drake is meant to come back when he's needed to save the country."

"Yeah, but you called him back didn't you? You said so, you banged the drum."

"You what...?" Brendan looked shocked at this revelation.

"Yeah I did," Jess tried to explain, "but don't you see, they would never have come back, either of them, unless they were actually needed, and that means we must all be in danger."

"And they don't know why they are here?" Brendan asked. "You mean they have no idea at all?"

"No idea Brendan, that's what we need to find out."

"You really banged the drum, Jess?" Brendan eyed her with wonderment.

"Yeah, I went back inside after everyone had left the building. I don't know what made me do it, but I heard it beating and I, well, I just felt forced to tap it."

"Jess!"

"I only tapped it very gently, I..."

"Me drum," Drake interrupted. "Thou girl didst rattle 'pon me old drum?"

"Yes Sir Francis, I did."

"And thou, Sirrah, wouldst share mine thoughts?" He eyed Brendan

157

with suspicion.

"Um, Jess seems to think I might be able to help, Sir," Brendan replied nervously.

"'Tis now I ponder why wouldst thou call me hither t' push draughts wi' this warrior o' the past," he gestured rudely and dismissively at Arthur and tipped the board out on Arthur's lap.

"I don't think you've come back to play draughts," Jess tried to explain, but she was cut short by Arthur, who had risen in rage from his chair.

"Dydy amsera adnabuoch 'ch Brenin,"(x) he protested.

"Oh that's the way he speaks by the way," Max explained unhelpfully, "it's Welsh or something like it. Rhys was able to talk with him because he speaks a bit of Welsh, and..."

"Max, why didn't you tell me earlier?" Jess looked furious.

"Oh it's alright, Rhys is coming back later and..."

"Unhand me thou knave," Drake spoke with urgency as he tried to prise off the firm grip which Arthur now had on him.

The King, fed up with Drake's lack of respect and recognition and his arrogant manner, had him by the shoulders and was trying to force the other to his knees.

"Adnabod 'ch Brenin,"(xi) he demanded through clenched teeth.

"Get off him," Jess protested, "you're not supposed to be fighting each other."

"Ca'r torc, ca'r cana chan Prydain!"(xii) Arthur used his brute strength to force the sailor into an uncomfortable curtsey in front of him as he demanded homage, and when he spoke again it was in a different language. "Aspicio orbis Britannicas. Adepto in vestri genua quod agnitio vestri Rex regis."(a)

Arthur forced his ring, with Caesar's face upon it, under Drake's nose, and the other, unable to struggle against Arthur's great bear-hug, kissed it and muttered a resentful reply.

"Meus liege Senior. Vos es vero Rex, Ego profiteer etiamnun Ego did noa punto is."(b)

"Exsisto iam quod operor muneris ut vestri populus,"(c) Arthur spoke back, and he let go of Drake slowly.

Once released, Drake quickly twisted away and straightened up. It clearly pained him to have been physically manhandled and he knew he had to regain face, yet he now had no doubts about whom he addressed and he was no novice to conversing with monarchs.

"Is ero an veneratio ut servo is populus praetor vos,"(d) he said elegantly, and then translated for the benefit of the children who stood in open-mouthed shock at what they had just seen. "Spake I, t'will be

158

an honour t' serve alongside the Great King Arthur."

Arthur nodded approvingly at Drake's words, but Max just stated the obvious.

"They spoke to each other. They actually spoke..."

"Aye, the King, like unto a real monarch, speakst the language o' Court."

"What, so you actually understand each other, Sir Francis?" Jess was amazed.

"Latin," said Brendan slowly, "they both speak Latin."

"Quite so, young Master. Hast I though him mad, though he casts drafts t' rival Queen Bess herself, but pon his finger bares he a royal ring o' Rome, a mark o' Kingship long lost."

"His royal ring of Britain," said Jess quietly.

"Aye, an' so too didst I behold it in those noble eyes, kingly qualities in abundance, nobility, reverence... Yet had the thought tarried wi' me from our first meeting..."

"Oh you liar," Max butted in, "you had no respect for him at all until he put you in a headlock. And anyway, I told you he was King Arthur hours ago."

"And well-met indeed." Drake brushed off the criticism. "Oh," - a look of horror filled his face as a new and terrible thought came to his mind - "but what knowst the King o' mine own great deeds?"

"Very little I should think," Brendan remarked, "he wasn't around for your bit was he?" Drake's face fell and Brendan hastily added. "But you've gone down in legend too, you don't have to worry about that."

"How could't be else?" The Sea Captain beamed. "I'll wager there hast been none whose deeds couldst rival mine own since mine departure for the Indies."

"Well there have been loads of great events and heroes since your time, Sir Francis," said Max carelessly, and the Elizabethan's response was merely to rebuff his comment by repeating his words with challenging vigour.

"Sirrah, spake I, I'll wager there hast been none who couldst rival mineself."

"Yeah, of course not," said Jess sarcastically, "but lots has certainly happened, and you would do well to understand it."

"The King must hear o' me," said Drake earnestly.

"Well you have to hear of everything else too, we'll tell you about everything that has happened since you went off to rest."

"Yes, good idea Jess," said Brendan. "Have you got last year's History textbook? We can use the pictures to help explain. After all, if they both understand how long they have been away, and all that has happened while they've been...wherever they've been, well, it might help them realise why it is they've come back.

They weren't alone for long, Rhys returned with his girlfriend, Rhiannon, and with the benefit of his translation and Arthur and Drake's common grasp of Latin, they were all able to bring themselves up to date.

Arthur spoke of his ancient Kingdom, of blood-thirsty battles with warring invaders, where limb cleaving weapons caused the blood to pour, and a wide-eyed Max was on the edge of his seat. Never had history grasped him so before.

He spoke of the counsel of Merlin, of his round table and the loyalty of his closest and bravest Knights. He spoke of Cai and Galahad and the pain of their loss at Camlan, and of Bedwyr and Gwalchmai, who Brendan, through his knowledge of the Arthurian legends, could identify as Bedivere and Gawain.

Max was surprised to discover that Sir Lancelot had never existed, and that the extent of the hero's quests had not stretched beyond the bitter struggle for very survival to searching for holy grails and glamorous tournaments.

Arthur spoke of his grief at Mordred's betrayal, and of his anger that the son of his own sister, Morgan, could turn on him the way he had. Of the final battle, the wound he sustained, and of his journey to Avalon.

He told the children of his waking, and his hope that he would find the garrison at Little Solsbury. But he didn't for a moment consider sharing all his thoughts of their first meeting with them.

It was the King's turn to be dismayed as Brendan and Jess took on the story and explained how the Saxons had indeed settled the land, but only to be invaded in turn by marauding Vikings and Danes as his own old people were pushed into the mountains of Wales. His eyebrows raised as he was told that the Saxon King Alfred had become known as 'The Great' and that his own old Kingdom was effectively re-drawn as Wessex. History had almost completely repeated itself, as the Saxons themselves had become in danger of annihilation.

Through the aid of the unfamiliar book and it's pictures the battle of Hastings was brought to life and he could easily identify the Saxons, he would know the axes and drooping moustaches anywhere, and he could see the central figure in the middle of the shield wall clutching an arrow stuck fast in his eye, as the Norman cavalry closed in and the strange looking infantry, with their odd triangular shields and oval helmets, clashed with his house carls all around him.

"Another invasion to get his head around," Brendan observed, and

160

he and Jess explained the crusades, the wars of unification and the Middle Ages with its mighty castles and powerful siege engines at a steady pace.

But when they got up to the Tudor period, Drake, who had waited most impatiently, picked up the tale himself.

His had been the Golden Age and he had helped make it so. He spoke of Henry the Eighth and his own Queen, Elizabeth the First, and Arthur listened intensely to his tales of the sea and the wonders of the 'black powder' of which he spoke so fondly.

Arthur was fascinated to hear of The Spanish Armada, another would-be invasion of his land thwarted, and so it seemed, according to the story teller, almost single-handedly by Drake himself. He was also intrigued to hear of Drake's voyage around the earth and his claims that the world was round, but such was the speaker's pompous style of storytelling that the King could not be entirely sure he could believe it, and every time he tried to turn the page over, which bore a picture of the speaker holding the globe, Drake would rattle on about Spanish gold and his exploits in the new world.

When Drake had been finally prised off the subject, Brendan and Jess were able to progress the story quickly, with every turn of a page. As Brendan reflected, it was hard enough explaining history from the fifteen-hundreds to Drake without having to explain fifteen hundred years of history to Arthur, but both men were fascinated by what they heard as the pages turned.

They were horrified to hear of the Civil War, of a nation which had taken so many painful years to establish turning against itself, and Drake could not fathom the treachery of a Parliament which could turn on its monarch, nor of the gall of 'this Cromwell,' to 'take off a Royal head.'

The pages continued to turn, through the age of restoration and the failure of the Gunpowder plot, to the quelling of successive Jacobite rebellions and the dawn of the Empire.

The pictures showed ranks of red-coated infantrymen carrying sticks that appeared to smoke, and eloquent gentlemen in huge, elaborate wigs directing troops from the backs of dashing chargers. The 'black powder' was again explained to Arthur by Drake, and he was amazed to hear of the great wars which had plagued Europe and of the huge battles which had ensued.

It was very much an abridged version of history, but Max had never thought it so interesting. One event so quickly led to another, and he smirked quietly to himself as Drake examined accounts of Trafalgar with scornful criticism, his jealously at the realisation that another

Admiral could possibly have conducted himself with bravery to match his own, was clearly all too hard for him to conceal.

"Thou spake o' yon Nelson putting both Don and Frog t' flight, canst really be so?"

"Well yeah," replied Jess, "it was a great victory. Napoleon wanted to invade England and he couldn't because virtually his entire Navy was destroyed."

"Probably the biggest naval triumph ever to have..."

"But t'were not craft in number t' match the Armada?" Drake rudely interrupted Brendan.

"Maybe not as many ships, but in numbers of cannons...."

"Ah guns, guns," a gleam of desire shone in Drake's eye as he greedily examined a picture of HMS victory, Nelson's own flagship with its intricate rigging and bristling rows of cannon. "Oh if t'were possible t' furnish me wi' a craft o' this ilk."

"It's out of date now you wally," Max laughed, "wouldn't last two minutes against a nuclear submarine."

"She still exists though, Sir Francis," Brendan explained, "down in Portsmouth, and I think they've made a replica of your own ship too, the Golden Hind."

"A pox o' the Hind," Drake spat. "Mine right arm wouldst I sacrifice for to have sailed such a craft."

"Funny that," observed Max, "Nelson did much the same. Proper hero, that Nelson," he stirred.

"Look, Sir Francis, it was a different age," Jess turned the page. "I'm sure if you'd been there..."

"T'was not an invasion," Drake interrupted firmly. "Trafalgar is but in the Dago-Don King's back-yard; t'was not an invasion o' fair England thwarted."

"Well they would have got there, Sir Francis, it was a very important battle."

"Be they in the channel, were't to load wi' an Army for invasion?"

"Well, no..."

"Then t'was not a victory t' match Armada," he said with pride and finality.

"As you like it," replied Jess with irritation, and with similar firmness she turned the page.

As sailing ships gave way to metal-hulled monsters and air warfare was introduced over the next few chapters, Drake's eyes grew even wider. How he longed to taste the wind up in the very heavens themselves, and both found it hard to believe that this was an age where outer-space could now be reached; it was a world beyond their wildest dreams. It was incredible to hear and all the harder to take in, but there was no denying that it was innovation and mobilisation, primarily for war, which had forced the pace all the quicker.

But what war? The events of the previous century were more numerous, intense and terrible than anything which had preceded them in pure scale alone. Greek fire, Arthur noted, seemed to figure rather highly as the pictures showed huge explosions, flaming tanks and blazing cities. Both men were amazed by the very notion of almost the whole world being plunged headlong into one great war followed by another in such a short time, and it brought it home to them just how out of date they really were. Guns and stalemate on the Western Front, then bombs and terror as Germany, a nation neither of them had ever known, (though Arthur noticed that Saxony was certainly part of it,) occupying almost all of Europe in a series of campaigns even more impressive than those of the Corsican, Bonaparte, a century before.

The realisation that Britain had somehow stood alone and defended itself successfully against first Napoleon and then Hitler filled both Drake and Arthur with pride. This 'Churchill', whoever he was, was a man they were as keen to meet as the 'Wellington' of the previous pages. But it was Churchill who had steered the nation, their own country, through what he described as its darkest hour. The evidence was all there, it had been rather too close for comfort, and whilst they'd clearly been needed they had not returned to save their people from what the children called 'World War Two,' why had this not been their time?

"But what would you have done?" Rhiannon asked them carefully. Being rather cautious of the two strangers, she had at first said little throughout the history lesson, but any doubts she had of their authenticity had been vanquished by their genuine reaction to the tale.

"What could you have done?" Rhys added, as he put his arm around his girlfriend. Drake and Arthur looked blankly at each other. "What could you have done with swords and cannon against a blitzkrieg? Nothing," he said dismissively.

"We didn't need you, anyway," said Max mischievously, hoping to get a reaction from Drake. "We got through it alright, didn't we?"

"Our ancestors did," Jess corrected him. "I don't know how we would have managed."

"It rather beggars the question though, doesn't it?" Brendan looked worriedly around the group. "As Jess said earlier, what are they doing here now? If you weren't needed then, in all that danger…"

"What danger are we facing now?" Jess finished the ominous sentence. They had explained the past, but they were still no nearer to

163

fully understanding the present.

Brendan scratched his head thoughtfully. "This really is going to take a lot of sorting out," he said.

(a)   Behold the ring of Britain. Down on your knees and recognise your King.

(b)   My liege Lord. You are indeed the King, I confess until now I did not believe it.

(c)   Arise now and do service to your nation.

(d)   It will be an honour to serve this people beside you,

(i)   I know not why I am here, yet we must sort this mess out.

(ii)   You speak Welsh then?

(iii)   I speak.

(iv)   But what do you mean Welsh? I speak the tongue of my people. I am Arthur King of the Britain's, and it is wonderful to hear one of my countrymen speak

(v)   What news of Caerleon? Gwenhwyfar? Is it as the children say? Is this really the future?

(vi)   A Roman game, I know this.

(vii)   Here is a game I can play.

(viii)   As it is,

(ix)   Divide and destroy, the legacy of Caesar.

(x)   It is time you knew your King.

(xi)   Recognise your King,

(xii)   I have the torc, I have the ring of Britain.

Chapter Ten – The Tower

Joe Banks was a proud man, an ex-Regimental Sergeant Major, and thirty years of army service had left him with an acute sense of loyalty, duty and discipline, as well as a string of brightly-coloured medal ribbons which rightly reflected his glittering military career, and were stitched in pride of place to the breast of his livery coat.

Joe's was one of the most-photographed faces in the country and this was why he took such pride in his appearance, though few knew or ever asked his name. His brilliant white sideboard whiskers and moustache were always neatly preened and clipped, his black bonnet was always superbly buffed out, and from his scarlet livery coat with the famous initials 'ER' embroidered on the front of it, down to his white stockinged, black-gartered legs, he was turned out immaculately. His black, silver-buckled shoes shone in the evening sun with all the dazzle of his old parade ground boots, and his 'partizan,' which he held firmly, and dead straight in his right hand, reflected the light on its many polished surfaces like a beautifully finished diamond.

Mr Joseph Banks held a position of great honour, and as a Yeoman Warder of the Tower of London he took great pride in seeing out his long career of service to the crown in style. He sighed contentedly to himself, for he would soon retire and join the ranks of the Chelsea pensioners with his own little cottage in the grounds of Windsor Castle, and he was going to relish it, for it would be just recognition indeed from the monarch he loved for all his long years of service.

Banks was a walking encyclopaedia, a living history book who could recite a vast wealth of knowledge about the Tower, its prisoners, and those who had died on its block. He had so much to tell about the monarchs who had built and lived in it, and of those who had tried to escape. Yet he'd lost count already today of how many times he'd been asked to pose, ramrod straight, to be photographed in his full regalia by delighted Japanese and American tourists who saw him merely as a novelty and didn't seek to delve into his reserves of informative dialogue. He often thought it remarkable that the majority of questions he was invited to field were so utterly mundane, and had lost count of how many times that afternoon alone he'd been approached by inquisitive children only to be asked: "Do you make your own clothes?" Or "Have you ever used your axe?"

One young man had come close to impressing him by referring to his medieval weapon as a 'halberd,' which technically it was, but the potential was lost as he failed to test the owner's knowledge. He'd asked predictably if he could pose with the Yeoman for a photograph, and the kindly old man had allowed the youth to hold the weapon whilst his mother snapped the two of them on her camera. He'd been right on hand of course, for as a Yeoman Warder he carried his arms as a sign of his office as well as in defence of the realm, and both the sword at his side and the 'partizan,' which he now held aloft with its studded shaft and head of axe and pike, were dear to him, and he could never risk the prospect of a tourist trying to make off with either. The day was drawing to a close and the number of tourists was dwindling, but Banks would not drop his guard until he hung up his bonnet at the end of the day.

Looking across the courtyard he could see two other livery-clad Warders approaching across Tower Green, and he presumed they were coming to relieve him in order that he could take a quick tea break before getting ready for the 'key ceremony', which the delighted tourists would be gathering for shortly.

The ceremony was a nightly event and living pageantry. The Chief Warder, whose job it was to lock up the castle at the end of the day, would approach the gate Banks manned with a lantern in one hand and a big bunch of keys in the other. The key bearer and his foot-guard escort routinely started their approach at exactly seven minutes to ten o'clock, and Banks, whose job it was to be sentry, had to be in position under the archway to the Bloody Tower ready to challenge them when they approached, as he had done virtually every night of the year, rain, snow or fine, for the last five years.

The ceremony had been performed every night for seven hundred years, and Banks, feeling privileged to be continuing the tradition, never failed to play his part with the same heartfelt enthusiasm. In fact, on the rare occasions when he'd been absent, on holiday or in bed with the flu and another Yeoman had been deputising for him, he'd still glanced at his watch at the relevant time and his mind had drifted loyally to events at the archway.

On the approach, Banks, as sentry, was required to challenge with a cry of: "Halt, who goes there?" Not the most challenging of lines, it was true, and with over thirty years of army service to fall back on the warning cry of the watchman was one he had made countless times on sentry duty in foreign, war-torn lands. But it was still a challenge, be it a very public one for the tourist's benefit, and Banks always ensured his tone of voice adequately reflected this.

The Chief Warder would then announce in reply to the challenge: "The keys." And Banks would then ask the famous question: "Whose keys?"

The Chief Yeoman Warder, charged with the duties of his office and in

possession of the current monarch's keys to the Royal residence, Castle and Prison that is the Tower of London, which contains among other things the monarch's own crown jewels, then varies his reply dependant on who it is that sits on the throne at that time. During the five years that Banks had been a sentry the Chief Warder's answer had always been the same: "Queen Elizabeth's keys."

Thus cleared, and with the keys being treated with all the reverence of the monarch herself, Banks would then announce: "Advance Queen Elizabeth's keys, all's well."

The Chief Warder would lock up the gates, and one of the escort would then play the 'last post' on a shining bugle, following which the remaining visitors, having witnessed the famous ceremony, would be promptly escorted from the Castle out of the only remaining exit. The keys would be hung up on their hook in the Queen's house, and the Yeoman Warder's duties would be finished for another day.

Banks always enjoyed the ceremony, and used his tea break before hand to check himself quickly in the full-length mirror which hung in the guard room to ensure that his appearance was as crisp and presentable as it had been when he'd turned out for duty at the start of his day. He also, being now advanced in years, welcomed the prospect of being able to empty his bladder before the formalities began, and considered his approaching relief a timely blessing.

However, as the two supposed colleagues advanced across the grass Banks couldn't help but raise a bushy grey eyebrow in suspicion. They didn't march in step, and instead of moving with proud straight backs and vertical weapons they seemed to lope along at a casual pace with the air of men who'd never pounded a drill square in their lives. The one on the left held his partizan almost horizontally, the weight of the head making it bob up and down clumsily in his hand, and the other held his awkwardly in what Banks could only assume was his weak hand, and had his bonnet off-set at a jaunty angle which revealed far too much forehead.

The taller, on the left, now let his partizan actually hit the turf as he lost the fragile remains of his concentration to a large male raven who busied himself trying to remove worms from the well-kept grass. Banks saw him turn and stride towards it purposefully and the other had to take his arm quickly to halt him and return his colleague to their route. After a few hushed and quickly spoken words, which Banks at a distance could not hear, the taller of the two, who had been treading down the backs of his shoes, was ordered to put his feet in properly by the other, and he having done so, the two fellow Yeomen drew up to him cautiously. Banks prepared to receive them, his back dead straight, as he stood on guard outside the White Tower in the centre of the castle compound.

He observed the two Warders with no less suspicion as they drew closer. The tall one on the left appeared to be dressed in a uniform far too small for him; the cuffs, which were supposed to be cut at the wrists, were halfway up his forearms and he walked uncomfortably now in the shoes which were clearly several sizes too small, wincing with each little step. Strands of ginger hair poked out untidily from under his bonnet and a large nose in the centre of his face drew most of the sentry's attention.

The other, whose buckled shoes were in the former parade sergeants opinion lamentably poorly polished, also wore his garters far too far down his stockings, and had made what could only be described as a feeble attempt to shine the buttons on his livery tunic.

"Um, come to relieve you," said the shorter of the two awkwardly, displaying a prominent set of teeth which fixed into a toothy and untrustworthy-looking grin as he faced the former Sergeant Major. The man seemed to be desperately avoiding eye contact and focused instead on Banks' magnificent moustache and authoritarian side whiskers.

Fighting the instinct and desire to ask: 'Who the hell are you?' Banks instead retained his discipline, and with a voice of composed professionalism challenged with a cry of: "Halt, who goes there?" He dropped his weight onto his left leg, bringing his right back into a position of defence, and his partisan out in front of him so it rested in both hands ready to swing. He didn't recognise either of these 'fellow Yeomen' and the Warder, in his primary position of guardian of the Tower, smelt a rat. He'd made his challenge formally and in a loud voice which alerted a number of tourists who were idly drifting across the courtyard.

"Er... Who goes where?" The buck-toothed one repeated the challenge as if in baffled greeting and in a questioning tone of confusion. "Um..."

"Well, two Beefeaters," his taller, big-nosed colleague cut in.

"Um, yes, er, that's right, two Beefeaters come to relieve you, my good fellow."

"'Cept yer not, are yer?" Banks observed them sternly.

"Erm..." The two men gave each other a quick glance; their costumes had certainly got them through the front gate unchallenged. Banks noted the taller male swallow anxiously, his protruding Adam's apple bulging up and down in his throat a tell-tale sign that something was up.

"Yer not Beefeaters, are yer," Banks spoke again firmly, but it was a statement not a question. He was fiercely proud of his position as Yeoman Warder and resented the term 'Beefeater,' which he considered derogatory.

"Um, are we not?" the tall man enquired nervously of the other.

"We are," the toothy one protested.

"Yer not Beefeaters," Banks corrected. "If yer anything yer be Yeoman Warders," he paused. "If yer are anythin', that is."

"Oh yes, certainly," the buck-toothed one responded, "Yeoman Warders we are, guardians of the Tower..."

"Custodians..." The other cut in.

"Yes custodians of the crown so forth etc... etc..." said the toothy one, gaining confidence.

"But are you?" Banks regarded them critically, not relaxing his pose even for a second. "'Cos I don't recognise yer."

"Erm... It's our first day," said the tall ginger one cautiously.

"Right, okay," but Banks wasn't letting up. He knew what it was like to take on important duties for the first time and the nerves involved, for he'd trooped the colour many times and changed the guard at Buckingham Place in his army days, but on each occasion before he'd started he'd made sure he knew exactly what would be expected of him. He'd not been made aware that any new Warders were starting today, and he tried to perish the thought that these two might be starting now, getting ready to replace him when he retired. Whatever these idiots said and however ridiculous they looked, there was one sure way to find out if they were genuine or not.

"Right," said Banks again in the same challenging voice, "if you are my relief... What's today's password?"

"Um..." The Buck-toothed one shuffled his feet and looked uncomfortable again as the fragile confidence he'd built appeared shattered.

"P-p-password?" The tall one replied uncertainly, though he meant it as a question and not as an answer, he'd not been prepared to be challenged in this way.

To his amazement and surprise, as well as to the obvious relief of his friend, the challenging sentry with the immaculate white whiskers stamped his feet back into attention in one swift movement, his weapon sliding easily back into position at his side.

"That's it," he said formally, "my apologies. Pass, friend."

"Well there we go then," the tall one swallowed again in jubilation. "Easy as that."

169

"Indeed, yes." Banks turned to march briskly off to the guard room; time was now short before the key ceremony and his bladder had nearly got the better of him. "Gentlemen," he added quickly, "I had not been informed you was joining us today. Joseph Banks, Senior Warder," he introduced himself.

"Ni..." The tall one began, but the shorter coughed loudly to halt him and instead spoke for both of them.

"Ronald Pleasance and Kenneth Marshbanks."

"Yes, delighted to meet you," said the other.

Banks shook hands with both of them quickly and added as he walked away, "I'll make meself available to speak wi' both of yers after the key ceremony.... Presentation is key, it's all in the presentation, and pride in the uniform." Banks hated a scruffy soldier, it pointed to a scruffy professional, and if these two really were going to replace him at the end of the month he had a lot of work to do between now and then to lick them into shape.

It still bothered him that something wasn't right about Mr Pleasance and Marshbanks, who behind the Warder's back now scuttled off in the direction of the Queen's House. To the old soldier the password was sacred, and though he'd had to concede that today's had been rather easy, they'd known it and that meant he'd been duty bound to let them pass. But Banks decided he would voice his concerns over a quick cuppa before the formalities of the key ceremony began.

When Banks arrived at the Guard House, however, the Chief Warder was nowhere to be seen. He rushed passed the Raven Master on his way to the lavatory and called out over his shoulder to his friend, asking him where the boss was.

"I d'know Joe," the raven master replied, he was himself in a hurry to put the birds, whose welfare he was charged with, away for the night. "Think 'e might be in the White Tower, 'e said 'e were goin' out t'do a quick circuit."

"Oh right, tar Harry... Oh by the way, did you know there are two new..."

But the Raven Master was gone to finish off his own duties and Joseph Banks had the guard house, complete with its kettle and full-length mirror, all to himself.

The exact location of the Chief Warder at that moment in time was the floor of a lavatory cubicle in the Queen's House, a building in the grounds of the castle where he had gone to collect the keys and await his escort. He sat with his back to the toilet and his chin on his knees. His hands were bound behind his back, his ankles were fastened

170

together, he had a gag round his mouth and faced a locked door which he couldn't reach to open. He opened his eyes carefully and was conscious of a stonking headache similar to the one he had acquired in the 'Yeoman's' bar the night he'd been promoted to Chief Warder.

This headache, however, had been less expensive and had been awarded to him courtesy of a strike to the head from behind when he'd been reaching up to collect the keys from the hook. The unexpected blow had seemed to come from nowhere, and due to the amount of pain the unfortunate Chief Warder was now experiencing, he reasoned it had to have been delivered by a strong, tall man, with a heavy implement.

His attacker had indeed used great force as he had wanted to make sure he knocked his target out cleanly, and for this purpose he'd used the shiny flat side of the partizan he carried. The thick, heavy side of the axe had done its job well, almost too well.

"You fool," the attacker's buck-toothed side kick had exclaimed in alarm as the Chief Warder had crumpled instantly to the ground, "you've killed the man."

"You said hit him hard!" The attacker had gone on the defensive.

"Not that hard, idiot," and for a few tense moments the buck-toothed man had knelt over the unfortunate victim, his upper lip twitching anxiously as he listened for breathing, before, with relief, he'd let out a sigh and given the thumbs up. "He's breathing, he's okay."

"Right, well lets get him hidden away quick," and they'd half-carried, half-dragged the unconscious Chief Warder into the toilets where the restraints had been applied. The taller of the two had taken his arms and the shorter his feet, and as a result he had been transported far from horizontally, due to the difference in height between them. The shorter man had then exited the cubicle with the castle keys in hand, leaving the taller inside with the victim.

The taller man had drawn the bolt across the cubicle door, locking it from the inside, before climbing out of the cubicle by first standing on the toilet and then scrambling over the top of the door to join his mate on the other side. He was clumsy, and as a consequence of his shoes being rather too tight, he'd stumbled when he'd first tried to stand on the seat of the toilet to gain the necessary purchase to bunk himself up and over the door. As he'd brought his second foot up to join the first on the toilet seat, he'd slipped, and his right foot had gone straight into the bowl.

Now, with one sopping and uncomfortable foot and the other just plain uncomfortable, the Yeoman Warder with the big nose, who'd approached Joseph Banks a few minutes before, stood in the lobby of the Queen's House and began to argue with his bald-headed colleague.

171

"Well let's go and get them now, we've got the key."

"No, we've got to wait until everyone's gone, we'll never get away with it if we try now."

"Fine, then let's just take the key to their cage and hide somewhere until the coast is clear."

"Well then, der brain," the shorter man held up the large metal ring with numerous heavy keys clinking on it, "you just pick out the right key and we're away." A sarcastic toothy smirk spread across his face.

"Erm..." The taller man swallowed and his Adam's apple jumped up and down in his throat. "Er..." He took the key ring and started fumbling through them clumsily as the other looked on with impatience. After a few seconds he realised it was useless, he'd never be able to tell which key was which, and with a frustrated grunt of 'blast it,' he thrust them back into his colleague's hands.

The grin of the shorter Yeoman spread across his face in a victory leer. "See," he said, "I told you it was a silly idea."

"Right then," the taller folded his arms in defiance, "so what do you suggest?"

There was a sudden knock at the door, and after an anxious glance at the other the tall man opened the door to reveal another Yeoman waiting outside, a shiny bugle in his hand.

"Can we help?" The toothy one enquired.

"Um..." The newcomer seemed surprised to see them. "Escort reporting to meet the Chief Ward..."

"Ah, well he's a bit off-colour today," the big-nosed, ginger one began to explain, but the bald-headed, toothy one quickly cut in.

"He's on colour, very much on colour and raring to go, just chomping at the bit to get cracking, he'll be out in a minute."

"Oh," the bugler looked confused.

"But he doesn't need an escort today," the shorter man continued, "good day to you," and he made to shut the door.

"But..." The bugle-wielding Yeoman held the door open. " He needs an escort, the keys always have an..."

"We are the escort," said the toothy one quickly.

"Yes, yes we're the escort," the tall one joined in, "very much so, the escort, yes... That's us."

"So good day to you," said the shorter man firmly, and after an irritated glance at his colleague, "he'll be out in a minute. When he's ready."

"Right, um..." The newcomer looked disappointed. "You two new then?"

"Yup," said the shorter man, and rudely he swung the door shut in

172

the bugle-carrying Yeoman's face. "Has he gone?" He asked the tall one after a pause.

"Yeah, we showed him eh, tail between his legs... And as I was asking, what do you suggest?" He turned and looked down his long nose at his colleague once again.

"Well, its simple isn't it? We'll just go round like he would, lock up the doors, turf everyone out, and then... We can go get em... We'll have all the time in the world to go through the keys later, there will be no one to stop us."

"Just like that?"

"Well how hard can it be? I don't see what all the fuss is about anyway, I mean, dressing up in these silly clothes, strutting about..."

"Yeah, in these damned uncomfortable shoes. Why can't I tread the backs down? They are so much more comforta..."

"Cos you stick out like a sore thumb dragging your heels, I told you, no one'll suspect a thing if we dress up properly, and it's only for a little while longer. Trust me my friend, all these Beefeaters are is glorified security guards. We just have to go round locking doors and whichever key we haven't used will be the one we need afterwards - it'll be a doddle."

"Well lead on, then," the other responded. "And don't forget his lantern."

The two set off across the compound, locking up the Bell and Byward towers on their way. They'd fumbled through most of the keys on the ring on both occasions in order to find the right ones, and as they approached the Bloody Tower they were at least five minutes late.

"Oh come on," said the impostor with the keys and lantern to his partizan-carrying escort.

"Its these bloody shoes," the taller hissed back in a muffled whisper, "I bet I've got terrible blisters already."

"Stop moaning and keep up." The supposed 'Chief Warder' had no sympathy and quickly strode on ahead, but as he came around the corner he was surprised to see such a large gathering of people.

"What the heck...?" His escort had seen them too.

"Just keep up, you'll spoil the show."

"But what are we supposed to do now?" The escort stopped and the key-bearer turned on him.

"I don't know. I guess we just carry on. Guess we just put on a show and try and enjoy the moment."

"Enjoy... In these shoes." The escort picked at his large nose anxiously.

"Come on, and leave your nose alone, they might realise something's up." They walked on with a little more purpose towards the Bloody tower.

Joseph Banks, in his regular position under the arch, couldn't believe his eyes. The crowd had gathered as usual, but for the first time in his career the Chief Warder was late. As the minutes had ticked by Banks had become more and more concerned; something was clearly wrong and he needed to get to the bottom of it. The problem was that he had a duty to remain under the arch, he couldn't leave his post, and were he to move away the crowd would quickly catch on that something wasn't right. He tried to reason in his own mind that there had to be some explanation for his boss's poor time-keeping - perhaps one of the keys had broken or one of the locks had been a bit stiff - but deep down he was a worried man. The ceremony always ran like clockwork and he feared something serious must have happened; he just wondered if the two sloppy new Warders were in any way responsible.

When he eventually did sight the key bearer and his escort rounding the corner, Banks' jaw dropped as he instantly recognised the approaching pair, and he almost lost his composure altogether. He recovered himself just in time to see the smaller, buck-toothed Warder, who carried the keys and lantern, actually stop and converse with the other. This was totally unprofessional, and was worsened by the escort, who picked his nose in full view of the assembled public. Banks was all for marching over and challenging them then and there, when the two started walking towards him again. The taller, almost on tip-toes, had lost his loping gate and seemed most uncomfortable.

Banks couldn't understand it, he had no idea where the Chief Warder was, and was now almost certain that the two approaching him were entirely bogus - they had to be, for it was only the Chief Yeoman Warder who bore the keys and lantern at the key ceremony. He breathed heavily, angrily, the blood pulsed in his veins and he felt the old sensations that he had on campaigns when combat was close at hand. He wanted to charge them, but he held his ground until the two impostors were almost at his gate.

"Come on, come on step aside," said the lantern carrier, looking rather flustered by the crowd. "Come on, got to lock up."

"Halt!" Former Regimental Sergeant Major Joseph Banks bellowed a challenge in his loudest parade-ground voice. "Who goes there?" In a second he had dropped into a defensive stance, his feet firmly planted with his weight evenly distributed for maximum stability. He brandished his weapon in front of him with its base on the ground and

174

the blade leaning towards the two as his eyes burned in fury.

"Um…" The lantern bearer paused. "Oh not you again," he replied impatiently. "Look I've got the keys, I've come to lock up."

"Whose keys?" Banks yelled his question knowing full well the impostor wouldn't know the answer.

"Er… The keys to the um… To the Castle," the taller escorting Warder volunteered. He may have guessed the password earlier, but that had been lucky, and no-one fooled Joe Banks more than once.

"Gimme them keys," Banks yelled ferociously.

The crowd gasped in astonishment as the sentry swung his partizan at the key bearer, and as the smaller big-toothed Warder had to physically duck under the swing to avoid his head being severed from his shoulders. They began to applaud as the lantern-bearer dropped both his lantern and the keys unceremoniously on the ground, and as he and his escort, who had quickly discarded his own heavy weapon, rapidly turned and fled with the white-whiskered old soldier in hot pursuit and shouting "Come back, you villains," at them in tones of burning fury.

"Bravo," one American tourist applauded enthusiastically.

"Great show," another whistled in approval.

"Hey, honey," the first tourist said to his wife as the three Yeomen disappeared round the corner, "same every night for over seven hundred years, and no-one ever gets hurt doing that."

"Yeah," she replied in wonder. "They must have to practise that, like, so hard."

As they reached Tower Green the gap widened between the two bogus Warders and their pursuer. Age was catching up with the old man, and the huge weapon he carried was an awkward shape to run with. He'd swung it at them several times but had always been just too far from them to connect, and swiping at fresh air had just slowed his progress further.

The taller of the two used the advantage to rid himself of his restrictive footwear, and once free of his shoes he quickly widened the gap from his colleague and their pursuer even further. He headed for the main exit, and was first outside the Castle walls, where he was panting and trying to catch his breath when the other joined him in safety.

Banks, having seen them off, stood just inside the compound grasping his chest and gasping for air, he simply couldn't keep up. Then it suddenly dawned on him in horror that the keys were now unguarded and abandoned by his unmanned sentry post. He panicked and felt torn in two between his duties to recover the keys and the need to alert the Police and get the impostors arrested, and then in realisation that their approach and flight could always have simply been a diversion to draw him from his post whilst another took the keys, he trotted back to the arch as fast as his aged legs would carry him.

He turned the corner to a huge round of applause from the crowd, who had loitered indecisively after his earlier disappearance, unsure of whether or not the show was over, and Banks was greatly relieved to see the keys still lying on the ground where they had fallen. He strode over, took possession of them and then requested politely for the crowd to leave by the exit. He was anxious to complete a tour of the Tower at once in the hopes of locating the Chief Warder.

Outside the Castle, the two bogus Warders heaved as they tried to recover their breath.

"How hard can it be," the taller repeated the earlier words of the other between heavy breaths. "How hard can it be, you said... You idiot, you almost got us killed."

"Look, we'll just have to find another way," the other panted beside him. His bonnet had blown off in the pursuit and beads of sweat ran in rivers down his bald head.

"Just have to find another way," the taller mocked his colleague by impersonating his voice in a sarcastic tone, "another way to get us killed, no doubt."

"Look I'm sorry okay, I didn't expect the old boy to blow up like that, and anyway it was me he tried to decapitate."

"Humph," the taller picked at his enormous nose again, and removed his own bonnet to reveal a shock of red hair. "We should have pinched the keys when the Chief Warder had hung them back up at the end of the ceremony, not before he'd even started it. You and your stupid ideas." He looked down at the other expecting him to admit his failings, but instead his friend raised his eyebrows so that folds of skin rippled up his face and onto his bald head, and a wide grin spread across his face. "Oh no, you've had another idea."

"Can you swim?" the toothy one asked.

Shortly afterwards, a lanky frogman and his mate, in jeans and a t-shirt, were standing together in the gathering darkness on Tower Wharf. The term 'frogman' must be used in the broadest possible sense, for the man wore a cheap snorkelling mask, breathing pipe and flippers, which had been hastily purchased from a market stall, and had otherwise simply stripped down to his vest and underpants.

In years past the main entrance to the Castle for a lot of its prisoners had been straight off the river Thames and through its most famous

176

point of access, Traitor's Gate. Many had entered by boat never to come out again, and the entrance is secured not by a door but by a portcullis, a huge metal grid which hangs from the top of the archway and down into the water. It had been many years out of use, but in times past the grid would be hoisted out of the water for the boats to enter under the arch, and the two men approached the outside of the gate now, the taller walking self consciously, his flippered feet pattering on the wharf. The other walked beside him half-crouching as if he didn't wish to be seen lest he draw attention to himself, (which was going to be rather difficult anyway when he walked next to a fully grown man in a snorkelling mask and his pants). In his hand he carried a crowbar.

"I look ridiculous," said the first man in protest. He had the face-mask and breathing pipe up on the top of his head to avoid it getting too uncomfortable until he actually needed it. "I feel ridiculous, too," he added angrily.

"Well, if you will wear a string vest," said the other scathingly, "and I agree, you're not exactly catwalk material, are you?"

"I didn't think anyone would actually see me in this vest," the ginger frogman defended himself, "and anyway, they are rather comfy."

"Rather comfy..." the other mocked him. "Honestly!"

"It's the flippers and all this that I'm on about," he pointed to the mask on top of his head, "it's this that makes me look ridiculous."

"Oh, so walking though the centre of London in your underpants doesn't?"

"Look," said the first man impatiently, "this is your hair-brained scheme, why's it me that has to go in the water?"

"Because," said the other trying as hard as he could to muster a look of genuine disappointment, "I can't swim, can I?"

"Can't you?"

"No," he said quickly. "Ready?" He raised his arms as if to push the first man into the water.

"Look, wait a minute..."

"It's perfectly simple, old boy." The shorter man made an attempt at reassurance. "You hop into the water, crowbar your way through the gate, and in. Once you're in you pinch the keys again..."

"That you dropped," the frogman butted in angrily.

"Yes, that I dropped, because the axe-wielding maniac was trying to cut my head off. You go to the main entrance, let me in, then we go bag the birdies and it's off into the night."

"Simple as that, is it?" The tall man spoke sarcastically for it didn't take a genius to see that it was he who would run the significant risks.

"Oh yes," said the other with confidence. "Clever, isn't it?"

The tall man reluctantly pulled the mask over his eyes and was about to put the breathing pipe into his mouth when he paused again. "And what will you be doing while I'm..."

"Slithering like an eel into the Castle..."

"No. While I'm risking my neck trying to get in."

"Oh, standing watch... Yes, I'll be the lookout."

"Oh, good on you." The tall man reverted to sarcasm once again.

"Look, we have to get this done, you know." He handed the crowbar to the unwilling diver. "The whole plan relies on us, they said so. They've put their trust in us, and they said we could expect to be rewarded in kind." He paused, stuck in a daydream of untold wealth, and a wicked grin spread across his toothy face.

"Right," said the tall man as he carefully gave his huge beak one last delicate clear out with his index finger, "I wonder what the rewards are for standing watch. I'll make sure I tell them that I'm the one who took the plunge."

"Well it is my plan, don't forget that."

"Huh," the taller grunted.

"Look, it's not my fault, if I could swim I'd be the first in there, you know that."

"Do I?"

"Yes. Right then, on the count of three. One, two..."

"Wait." The diver took a step out of reach.

"What now?" the other exclaimed impatiently.

"Erm... I'm not ready."

"Why not? Look, there's no-one looking, let's just get on with it."

"Need to do my breathing exercises," said the reluctant diver, trying to find an excuse.

"Need to... Don't be ridiculous, man, it's little more than a puddle."

"As a non-swimmer you wouldn't understand, and anyway it's gonna be cold in there and the water's filthy - can't I get greased up or something?"

"You're not swimming the Channel, you know."

"Alright, alright, just let me take my time." He braced himself and started taking long breaths.

The other sighed to himself in frustration that his friend was constantly delaying the inevitable, looked at his watch for a few seconds and turned on the diver again. "Right, on the count of three," he stepped towards him. "One, two..."

"No..." The diver backed away from him again, but this time he tripped over his own flippered feet, tumbled from the wharf, and entered the water horizontally and on his back with a resounding splash.

The other had hoped his friend would lower himself stealthily into the murky, mud-brown river water, making no noise which might draw attention to them, but now that he was finally in after all the delays he looked down at his colleague with a mischievous grin and chortled to himself.

Below him in the water the diver splashed about, stirring up the filthy, murky-brown soup he floated in with flailing arms. He coughed several times and squirmed desperately.

"F-f-f-f-freezing," he declared, between coughs.

"Well, get on with it then," his unsympathetic overseer replied impatiently. "You haven't dropped the crowbar, have you?"

"N-no, I've g-g, I've got it," said the diver as he sploshed towards the portcullis. He latched onto the grating and held on to the slimy bars, trying to catch his breath as his body convulsed against the cold.

"Can you squirm through?" enquired his warm and dry colleague on the wharf. A quick glance around had confirmed that a young couple were approaching hand in hand, and he knew they wouldn't have long.

"Of c-c-course n-not," replied the man in the water, "f-far too narrow t-to get through. That's the whole point, idiot."

"Right, well crowbar it open then, widen the hole. No, not there, below the water line where no one will see it... Look there's someone coming, you're going to have to get under, use your snorkel." The speaker had been bent over looking into the water and giving his orders in a stage whisper lest the passers by would hear him as they approached, and as his colleague disappeared under the water he straightened up and smiled at the couple as they passed him by. "Good evening," he greeted them, desperate to give off the impression that nothing was wrong and hoping to divert their attention from the snorkel pipe which was breaking the surface of the sloshing water next to the gate.

"Strange bloke," remarked the girl to her boyfriend when they were safely out of earshot, "very odd talking into the river like that."

"Well there are all sorts in London," her partner conceded, and they walked briskly away into the night.

Seconds later a head broke the surface of the water. "Y-y-y-useless," exclaimed the frozen diver in frustration.

"Well you can't be doing it properly."

"W, w-ell you've never t-tried crow-baring open a secure metal grating under water in the dark," the floundering diver protested.

"Well... Just swim under it then." Yes, he thought, that might work, he should have thought of that before. "Just swim under it, man, it can't go all the way down."

"All, a-lright, I'll try." The diver let go of the crowbar, committing it to a watery grave on the river bed, took two deep breaths, and having replaced the breathing pipe in his mouth he dived to the bottom. His flippers popped out of the water as he turned over to begin his decent, and in a second they were gone.

The look out on the wharf watched the line of bubbles anxiously. They quickly stopped. There was a pause. The water went still. Another bubble, and again a brief pause. It was probably just for a matter of a few seconds, but to the watching man on the wharf it seemed like hours. He was just beginning to wonder if his colleague had made it into the Castle when the soaking ginger head broke the surface once more.

The diver coughed and spluttered like never before; he fought for breath and thrashed around in the water like an unwilling dog who'd been forced into a bath.

"Uh, uh, k-huh, argh." He splashed his way to the side, and the look out, frustrated that 'Plan B' had also failed so spectacularly, helped to pull the failed diver out by latching on to his slimy forearm.

The tall man, having been hauled up, coughed and spluttered for several minutes. He sat on the side shivering and blew his nose, and half the river seemed to dribble out of him as he coughed and wretched on the wharf.

"There, there," his bone-dry accomplice patted him reassuringly on the back. "Couldn't get under it, eh?"

"Ob, k-hur. O-bviously not." The dripping man coughed. "F-far too deep, wasn't it. the g-grating goes right d-down to the bottom, I knew it would."

"Well, it was worth a try I s'pose."

"F-for you maybe." The tall man shivered uncontrollably; he was angry that no thought had been given to supply him with a towel to dry off with after his frolics in the water. "Y-y-you idiot. I'm just too big, y-you might have got through there."

"What, with my back?"

"What back?"

"My bad back."

"Your...?"

"You know, the bad back I'm always going on about," the shorter protested, mentioning for the first time the perfectly functioning back he'd never complained about before. "Anyway, you're the idiot."

"M-k-hur. M-me!" The diver coughed again.

"Yes, once you're deep under water the snorkel doesn't work, you can't breathe through it once the top's under the surface."

"I for-forgot," protested the tall man as he got to his feet, dripping everywhere. "S-so how are we g-going to get in now?" he asked quickly, trying to take the subject matter away from his own stupidity.

"Hmm," the shorter man thought to himself, and he voiced his thinking aloud. "Well we can't get through it, we can't get under it..." Another wicked grin spread across his face. "Can you climb?" he asked.

Shortly afterwards the two men were back and standing outside the Castle ramparts, though this time they both wore dark boiler suits, assault boots and balaclava head-coverings. A compromise had been reached; the taller man would indeed go over the wall, but the shorter man would be going with him, bad back or no bad back.

They carried with them the tools of the burgling trade: a pair of bolt croppers was held by the smaller man, and he would need to tuck these into his belt as he negotiated the wall, he would need both hands for climbing. The taller man held a coil of tough nylon rope attached to a grappling hook, and he had a large sack folded down and tucked into the pocket of his boiler suit to contain their swag. This caused the other to snigger to himself as they prepared to attack the wall, due to the unsightly bulge it created at the front of his colleague's trousers.

"Right," said the tall man in preparation. He looked up at the wall as if to measure the length of the throw required to pass the grappling hook over the battlements, and the angle required to gain a purchase. He swallowed hard and the other could clearly see the shape of his enormous Adam's apple moving up and down as a great lump under the balaclava. "I'll throw the grabbling - hoo-ckh!" He sneezed loudly, and snot flew out of the huge nose, which also stuck all too obviously out of the balaclava nose hole. His ginger hair might have been hidden away, but his companion, who was similarly displaying a hideous set of teeth, hoped the tell-tale nasal feature wouldn't give them away. "I'll - huchoo." He sneezed again, but continued to speak through his rapidly blocking nose. "Throwb de grabbling book ober the wall. Den we climb ober. You furst," he was insistent on this, "den be."

"Uh," the other tutted under his breath.

"Ib's not by fault. I'b gob a cold combing on fwom dab freezing wabter," the speaker protested. He wiped his nose with the back of his hand; his cold was getting worse by the second and he must have swallowed a cocktail of unpleasantness in the Thames. He was still shivering as he continued. "Once on the badtlebents we use the

181

grabbling-book to attach to the obtside wall and be lowber ourselves into the Castle. Be run-b to the Beauchamp tower, you buse de bolt grobbers to bet us in, I'll bop dem into de sack. Ben ibs back ub the wope and onto the badtlebents abain. Be rebverse de grabbling-book and blower ourselves back out and into de b-night. Uh... uh...a-choo!" he sneezed again.

"Excellent plan," the shorter man agreed as he wiped aggressively at a globule of snot which had flown from his colleague's nose and had landed on the chest pocket of his own boiler suit.

"I-it'll be b-like the Bless-A-Bless," said the taller man excitedly.

"Like the what?"

"De Bless-A..."

"Oh, yes I see, like the special forces."

"B-yes."

"Or we could of course just go and get the keys once we are in and then we can let ourselves out." The other looked almost disappointed at this suggestion. "Right then, old boy, let's get on with it, and not a moment too soon."

The taller man snorted as he tried to clear his nose, he swung the grappling hook under his arm a few times to get used to its weight and then he let it fly... It soared up towards the battlements, fell short, hit the wall and fell into the moat.

"Urh," his fellow burglar shook his head.

"B-well, ib's nob-t gowing to be easby." The thrower made two more fruitless attempts, and on his fourth throw the grappling hook at last dropped out of sight between the castellations on top of the wall. A tug on the rope proved it was sound, and moments later the two desperadoes were climbing the rope and scaling the wall.

Chapter Eleven – All Met

As the train rumbled along the track and the fields and trees flitted passed the window in the failing light, Julian Finch sipped his coffee and tried to get comfortable. No first class compartment on an international train for him, just a corner seat on a normal car on the First Great Western 'express' service from Paddington to Bristol.

He had time to kill before he departed the train at Bath, but he was so tired he found it difficult to concentrate on the bundle of documents he'd planned to work through to while away the journey, and so instead he replaced them in his briefcase and sat back in the firm seat. The report the Commissioners had requested on the effects of intensive cod fishing in the North Sea would have to wait, he was no expert himself and the collection of scientific Marine Biologist's thesis's, dissertations and articles were far too heavy for him to compile the gist of them into a simple report for his masters at the end of a hard day.

In any case Julian knew the report wasn't going to tell them anything that wasn't obvious already. Dwindling fish stocks were running out fast, and trawling was responsible. Quotas were all very well, but it became ridiculous and wasteful when fishermen were throwing an excess back into the sea to prevent themselves from being penalised for exceeding it. The problem with trawling, as Julian saw it, was that it just lifted a whole section of the ecosystem out of the water at once and destroyed it beyond repair. The net could not discriminate between the species it caught, and the very considerable damage that man was doing to life in the sea could not be doubted. The mouths of an ever-increasing population had to be fed, however, and there seemed little chance that trawling would be subject to a ban in the near future whatever the recommendations of the report, which he knew could only realistically cite fish farming as an alternative. To Julian the reports objective of finding an answer to the questions about the 'sustainability of renewable fish stocks' should perhaps simply have been replaced with the question: 'how much longer can we go on like this?'

He wondered why the Commissioners were so eager to waste his time on reports like this, for serious as the situation was there was little he could personally do to assist it. It annoyed him that those in authority didn't just listen to the experts themselves, and instead choose to read abridged reports composed by Civil Servants like himself with no expertise, whose job it was to do their homework for them and present it to them in the most simple of terms - but leaving the odd buzzword in, of course, so that when the politician spoke on the subject they would sound as if they understood all the intricate ins and outs of it.

Julian lifted the lid delicately from his coffee, hoping not to spill it, and raised it to his mouth. A jolt of the train caused him to jerk and swallow considerably more of the scalding liquid than he had intended, and as he put the cup down again on the table in front of him he winced as the pain registered on his tongue and the roof of his mouth. It didn't seem to matter what time he got the train, the coffee was always much too hot.

He couldn't relax and his attention was instead drawn to a newspaper neatly folded on a nearby table and discarded by an earlier commuter. He picked it up and flicked through it hoping to find distraction, but instead saw only bad news, words of woe and echoes of doom, and most of it on a theme he would happily have left behind in the office; that of the environment.

As he first unfolded it he was greeted by the headline 'Mammoth Hole In The Ozone Layer Can Never Be Healed' plastered across the front page, and the satellite picture beneath it showed the extent of the damage already caused to the earth's atmosphere. He browsed it quickly - it was hardly new news - and having turned it he was greeted by the broad, smiling face of Sir Denis Hitoadie, Duke of Man, printed on the inside page. The accompanying article advised that his Grace was one of Britain's two European Union Commissioners, and that he and his colleague, Sir Morgan Dredmor, would be presenting the new European Environmental Act to the European Commission in Brussels today. The editorial questioned what answers the EEA would present to the environmental crisis and how it planned to tackle the causes of climate change. Indeed, Julian thought.

The picture of the Duke was old, and he knew it well as a copy hung in the Commissioner's office. It had been taken eighteen months ago at a multi-agency conference and showed the Duke several stone lighter and in a Churchillian pose with cigar in one hand as he waved to the camera with the other. No doubt the picture's nuances and flattering depiction of his shape would serve for the inclusion of this particular picture to find favour with his Grace. Julian smirked, for the picture could only mislead the reading public. The subject's appearance was so clean as to be completely out of character, there wasn't a splash of food on him, and he was dressed in a crisp, clean suit. The reader would assume an impression of a man who strove tirelessly and heroically for the betterment of the nation, a figure of serene authority with whom the buck stopped and in whom they should have confidence; they wouldn't see the selfish, greedy, port-swilling toad for what he was. But then again, he reflected, how well does anyone know anyone else? The Duke was his boss and it was his business to be about the Duke's business, but he didn't know the full extent of his dealings in Brussels, and he would personally know even less if his Grace's snivelling vassals Rindburn and Sludboil hadn't let on as they had.

The rest of the paper seemed to expand on the ominous theme of the front page; excessive carbon emissions causing damage to the delicate fabric of the earth by contributing to the ozone problem, global warming being spurred on by the gap in the atmosphere and the effects that inevitable climate change will have on us all. It foresaw rising temperatures leading to huge areas of the planet being affected by draught, and whole nations by starvation while seasonal disruption led to flooding elsewhere. It also suggested that various tropical diseases, so far non-existent on our continent, would be able to incubate in Europe if temperatures were to rise just a few degrees more. Whole species would die out as their habitats became too warm for them and the food sources they rely on. The risk of killer smog in East Asia was set to get worse as industry in that part of the world grew, and the impact of industrial development on the environment could not be underestimated. Deforestation of the mighty rain forests of South America was effectively choking the earth's lungs by restricting and incapacitating its ability to be able to cope with all these challenges. The melting of the polar ice caps would put the whole eco-system out of balance and water levels would rise causing a serious threat to low laying densely populated areas. Tsunamis and flooding could claim hundreds of thousands of lives a year, and large areas of land worldwide would be lost forever under the rising sea.

'We have to be greener,' the paper said, and the Government were quoted as planning to punish those who caused excessive pollution. It acknowledged that there were constant campaigns on the radio, the television, everywhere, telling people to use less energy, yet it cited the problem that the population continued to expand. Brown and green belt was continuously being developed and turned into soulless housing estates where every new household contributed to the problem, all using energy, consuming and regurgitating more waste than their councils could cope with.

Julian sighed. He tried to do his bit; Patricia ran the washing machine at low heat and never overfilled the kettle, and he was always going round after the kids turning lights off and trying to recycle what he could, but he had to wonder how much of a difference this really made.

The business supplement was full of it too and centred on the

185

supermarket packaging war. Less plastic packaging, the paper demanded, more biodegradable which would break down naturally over less time, and all this aimed at a consumer who doesn't want the stupid packaging anyway, and certainly doesn't want to pay more for 'green' packaging.

It didn't make very encouraging reading, so Julian turned to the sport supplement instead. The back page was a blur of Australian cricketers celebrating a one-day Ashes warm-up game at England's expense, and knowing that Max would be disappointed, Julian folded the paper away and reverted to looking at the lights out of the window as the train entered Bath on its way to the station.

All this environmental talk and yet no action, he thought - it really was a crisis and a challenge to the whole world, yet as a whole the world did nothing about it.

He departed the train and set off on foot in search of his car, passing shops and department stores all brightly lit up inside, despite the fact that all the doors were locked and the staff had long gone home. He knew it was all to deter thieves but it really made his running round the house switching off lights look ridiculous - his efforts were all for nothing if huge chains insisted on wasting energy like this round the clock. He was firmly of the opinion that we all had to work together on this one, and he just wondered how the Commissioners planned to do it.

He drove home in thoughtful silence; in fact it didn't even occur to him to turn his radio on, and he certainly didn't miss it. He was in a surreal, almost trancelike state brought on by his tiredness, and as he arrived home at his own front door and saw the warm inviting glow of the light within, he smiled happily to himself at the prospect of the quiet, relaxing weekend ahead with his family. They were what mattered. His pressurising bosses had been making work too much of a priority in his life, and he could, for a few days at least, leave the stress of it behind. Benji came bounding up to meet him at the door but no one else seemed to hear it. Perhaps the kids were playing and Pat was cooking the dinner, but no. As he walked into the lounge he saw his son deep in conversation with a very curiously-dressed fellow, and sat either side of the coffee table they each took turns at tapping a coin across the table, each towards the other. Indeed to say they were deep in conversation was not entirely true, for as the stranger spoke words of pompous self-congratulation in excited and enthusiastic tones, Max sat, open-mouthed and wide-eyed, lapping it all up and hanging on every word.

"'Twas a blazing hell o' thunder an' shot," the stranger recounted, pounding his fist on the table as if to give his story more authenticity, "a mariner o' mine no more advanced in years than thyself, young Master, were spread all o'er the quarter deck in the blink o' an eye."

"In front of you?" Max asked in ghoulish fascination.

"Aye, Master Max, he stood but two foot hence adrift o' me, an' whence the Don ball spread his limbs o'er every corner o' the deck, an' drenched us all in English blood. T'was only his feet that remained where he stood in defiance most bold o' the Don invader, and in demonstration most loyal o' his love for his Captain."

"Wow, they would really follow you anywhere," Max said in awe.

"Aye, an' to a man didst the whole ship's company, to the very bowels o' the cauldron o' firey hell, an' back t' glorious victory. For was there smoke, young Master, cloudy smoke consumed our every waking moment an' filled our nostrils wi' brimstone most foul. For takest courage t' stand on deck on account o' the smoke which wraps' self round a man like to the cloak o' night. An' though the way o' man's agony in death is hid from his eyes by the most unnatural fog, 'tis always close, an' searches for him in the mist, then fly's it at him like to a phantom o' hell and claims him for his own."

"Such bravery..."

"Aye, a boldness hitherto unbeknown, for mine own ears were shut for the force o' the Don pounding. But whence thou ist Captain, an' pon thee bare the eyes o' the fleet, thou must letst thy fortune run its true course. I stood aloft an' raised the spirits o' mine crew wi' words o' encouragement lest the force o' the battering put their hearts t' flight. 'Twas wi' steady head an' courage abounding didst I give mine orders, an' as the splinters flew around mine ears didst I vent mine rage."

"Splinters?" Max interrupted, for these didn't sound too dangerous.

"Aye, for no hazard is there more perilous than t' the flying splinters o' a vessel struck wi' cannon shot."

"Really?"

"Indeed, young Master, for very logs o' wood be hurled amidst the deck - some to take off limbs wi' them, some t' embed em'selves deep within thine tender flesh. Below deck be hell incarnate wi' splinters in the smoky darkness, an always noise. Above on deck the very rigging doest plunge upon the unsuspecting soul, an' splinters an shot alike can carry for leagues afore they be spent an fall t' be claimed by the rolling sea." He paused a moment for effect; he could see the boy was gripped. "Aye, tis nought that keepst aboard the attentions o' the barber surgeon like to the carnage o' the flying splinters."

"And do the splinters...?"

"Mine orders, young Master, mine orders," the speaker was insistent and clearly didn't like interruptions to his recitals too readily.

"Oh yes, the orders you were giving, go on."

"Aye, in the very face o' the fiery storm didst I stand tall an' broach mine orders," he coughed to gain the full attention of the one child audience once again and as if preparing himself to re-live the incredible moment. "'Bring her about,' didst I bellow in mine fury, mine bows t' bare o' the Don galleon's prows. An' boom, mine guns didst reap a vengeance most terrible o' the Don Captain's hull an' fore-castle that butchered were both Dago mariner and soldier alike swept from the deck, an' thus didst mine smaller crew an' humble vessel board an claim for the Queen the largest ship afloat 'pon all the seas, those charted an' those hitherto not so. Some said t'was erratic, but 'twas in troth glorious, noble, heroic..."

"Ahem," Julian interrupted as he stood awkwardly in the doorway.

"Oh, Dad," Max suddenly realised his father was home, and turned to him with enthusiastic welcome. "This is a friend of mine," he announced matter-of-factly, but unable to withhold his excitement. "Sir Francis Drake."

"Really!"

"Indeed, Sir." The stranger rose and Julian was able to take in his whole bizarre appearance, from dry-again neck ruff to sword and buckled shoes. "Admiral Sir Francis Drake, sailor, adventurer and favourite o' the Queen at thy service." He gave a bow and nod of his head in respectful acknowledgement of his host. "And may I offer mine humblest and most heartfelt thanks to thee for the fine hospitality o' thine house, which even now I tarry to enjoy."

Julian wondered if the visitor could do anything humbly but offered him his hand and a single word of puzzled "Welcome."

"Thou hast heard o' me I'll warrant, so too I'll wager mine deeds, trials an' exertions be by thee also known."

"Oh, yes, first-hand," Julian replied, trying to keep a straight face as he caught his son's eye.

"Aye, but thou hast even now been privy t' mine recollections o' triumph o'er the Don Armada's flag ship," Drake caught on quickly.

"Oh, was that it?"

"Aye, mine taking o' the Duke o' Medina Sidonia's flag ship, the Don Armada put t' flight. Thou art familiar wi' the tale o' England's savin'?"

Julian thought back to his own distant classroom coverage of the event and retrieved the famous contemporary quote of the Queen herself. "God blew, and they were scattered."

"Aye, thou knowst it." Drake seated himself, looking a little dispirited, for after all his dramatisation his host's well known quote placed all the credit with the only being he seemed capable of accepting was superior to himself.

"And he told me all about the Spanish gold, and the burning of the King of Spain's beard, and when he sailed right round the world and everything," said Max.

"Aye, shalt I recount the singeing o' the Don King's beard for yon ears t' behold?" Drake offered enthusiastically. "'Twas fire ships, hulls aflame I sailed amongst the Don fleet while all hands were abed, an' like wolves unto the sheep fold didst they..."

"Um, not just now," said Julian politely. He wondered just what the hell was going on - it was as if he had entered a madhouse. "And what are you doing anyway, Max?" He indicated to the ten-pence coin which now rested halfway across the table.

"'Tis but a game o' shove ha'penny," Drake ventured lightly, "goody Finch hath outlawed all wagers, there be no harm in't."

"Oh, of course it is," Julian sighed wearily to himself. He had to find his wife, had to get a sensible account of what was going on.

"Yeah Dad," said Max excitedly, "it's an old Elizabethan game 'cept they don't make any half pennies anymore, so Drake said what about..."

"Shove groat," the visitor spread his hands as if this had been the obvious thing to suggest.

"And I said..." he looked across at his guest as if to relive the joke, "you'll be lucky." They both laughed. "It's pretty cool, isn't it? I mean he really didn't have a clue, what with coming back from the past and everything."

"Um," Julian smiled; this was ridiculous. "Well, that's inflation for you," he nodded to 'Drake' and then added in an aside to his son: "Be careful of the table though, there's a good fellow, if you scratch it we both know your mother will have your head." He turned to leave but suddenly remembered that he had some news for his son. "Did you hear the score in the cricket?"

"Nope, 'spect we lost," Max replied sounding uninterested.

"Yes by, um, four wickets I think."

"Oh." Max, unusually, didn't seem to care.

"Looks pretty bleak for the series now."

"Yeah," his son responded, but his attention was fixed on the coin which he batted across to his opponent's side of the table once more.

Julian Finch made his way to the kitchen in search of his wife, but instead found his daughter sitting at the kitchen table and reading a newspaper to another strange visitor. The man sat next to Jess, who had

189

the paper spread out in front of them, and he seemed to be very intently studying the pictures whilst his daughter read aloud. Across the table sat his wife's nephew, Rhys, who was holding hands with an attractive young woman, and as Jess paused in her reading Rhys translated the words to Welsh. The stranger, who back in his own washed and dried clothing looked like a costumed model from a medieval museum, nodded his understanding of Rhys' translation. Another boy, who Julian hadn't met before, stood over Jess looking eager and excited. It was he who noticed Julian's arrival first, and suddenly, looking rather less comfortable, he straightened up quickly and smiled awkwardly.

"Oh, hi Dad," his daughter greeted him, looking up.

"Evening all - hello Jess, hello Rhys."

"Alright Jules," Rhys returned the greeting.

"Oh dad, this is a friend of thee, Brendan, and this is Rhiannon," she introduced the other two.

"Yes, of course," Julian smiled at them both, "I think we may have met once before," he greeted Rhiannon more formally, yet annoyed with himself for not recognising her straight away.

"And this is King Arthur," Jess continued coolly, as if introducing her father to just another school friend.

"Of course it is," said Julian in bewilderment, "how nice to meet you," and he extended his hand without even thinking. He felt like he was going through the motions of a dream - perhaps he'd fallen asleep on the train and would wake up in a minute. But the stranger, who still wasn't suitably skilled in the exchanging of modern greetings, rose and clasped Julian's whole forearm with his powerful open hand. He shook the whole of Julian's arm just once and very firmly, a jolt which almost brought Julian back to himself.

The stranger, a small but stocky man with wild, grey streaked, wiry dark hair and a glistening twist of gold at his throat, fixed Julian with the most intense eyes the Civil Servant had ever seen, and with a deep voice and in tones of real sincerity he said something no doubt profound, but which Julian couldn't understand at all.

"Um." Julian blinked uncomfortably, he knew he was tired but he had to pull himself together. This just couldn't be happening.

"He says he's, um... Very privileged to meet you. He um... Wants to express his, erm, heartfelt thanks for your hospitality, and to er compliment you on your... On Jess and Max. He says they are a tribute to you, um, a credit, you know what I mean," Rhys translated automatically and unbidden.

"Right, um..." Julian was stunned.

"He um, he really is King Arthur," Rhys continued awkwardly, "he's come back you see, come here." Unsure of how best to break the ridiculous news he just stated the obvious.

"So I see... Good!" Julian had a headache now, which had sprung on him suddenly and was really beginning to take hold, a thumping at his temples. "Um." He really didn't know what to say, so he turned to Jess and asked simply "where's your mother?"

Patricia Finch had retired upstairs for a long lie-down. Her husband found her stretched out on their bed with her eyes shut, and as he entered the room she looked up quickly and welcomed him with a relieved sigh and an almost pitiful "Oh thank goodness you're home," in an exhausted, strained voice.

"Headache," he muttered feebly as he removed his tie and jacket and sat down beside her.

"Yes," she replied.

"No, I've got one," he said gently.

"Oh." In one movement his wife had passed him the tablets. "Join the club. I've got two, downstairs." She shook her head slowly and shut her eyes.

"Yes, I've just met them. Um, who are the children's entertainers?... Very authentic."

"Oh I wish they were," she replied, "two total loonies. Well the one Rhys turned up with is at least rather charming and polite, but the other is quite the barbarian. Jessica and Maxwell brought him home yesterday, apparently he slept here last night," she shuddered.

"Oh right," Julian responded casually. The truth of the matter was that he still hadn't taken it all in.

"Yes nice of them to tell us, wasn't it? I mean you bring your children up, you try to warn them about strangers, and what do they do? They find a tramp in the woods who is clearly barking mad, doesn't speak a word of English, armed to the back teeth and probably on the run from the police, and they hide him from me in my own house."

"Well, I suppose..."

"What the hell are we going to do?" asked Patricia desperately. "Jessica has kicked up a right stink already, she wants them to stay. They have to leave, darling, you have to tell them to leave."

"So, um, who are they, really?"

"Well Sir Francis Drake and King Arthur supposedly," Patricia replied sarcastically, "that's all they'll say, and the children really believe it too."

"Right-ho." Julian walked to the basin, ran the tap until the water was running really cold and splashed it on his face. "Ah," he gasped, bracing himself as he splashed himself again in an attempt to shock himself out of the daydream. "And I have to get rid of them, do I?" He smiled at his wife, who looked almost as exhausted as he felt. Such are the privileges of fatherhood he thought, for he had seen how taken his children were with the strangers and he knew the decision would not be a popular one.

"Well, what was I supposed to do darling?" Patricia asked with her eyes still firmly shut. "The last thing we want, Julian, is the police turning up - I mean, what would the neighbours think? And what other alternative did I have?"

"But they aren't dangerous, are they?"

"No," she sighed. "Not so far, and if they are acting they're good, I mean they really don't seem to know where they are."

"Oh," he pondered. "And Rhys brought one, you say?"

"Yes, he said he found him on the motorway, the Shakespeare look-a-like."

"And the kids just found the other?"

"Yeah, yesterday in the woods, or so they say. I just don't know what to believe Julian darling, I really don't."

"Bit of a strange coincidence, isn't it?"

"Oh hang on a moment darling," Patricia Finch sat up in bed, "you can't really think…"

"Just, just give me a moment to think," he waved his wife to silence. "Arthur, Drake," he mumbled to himself. They had certainly looked authentic in their period clothing, and when he'd overheard them speaking they'd sounded authentic too. He had, after all, overheard Max and his visitor in conversation without either of them knowing he was there; they were certainly keeping up the charade well.

"They're just legends," Patricia interrupted her husbands thought process, "Drake and King Arthur are just legends, Julian, any old eccentric could try to impersonate them."

"Yes but at the same time, what are the chances? It just doesn't fit, Pat. I mean Jess and Max couldn't pull off a stunt like this, and if it is all an act why would they hide them from you? Why would they hide them from anyone? And if they have been fooled, Rhys turning up with another one, its just uncanny. And come to that - what's in it for them anyway? Why would a grown man pretend?"

"Oh come off it, Julian, we both know strange men will do anything to befriend children… That's it, they must be perverts, get them out…"

"Hang on a minute. Max and Jess found one and brought him home, Rhys picked up the other - it wasn't as if they came knocking, was it? I just don't know what to think, but we mustn't jump to conclusions. If these are a couple of exhibitionists why would they choose to come here, to our house, our kids?... And you say the children are convinced they're real, that they've come back, even Rhys has said..."

"They're just legends, Julian," Patricia insisted.

"Yes, you're right," he snapped his fingers enthusiastically and felt much more alert. "There are legends about both of them, legends that they will come back. Arthur is the once and future King, isn't he? And Drake too, I remember it from school now, something about a drum..."

"Oh, not you too! These aren't living legends, they're just weirdos, if you know it any impostor would know..."

There was a knock at the door which halted the conversation, and Jess entered the room tentatively.

"Daddy you mustn't make them leave," she said quickly.

"Oh Jessica really, not again..." Her mother was utterly frustrated.

"You can't," Jess pleaded, "not until we find out why they're here."

"Yes well, I do need to speak to them really, Jess, to - well, to see what they say about that," said her father gently, "why they're here, and well, who they really are, actually."

"They are who they say they are, and they don't know why they're here themselves," Jess continued earnestly, "they really don't, they both say they just woke up, and well... here they are."

Julian Finch smiled at his daughter. "Just like that, eh?" he asked her softly.

"Yeah, but..." Jess felt so stupid, and her father, who himself could scarcely believe they were having this conversation, could see in his daughter's face that she looked genuinely frightened. "They are meant to come back Dad, when the country's in trouble... They are meant to come back and save us."

"Yeah I know, Jess," he replied soothingly, "I remember the old stories too, but..."

"It is the real Arthur, Dad, you have to believe me, you have to believe him. He can't even understand English, he's never been in a house before, all you have to do is turn the lights on and off and he freaks out. Rhys can talk to him, though he says Arthur's Welsh is very different to his own, and we think he speaks some Latin too. Drake said he recognised it."

"Oh really!" Patricia Finch rolled her eyes in desperation.

"He thought we were Saxons to start with," Jess pleaded; she was desperate for her father to believe her. "He was terrified when we found him, he held a knife to Max's throat..."

"Hah!" Patricia gasped and put a hand to her mouth in shock.

"It's alright, Mum, but if I don't tell you all this you'll never believe me. He came to try and find his fort, he had no idea how much time had gone by." She was talking so fast she was gabbling now and was getting more and more distressed. "There's a place called Caerleon near where Rhys lives, they've been talking and it turns out there was a Roman fort there once, though its ruins now. When the Romans left it became a British stronghold. It was Arthur's Camelot, Dad, you should have seen him, when Rhys told him it isn't there anymore, he just, he went all quiet and started to cry... It's really him, Dad." Her eyes pleaded with him and it was clear she wasn't going along with a joke, she really believed it; this had scared her and she needed comforting."

"And the other one, um, Drake?" he asked carefully. "I mean both of them turning up..."

"Well that's just it, don't you see? It has to be really happening because they're both here."

"Oh really!" Patricia Finch reached for the aspirins once more.

"No, Mum, you don't understand, they are both meant to come back when the country needs them. The country must really be in big trouble for them both to have come back."

"Double trouble?" Patricia looked confused.

"No, she means genuine trouble," Julian explained. "What Jess is saying is it gives the return of each one more authenticity, more plausibility. Did they know that the other had come back too?"

"No."

"And you found them at different times in different places?"

"Yes, they can't have arranged it, they don't even like each other, they're both here for the same reason..."

"So the reason must be genuine."

"Exactly." But from her mother's facial expression Jess could see she looked far from convinced. "Mum, the country really is in trouble, that's why they've come back, and that's why we can't just make them leave. Don't you see? It explains everything."

"Well, it doesn't explain what this mysterious trouble is."

"And it doesn't explain why they are here." Her father emphasised the last word.

"Yes Jessica, darling, why have they come here, to our house? There must be a million places they could have gone."

"Why Drake?" Julian asked carefully. "If there is a genuine threat to the nation then as we have just established it would be no co-incidence that he should also have come back, but why here? I mean it's a bit weird that he should end up here too, Rhys or no Rhys. Does Drake know himself?"

Jess shook her head and her eyes filled with tears.

194

"It's okay, there, there, its okay, darling," her father tried to comfort her. "I'll go and ask him myself."

"It's my fault," Jess blurted as if suddenly letting it all out, and as the tears rolled down her face she threw her arms around her father and hugged him desperately as if he could make it all better.

"How's it your fault?" He asked gently.

"Rhys found him, Rhys brought him here," Jess explained between sobs, "but I called him back. He had to come here, I think he had to come to me."

"What on earth do you mean?"

"I banged his drum... In Buckland Abbey, on the school trip... It was his house, his drum was there...The legend is that..."

"If you bang the drum he will return," her father finished the sentence for her.

"Yes," Jess wiped her eyes, "but I don't understand it - he's only meant to return if the country needs him back."

"It's alright." Julian kissed his daughter's forehead; he could feel her hot tears and could fully sense her fear. "But why did you do it?"

"I, I don't know," Jess knew she could never explain what had drawn her to do it. She'd been dreading telling her parents what she'd done because she'd been afraid they would blame her, but in her father's arms it didn't seem so hard to try. "I, I just, I was drawn to it, I couldn't stop myself, I didn't want to but... I, I just had to, I just did it... I... When he came back I thought he was a ghost, I thought he'd c-come to g-get me." Jess pressed herself against her father's chest like a small child seeking reassurance and protection, and her mother could now see how upset her daughter really was.

Patricia Finch, reluctant as she was to accept the story, cuddled her daughter too and tried to give her comfort. "It's alright Jessica, its okay, my darling girl."

"It's not Jess' fault," came a voice from the door, and looking very uncomfortable to be interrupting this emotional family moment, Brendan Johnson showed himself in the doorway. "What I mean, Mr and Mrs Finch, is that while she did bang the drum, Jess felt compelled to do it. It was as if, as if Jess was meant to be the one to do it... I think it had to be Jess, and it was out of her own control."

"Well it certainly isn't like Jessica to fiddle with things in museums," Patricia spoke sternly. "Maxwell might have done it purposefully just to try and bring him back if he thought it might work, but Maxwell wouldn't consider the consequences."

"I think the consequences might have considered Jess," Brendan answered boldly. "According to the legend it wouldn't matter how

195

many times anyone beat the drum, if there was no danger facing the country Drake would never have come."

"But the drum called me," said Jess, who blew her nose noisily and wiped her eyes on her father's handkerchief, "I heard it sound, it drew me to it, it was as if it willed me to beat it itself... And I, I just had to..."

"Exactly," Brendan smiled as confidently as he could. "Perhaps the drum knew, perhaps Drake himself knew, there is some danger looming and we had to have him back... You had to get him back Jess, you've done nothing wrong."

"Right," said Julian straightening up, and coolly, as if nothing had happened he said, "Well that's all sorted out then. Now we know who they are we need only establish what this mortal peril is that they've come back to face."

Patricia Finch looked at her husband blankly as if she didn't know quite how to respond.

"So, they can stay?" asked Jess hopefully, still wiping her eyes.

"Well, for supper at least." He looked at his wife, who nodded in reluctant acceptance. "And we'll talk and see what we can come up with. Now darling," he asked Patricia as he looked round the room, "where did I leave my jeans?"

Rhys Jenkins was handed a roll of banknotes by his uncle and was despatched to the takeaway with an order for nine bags of fish and chips. When he returned with the supper he found the others sat snugly around the kitchen table, talking amongst themselves and waiting patiently for their food. In his absence they had been discussing the circumstances which had brought them all together.

Julian Finch had studied basic Latin at school, though he had thought that once graduated into long trousers he would never have need of it again. He'd certainly never thought it would ever be of any use to him when he'd been forced to learn it and he'd never had cause to draw on it since. Yet he now brought the arduous hours of boyhood spent learning Latin vocab back into the forefront of his mind, and found himself rather bizarrely conversing not with another unfortunate schoolboy, but with a sixth-century King and an Elizabethan Admiral.

Max, highly amused by his father's linguistic application did his best to avoid anyone seeing how impressed he was by simply taking the micky instead.

"Who threatens the peace o' the Queen an' her people? What foreign churl wouldst seek war pon our soil? An' wherefore is the sovereignty of our fair isle endangered?" Drake had asked the question in Latin and it was considered by all.

"It's Summer. Harvest time," Arthur had added. "The men will be in the fields, we need more time to raise a war-band. What number is our standing army, Julian? For we must locate our foe and know his own strength before we decide where best to rally our forces."

"Well that's just it, Sire," Julian had replied, unsure of how best to address the ancient King, "we don't know who's out to get us or where they're coming from. I mean we have enemies, extremists, fanatics, but they're terrorists, we aren't at war with any recognised Nation State at the present time, and although the Home Office keeps trying to describe the security level as high-risk there's been no indication of any imminent strike."

"Well, where are these terrorists?" enquired the King. "We must pick our ground to face them, there's so much to do." Arthur had become excited, and banging his fist on the table he'd risen to his feet and spoken with passion. To Jess, who couldn't understand a word he was saying, he'd looked revitalised, as if he thought he could put all his grief behind him by throwing his energies into one last great campaign. "I shall raise my standard and call all Christendom to me. This requires logistics and planning. We need armour, weaponry, discipline, leadership, a chain of command. We need horses, archers, oxen to carry the baggage and all that is required to keep an army in the field. We need fodder for the animals, rations for the men, and a means to finance this endeavour. Scouts must be sent out, for we need intelligence. When the foe falls upon my shield wall I wish it to be on ground and terms of my choosing; we must be ready."

"Aye, an' the battle must be joined at sea," Drake had cut in. "The invader canst not be given leave t' set a foot 'pon our sacred shores. Shalt he be hounded, raked wi' ball, driven off an' sunk afore he can land but one jolly boat ashore, his whole army drowned lest yon shield wall be humbled an' put t' flight, cut likest t' dry grass by his black powder an' shot." Drake had sneered at Arthur and began to strut like a peacock around the room. "Thou knowst nought o' the sea, mine ancient monarch. 'Tis mine own destiny which calls an knocks at the door o' victory an' fortune. Goodwife Finch," he'd turned to his hostess and reverted to his Elizabethan English, "bringst thou thy Don sherry that we shalt all drink mine health, Admiral Drake, terror o' the seas, scourge o' the Queen's enemies an' defender o' her humble subjects."

"They will break through while you stand and prance in front of the mirror," Arthur had mocked him, "as you gaze at your own reflection and salute your own misplaced greatness the enemy will simply sneak round behind you. What size your fleet, Drake? What bottomless inventory of resources have you at your disposal? You have my blessing to sit in the sea and be our first line of defence, but we must know and understand our enemy before complacency gets the better of us." Drake had just gawped, rather taken aback by the put-down, as Arthur had continued unabated. "No, I must away to Brittany, there are many men loyal to me there, and then to Caerleon and the valleys beyond, when the threat is known the men will come forth from their homesteads... Oh to gaze on Caerleon ..." He'd re-seated himself and a more sombre expression of reflection had spread across his face.

"Man canst not face cannon wi' shields," Drake'd piped up again. "Old Arthur o' Albion livest in a dream world. A pox o' the old man's spurning! I carest not be he monarch or nave, I shalt cut the tongue from his mouth were't to utter one slur more 'pon mine reputable deeds."

He had spoken in English as if playing to an audience, and Jess, who had thought it rather cowardly of Drake to make this last pledge in a language Arthur couldn't understand, picked up the theme herself.

"You can't face machine guns with cannon either."

Julian Finch, in his broken Latin, had brought the grim reality of their predicament back to the arguing, time-lost pair.

"They could come from anywhere, they could bomb us from aeroplanes, they could land tanks. You speak of knowing our enemy, knowing their strength, but if it is terrorists we must look out for, then they could already be here. They live in the community, they hide in small groups, they make explosives, they blow people up when they aren't expecting it, they won't meet either of you in pitched battle. These guys have much more sophisticated weapons than anything we might have at our disposal, and they could strike anywhere unannounced. We can call the Police, the Army, but if this risk is imminent then who knows. They might have chemical weapons, perhaps even a nuclear device; perhaps it's even primed and ready to go."

"Nuclear?" Drake and Arthur had both frowned, they had no idea what he was talking about, but they could see the look of concern on their host's face and it worried them.

"One bang is all it takes," Julian explained. "It's radioactive, you wouldn't understand it, I can't understand it... It's just incredibly dangerous. One blast of sufficient size could take the whole country out in seconds. They'd both looked blankly at him, they couldn't begin to understand such things so Julian had tried a few lame attempts to put the scenario in terms he'd hoped they would. "Like a ship's magazine," he explained to Drake, "or, or a fire arrow which just burns everything up spontaneously... It would be hell," he'd said simply. "Just like hell opening up like a trap door and burning everything up in one go."

That had them worried. These were words which struck a chord with both visitors, they could relate to the image, and it frightened them. Max didn't help though, he'd collapsed in stitches.

"S-sorry," he laughed as Benji ran to the door yapping in welcome of the returning Rhys. "I c-can't control it any... anymore. Do you... Do you know what you sound like?" Max held his gut and rocked as he looked at his father.

"Maxwell Finch, this is serious," his mother grabbed his arm.

"But he sounds so, so silly... It's hilarious, you ha ha, you speaking Latin. Aha, ha ha..."

"Max stop it," Jess scolded him.

"No," Julian smiled, "Perhaps he's right. We should try to be a little more light-hearted. And anyway," he turned to his guests, "we won't get anywhere fighting amongst ourselves. Let's at least get this food inside us, while we all still have tongues to eat it," he glanced at the impetuous Drake, who sat back, arms folded.

The meal was a first for both guests, but they seemed to find it palatable and there was less left to take off his fellow diners' plates than Max had hoped for.

Drake cut the glistening batter from his fish to expose the fleshy white fillet beneath, but it was the chips he approached with caution.

"From which vegetable be this food begotten, Goody Finch?" he asked as he poked suspiciously at his chips with his knife. "Or be it not begot but grown in state?"

"It's a chip," said Max unhelpfully with his own mouth overfull, and he left his sister to explain further.

"It's just potato, sliced up and deep fried. It's got salt and vinegar on it, try it, you might like it."

"Potato," Drake said in surprise. "But 'tis the root Raleigh brought oe'r from the new world." He impaled one on the strange four pronged fork, which his hostess had set before him, and brought it to his eye to examine it more closely. The others were all eating it, Arthur greedily, with his fingers, and the children were wolfing it down so it had to be alright. "I recall, didst I spake unto the Queen 'twould... Ahem," he coughed and quickly corrected himself. "Meanst I, I recall Essex spake unto the Queen 'twould ne'er catch on."

"Oh yeah," said Jess, "well you were... ahem,," she pretended to cough too. "I mean Essex was wrong about that, wasn't he?"

"Looks like you've been wrong about a few things," said Rhys, and instantly regretted it, hoping that Drake wouldn't mention the smoking in front of his Aunt. Fortunately Brendan spoke before Drake could reply.

"Yes its our national dish now you know, fish and chips."

"And curry I fear," Julian added, "but I think that little surprise can wait for another night, we don't want anyone to think we are trying to poison them."

"Don't you want them, then?" Max asked as he made a lunge at Drake's plateful with his fork.

"Hold, young Master." Drake brushed the invading fork aside with a sweep of his knife, and then cautiously he brought a forkful of chips to his mouth. He chewed carefully, enjoying all eyes but Arthur's fixed upon him, for the King was busily swallowing up the debris from his own plate; he'd never tasted anything like it before but it certainly wasn't going to the dog.

"'Tis good," Drake announced after a thoughtful pause, "enough salt t' keep a mariner at sea for o'er a month be charged on every forkful, but 'tis good indeed."

"I thought they'd like it," Rhiannon said quietly to Rhys, "I told you they would."

"Yeah, yeah," he said in response, and then to his cousin, "Bad luck Max, there goes your chance of seconds I'd say."

"You can have a bit of mine if you want, Max," Brendan made the offer, though in truth, although he could easily have accommodated his whole plateful. He had already made the decision to leave some so as not to seem too greedy. Max needed no second invitation and took rather more off Brendan's plate than he'd hoped and anticipated.

"To mine ear and eye," Drake leaned over the table towards his hostess, "yon King hath a manner for consumption like to a sow in pig."

Arthur's lack of table etiquette had not gone unnoticed by Patricia, and although she'd grimaced as he'd hacked his fish to pieces with his knife and piled food into his mouth with his fingers, she had deliberately maintained a front of unconcern in order to try and make Arthur, who now lounged back in his chair with one hand on his gut and the other picking at his teeth, feel comfortable.

"Well, Mr Drake, we must try to remember where he's come from, mustn't we?" she replied.

"The Dark Ages," said Rhys simply, but any attempt to make excuses for the King were totally foiled as he emitted a huge belch, and a look of contentment crossed his face.

"Cool!"

"Don't get any ideas, Maxwell Finch," Patricia turned on her son, "you must not be influenced by such crudity."

"So mum," Jess latched on to her mother's previous comment, "you agree then. They really have come back, they really are who they say they are?"

"Well I, I didn't say..."

"How many mad men speak Latin around the dinner table?"

"Who hasn't heard of fish and chips?" Max added.

"Or table manners?" Rhiannon piped in. "He doesn't even know how to use a fork."

"Or terrorism, planes, bombs, tanks?" said Brendan.

"Well I, I didn't... That is to say, I never..."

"The Jury is still out," said Julian Finch firmly in a tone designed to put an end to the table-wide assault on his wife. "The coincidences appear more than circumstantial, they deserve the benefit of the doubt and will stay until we've had a chance to sort this out." The children cheered in victory, and seeing the delight in their faces Drake and Arthur both smiled in understanding. "Besides, darling," Julian added to reassure his wife, "it's not every night you have a king sit at your table, is it?" She smiled feebly back at him and tried not to look disappointed, but deep down she knew it was the right decision.

Arthur, who perhaps had sensed that his board and lodging had been hanging in the balance, rose from the table and knelt before his hostess. Taking her hand with a gentleness and sensitivity he'd not exhibited since his arrival, he kissed the back of it to signal his gratitude and nodded his head to her as he rose. He was truly grateful for the way the children had befriended him, for they had already showed him so much of the strange ways and times he had returned to, and their father was now proving a useful source of information and stability. He slapped his host warmly on the back as he returned to his seat, almost knocking Julian off his own chair and causing him a coughing fit. Arthur could see that this Finch was a good hearted man, a true patriot who could so easily have chosen to turn him over to his enemies, and he suddenly began to think that perhaps it was no accident that he sat now in this man's home. For whilst it was his destiny to return, perhaps his own fate was bound up with Julian's, he knew he would need people loyal to him if he was to succeed and counted himself most fortunate to have found the Finch's.

As Patricia wiped the greasy deposit from her hand, which as a sad consequence of his inability to master cutlery Arthur had transferred to her from his own fingers, Drake also rose. Desperate not to be outdone by the scruffy barbarian, who he lamented had beaten him to it, he stooped into a hugely over-exaggerated and elegant bow, ruffling his cape out behind himself as he too came down to take and kiss the lady's hand.

"Goodwife Finch," he spoke sincerely and with feeling as if addressing his beloved Queen, "'tis an honour indeed for as humble a seaman as mineself to find such a welcome within thine walls. I shalt call all such blessings on this house as God willing shalt provide, an' proffer to thee, goody Finch, mine most eternal gratitude in all perpetuity." He stroked her hand warmly as he rose, and Patricia blushed at the flattery.

Max and Brendan turned to each other and Brendan coughed under his breath as he said simply, "Humble!"

Max more crudely mimed the putting of fingers into his mouth, as if Drake's courtly approach made him feel sick.

"Well um, what now?" Asked Patricia Finch in embarrassment.

"Well," Julian pondered his options aloud. His long and tiring day had become all the more complicated since his return home, but in all the confusion he'd shaken off his headache, and this if nothing else was reason to celebrate. "A beer, I think."

"Men!" Patricia shook her head in disbelief.

"Well, how better to entertain such distinguished guests? Only being hospitable, Pat," he grinned. "Max, my boy, go and get some beer from the cupboard, the decent bottled stuff, oh, and a bottle-opener."

"Oh, can I...?"

"No. But mum might make you and Brendan a shandy if you ask her nicely. Bring one for each of us, me, Arthur, Drake and Rhys, four, Max..." he called after his disappearing son.

He needn't have worried about Max miscounting, for when he returned he carried two boxes of bottled beer and placed them on the table with aplomb.

"Ah, ale," Drake's face lit up at the sight of the Alban liquid in the bottles, "now canst we partake o' a counsel o' war."

"Right, I see." Patricia Finch rolled her eyes and started to gather up the plates from around the table, "I suppose I'd better get some beds made up too." But she wasn't alone. Rhiannon and Jess took the hint and got up to assist her as Julian passed the beer round.

"I think tomorrow," Julian smiled knowingly at his daughter, "that these two gentlemen will need a trip to town, they may look a little less conspicuous in contemporary clothes...."

"Ah now, Dad..." Jess tried to explain.

"Especially as my jeans clearly didn't fit."

He smiled at her again, and Jess, so relieved that her father had made it all so easy for her, gave him a hug, a kiss on the cheek, and said gently in his ear: "Thank you for understanding."

It was true that both guests were much broader and stockier than their host, though King Arthur was also considerably shorter, and both made light work of their beer using their bulk to easily slosh it away. They were both on their second bottles as Julian tried to explain the importance of assimilation.

"You will need new clothes," he explained in Latin. "Modern clothes will be very important because we won't want people to work out who you are too quickly."

Arthur nodded in understanding, but Drake, reverting to English, rather missed the point.

"But 'tis for the very reason o' recognition that Drake hast returned unto thee," he ventured carelessly. "'Tis Sir Francis the nation calls, not a lowly serf. To no nave doest the nation bid return but to her hero, mine own true self whom she keepeth close unto her heart."

"Yeah but you've got to wait until the time is right," Rhys tried to explain, "we can't have your cover blown too quickly."

"It's still you two under the clothes," Brendan added.

"Precisely," Julian continued. "But we can't reveal your true identity yet, at least not until we know who the enemy are. It's as I explained; if they are terrorists then we will play at their game and keep you secret until the time is right. Announce you too early and you would be all over the TV and the papers, in minutes every one would know you were back."

"Mine fame wouldst be widespread." Drake brightened at the idea and his face lit up.

"All in good time, Sir Francis. Whoever threatens us probably has no idea you have returned, we should keep it that way and know our own enemy before we make you known." Julian turned to Arthur, who had missed out on this last exchange, but Rhys, speaking Welsh and keen to remain useful, quickly translated for him.

As Rhys explained the importance of the element of surprise Arthur nodded approvingly and gulped down his ale. It wasn't mead but it was good, and as the ale coursed through his veins he was elated at the prospect of campaigning and felt heartened that here he sat around a circular table with loyal men he could trust. Well, he reflected, two men he could trust, two boys of noble character and a blithering peacock, but Drake knew the sea and it would be foolish to dismiss his usefulness. He too was a legend in his own age, and whilst Arthur found it hard to see just why and how he had been so successful, he knew he must also have returned for some purpose. Time and the revelation of destiny would tell all, and if he was half as brave as he kept indicating, Drake should prove a formidable ally in battle.

What frustrated Arthur was Drake's apparent inability to see where everyone else was coming from. United they stood more chance, but he feared that Drake's sense of adventure might get the better of him and lead him after his own glory. Finch's counsel seemed good to him, and keen to voice his approval the King spoke firmly to Drake in Latin.

"We will assimilate as would a scout and better shall we know our enemy, but we shall retain our own clothing underneath the modern vestments so when the time and place be right we can reveal ourselves, and so shall we take the fight to our people's enemies."

Drake took it in. There was no denying the sense of this logic, for they had to lie low for their own safety, at least for the moment, but he cast his eye mournfully around the table at the drab and simple looking clothes of his fellow drinkers. Master Rhys had told him that his own britches were 'designer,' whatever that meant, but compared to his own gaudy attire they held little appeal to him. He consoled himself by considering the pure elation of being able, in a flash, to transform himself, and he smiled as he pictured the terror on the faces of his enemies when they realised it was no normal Englishman but 'El Draque' whom they faced.

Max, who had finished his shandy almost as quickly as Arthur had finished his beer, asked his dad quickly if he could have another, and Julian, who did not want his son to feel excluded, replenished his glass, but ensured that the mixture was more in favour of the lemonade this time. Brendan, who had been sipping at his own politely, could see the disappointment register on his classmate's face as Julian mixed the drink.

"Hast thou no small beer for thy charges," Drake asked, "that thou doest add water to thy offspring's cup?"

"No," Julian explained, "but this is more than strong enough for young Max here."

"Small beer?" Max enquired.

"They used to make several brews from the same mixture," Brendan informed him, "each one was slightly weaker and the weakest was called small beer. Because boiling the water to brew the beer got rid of infections they drank lots of beer in Drake's time, as the normal water was so polluted."

"Cool," and Max eyed Brendan with a new respect. He'd always thought him a geek, the uncoordinated kid who was always last to be picked for sports teams - he was a swot, and why else would he get on with his own swotty sister? But to know so much about brewing and beer, perhaps he wasn't the square he'd always taken him for.

"Polluted water, then," said Rhys, "and polluted water now, not much difference really is there? It probably had less chemicals in it then even if it has less bugs in it now."

"Aye, and thou canst draw water from thy very tip," Drake indicated to the sink behind them.

"Tap," Max corrected him with a snigger.

"Canst thou but imagine the smell that comest from a barrel o' water whence after fourteen months at sea 'tis opened and passed for t' parch the thirst o' a moaning, sun soaked crew? 'Tis o' a like t' lead unto mutiny; oft have I thought t'would be better t' suffer't an embrace the crippling thirst."

"Taste it," Max offered, pushing his glass across the table and into Drake's hand.

"If thou wilt." Drake took the glass, and opening his throat wide he tipped the contents into his mouth as he leaned his head backwards. His intention to down the drink in one movement, thus demonstrating his manliness, backfired badly as the lemonade tickled in his gullet and shot up his nostrils.

Coughing and spluttering, he returned the glass to the table as the contents streamed from his nose, and the Elizabethan adventurer, scourge of the Spanish fleet and terror of the seas, was reduced to coughing fits between eruptions of "poison," and "thou trickster, knave," and "churl," whilst all around the table heightened his embarrassment by laughing at his misfortune raucously. His host explained that he'd "only done the elephant trick," and the tubby boy that "Lemonade is full of bubbles," but this made him feel little better.

Just as he was getting over it Patricia Finch re-entered the room, brandishing a small silver-coloured box. It having been decided that the guests were to stay, she was keen to preserve the moment forever in order to add it to the family album. Patricia thought an un-posed photo would be best, and gave no warning before taking the picture. The resulting flash of the camera startled Arthur, who thought for a second that a lightning bolt must have severed the room, and Drake, who presumed a pistol must have been fired braced himself for the impact of the bullet and sound of the explosion in the mini-second after the flash registered, but no noise came.

After the camera's function had been explained and the digital image reviewed at length, several more highly posed photos were taken and the fear and uncertainty of the unknown peril facing the country was once again forgotten as another modern novelty provided complete

205

distraction. Drake demanded the opportunity to pull all kinds of faces for the 'instant portrait' box and recounted the hours he had stood as the great painters of Europe struggled to replicate his noble pose and expressions of grandeur.

Arthur, who detached himself slightly from the good-humoured banter once the wonder of the device had been revealed to him, sat in thought considering yet again his purpose in this much changed world as another all too real demonstration of how times had changed was brought home to him.

Julian Finch, meanwhile, noticed the time and switched on the television in the hopes of catching the evening news. Discussion had revealed little of any potential threat and he wanted to see if any breach of national security had been spotted by the media.

They were just in time to see the end of a report about the devastation caused by flash floods in Bangladesh before the anchor man moved on to the next article.

"And sticking with the environment, the European Commission signed up to the European Environmental Act today in Brussels. The Act is set to commit the European Community to take positive steps towards combating climate change." The pictures cut to show images of Britain's two Commissioners greeting their European colleagues and lining up for a photo shoot, but the anchor man's voice continued over the pictures. "Britain's two Commissioners, Sir Denis Hitoadie, the Duke of Man, and Sir Morgan Dredmor, currently hold the directive on environmental policy, and they are thought to have been instrumental in the instigation of the Act."

"Hey, isn't that your boss, Dad?" asked Max, as he recognised the Duke of Man's enormous shape in centre screen.

"Yes, Max, that's the toad alright."

Jess noted another figure looking on in the background. She instantly recognised Sir Morgan Dredmor as the VIP at Wookey Hole, and a shiver ran down her spine as she noticed the same sinister sneer crossing his face as he watched his colleagues with approval.

"The signing of the Act today gives it the Commission's endorsement and prepares the way for the European Council to sign up to the Act on Monday. But whilst the Act sets out Europe's intentions to deal robustly with climate change by reducing emissions and pollution and dealing with waste more suitably, sceptics fear it does not adequately provide for how these objectives will be achieved. Well, earlier today at the press conference Britain's Commissioners had this to say…"

The programme cut to show footage of Sir Denis Hitoadie and Sir

Morgan Dredmor standing at a lectern and preparing to address Europe's press. The Duke clumsily shuffled his paperwork with his fat fingers and cleared his throat thoroughly before starting to read out his prepared statement.

"Today, the groundwork for a new Europe has been set. This will be a fresh smelling, toxin-free continent, free of pollutants, chemical and nuclear waste. A Europe fully capable of dealing with all the by-products of our modern consumer age and fully equipped to generate a significant percentage of its energy supply from natural and sustainable means. The future is upon us, and the Commission today, as one man with one mind, are united behind the concept of fully embracing this vision of the future." He finished speaking and glanced down at his notes in front of him as he folded them away. His body language was a clear indication to the assembled journalists that he was not inviting questions, but this wasn't going to stop them.

"Your Grace," a voice piped up off-camera from the back of the room. "Terry George, BBC. What is Britain's place in this new Europe?"

Hitoadie made no attempt to answer, but Sir Morgan Dredmor fielded the reply and fixed the camera with a cold icy stare.

"Britain has a most exciting place, a central role, a pivotal role in our combined vision of the future. It's fair to say that Britain will be at the centre of policy."

"Toby Grant, ITV," another voice shouted up. "Do you expect the European Council to sign up to the Act unanimously on Monday?"

"I fully and confidently anticipate that the Council will take the lead of the Commission, and that they too will endorse the Act and make their commitment to the cause known."

"But what are the policies? What measures are being considered to bring about the aims of the Act?"

"Such measures as are necessary will of course have to be considered by the Commission in due time. The Council have every confidence in the Commission to do what is best for Europe, as seasoned politicians and experts in their field." Sir Morgan's voice was cold and frosty. "I have spoken to the Prime Minister personally and he has been fully supportive of the aims and intentions behind the Act. He has made it very clear to the Duke and myself that he is behind the concept of this legislation. I anticipate that likewise the rest of the Council will rightly back the Act on Monday; it is time we took positive steps to clear up our continent."

"Tom Bowes, Channel Four," came another voice. "Sir Morgan, yourself and the Duke are the Commissioners with the Directive on the environment - surely you must have some idea as to how the aims of the Act will be made a reality?"

"I'm not at liberty to discuss any such position," Sir Morgan scornfully brushed the question aside.

"You must have some idea," came another unidentified voice.

Sir Morgan looked irritated now, but decided to present a simple closed reply.

"It is not procedural for full secondary legislation to be in place prior to primary legislation being passed," he said, but after a smirk he couldn't resist but expand on this, if only in the hopes of preventing any further questions. "You can, however, rest assured that any changes made will be for the common European good. We, as Commissioners, aren't meant to seek nor take instruction from any government or other body, it is the citizens of our continent for whom we act. I can however advise," he hinted, "that expensive methods of recycling are to be urgently reviewed in favour of increased landfill."

"Will there be sacrifices to our lifestyle?" another voice chipped in.

The Duke of Man took this question, though it was clear from his posture that he had every intention of terminating the press conference before it became any more heated. Unfortunately for him, his attempt to appease the press with an uplifting positive reply backfired and proved only to bait them further.

"There are always sacrifices for a noble cause," he began. "And for the greater good of our Europe, and indeed our World as a whole, we must be prepared, when the time comes, to make those minor sacrifices as are necessary to ensure the future of this planet for our children and our children's children."

"What sacrifices?" someone shouted.

"What changes?" blurted someone else.

"What stage is the secondary legislation at?"

"How will the Act change Europe?"

But to all these, Sir Morgan Dredmor simply waved his hands and shook his head. "No more questions, gentlemen," he said abruptly, "but thank you for your kind attention." The two British Commissioners were seen quickly scurrying from the room, and as they left the Duke could be seen warmly slapping his colleague on the back as if they had come through a real trial, a test of their metal at the hands of the assembled press.

"Well, after that heated press conference what's your take on it, Roger Lineen, our correspondent today in Brussels?"

The news reader passed the focus to their 'man on the ground', and Lineen, who stood pictured outside a very important looking building, paused a moment as the end of the link registered through his earpiece, and then began his reply.

"Well, as interesting as that press conference was, it really hasn't shed any light on how the Act proposes to make those changes. You heard the Duke say there that this will be an exciting new Europe, and he also implied at the end that there will be some changes. However, whilst the Duke referred to the concepts as noble - and I don't doubt they are, as tackling climate change, waste and pollution must be high on all our agendas, and it's encouraging that the Commission are so committed to that - Sir Morgan listed landfill, recycling and sustainable energy sources as priorities but declined to divulge any further information as to what will actually be done to make Europe this cleaner, fresher place."

"So, how will this policy be decided?" asked the anchorman from the studio.

"Well, of course if the Council, which is made up of representatives, usually the Premiers, of each Member State, signs up to the Act on Monday, they will make the European Environmental Act, or EEA as it has become known, law. If that happens then the responsibility passes back to the Commission to generate any secondary legislation; that's any additional laws which might be needed to make the aims of the Act a reality."

"And presumably, Roger, as Commissioners with the Environmental Directive, a kind of portfolio of the environment, Sir Morgan and the Duke of Man could prove instrumental in devising any such additional laws?"

"Yes indeed, and it's hard to believe they don't already have some idea of how they will instigate it. They appeared there to dodge a few questions on the subject but both are canny politicians and I don't doubt that the Duke and Sir Morgan will have a very important part to play in any future changes to European environmental policy. If the Act is passed, we will really be in their hands.

"What's also interesting is that a full draft of the Act hasn't been made available to the press, and as such it's very hard for the media to accurately report back on any proposals made by the Act."

"This is boring," said Max carelessly, "can't we turn over?"

"Just a moment, Max." Julian sat transfixed, this was the very same Act he'd been working on, the draft of which he'd been tasked to proofread, and even he had not been allowed to see a full text version. The closest he'd got to seeing the missing Protocol Fifteen had been when Hitoadie had covered his copy of it with the Financial Times when Julian had taken the finished draft to the Commissioner's office.

"I think we can anticipate that the Council will sign up to the Act," Roger Lineen continued. "Sir Morgan certainly seemed confident that they will, and it's to be expected. They have, after all, already discussed the proposed Act in its very early stages, as did the European Parliament, whom you may remember raised some initial questions regards the potential placement of wind farms in the Bay of Biscay. The current Act has obviously been re-drafted following that. The Council are supposed to take instruction from the expert Commissioners, not the other way round, and the Parliament have now had their chance, so there is really nothing to stand in the way of this Act becoming law. All agree it's about time Europe committed to doing something about the environmental crisis."

"Roger, thank you very much," said the newsreader as the pictures cut again to the comfortable studio. "The Government have announced radical plans to overhaul the schooling system in England and Wales..." But as he continued with the next article, Julian Finch sat dumbfounded by what he had just seen and heard.

"Sounds like a done deal," said Rhys, who like Max found the whole thing very boring.

"Yes," Julian observed, "they've certainly whisked it through pretty quickly."

"Is that what you've been working on?" Max asked his father.

"Well not me personally, the Commissioners have been drafting it, they've worked really hard. I've just been checking it through really. There's really something not right there, they really ought to be more open about the Act - not disclosing it to the press is just odd."

"Politics is boring," Max declared as he tapped Drake on the shoulder and reached for his Playstation games console. "Let's play..."

"Ah, but Statesmen make fine sport, Master Max, whence poor diplomacy leadeth man unto the glories o' war."

"Politicians only like war, Sir Francis, because they can play with other people's lives," Jess rebuked him, "other people's countries, and usually without even getting their hands dirty. You soldiers and sailors are just like pawns, like chess pieces to the politicians."

"Mistress Jessica, mine own destiny be within mine own grasp," Drake defended himself.

"Of course," said Jess under her breath, "but you're a pirate, aren't you?"

Arthur, curious to know if any news of the enemy had been gained, asked Julian quickly in Latin. He was disappointed to learn that it hadn't and, bored of the television and the constant chatter which he couldn't understand, he busied himself by flicking through some colourful reference books which Jess had thoughtfully provided for him.

Patricia Finch took her hostess duties very seriously, and entered the room again with the announcement that beds had been made up for Drake and Arthur in the garage, and for Rhys on Max's bedroom floor. She also declared that she would be taking Brendan home shortly as his mother would 'no doubt be wondering where he was.'

Rhys whispered a few words to Rhiannon, and then likewise announced to the room that it was probably time he dropped her off at home too, and Rhys, Rhiannon, Brendan and Patricia left for the cars after hurried goodbyes.

The news had moved on to the sport and was covering a debrief of England's capitulation at Lords in front of Australia's mighty bowlers, but to Julian's surprise Max was too busy explaining how to operate the games console keypad to Drake to even notice.

With the sport report completed, the weather man was interrupted as the news reader dramatically announced that there was breaking news:

"This just in." He read the autocue almost in amusement. "Security staff at the Tower of London have just announced that the Castle has been burgled tonight. "But the thieves did not make off with any valuable works of art, and they made no attempt to take the crown jewels..."

The pictures showed brief CCTV footage of two figures in boiler suits, and with balaclavas covering their heads, bumbling along the Castle battlements. One carried a sack over his shoulder, and the other tripped over his own feet and almost fell flat on his face before the two disappeared out of shot by hopping over the wall and lowering themselves down a rope.

"The sack is believed to contain the Tower's ravens. The birds are crowd favourites and are residents of the Castle and have been confirmed missing in a statement from the Tower tonight. I'm told it's unclear at the moment why the birds might have been taken, and if anything else has been confirmed as missing... And we will have more on that breaking news and on our main headlines on our twenty-four-hour channel throughout the night."

As the ending music for the news began to blurt out, Julian switched the television off. "Strange, that," he said.

"Dad - that's it." Max was wide-eyed and earnest.

"What do you mean?" Julian asked him, and both he and Jess eyed Max with expressions of concern.

"The ravens," Max began, "the legend says that when the ravens leave the Tower the country will fall. I've been there, me and mum read

211

it ourselves. Someone's stolen the ravens, don't you see? It means…"

"The enemy have started to make their move," Jess finished the sentence. "They have begun their preparation, their strike could be about to come, it could come any minute."

Whatever this danger was that Drake and Arthur had come back to save the nation from was almost upon them. Only the unknown, unseen, unheard enemy knew where their strike would come, and their plan was now clearly in operation.

"What's all the flapping about?" Arthur asked of Drake in Latin.

"Some birds have gone missing," the other replied. "I see nothing to squawk about," and the two shrugged their shoulders, oblivious to the potential peril indicated by the invoking of the old superstitious myth.

Chapter Twelve – Julian's Dream

That night Julian Finch, tired as he was, couldn't sleep. His mind was alive, his brain racing as he tried desperately to keep his body still, but he just couldn't stop thinking.

He needed more time, more time to work out what the danger was, and where it was coming from. It was clear that if Max was right and the taking of the ravens was significant, then their absence coinciding with Drake and Arthur's arrival had to suggest that the unidentified enemy was closing in, for if their attack was not imminent why would Drake and Arthur be under his roof?... And why his roof anyway? What had brought them here rather than somewhere else?

He rolled over, as he'd done so many times already since he had got into bed, and shuffled his position in another desperate attempt to get comfortable. He was getting frustrated with himself now, but had to take great care not to nudge and wake the sleeping figure of his wife beside him.

He positioned himself side-on with his eyes tightly shut, and tried to blank his mind. He hoped sleep could finally take him and he told himself that in the morning, when refreshed, he would find it so much easier to think things through... Blackness, but only for a few seconds. The harder he tried to think of nothing the harder it was for blankness to clear his thoughts, and then, as if there was nothing more unpleasant to disturb his attempts of peace, the grinning, disembodied face of Trevor Rindburn came prancing into his head, the yellowing teeth protruding from his mouth to show their blackened tops in a filthy leer. "Heroes," the pseudo-image announced in Julian's troubled mind. He immediately tried to dismiss the image, but he could not. "That is the depth of our leader's great genius," the lifelike Rindburn continued in an echo of the conversation he'd exchanged with the real personage over lunch earlier in the day.

It had been only hours ago, but it could have been an ice age away to Julian, who tried to banish the leering face from his mind in one last bid to be swallowed up by sleep. He tried his best, but within seconds the bodiless, big-nosed visage of Nigel Sludboil drew up alongside the toothy Rindburn in Julian's mind's eye. "Already decided, isn't it," Sludboil announced with all the vigour and enthusiasm that he too had demonstrated in Julian's small office earlier in the day. "What do you think all these private meetings have been about...? It won't be worth your job to get cheeky with us. There are going to be some changes around here shortly." The flashbacks continued, and Rindburn's hovering head chipped in again to add to them. 'Great men both, and wise, truly blessed with a vision of the future.'

Julian sat bolt upright in bed, lifting the duvet and causing Patricia to groan in her sleep and roll away from him in an attempt to keep warm. As his mind returned to full consciousness the Duke and Sir Morgan came to prominence in his waking memory. "Cheers." They tapped glasses together once again in a replay of their toast to their precious Protocol Fifteen... Protocol Fifteen, Julian thought, what the heck was in that document? He had to get his hands on that last section of the European Environmental Act, had to find out what it was all about.

"The EEA and what follows is all for the greatest good." Sludboil's clumsy salute to his masters registered once again in Julian's brain... "What follows," Julian whispered to himself - they had said pre-drafted, pre-arranged... "Drafted and agreed on." The image of Sludboil let slip once more, that's what he'd said... Secondary legislation already in place, or at least pre-agreed and ready to bring in.

"Here's to NESA." The two images of the British Commissioners raised their glasses once more in his memory as he flashed back to his view of them seated in their office through the open door. "Protocol Fifteen is none of your business, Finch," the memory of Sir Morgan sneered at him now, and the fat toad, comfortably reclined in his huge arm chair, chortled at him once more. "Ah, the old elusive Protocol Fifteen, eh. Don't worry about that, Sir Morgan and myself have written that up personally."

Julian clicked his fingers; it had been staring him in the face. Clearly all the private meetings Sir Morgan and the Duke had been having with the other Commissioners had been in order to broker a deal, not just for the EEA, but for "what follows..." - NESA.

'NESA', whatever it contained, had to be the secondary legislation they were going to bring in on the back of the EEA. The Commission were up to no good. They knew exactly what measures they would bring in once the EEA was passed and they were keeping them from the media.

He lay back, flat on his back with his feet crossed over each other and his arms folded under his head. It could be nothing, he told himself. It could bear no relation to Drake and Arthur's appearance, but Protocol Fifteen was a section added to the Act by his bosses and agreed to by the rest of the Commission. He hadn't seen it, the press hadn't seen it, and he was sure the European Council hadn't seen it either.

The image of Rindburn suddenly interrupted his thought process again, as if on cue to confirm his own suspicions. 'Lord no, Finch, have you ever known a Politician to actually read legislation?'... That was it. He had to see it, had to get a copy of it, and he thought he knew where he might be able to find one.

Once more Julian closed his eyes and tried to relax; gradually his heart rate slowed as he pondered his options more carefully. He would try tomorrow, and regardless of what he might find he knew from the raven's disappearance that he would have little time to plan his next move from there. He thought, he planned, he racked his tired brain long into the night, and at some small hour, and without even realising it, Julian Finch finally fell asleep.

The morning was bright, the clear sky letting the sun warm the bedroom, and Julian Finch had overslept. Woken by the sounds of healthy competition from outside, he made his way downstairs to find his hard-working wife clearing away the breakfast things while his enthusiastic son was doing his best to introduce his two eccentric house guests to the delights of 'headers and volleys,' in the back garden, the yapping Benji snapping at their heels.

Drake, who appeared to have grasped the intricacies of the simple game, was showing a keen interest combined with a worrying lack of coordination, while Max was desperately trying to include Arthur, who clearly wasn't so interested, by taking every opportunity to pass the football to him.

Letting out a victorious whoop, Drake struck the ball full pelt with his right, causing it to ricochet noisily off the garden fence, and his hostess, who was filling the dishwasher, to take a sharp intake of breath and hold her head in her hands.

"Do watch the flowers, Maxwell," she shouted through the kitchen window.

"Sorry Mum," came the quick reply, and just as the reluctant Arthur spotted his host and a good excuse to get out of the game, Max neatly headed the ball to him, forcing his prolonged participation. The ancient King swung a short, stocky leg at the ball but missed it completely and fell heavily to the ground, to the delighted yelps of the Elizabethan sea Captain.

"Morning, darling," Julian Finch greeted his wife, with a wince in Arthur's direction.

"Oh, how much longer will this go on?" Patricia let out a sigh, she was clearly distressed and the demands of the hostess appeared to be getting the better of her.

"Well, we can tell Max to stop."

"No. Not that, them. How much longer will they be here, Julian? It's like trying to provide for a small army every meal time... I did porridge in the end, mountains of it. I've never known such an appetite as Arthur's got... I'm not sure I can cope with it much longer, thank goodness Rhys didn't stay to breakfast."

"Not long, Pat, I promise." he put a comforting arm on her shoulder, "I think I may have worked out our next move, anyway."

"Really?" She looked relieved.

"Well, I'm not sure, perhaps I haven't, but it's worth a try. I'm going to have to go into the office later."

"On a Saturday!" His wife looked aghast. "You can't, not on a Saturday Julian, you can't leave them all with me."

"Oh I won't, they can come with me."

"What, both of them?"

"Yup, and the kids too."

"But you can't, you can't take those two ruffians into the office, they'll think you've gone mad... And what about security? They'll never let them into a Government office."

"Ah yes," he conceded as he put two slices of bread in the toaster and grabbed himself a plate. "Well we'll leave it till later of course. Yes much later, we'll go tonight."

"And in the meantime, what will we do with them all day? I don't like it, Julian, I feel like I'm hiding them."

"Well we'll take them shopping," he replied quickly "they've both agreed to wear modern clothes and we'll need them to fit in later."

"Oh," she sighed again. "There's no getting through to you sometimes - am I the only sane one left to reality? These two just turn up unannounced, I can understand the children getting sucked in, but you! I just can't believe you've been taken in so easily, they could be a pair of crooks."

Julian looked at his wife carefully and fixed her with an open, honest expression. "I believe them Pat. I don't want to, but I do. This country could be in terrible trouble, they wouldn't be here if it wasn't, and we have to help. I suppose it's our duty." He tried to put it in terms she would understand.

"But the kids," she spoke with a quavering voice and her eyes filled with tears, "why must the children be involved? If they are whom they say they are... Jessica and Maxwell could be in frightful danger... Why did they have to come here, Julian, to our home?"

"I really don't know darling," he spoke soothingly, "but they've come to us for a reason and the kids just seem to be bound up in it all. After all, Max stumbled across Arthur, and Jess has told us how she called Drake back. Maybe it's just fate, who knows. But we have to let it run its course. I'm sure it will all be revealed soon."

"So why the office?" She wiped at her eyes and sniffed back her tears as she tried to compose herself.

"There may be something there which I think, I hope, might have something to do with it. It could be nothing but a wild goose chase, but just in case it's the clue we need I'm going to have to take them all with me - who knows what might develop from there."

"But Jessica and Maxwell too," she protested.

"Do you honestly think I'll be able to stop them?" he grinned, and as his toast popped he retrieved it quickly and seated himself. He unscrewed the marmalade, spread it over the hot toast and took a large bite. "I'll look after them," he said with his mouth full, and having chewed and swallowed he added thoughtfully, "We have two legendary warriors to protect us; what is there to be worried about?"

With a smack the football bounced heavily off the patio doors and Patricia Finch, letting rip her frustration, yelled in a voice which would rouse the neighbourhood.

"Maxwell Finch, will you stop it now!" Rather sheepishly her son, the King and the Admiral left the ball and quietly filed back into the kitchen. "You've wound the dog up," she continued, "and you've wrecked half my geraniums. Now stop before you break something." Jess, who also appeared as if summoned by the shouting, busied herself by quietly helping her mother clear the rest of the bowls and plates from the table.

"We've been careful, Mum," Max tried to explain, but his mother just tutted back at him.

"Honestly, it's a miracle that greenhouse isn't smashed to smithereens the way you go on out there - and who's been digging in the flowerbed?" She pointed to the hole Arthur had made on his first afternoon before Max had introduced him to the rather more comfortable toilet.

"Um, Benji," Jess lied quickly, trying to draw a bit of flack away from her brother, "I saw him digging yesterday." Lying was not something that came naturally to Jess, and she could see her father looking at her knowingly.

"Well you shouldn't stir him up like that," Patricia went on. "Sit down quietly you lot, I need a break."

"'Pon my troth, goody Finch," Drake began eloquently, "'twas all in good sport there was meant no ill in't. An' if by ways o' use we merrie band hath soiled thy peace, we pray of thee thy pardon. For 'tis ill indeed t' reap displeasure o' one so fair."

"Yeah, I'm sorry too, Mum," Max added, and Arthur, relieved that

217

the game was over, seated himself next to Julian, and to Patricia's amazement hungrily consumed a slice of toast handed him by his host.

"How does he have any more room?... If you'll excuse me, I've things to do upstairs," she said as she took her leave of the others in the kitchen.

"Your mother's just a bit stressed out, it's all been a bit of a shock to her," Julian said by means of explanation. "I'm taking you all into London later," he added casually.

"Cool," said Max, "The zoo? The war museum?"

"No, Max, the office, but it might prove interesting. First however, we're going to take Drake and Arthur into town to get them some clothes that fit - we can't take them to London looking like, like they do now."

"Right," Max smirked, "people'd think they were street entertainers or something."

"Exactly, so be a good chap and see what you can find upstairs, will you? Any old clothes of mine that they can slip on for now will do, just until we get something which looks better on them." Max, happy to be given a task to be getting on with, bolted upstairs, and his father poured himself a cup of lukewarm tea. He looked at his daughter mischievously and smiled. "Clever dog we've got haven't we? To master the use of a trowel, and with no opposable thumbs!"

Jess just smiled back at her dad and took a seat on his other side. "What's in the office, then?" she asked quietly.

"Ah, well, that's what we have to find out. A piece of the jigsaw, I hope. Switch on the news a minute, we'll see if it gives us any other clues."

As the screen tuned in the studio presenter, on his comfy sofa, thanked the guest he'd just finished speaking to - a middle-aged female nutritionalist who'd been attacking the nation over its breakfast table about the state of its diet - and turned to the camera.

"And now more on last night's quite remarkable burglary at the Tower of London," he announced as the familiar CCTV footage of the thieves in action was once again brought up on the screen.

"Now it's hard to believe I know," the presenter continued light-heartedly, "but the pictures there show the two thieves making off with a bag of swag, and it's understood that they haven't taken any treasures or valuable antiquities. Instead Police confirm it's only the Tower's ravens which have been taken, and there is some speculation that as the birds are a tourist attraction, pranksters might be responsible. Our reporter Reggie Burrows is at the Tower."

The picture cut to Burrows, who stood microphone at the ready on Tower Green.

"Well, yes Chris," Burrows linked in, "and I suppose it's fortunate that having breached security no attempt was made to raid the jewel room. However, to the Beefeaters here, and the Raven Master especially who has direct responsibility for the birds, this is a very serious theft indeed. There have been ravens here since before the reign of Charles the second and legend has it that if the birds leave the Tower the country will fall, so make of that what you will, but it perhaps supports police suspicion that this might be a student prank."

Jess and her father exchanged scathing looks; she couldn't believe that the news channel could treat this like a simple joke.

"I have a witness here with me, Mr Joseph Banks."

The camera turned on Banks, who was dressed in his full Yeoman regalia, and although he was made a little uncomfortable by the presence of the camera crew his beard and uniform were as ever immaculate, he straightened his back and puffed out his chest to display the row of medal ribbons across his tunic.

"Mr Banks," Burrows turned to face him, "I understand you are one of the Beefeat..."

"I'm a senior Yeoman Warder here at the Tower," Banks interrupted.

"Oh, sorry, my mistake. But I understand you were on duty yesterday afternoon when a suspicious incident occurred involving two bogus Beefeaters. What happened yesterday?"

"Um, well. Them were these two impostors see, walked into the Tower they did, bold as brass an' cocksure o' 'emselves. Tol' me them was come t' lock up the Castle and had 'em keys wir'em too if you please. Must 'ave attacked the Chief Warder t' get 'em, 'cause he were found tied up soon after."

"Yes that's right," Reggie Burrows cut in, "the Chief Warder had been knocked out and tied up and the two intruders had taken the Castle keys from him, but you saw them off I believe."

"Oh aye, I knew sommat was up 'cause I'd challenged 'em earlier on like. An' when them's come up an I shout's halt who goes there, the impostors didn' know whose keys they had wir'em."

"Well they had the Castle keys, we've already established that," Burrows interrupted impatiently."

"Aye, but at the key ceremony them's supposed t' say Queen Elizabeth's keys, its Queen Elizabeth's keys they has wir'em."

"Oh I see."

"Ah, an that's what's got me suspicious like, I weren't havin' none o' that." Banks smiled awkwardly at the camera, and Burrows, who was finding him rather hard work, prompted him quickly.

"No, because you saw them off, didn't you?"

"Aye, that I did. Did me duty good an' proper, chased em' out o' the Castle an' recovered 'em keys, her Majesty's keys. I puts 'em back where they belongs, an' what does I find but the Chief Warder all tied up, an' wir'a splittin'headache."

"And then of course the keys were stolen later the same night by the offenders caught on CCTV. Has anything like this ever happened before?"

"Well not in my time no, not known anything like it in all me years o' service, that's the shame in it. The ravens gone, they be part o' the Castle them ravens an' all them legends which goes wir'em." Banks shook his head sadly. "Yup, first theft since Colonel James Blood took the crown jewels on the ninth o' May sixteen..."

"I'm afraid I'm going to have to stop you there," Burrows cut in, keen to prevent the old man launching into a lengthy anecdote, "but just one last question. What's the feeling amongst the staff here? I mean it's got to be quite embarrassing that something like this has happened, isn't it? Especially after the earlier suspicious incident you have described."

"Well aye, it's a debacle an' them security monkeys are t' blame, it's appallin', civilian security staff takin' over once the Yeomen Warders 'ave gone off duty. Calls em'selves guards," he continued through clenched teeth as his face began to redden. "Them knows nought o' guardin', 'bout as useful as a chocolate bayonet on desert exercise..."

"Yes, thank you, Mr Banks," said Reggie Burrows quickly as he moved away from the former Regimental Sergeant Major in order to distance the camera from his on-going rant. "Also with me is Detective Inspector Michael Dodds from the Metropolitan Police. Good morning to you." The camera panned across to cover a smartly-dressed middle-aged man in a suit, who looked every bit as uncomfortable as Banks had initially been when the camera first turned on him. "Inspector, I understand you are keen to speak to the two bogus Beefeaters from yesterday. But this is a student prank surely, they are probably trying to pull off some stunt, aren't they? Perhaps they'll try and ransom the ravens back, or maybe they will reappear at the Edinburgh festival or something..."

"No, so far as we are concerned this is a serious offence. Two separate incidents have occurred which appear connected and a staff member has been assaulted in the commission of the offence. We therefore believe we are dealing with organized criminals and urge anyone who knows who these people are to come forward."

Dodds was in truth rather thrown by Burrows' rather dismissive approach, but he'd recovered well, and Banks, who looked rather down hearted, walked aimlessly round behind them and into the back of the picture.

"In terms of national security," the Policeman continued, "this is obviously a Royal Castle, a National landmark, and it is also clearly a huge cause for concern that security has been breached in this way." Banks could be seen to nod in agreement as the Detective continued to speak. "A witness has described the two men from earlier in the day as..." He glanced down at his notes. "A scruffy bunch of misfit reprobates, one tall with a huge protruding bulbous nose, um. And the other, um, shorter with a high forehead and very pronounced and protruding teeth like a um, like a row of gravestones in a military cemetery." It was clear that the Officer was a little uncomfortable passing the descriptions, but it was also fairly clear, as Banks nodded his head enthusiastically, just who the description had come from. "Um, both middle-aged white males," Dodds added quickly, "and they don't sound like students to me."

"Well, there you have it," said Burrows quickly as the camera turned back on him. "Back to you in the studio, Chris."

As the face of the studio newsreader once again appeared on the screen, Jess switched the television off and turned to her father angrily. "Doesn't look like they are taking it very seriously, does it?"

"The police, what office bare they?" Drake asked curiously.

"Um, Officers of the Crown," Julian answered him.

"No not the police," Jess continued in frustration, "the news people aren't taking it seriously."

"Well then it's lucky we are," said Julian, and he sipped his tea thoughtfully.

"If only they knew that Drake and Arthur were here, Dad, they might realise what trouble we're in, and someone might be able to work it out."

"You're right, Jess, they might," he finished his last mouthful of toast and folded up the paper, "but we've got to be careful about letting our secret out. After all, if they won't take the theft of the ravens seriously are they really going to give any credibility to a claim that Arthur and Drake have returned?"

"So hath I spake," Drake stood in dramatic fashion once again, "give unto Drake the very stage an' all doubters shalt I turn unto our noble endeavour."

"Yes, but when the time is right, Sir Francis." Julian felt much more comfortable addressing his guests now, "Patience is crucial. As we agreed yesterday, we must first establish the purpose of your return, identify the foe you have returned to face…"

"The media is very powerful, they cannot be underestimated, but we need to use them for maximum effect at the right time - they could just as easily destroy us, make a mockery of us and turn people away from taking you two seriously. That's why we need to keep our heads down and get you some smart clothes that fit, we're going to London later and I'm not sure where events will lead us from there."

"T' Greenwich, t' Court, t' present our case unto our sovereign lady the Queen herself?" Drake looked excited.

"Um maybe, though not just yet. There's some paperwork I want to try and get hold of first."

"Ah, a document, a writ, a Royal warrant?"

"Of sorts, yes."

"Wow." Jess sat open-mouthed. "Do you really think the Queen might get involved, Dad? Do you really think we might meet her?"

"Well Jess I just don't know, but I think Arthur here might pose a bit of a shock for her." The king, who had been sucking marmalade off his fingers, sat back in his chair and belched loudly.

Max reappeared with his arms full of clothing. "Will this do, Dad?" he asked as he spread a number of his father's old tracksuits and gardening clothes on the table.

Arthur lifted a pair of lightweight trousers in the air and eyed them suspiciously. "They weigh nothing," he observed in Latin, "these will give us no protection to the sword thrust of the enemy."

"They are just for comfort," Julian replied in the same language, "you can wear these to town where we'll get you some formal clothes which will fit your own size. You can wear your own clothes under the new ones if you want to, but you'll need a disguise if we are to get you into the office un-noticed."

"Office?"

"It's where I work, an official place. I'm a scribe of sorts," he tried to put it into words the King might understand. "I work in a huge building in London, we've got to get in there without drawing any attention…"

"Ah, Londinium." The King looked delighted; there was to be action at last, his adventure would soon start.

Drake prodded one of his host's old gardening tops with a look of abject disgust on his face. "If thou thinkst Admiral Drake wilt scuttle abroad in peasant garb thou art much mistook, Finch. For here standeth in splendour a Knight o' this realm," he ran his hand up and down his finely embroidered sleeves as if to illustrate his point, "an' thou wouldst prescribe unto he the attire o' a common seaman."

"Well, thanks very much," said Julian with a smile. "I know I may not have the finest wardrobe in Somerset, but that's the whole point, Sir Francis. Look, we've been over this, we need you to blend in - just until we get you to town, anyway. Once we do we'll get you the smartest suit we can find."

"I thought the Tudors liked dressing-up," Max observed clumsily.

"He does, Max," said his sister. "It's dressing down that he's objecting to."

"Thou hast it, Miss Finch, thou art sharp o' mind Jessica, and thou knowst the heart's o' men."

"I should hope she doesn't," her father grinned, "not yet anyway."

"Bet she knows Brendan's heart," said Max trying to wind her up. "Oh look, she's blushing."

"A-har! There be sport in't" Drake only made things worse as Max whooped in delight, "pon my troth, Mistress Jessica, young Brendan looks after thee wi' the eye's o' a pining hound."

"I think he's a sound lad," Julian tried to deflate the situation, "certainly knows his history…"

"He'd rather learn Jess's biology," Max laughed.

"That'll do, Max, stop embarrassing your sister. Now which of these clothes are for who?"

"Well, these are best for Drake," Max passed his guest an old tracksuit, "and this old jumper and the cut-off jeans - sorry Dad - will be the best fit for Arthur."

As they all trooped out to the car, Arthur initially held back rather uneasily. He was highly suspicious of the monster on the driveway. His host, however, jumped in the front undeterred, and when he ignited the engine the rough growl from the monster's bowels and the sudden puff of acrid smoke made Arthur jump back in surprise and reach for his dagger.

To his amazement, Max, in a sudden movement, reached forward and simply ripped the beast's stomach open very matter-of-factly. The boy hopped in and beckoned at him to follow. Arthur decided quickly that it had to be safe, and not wanting to show any hesitation in front of the Elizabethan Admiral, yet with his heart pounding, he boldly lurched in beside Max on the back seat.

Luckily for Arthur, Drake hadn't noticed any reluctance on his part, and instead clapped his hands in glee as Jess jumped in beside Arthur and shut the door leaving the front seat for him.

"A motor cart, like to that o' Master Rhys. Oh 'tis a means o' conveyance Sir Francis knows well; canst I take to mineself the reins, Finch?"

"Maybe on the way back," Julian replied, trying not to upset him. "It's best if I drive, Sir Francis. I know the roads, you see."

"Ah, but 'tis aright she be piloted by one who knows well our path." Reluctantly the Admiral took his place in the passenger seat, but almost before his bum had hit the seat he was making a further plea. "Canst I then be first mate aboard?"

"Um, yes, I'd be honoured."

"You should start at the bottom," Max teased, "got to work your way up from cabin boy you know."

"Mutiny," Jess sniggered, "and we haven't even got off the drive."

"Aye, launch her Finch, and be quick about it, for we must be about our business."

Arthur grabbed hold of Max's arm as the car started to move, but when the boy looked at him in bewilderment he made a show of trying to steady himself rather than seek reassurance, and as they progressed towards Bath City centre he started to relax a bit, though the build-up of traffic, houses and people made him feel a little out of his depth, and he decided he would stick close to his hosts when they disembarked.

They made a strange group as they walked along together, Arthur in the cut-down jeans and an old rugby shirt, (which was far too long for him in the arms,) and Drake, still with his pearl earring but dressed in a tracksuit which was baggy in the leg but far too tight across his broad shoulders. For all his protestations when he put the clothes on, Drake was secretly enjoying the loose material around his legs, for it was his first time in long trousers, and although he had lost his swagger to an awkward trudge in the unfamiliar trainers, he was in buoyant mood just to be out and about.

Arthur was totally amazed by the scale of the buildings and the huge number of shoppers who busied themselves all around them, whilst Drake, who was familiar with the bustle of crowds, was in awe of the grand Georgian buildings, the wideness of the streets and the colourful shop windows. Both were like fish out of water and gawped at the towering stone and glass-fronted buildings and the mass of humanity which passed in and out of them.

"This is not the Aquae Sulis known to me," Arthur had spoken in Latin as they had crossed the river Avon into the city. In truth he felt intimidated by it, for when last he had left this settlement it had been a small town of wood and wattle dwellings and he had been leading out an Army to shouts of 'Dduw a Artos at achub Prydain,'(i) on his way to inflict a heavy defeat on the Saxon invaders at Dyrham.

Bath had been in decline since the Romans had left, but the bath house had still been operating and it had remained comparatively affluent and in a strategic position, a good place for his troops to unwind between battles and long marches. Yet now he felt defenceless in the face of circumstance, the extent of the changing times came back to him again as he walked through the Abbey courtyard, the huge church loomed high into the sky and a place which had once been so familiar now frightening him.

He felt so insignificant amongst all the towering buildings. He was a King yet felt like a grub on a meeting hall floor, and more humbling still, he felt foolish. He cursed himself that he had been silly enough to hope that his folk might still be in these parts, that his garrison at Little Solsbury would welcome him with cries of 'Artos Rex.'(ii) Today he was just one of thousands of Saturday morning shoppers in just one of many thousand such town centres in the country. He felt dispirited, sombre, yet kept his composure and tried to stay close to his host, Julian understood this world and its people, and although he, Arthur, might still have a part to play in it, he knew now for sure that he would be dependent on Julian Finch to guide him and give him the signal.

While Arthur chose to remain quiet, his fellow time-traveller could not contain his excitement, and had to be forcibly dragged by Max and Jess passed every shop and window display that grabbed his attention. Never had he seen such a vast array of different premises; book sellers, hostelries, cloth merchants, butchers, bakers, and shops selling odd-looking gadgets which Max explained to him were 'mobile phones' and 'electrical goods,' whatever they were. He wanted to enter them all and sample their wares, and though he had no idea what a 'card shop' was or what 'DVDs' were he was like a puppy on his first walk, a little cautious but desperate to stick his nose in everywhere. It was all new experience and Jess and Max between them had to literally steer him past every distraction as they tried to reach the clothing shop they were headed for.

Max pointed out a juggler at one point to stop Drake sprinting off into a shopping arcade and getting lost, and it was with reluctance that the Tudor sea captain obeyed the teenager and joined the crowd surrounding the performer.

"Pretty good, isn't he?" Jess urged.

"Wish I could juggle like that," Max added, "bet I could earn a few quid off a crowd like this. Bet you've never seen so many people, have you, Sir Francis?"

"Thou art a noble child, Jessica, and thou Maxwell art filled wi' all the zeal o' any numbered amongst mine crew, yet thou art counted hither wi' one who many times hath trod the banks at Greenwich, an' there be no crowd nor company 'pon these shores t' rival them that fill the Thames-side cock pits."

"Cock fights!" Jess looked disgusted.

"Aye, and t'was ne'er more loved a sport in all Albion."

"Not more popular than football, surely?" Max couldn't believe it.

"Ah, football be a pursuit o' the provinces. Cockerel fights be the love o' the townsfolk. The blood pumps an' the heart beats like to a drum in battle, the birds dance an' cut, the crowd roars, an' all rise, gentlemen an' rogues as one, t' witness groat an guinea be won an lost as the feathers fly."

"Sounds exciting," Max was wide eyed.

"Sounds brutal." His sister was less impressed.

"There, Master, wilt thou find sport, an' there Mistress Jess wilt thou find a crowd an' folk o' such an ilk as to none other." He shook his head slowly as he made his point. "'Master Drake,'" he impersonated one long dead, "'a seat by the ring for one such as thee.' Churls all, and vagabonds to a man." He smiled at his memories. "Such folk wouldst take thy coat an' seat thee in finery, yet then, as thou sat an' cheered thy cockerel, wouldst them same, whom thee had seated, then cut from thy britches thy purse as the ring bore thy attention, an' sneak as thief to the nearest Inn.

"An thou wouldst chance upon them an hour or three hence consumed by ale levied from thine own estate, yet filled anon wi' guile. 'Good morrow t' thee Sir Francis,' wouldst speak the thieving churl, 'hast thou good fortune in the ring?'"

"Sounds like a dangerous place to me," said Jess, voicing her disapproval.

"'Tis but the play o' infants t' the terrors o' the open sea," Drake dismissed her concern.

"Just imagine it, Jess," Max was trying his best, "the danger, the squalor..."

"Don't encourage him, Max." She turned to her brother. "We live in a civilised world now, we don't go round killing each other, stealing off each other and watching defenceless animals tear each other apart for our own entertainment."

"Well it sounds exciting to me, and anyway Drake and Arthur were both fighting for their own freedom at the time, their enemies would have killed them if they'd caught them - it was a bloodthirsty age."

"It was, Max, but I'm happier living in the here and now thank you very much." She was insistent. "I quite like the simple pleasures we take for granted, heating, lighting, the chance to drink fresh water and shower when I want to. But if you want to go back to a time of disease when people used to throw there own poo out into the street you can team up with your new friend and go and visit his dentist."

"Kids, keep an eye on him," their father's voice interrupted their arguing, and Julian pointed to their charge, who had made his way off to the other side of the crowd and was starring wide-eyed, and without an ounce of subtlety, at a number of ladies who were clapping the juggler. "Catch up," Julian called to them again, and he and Arthur continued up the street and into the clothing shop.

As Jess and Max once again united in purpose to take hold of Drake and usher him after their father, all he could do was rant in excitement and concede that whilst the crowds at the Cock pits were, 'like to none other,' never had he seen 'in number such wenches, and so buxom, as mine eyes hath beheld yonder.' Raleigh would never believe him he said, were he to tell him of the wonders he had beheld.

Inside the shop the Tudor peacock was both amazed and disappointed. In his own age clothing had been a way to display wealth and status, the rich wore embroidered outfits in fine colours and all tailored to their own specific dimensions. Even his undershirts had been of fine lace and the premises he shopped in were small and manned by skilled craftsmen. Inside the enormous modern high street clothes shop he couldn't take in the huge range of fully-stitched and finished clothing displayed on rack upon rack in every shape and size.

He followed his host past colourful children's clothes and elaborate ladies dresses which left little to the imagination, and into the gentlemen's section. They passed casual trousers and tops, like Julian and Max were wearing, to a section of the shop which didn't excite him at all. He cast his eyes around the formal and business section with scepticism, and then horror. Row upon row of plain blue, black and grey suits, no splendour, no colour, just plain boring, and next to them, hundreds of black and brown leather shoes, all gleamed with polish, but there wasn't a silver buckle in sight.

"Wherefore hast thou led mineself an' yon ancient King across town t' this, Finch? Methinks thou art jesting, for I beseech thee, makest not thy heroes don such drab an' dull attire."

Julian just laughed at the seafarer's anguish and selected a suitably-sized blue business suit for him from the rack. "Here, it won't kill you, take it behind that curtain over there and try it on."

"'Tis plain," Drake was aghast, "'tis dour and hast no life in't."

"Alright," Julian replaced it on the rack and selected a pinstriped suit instead. "This one has a bit more colour and it'll be nice and baggy for you to keep your own clothes on underneath, try this."

"Ooh executive," said Jess enthusiastically, but Drake wasn't going to be easily convinced.

"There be more life in yon statue," Drake protested, as he indicated to a clothes dummy who stood rigid on a plinth surrounded by mirrors.

"I know how we can give you some colour," Max grinned, and selected a bright purple shirt from the shelf. "And a tie," he said carefully, "now which one?" He took a selection.

"Oh, and cufflinks," Jess added excitedly, "and a nice colourful handkerchief for your top pocket."

"Come on, Sir Francis," Max led him to the changing rooms, "I'll show you how to put it all on."

Julian Finch selected a standard grey suit for King Arthur, a light blue shirt and tie, and explained to the King in his broken Latin that these really were the clothes of the age. The King nodded as he followed his host to the changing rooms, and reminded Julian that he had seen him in just such an outfit when he had come home the previous evening.

Jess, waiting patiently the other side of the curtains for the two transformed national heroes to re-emerge, could hear grunting as Arthur fumbled with his shirt buttons, and protestations from Drake, who grumbled loudly as Max handed him a tie.

"Wherefore be this donned, and how?"

"Um, well," Max thought carefully but couldn't really come up with an answer. "I don't know really, it's just meant to be worn with a suit that's all, I guess people only wear them because it's expected that they will."

"Then be there no purpose," Drake challenged with a heavy frown, "I shalt not don it."

"It's colourful though, isn't it? And, um... It's a mark of how important you are," Max recovered quickly, "bit like a coat of arms or something," and he could see the lie was grabbing Drake's attention as he held out the selection in his right hand. "Yes, um, a blue one means you're not very important," he dropped one from his hand, "but a yellow one," he glanced at the next, "um, with red on it, yeah, that means you're a very important person indeed..."

"Ah!"

"And a um, a pink one, with, um... green stripes on it... like this,"

Max held up the most ghastly tie he had ever seen, "this would mean you are really top dog, a really important person, like a celebrity or something."

"Ah-har, like to a badge of office!"

"Exactly," said Max, more in relief than triumph, yet knowing that he had brought the Admiral round. "So here we have it, the tie for you," he winced as he put the ghastly coloured thing around Drake's neck. "Yup, this is the one." He tried to sound convincing.

"'Tis aright," Drake clapped his hands in glee. "How doest one knot it? Bowline or reef?"

"Um... I'll show you," said Max as he put the finishing touches to Drake's transformation and tucked the tie in under the jacket.

It was to a tactful round of applause from Jess that Drake emerged. "Very smart, Sir Francis, it makes you look so, powerful, so um, important." She caught her brother's eye.

"Well, there be the rub," the sailor smiled. "For by troth so shouldst a favourite o' the Queen appear."

Arthur came to join him, though he looked awkward and very uncomfortable; he had retained the twisted torc at his throat and it was clear that his collar was a little too tight around it. Drake had moved over to the mirror where he was admiring his reflection and was checking out the pointed-ness of his beard, and a dispirited Arthur checked his own appearance quickly before turning to his host and accepting in Latin that it would have to do.

"It will get you into my office anyway," Julian smiled back. "Time to march on London."

The clothing was removed from the two legends and Julian's old clothes put back on for the walk home. Getting Drake out of the suit was almost as hard as getting him into it had been, for he seemed disgruntled that having only just been given the respect he was due it was to be just as suddenly whisked away from him.

"But we have to pay for it," Jess explained, "you have to take it off so Dad can buy it, you can put it all back on when we get home." Not for the first time she reflected on the similarities Drake posed to some difficult children she'd known. "You'll need some smart new shoes as well."

As they arrived home the sun broke through the clouds, bringing all the promise of a long summer afternoon.

Patricia Finch sat in a deckchair in the back garden with a large glass of lemonade in one hand, a pen in the other, and the crossword page of the newspaper draped across her lap. Sat next to her a little awkwardly, yet whispering sweet nothings to each other regardless, were Rhys and Rhiannon, Benji the dog was splayed out in the sun at their feet. They had been a little disappointed to hear that the others were all out when they arrived, but had decided to stay and await their return.

Behind Patricia a curious collection of clothing was drying on the washing line. Drake's doublet and hose swayed gently in the breeze next to the Coptic dalmic, cloak and woollen leggings of the ancient King; anyone with a bird's-eye view of the back garden might have thought the household were preparing for a fancy dress party.Patricia had wasted no time and had seized the moment to cram the clothes into the washing machine the second her guests had left the house. For whilst Arthur's clothes had already been washed once they had still been grubby, and Drake's clothing had had a sharp and wholly unpleasant smell about it. She had wondered whether he bathed more than once a year and had suggested the previous night to Julian that she burn the lot to avoid a louse infestation. He'd advised that she wash the clothes instead to avoid any ill feeling, and she relaxed, at peace with herself for having done something to make the two guests more presentable.

Stuck in his Aunt's company Rhys had been rather bored, and he stood in greeting as his cousin, Max, led the returning group back to the house.

"Hail an' well met," Drake greeted them to great amusement, and Arthur greeted Rhys in Welsh to the effect that he had returned and was ready for battle.

"Really brings you up to date," Rhiannon laughed at the sight of the two historical figures in Julian's old and ill-fitting clothes.

"All the way to town to get clothes and you bring 'em back looking like a couple of scarecrows. Took them to a charity shop did you Max?" Rhys teased. "I can see I'm going to have to give you a few fashion tips."

"These happen to be my clothes," said Julian, looking genuinely hurt.

"Yeah, we've got some proper smart suits in here Rhys," Max ran over to show his cousin the contents of the large plastic bags he carried.

"Oh right," Rhys was rather surprised as he took in the pinstripe, "and what are all these in aid of?"

"It's so they can fit in," Jess explained, as she played with the bouncing Benji.

"What, in Weston-Bissett on a Saturday afternoon?" Rhiannon sniggered.

"No, in my office this evening," Julian spoke in a serious tone intended to remind everyone of the business ahead. "We're going to London later, there might be something in my office which I want to get hold of."

"Yeah, and if you're coming with us..." Jess began.

"I am coming with you - we can come, can't we Jules?"

"Oh you can both come, Rhys," Julian assured him, "we're going to be needing you."

"But if you're coming," Jess continued, "you'll be needing a suit too."

"Good point," Julian reflected. "I don't suppose you brought a suit with you, did you Rhys?"

"Er, no, but I've got loads of dead smart suits at home like."

"But not here... No matter, you're about the same size as me, you can borrow one of my spare ones," Julian grinned. "I'm sure you won't look like a scarecrow."

Rhys looked rather downhearted by this but Rhiannon clutched his arm affectionately and whispered in his ear, "Serves you right."

As Julian ate his lunch he tried to remind himself that timing was everything. Although it was a Saturday they had to wait till it was getting dark and the office would be empty and manned thinly by security. But the waiting, the time-killing was making him nervous; it reminded him of the first time he'd batted for the school's first xi and every job interview he'd ever had. He wanted to just get on the train and go, but the clock-watching, the butterflies in the stomach, were spoiling his appetite.

His guests, in comparison, were both eating ravenously and appeared to be revelling in the tension as the excitement intensified. For each of them the anticipation of actually going to London, of actually progressing their quest was what they had come back for. To them this was the eve of battle and the waiting it brought was no strange sensation. Both maintained a dignified calm at the table, for they appeared to have made peace with themselves, and perhaps for the first time properly, with each other. And when the food was finished they nodded their thanks to Patricia and led Max and Rhys outside to educate them in the skills they thought they might need for the battle ahead.

Patricia Finch looked out of the kitchen window in horror to see her son, who was holding a dustbin lid in one hand and a cricket stump in the other, being taught a harsh lesson in hand-to-hand combat by the ancient warlord, who was similarly armed with poor substitutes for

Caledfwlch and Wynebgwrthucher. Never losing complete control, and with gentle care, Arthur demonstrated to Max how to shield the blow of an opponent and run him through under his unprotected sword arm before Max even realised that his own fierce blow had been deflected. But Patricia protested as they battered at each other and the crashing noises reverberated around the garden.

"He'll kill him," she implored her husband to put a stop to it. "It's far too rough, poor Maxie."

But Julian tried to reassure her by explaining that the old warrior was being gentle and that Max was hugely enjoying the simulated combat.

"Look, darling, that's King Arthur out there. He could be much more ferocious than that, and you only have to watch to see that every time Max tries too hard he makes him stop. Max is loving it, it's every boy's dream to be one of King Arthur's Knights... Actually, I'm rather jealous,"

"Ugh, boys and their silly little toys!" Patricia rolled her eyes at her husband. "If he gets hurt it will be your fault."

"Oh I don't think Max will hurt him," Julian joked, but his despairing wife left the room tutting to herself.

Rhiannon looked on as Drake and Rhys duelled at the other end of the garden. They carried no shields but stood on light feet with a beanpole each and fenced with the longer, lighter weapons which better replicated the swords with which Drake was most familiar.

"Attired thus, 'tis true, an' be it known, Master Rhys, the point o' a weapon balanced such as these wilt beat the edge o' yon foes bladed strike."

"So stab him, don't slash him," Rhys voiced his understanding somewhat more crudely.

"Indeed, thou hast the jist," Drake slapped him on the back, pleased to see that the principles had sunk in so quickly.

"You'll get them killed," Patricia Finch stood in the upstairs window, and put her hand to her mouth as Drake discarded his beanpole and handed Rhys his own sword so the teenager could feel its balance.

"'Tis but extension to thine arm," he explained, "take unto thy mind the weight o' it, an' to thine eye inter the range o' thy thrust."

"They aren't teaching them how to die but how to defend themselves," Julian explained as he climbed the stairs to seek out his wife. "I don't know what we are letting ourselves in for, Pat, but if it comes to a fight who better to protect us?"

"Do you think it will come to a fight?" Patricia looked distraught.

232

"No," he said quickly, "I don't know. I don't know what we might find in that office," he conceded, "we might come back later with no more clue than we have now."

"But if you do get somewhere?..." Her eyes implored him.

"I just don't know," Julian answered truthfully. "I don't know where it might lead us... But I'll take no risks, I've promised you that. I'll keep the children safe."

"Well," Patricia spoke uncertainly as she wiped a tear from her eye, "should I not come with you?"

"Oh Pat," Julian was unsure of what to say in response, "your heart isn't in it, and anyway I shall be needing you at home. If anything does go wrong," he said carefully, "I might need you at the other end of the phone to call us help. If we need you, Pat, I'll call you, and you'll be there for us, won't you?" She nodded silently as he spoke. "Benji might be glad of his supper too, you know," Julian smiled.

"Well then," Patricia tried once again to put a brave face on things. "I can see your mind is made up, if you are all going to London and you don't know quite when you might come back... I suppose I'd better be packing you some sandwiches for the journey."

"That's the spirit," Julian kissed her. "I'll do my utmost to keep Max out of them, at least until we reach the office."

With her mother busy in the kitchen, Jessica Finch approached her father on the upstairs landing with a pleading expression on her face. "Dad, I really think Brendan ought to come with us too."

"Look, Jess, I'm really not sure," he lowered his voice so his wife wouldn't hear. "This really could be dangerous. It's bad enough I'm taking my own children, but someone else's..."

"But dad Brendan is part of this too, he was with us last night, he knows all about Drake and Arthur and he was with me the day I hit the drum... Well not actually with me when I did it, but he was paired with me as we went round," she explained. "He knows a lot about both of them, Dad, he really does, and I just know he's going to be helpful."

"Well I know what you're saying Jess, but... he was here last night, do you think he'll tell anyone about what he saw?"

"No, I don't," said Jess firmly. "Brendan isn't like the others dad, he's not like Tommo Lydon or Mark Thompson, he's not like any of Max's friends, not like any of the other boys. I had to keep Max quiet because if one of that lot knew they'd all know by now, that's why I haven't told Abi Saunders about them, but she probably won't want to speak to me for the rest of the holidays now because I didn't go to her party last night."

"No bad thing that," said her father wisely. "What is it about kids today...?"

"But that's just it dad, Brendan isn't like that, he's loyal, he's trusting, and... We ought to give him credit for loyalty like that."

"Yeah," her father responded quickly, "you're right Jess he is one of us, he was with us last night. Call him up and tell him to get over here sharpish."

When Brendan arrived shortly afterwards it was with an understanding that made Julian glad he'd agreed to Jess's request that the tubby teenager be included.

"I didn't think you were going to call," said a rushed Brendan rather out of breath. "But I saw the news this morning, the ravens have been stolen from the Tower of London, everyone knows the country can't fall while the ravens remain so it's obvious that someone must have taken them on purpose and in preparation. It confirms what we all thought - there is about to be some sort of invasion or coup any moment."

"The ravens?" enquired Rhys in ignorance, and as Jess and Max explained the significance of their disappearance to their cousin, Julian considered Brendan's last remark carefully.

"A coup - you could be right, Brendan. It could be an attempt to seize power from within. Perhaps we've been looking outwards for an inward enemy."

"Well I was just about to phone you, you see I've been thinking and whoever has taken the ravens obviously knows all about our traditions. I hope they haven't anticipated Drake and Arthur returning. I was going to call," he said again lamely, "but I thought you were all busy."

"Oh, we have been," said Jess. "Dad's got suits for Drake and Arthur and we're all going to London in an hour or so to dad's office."

"I think there might be a clue there, Brendan," Julian explained, "and it might just support your coup theory."

"And I can come?" Brendan looked ecstatic, he'd never been included in anything exciting ever before."

"We want you to come," Jess smiled at her friend, "don't we, Dad?"

"Sure," Julian gave the youngster a reassuring grin.

"And what am I to tell Brendan's parents?" Patricia Finch appeared from the kitchen, a piece of bread in one hand and a knife covered in spread in the other. She might have still been making the sandwiches, but she'd kept an ear to the conversation in the other room.

"Um, tell them..."

"Am I to tell Mrs Johnson, Julian, that you have whisked their darling little boy off to London and that you don't know what dangers you are exposing him to?"

"Goody Finch, 'pon my troth holdst thou no fear," Drake answered for his host. "Impart 'pon those persons concerned that Master Brendan be bound unto Putney wi' brave company, an' numbered 'mongst they that be counted: Sir Francis Drake an' ole King Arthur."

"Yeah, Mum," said Max simply, "just tell them that he's gone to London with Drake and Arthur."

"Fiddlesticks," said Patricia. "I'm exasperated with the lot of you - can't you try to remain in reality one moment, Maxwell? This is serious. Mrs Johnson will go spare if she finds out her son has gone gallivanting off to London at the drop of a hat."

"Look, Pat," Julian spoke calmly, "just tell her I'm taking the kids up to London to see my office. It's in Whitehall so I'm sure she'll be impressed, what with young Brendan being an aspiring politician and all." He turned to the others. "Time to get ready you lot, we leave soon."

(i) God and Arthur to save Britain.
(ii) Arthur King.

Chapter Thirteen – The 19:45 Service to Paddington

Drake and Arthur were as quick as they could be at dressing themselves, and Sir Francis was delighted to be free of the tracksuit and back in his own clothes, though the freshly-laundered smell made them a little unfamiliar. They needed a little help in squeezing their new suits over the top, and Max had to persuade Drake to keep his ruff in his pocket in order that his shirt collar could be done up and the gaudy tie fastened. The King, who wore his dagger, Carnwennau, strapped to his calf under the trouser leg, had seen the wisdom in abandoning his cloak, but still bore a somewhat unsightly bulge around his waist where his chain mail, tucked under the trousers, made him look like he was carrying a rather saggy spare tyre. Drake's sword had been wrapped up in a cardboard tube by Jess, who had also covered the handle in matching brown paper. Both had been insistent on taking their weapons, and disguising the sword as a parcel was the best thing that Jess and Brendan could think of.

When the time came Julian Finch ferried Rhys, Rhiannon and Jess down to the train station, and returned to pick up Brendan, Max, Drake and Arthur. In his short absence Max and Brendan had raided the garden shed and had compiled a strange assortment of tennis balls, footballs, cricket balls and even an old beach ball on the back lawn. As Julian entered the garden to chivvy them out he found the foursome engrossed in competition, as each rolled a selection of balls from behind a hastily scratched marker in an attempt to halt theirs nearest to the table tennis ball which Drake had thrown out as the jack.

"Bowls," Max explained as he registered the look of confusion on his father's face, "it was Sir Francis' idea."

"Aye Finch," Drake grinned at him as he let fly an overcooked tennis ball which rebounded forcefully off the back fence, "be there time t' finish the game?"

"The train won't wait," Julian explained, and with a round of kisses and 'good lucks' from Patricia they boarded the car. Julian looked back over his shoulder to see his wife tearfully waving them off, the 'radiant blessings' called upon her by Drake still ringing in her ears.

When all were united on the London-bound platform at Bath Spa Railway Station, Julian took himself off to the ticket booth, and Rhys, taking advantage of his uncle's brief absence, quickly lit up a cigarette.

Arthur looked on in wonder as the young man took the little fire stick to his mouth and then breathed dragon-like smoke from his nostrils.

"Hast thou a surplus o' thy tobacco sticks?" Drake asked, and when offered, the Elizabethan Admiral removed a cigarette from the packet with a dramatic flourish.

Arthur watched with curiosity as Rhys ignited the seaman's fag from his own, and as Jess, with a look of abject disgust on her face, took a step away from Drake as he took a puff on it. Perhaps, he thought, this might be some kind of per-battle ritual, some communal activity the men would share in before baring arms. After all it had been said that the ancient Greeks would oil themselves, the old Celtic tribesman had spiked their hair and painted their bodies with woad to frighten their enemies, and his own stout hearted army used to fortify themselves with mead on the morning of battle to fill their hearts with fire and numb the pains to come.

Sure that this had to be some kind of tradition, yet wondering why they hadn't waited for Julian, Arthur was about to ask for one himself when Drake doubled over in a fit of coughing, the smoke spewing out of his mouth. Did the man ever stop exhibitioning himself?

"Archkh, 'tis a rough blend, Master Rhys," he declared and coughed repeatedly.

This in turn caused Jess to start coughing as Drake's secondhand smoke engulfed her, and she turned angrily on her cousin to remonstrate with him. "Why do you have to smoke those? You know they're bad for you."

"I like them," said Rhys defensively, yet with a trace of amusement in his tone as he smirked at the suffering Admiral beside him.

"But why do you have to smoke them near me? You know I don't like them. You haven't smoked around my mum, I bet she doesn't even know you smoke."

"Yeah, I haven't seen you smoke around Patricia either," Rhiannon joined in.

"Because I know she doesn't like it."

"Because you know she'll take them off you," his girlfriend teased.

"Well now you know that I don't like it either," said Jess with finality, "so don't smoke around me."

"I like it," said Max quickly. "That is, I don't mind it." He looked around quickly but there was no sign of his father returning from the ticket booth. "Rhys, could I..."

"No." Said Rhys, Jess and Rhiannon together.

"Er, you're too young mate," Rhys added kindly. "Too young for the criticism it brings, anyway."

Drake took another long puff on his cigarette and immediately doubled over again in a further fit of coughing, to the great annoyance of an old lady who sat alone under the Station clock. This decided Arthur's mind for him. He would pass on the fire stick and would thus retain his quiet dignity, but if Finch had brought some mead with him he would certainly have a draught of that.

"I thought you used to smoke a pipe," Brendan enquired of the Tudor time traveller, "aren't you used to it?"

"Ah, 'tis true, yet not so. Bring unto me mine pipe an..."

But in a flash Rhys, who had sighted Julian returning, had swiped the dog-end off his friend, and there being no bin immediately available, he plunged both his own and Drake's butt onto the tracks below the platform.

"Oh, Rhys," Rhiannon wasn't impressed.

"That's littering now," Jess chastised her cousin. "First polluting now littering, who's going to clear that up now?"

"Oh come on, Sis, it's only a little..."

But Max's attempts to come to Rhys' aid were interrupted by Jess; for her, littering was a serious matter. "It all adds up," she said firmly, and he didn't argue, for Jess had led a small crusade the previous term to clamp down on litter at school, and as Julian returned with a handful of tickets, Rhys quickly changed the subject.

"Just in time, Julian," he said quickly, distracting all eyes from the smoking cigarette butts to a distant train which had appeared down the tracks and was edging ever nearer.

"Good," Julian smiled as he handed the tickets round, "good timing."

The huge train approached as an enormous terrifying and noisy serpent, and though Rhys had tried to prepare Arthur, it was quite beyond anything the King had imagined. He impressed himself however by keeping still and composed, doing his best to show no fear but to give the outward impression of a seasoned commuter preparing to board the thing as part of a boring daily routine.

Drake, in comparison, was hopping up and down and whooping in excitement, making a most curious display of him in his pinstripe suit. For him the adventure brought nothing but prestige and stories from the start, and were he to recount the journey, Jess thought to herself, no doubt he would have ridden the wild serpent's back all the way to London, having first harnessed it and made it yield to his every bidding.

As they boarded the carriage, Arthur tried his best to give off an air of coolness as he took a seat next to Max. Certainly the experience would have phased him even more a few days previously, and it was a credit to him that against his every instinct he was acclimatising well to this unfamiliar modern way of life. The Finch's gave him confidence, but he would never be able to emulate the reckless and impetuous nature of Drake, and nor did he share in a fraction of his vanity.

The carriage was fairly empty; a huddle of people sat at the far end, but otherwise they had it to themselves. Opposite Max and Arthur sat Drake and Julian, and across the aisle Jess and Brendan sat uncomfortably as Rhys and Rhiannon cuddled together in front of them.

"So what exactly is it that we are expecting to find in your office, Jules?" asked Rhys.

"We'll see," Julian replied, "I've just got this hunch that there might be some papers there which might shed some light on a few things - that is, if they are there, and if we can find them."

"But how will we know where to look?" Max questioned.

"Well, I think I can narrow it down. I think I know which room we want anyway."

The train suddenly and very quietly lurched forward, and then at a crawl began to move. Max watched as confusion broke out on Arthur's face as the King looked out of the window at the platform. The King rose to his feet and demanded of Julian in Latin

"Humus est amoveo."(a) And of Rhys, in Welsh "Beth actia chan r Andras ydy hon? Bod 'n weledig beiddia 'ch."(i)

"Mae na swyngyfaredd, bopeth ydy ddirwya,"(ii) Rhys tried to calm him.

"What's going on?" asked Jess, looking worried.

"Yeah, is he ok?" Rhiannon spoke anxiously.

"He'll be fine," Julian explained to the others, "The train has confused him," and as Rhys spoke to Arthur in soothing and reassuring tones Julian Finch explained to the others that Arthur had mistakenly believed the ground, and not the carriage, to be moving past them.

"He's alright now," Rhys confirmed as the King re-took his seat, but as Arthur tried to settle and not to look too embarrassed, Drake was not helping matters. Impatiently, the Sea Captain bobbed up and down in his seat demanding more speed be made.

"'Tis slow Finch, canst not we make more knots? Dog traps hath I known to makest wi' more haste."

"It'll speed up," Max assured him, and as he spoke the train gradually picked up momentum, and with an ever-progressive clatter it broke out of the town and down the track at increasing speed. "Faster than a car isn't it, I bet you've never gone so quick," he smiled.

"Canst but hope on a fair wind," Drake declared, and as the train picked up even more speed it made the bushes close around the track pass in a blur. "'Tis a fair wind we hath behind us now," he whooped again, and like an irrepressible little boy he was off around the carriage, going from window to window, pressing the point of his beard up against the glass to look out at the passing trees, embankments and houses. "Not much chance of a fair wind behind me," Max giggled as he emitted an audible fart which brought on his sister's displeasure.

"Honestly, it's like going on a trip with a couple of four-year-olds." She crossed her arms grumpily, and as the smell wafted towards her she rose to her feet and set off down the carriage to retrieve the pinstriped lunatic. She returned moments later leading Drake by the hand, like a wayward toddler, back to his seat. "You can see it all from right here Sir Francis," she explained "it's the same view, every carriage moves past it all."

Jess re-seated herself next to Brendan, who shuffled his feet uncomfortably opposite the whispering Rhys and Rhiannon.

"Are you sure Arthur's alright?" Brendan indicated to the King, who sat bolt upright, the knuckles of his stubby, powerful hands showing white as he gripped the table top between them, a look of grim determination on his face as the world flashed by outside. "He looks a bit motion sick to me. Maybe it's all the layers he's wearing."

"Aha!" Drake cheered as the carriage entered a tunnel, and whilst the lights within stayed on, all around was plunged into darkness. The change in pressure led Arthur to frown, and Drake to question the King's 'sea legs,' but Julian explained in Latin for the benefit of them both that this was a tunnel and they would soon be out of it.

"It's like the world is closing in." Arthur tried to compose himself, he was fighting nausea, and though undeniably nervous, he didn't want the others to mistake it for fear. He took reassurance from the apparent lack of concern of his fellow passenger's faces and voiced his amazement, in the Latin tongue, at this incredible experience.

"Merlin often spoke of such things, the passing of the world in a flash, it's like being in a vortex."

"Well it's certainly saving us time," Julian explained, "and we'll be getting out in a different place." And with a 'vooching' sound they were just as suddenly out of the tunnel and back in the late afternoon sunlight.

They broke out of the trees, and Arthur visibly relaxed as the view increased and fields of green pasture and ripening corn opened out to each side. He tried to settle in his seat, and feeling less enclosed and being able now to see. His stomach settled also, though Max did notice him flinch with every little bridge and tunnel they passed through.

"Who's for a sandwich?" Max asked as the train began to slow into the first station of the journey. He held the bag open on his lap, and like a successful contestant at a lucky dip dug his hand in to withdraw it, clutching a big bag of crisps as a satisfied smile spread over his face.

"Really, Max, not already," Jess spurned him.

"Yes, you can't be hungry already Max," their father added in tones of amusement, "we've only been going ten minutes."

"Brendan," Max called, and ignoring the protests he chucked the crisps onto his fellow traveller's lap.

Brendan, who'd been feeling a little peckish, tried not to look too disappointed as Jess took them straight off him and handed them to her father, who returned them to the sandwich bag.

"They may have to last us," he explained.

"Why?" Max challenged, scowling at his sister. "Because Miss bossy-boots says?"

"No. Because we didn't bring them just to eat straight away."

"Ah, 'tis true wisdom," Drake spoke authoritatively, "for 'tis like to a voyage in seas uncharted..."

"We'll have to ration it," Rhys joked, but Drake was being serious.

"Aye, we mayst Master Rhys. An' unto thy charge, thus for thy pains, do I appoint thee quartermaster."

"There we go then," Julian lifted the picnic bag off his son's lap and entrusted it to the care of his wife's nephew. "A very wise appointment if I might say so, Sir Francis," he smiled in amusement, and then to Rhys he added quickly: "Half a piece of bread a day and a pickled onion should see young Maxwell through!"

"Dad!" Max didn't find it funny, and neither did the Tudor Sea Captain.

"'Tis not subject t' merriment Mr Finch, oft hath I strung pon a yard arm those men o' mine crew, who greed ravaged an' gripped by hunger, turned vagabond an' thief."

"Did that often happen?" asked Brendan, wide-eyed. "Did sailors often try to get at the rations on long sea voyages?"

"Ah, whence hunger doest grab at thy belly an' thirst doest upset the balance o' thy mind in the tropical sun, 'tis danger," Drake spoke dramatically, once again enjoying all eyes being upon him. "'Tis more danger at hand 'mongst a famished crew, an' mutinous thought, than there be terrors in the deep nor death in the winds above."

"A storm would certainly wreck a ship," Brendan challenged, "but how..."

"Wi' united purpose canst a storm be fought," Drake parried, "a crew that fights itself, that be torn asunder by a vagabond or three, be

241

bent on its own destruction."

"And they will all be weaker, they will all suffer if one selfish man pinches all the rations from the others," Rhys added, "that's why you had to make an example of them, right?" He grinned at his cousin. "I recommend Max gets three thousand lashes," he joked.

"Indeed, spake like a quartermaster o' the Queen's own fleet."

"Look, I wasn't pinching anyone else's," Max defended himself looking hurt, "I was handing it round."

"I know you were," his father chuckled, but Drake was still in control of the conversation.

"Be not it said that we shouldst find London at peace," he spoke seriously, "for be it so that we must raise a siege, there couldst be scarce a crust within her noble and ignoble walls."

"Oh I think there will be food in London," Rhiannon sniggered. "There's usually a bit of choice anyway, and if the enemy have already attacked London I think we'd know about it by now."

The train drew up to the platform at Chippenham station, and to those aboard the small group waiting patiently on the platform appeared to stare into space as the carriages flitted past them. With the brakes applied fully the train screeched to a halt, and the doors opened to let a few on and even fewer off. Arthur rose with a look of relief and Rhys had to explain to him that this was just a brief stop and that there would be many more before they finally arrived in the Capital.

Arthur settled again as the journey continued, and as the others talked amongst themselves, rather hindered by the language barrier, he, Julian and Drake kept up a flowing conversation in Latin about tactics and how best to deal with a powerful enemy, how to deliver the killer blow when you are outnumbered and the odds are stacked against you.

Julian felt his way uncomfortably through the unexplored realms of military campaigning; he felt he should pinch himself, for here he was sat with these two and hoping to unearth whatever it was that threatened the security of his nation. It was like a dream and yet it was a nightmare, he felt such an unlikely hero, nervous and apprehensive, but as the two legends reminisced of past glories it bolstered his confidence hugely.

"At Coed Celyddon I sucked them into a trap," Arthur recalled. "Thousands of Saxons bore down upon us, thicker than the corn in those fields, and my small band like bait in a trap stood at the bottom of the wooded gorge. It was loyalty which saved us, for I had put two wings on the army of equal strength, and both were hidden in the woods in ambush. As the enemy bore down the gorge and drove towards the centre to drive a wedge through my thin ranks my men held to the last moment when the wing men came from the hills above, from left and right, and flung a hail of spears and rocks upon the enemy. The Saxons couldn't move - they had nowhere to go and couldn't swing their axes for the weight of their fellows penning them in like sheep in a fold. My band could so easily have turned and fled, but when the wings descended upon them to cleave carnage amongst them my band cut loose and wrought death to our sworn foe. It took guts to spill guts that day, faith in our fellows to come to our aid, and I've never been so glad to see anyone as I was to see Cai and Gwalchmai appear on each ridge of the enemy's flanks."

"'Tis discipline indeed," Drake commentated, "an' timed so sweet as to let fly havoc when the time be aright. Each gunner by his cannon has an itch t' give fire when his enemy is in range, yet discipline must stay each hand until the foe be close at quarter. Only then wouldst I bark mine order, only whence mine foe sits just across the water an' his deck be cluttered wi' all hands. Whence couldst I see each face, each yellowed tooth an' pockmark, then, an' timed afore mine foe wouldst have a like to shout as I, wouldst I bellow 'give fire,' an' look on as didst my guns sweep his deck like to skittles in an ale house. No tavern floor couldst soak up the blood o' such slaughter. For whence the wind doest lift the smoke o' battle, like line on line o' child's poppets, twisted in death, doest the foe lay broken."

"Brutal," said Julian. It was the first time he had sensed anything but a glorifying joy from Drake as he told his stories. The children weren't listening now, he was telling it like it was, and for once was not trying to impress either himself or the ancient King. For in the brutal world of professional killing Arthur had been as proficient an expert as himself, he'd been there and done it, and not with the aid of gunpowder but with the sharp edge of a sword.

"The men must have faith in their leaders," Arthur observed softly. "They must do their tasks unfailingly, unquestioning, for their leaders plan may not be revealed to them. They may not be privy to his wisdom but they must have faith in his judgment and the cause if they are to complete the tasks they are given and the end is to be reached."

"It be so," Drake agreed, "for 'pon my chest within mine cabin be laid mine chart for mine eyes alone t' behold. Yet say I unto mine crew 'take in the top sail,' or 'three degrees leeward,' an' 'tis wi' a faithful heart do they mine bidding."

"And so it was the summer before Dyrham," Arthur spoke sadly, "Merlin's last summer. United, the Saxons occupied a hill, having pursued us for many weeks. They numbered five war bands in total, at least four times our number, and they were desperate to bring us to battle before the harvest needed to be gathered in. For my men it had been shame to run, fleeing in the face of the Saxons and not turning to fight them. Merlin and I sat with the counsel - we couldn't hope to win if we stood against so many - yet morale in my ranks was at breaking point, and I needed to give them a victory if they were to take up arms again in the spring. Many times the counsel petitioned for battle - Bors, Bedwyr - yet Merlin spoke against it. In his wisdom he knew we could not stand, and he spoke of a dream in which he'd seen the starry host, vast in number, twinkling brightly in the sky.

"I looked across the valley to the Saxon encampment. They had closed upon us and I could see the fires of their vast horde burning bright in the dusk. The number of their fires sparked fear in the hearts of my men, so I ordered the same.

"I ordered each man to rise and cut wood from the forest behind and to lay his own fires, not one between many, for it is the custom for warriors to gather around, but many fires for each man. I ordered each man to lay and tend three fires, to spread them out well and to keep each stacked up and burning all through the night.

"Come daybreak my men were exhausted, but the enemy feared we had mustered such a host as they couldn't stand against it; their warlords lost heart and with the dawn they scattered, some leaving their burnt supper cooking on their fires.

"My men, weary as they were, entered the Saxon camp soon after, and full of fury pursued the scattered foe. Bent on revenge for all the running we had done, and hungry for the victory they craved, they set about the Saxons and revelled in the slaughter. Merlin's dream had broken their spirit."

"Aye," Drake nodded in agreement. "For victory, success, gold, wilt a churl do his master's bidding. Yet whence he feels the cold, when hunger bites at his gut he be like to a beast, stubborn like to a mule an' full o' groaning."

"As my men that night. 'Why must we tend so may fires? We are tired and tomorrow we die, can not we sleep at peace while we can?' Merlin told them in death there would be time enough for sleep and through toil might they earn their peace. In faith they did my bidding and their perseverance brought us victory."

"Aye, there be no allay like to good counsel."

"So you see, Mr Finch, Julian." Arthur looked across at his host. "We are in your hands now, we do not understand this world, but you know it and you must lead the way for us to follow."

Julian felt his throat tighten as the poison chalice of leadership was handed to him, and he coughed uncomfortably, unsure of what to say in response.

"Even I know not what waters lie ahead," Drake too conceded humbly, "you must be our pilot, Finch. Thou shalt fight along side us, yet must we trust in thy counsel unerring to guide us through the sounds. For victory an' deliverance from servitude strive us three together."

"Well, I'm honoured," said Julian slowly, and Drake really did seem as good as his word, for once he seemed prepared to listen to wisdom and wasn't trying to compete with, or out do, anyone else. "Well we certainly need to work together if we are to get anywhere, strike while the iron is hot I suppose."

"Aye, surprise, 'twas speed an' surprise didst scatter the Armada," Drake smiled. "Fire ships t' break them up an' strike fear into their very hearts, an' a merrie chase didst follow."

"Basic warfare," Arthur grinned. "When we face a mightier foe than ourselves we must first divide him up, partition him, and then squash him little bits at a time."

"It comes down to the same problems though, my Liege, it's all very well if we knew we were facing a huge army, but when our enemy is unseen, unknown..."

"There are other ways to divide your foe - you must make the war lords turn on each other. There's always tension in any meeting of war lords, there always was from the time of the ancient tribes until today. Each war lord has his own pride and he has his own agenda, they all wrestle for control, and like the old Roman siege engines and artillery you need only overstretch the tension and they will snap and break apart. Like a pack of dogs they will turn on each other, for each war lord must keep the loyalty of his own men to remain in control. If he loses the loyalty of his following they will kill him and replace him, like a wolf pack when the Alpha male is past his prime, the pretenders will oust him, and if he stands to fight they will tear him apart."

"So how do you ensure disloyalty?"

"There are many ways. For a start you can attack the material needs of your foe. Were I pursued by three Saxon war bands I would leave enough food behind for one, each leader will seek to provide for his own, and will challenge the others to seize what he can."

"Your rationing argument again, Sir Francis."

"Or Finch, canst thou attack thy enemies wealth. The Don King had not a groat for to build a fleet, for whence had he sacked the Indies an' sailed his ships homeward filled wi' all the gold o' the New World, didst I then attack an' take it from him. For there are those who denounce me an' cry 'Drake the pirate,'" he gave Jess a sideways glance, "yet were his Panama gold not carried unto Queen Bess there wouldst in Cadiz be an' Armada threefold in size, an a threat therein too mighty for the stout-hearted sailors o' England, though there would have been glory in the fight."

"Men fight for money," Arthur observed. "My men fought for their land, their kinfolk and their very lives, but Rome was built on a professional army, each legionary paid in wages and hoping to retire to lands of his own at the end of his service. The raider seeks plunder..."

"An' the loyalty o' the mercenary soldier can be bought for any price," Drake interrupted, "like to a hog at market, out-bid thy foe an' his services shalt be thine whilst thou hast gold enough for his purse an' ale enough for his gut."

"So take your enemies' money and..."

"Aye, thou hast it, Finch. Seize his war chest, cut his purse strings, make thee a hole to empty it, an' as his coins fall out see too his forces dribble away, for canst he not deliver. Greed be the undoing of many."

"But some fight for causes," Julian considered, "for ideologies, beliefs..."

"Then attack the causes," Arthur fixed him with a stare, with hard uncompromising eyes. "Make him doubt his leaders, his motives, his beliefs, make him doubt himself. It's about trust, Julian - if they don't trust each other they won't function, they will turn on each other and they will fail. You can send spies into the enemy camp, you can spread rumours of disloyalty, rumours of greed. Not all battles are won on the field and not all battles even come to the field, if we can turn the enemy on himself we may not have to face him."

There was silence, just for a moment as Julian and Drake reflected on the King's last words.

"Thou hast around thy neck thy old torc, an pon they finger bare thee thy signet ring, the seal o' thine office," Drake broke the silence, "but thou hast also the bearing o' a King. 'Twill be high honour, Artos Rex, to do battle beside thee." And he really meant it.

At the back of his mind Julian feared how he would cope if his own metal were tested, if the moment came would he have the courage to face the danger? He didn't know, but he wouldn't be facing anything alone and the presence of such distinguished company encouraged him. Even so, he now felt the burden of responsibility more keenly then ever, it was quite an experience to be told by two such heroes that they sought guidance from him. And as they both looked at him now almost with expectation, he felt huge pressure to say something significant, to make a rousing speech or to do something momentous. Instead he feebly repeated the lessons of his tutors to demonstrate his understanding.

"So to scatter the enemy we must time it right, we must vary the line of attack and we must rely on surprise. We'll need unfailing discipline and an unbreakable nerve, and we must do anything we can to pull his feet from under him." He thought it sounded lame, but Drake and Arthur beamed back at him.

"So show us what to do: take us to him, Julian, and let us loose," Arthur smiled, then sat back and immersed himself in his own wallow of thought.

"I wish I could understand what you've been going on about, Dad." Maxwell Finch brought his father back to reality. Max had been left out in the cold a bit as Jess and Brendan and Rhiannon and Rhys had been engaged in more private conversations on the other side of the aisle, and the constant babble of unfamiliar Latin in his ears had begun to irritate him.

"I wish you could understand it too, son, in fact I'll talk to all of you lot later - these two really know their stuff."

"You know what you have to do," Jess looked at her brother, "it might take a while, but..."

"I'm not learning Latin, Latin's dead," Max protested.

"Arthur appears to be living proof that it's very much alive."

"Come off it, Sis."

"You could always learn Welsh, cuz." Rhys smiled, "I'll teach you myself if you like, then you can chat to Arthur and just translate to him what Sir Francis is saying."

"Or perhaps Sir Francis would like to learn too," Rhiannon suggested, "then you could all understand each other."

"Well everyone might as well learn modern English then," said Max defensively, "then everyone could understand each other." He felt they were all ganging up on him.

"It's been tried before, you know, Max," Julian explained. "One ruling power after another has tried to ban the use of native languages, each making it's own speech that of the administration, of the law, of the religion of the land."

"They even tried to ban Welsh-speaking in the last century," Rhys agreed, "but it backfired."

"It always will," Julian nodded. "Repression always invites resistance."

"Arthur's no outsider, you know, Max," said Brendan. "This is his country too - in fact he was here first."

247

"It doesn't matter who was here first," Jess spoke wisely. "This country belongs to all of us, we should all want the best for it and each other. We all have to try and get on, and we all ought to make efforts to understand each other better, it's just lazy not to try, and it's totally hypocritical to expect everyone else to adapt to suit us."

"Oh yeah," Max challenged, "well you can get off your high horse, I don't see you speaking Urdu or Hindi. I think it would be much easier if all the parlez-vous and gratsi-gratsi's were made to learn English, it would cut out half the rubbish we have to learn at school anyway."

"Well you would, my little imperialist," Julian smiled at his son, "anything to spend less time in the classroom, eh?"

Jessica Finch just shook her head at Brendan in disregard for what she saw as her brother's narrow-minded attitude. This conversation had echoes of Mr Jarvis lecturing to Nick Bovis and Lizzie Taylor, and in many ways her brother's argument made the teachers' point.

"Look at me now," their father continued. "I never thought Latin would be useful, and here I am using it."

"Yeah, that's an everyday use for classical languages that is, Dad, talking with medieval kings on trains."

"He's not medieval, Max," Jess corrected him, "he's Romano-British."

"I couldn't care if he's from outer-Mongolia, that's not the point."

"Well technically there's no such place as outer-Mongolia, there's the Gobi desert and there's..."

"Brendan, I couldn't care less, I'm just saying it would be much easier if everyone spoke English."

"It's certainly an interesting suggestion." Julian tried to calm the exchange down with compromise. "I'm sure a lot of nations would agree that a common language would be useful just as Latin once was, after all effective communication helps us understand a lot of cultural differences. But I'm not sure they'd all agree it should be English."

"You might find they all insisted on us learning French," said Rhiannon.

"I'm no good at French," Max spoke in defiance.

"Well what about something more obscure? Romanian, Egyptian..."

"Oh please! You mean I'd have to suddenly learn how to draw as well."

"Modern Egyptian isn't all in hieroglyphics," Jess was despairing. "You can be an idiot at times, Max, you really can."

"Latin was once just such a common language, a language of trade, of literature, of religion," Julian tried to get through to his son, "that's why Arthur spoke it, as did many educated nobles within what had once been the Roman empire. Drake learnt it because in his time it was the language of court."

"You mean judges had to speak it?" Max sneered. "That's not very fair on the people on trial, is it? It's hard enough for them to know what's going on, what's being said with all that legal mumbo jumbo, but in Latin..."

"No, in the Monarch's court. It was a kind of international language of diplomacy. King's, Queen's and nobles learnt it so they could communicate with other Kings in other countries. It saved going through interpreters all the time and meant they could speak to each other directly when they met. It certainly would've helped develop trust - I mean, imagine the mischief interpreters would have been able to cause if they'd wanted to, or the problems that might have arisen through miss-interpretation. But in fact, Max, a lot of that mumbo-jumbo still spoken in law courts is Latin. It's formal, you see."

"Well, that's very silly because no one can understand them," Max countered in defence. "I mean, take animals for example - in all our biology books they have an English name and a Latin name as if that's their real name. That's stupid. I mean, the name they're given is what they're called and what we understand them to be. I mean, a wolf's a wolf, why can't we all call it a wolf instead of a... um..."

"Canis Lupus."

"Exactly," Max folded his arms defiantly, "That's stupid, it's a wolf, call it a wolf, how are people supposed to know what you're talking about."

"But that's the whole point, Max," his father tried to explain sensitively. "It has a Latin name so that all peoples, all scientists and biologists of all nations and speaking all different languages, can all refer to it in Latin, and then they all know exactly what species they are talking about."

"Well, I still think it would be better if everyone just spoke English."

"Because you're lazy," his sister cut in.

"And what are you doing about it then?" Max turned on her. "You only do French at school, same as me."

"Brendan's getting Spanish lessons after school," she replied casually, "I thought I might learn with him."

"Oh, very cosy," he mocked sarcastically.

"The Don tongue," Drake sounded impressed. "The Dago speech be foul an' twisted, yet wouldst I too, Drake, be keen of mind to yoke it."

"See," said Rhys, "even Sir Francis knows it would be useful if he could communicate with his enemies in their own language - it might even spare a few lives, eh?"

"Think on." Drake's eyes were alight and a wicked grin had spread across his bearded face. "What damage couldst be done were even I to yoke the Dago tongue and with it plough deceit an' destruction. Couldst I listen to Don prisoners in discussion an' take to mine ears their secrets. I couldst spread amongst them such rumours as wouldst make them cower at the thought o' the open sea. Couldst I even play the part o' a Don Cap'n an' sail mine ships t' dock in Panama under a stinking Don flag, t' spake unto them as would their own an' order, 'fill the hold wi' gold.' Couldst then I sail away freely, an' not one shot fired, for Plymouth t' drop mine cargo, yet return wouldst I 'pon the next tide."

"Very honourable motives to learn another language," observed Jess shaking her head.

"But what is modern English anyway?" Julian turned the subject back to Max's original suggestion. "After all, you made a good point, language is merely a means of establishing a communication, to ensure mutual understanding, that's why it's always developing, always changing."

"New words," said Brendan, "they add new words to the dictionary every year."

"Indeed they do," Julian agreed, "I mean 'chav' didn't exist in my day," he said the word awkwardly, "and there are loads of other words which have almost completely changed their meaning. 'Cool,' and 'wicked' for example, and 'far out.'" He said each word as if he was still profoundly uncomfortable with their new meanings, and sounded rather square as he did so.

"Or 'gay,'" said Max quickly, thinking himself very funny.

"Exactly," his father agreed, yet remained serious. "That would be another example, and it's no surprise you thought of it."

"Bet you were very gay on your voyages, Sir Francis, weren't you?" Max turned to Drake, but couldn't stop himself sniggering.

"Verily, at times," Drake replied, though he looked a little confused. "There camest times on each voyage whence mine whole ships company were full of merriment an' danced most gaily."

"You see," Julian continued with a straight face as his son rocked backwards and forwards with laughter, "meanings change as the language develops. Our society is much more integrated now than it was when these two were doing their best to prevent it being so. It's multicultural now, and as such it's no longer just about languages but about common understanding and respect, that's what's important if we are going to survive."

"Max," Arthur turned to the lad and put his hand out as if to demonstrate that he too was making a great effort towards unifying the group. "My friend Max," he said slowly and with great difficulty, straining out the words awkwardly, hoping he was saying it right, hoping he would be understood. Then a huge smile spread over the king's face as Max, humbled by his own lack of effort, took the King's hand and shook it warmly.

"You're my friend too, Arthur," he said, "Artos rex Britainicus."

Jess was enjoying their vantage point from high up on the tracks to peer nosily down into people's back gardens, into their private lives, and was commenting to Brendan about how 'that garden was overgrown,' or 'they must have small children, look at that climbing frame,' or 'they've got a nice pond,' and 'did you see that ugly extension?' But ignoring the babble, Arthur gazed out of the window as the surroundings began to change more totally than anywhere else he had stopped so far.

Outside the slowing train it was all becoming much more built up, and it was fascinating to him to think that each one of the many rows upon rows of houses could each contain a family, or several families as Julian had explained. For some of them were 'flats' - a strange name for a strange concept, stacking one dwelling on another - but he could see for himself that space came at a premium.

The buildings sprawled out in every direction as far as the eye could see and he could see huge towering structures far off which caused him to completely lose his sense of perspective. He just couldn't fathom how so many could live in one place or how a garrison could ever be rallied and deployed to cover such a huge city successfully. He felt as if he was being sucked on and on into the heart of it by this 'train' he was sitting on, and the City, so big, so imposing, made him feel so, so, small, and he'd never imagined that any city, not even Rome, could ever be on such a scale. As the train slowed gently into London's Paddington station his heart beat fast in his chest. His moment could be coming, he had to find strength, had to rise to the occasion.

Drake too gazed in awe as the City around him displayed itself. "Old London town," he declared sadly, "wherefore hast thou become so altered?"

"S'pect it's changed a bit, hasn't it?" said Max unhelpfully, and his comment provoked a critical 'tut' from his sister, who considered it so obvious as to not need voicing.

"'Pon my troth," said Drake loudly, "be Runciman's tavern yonder at Putney Bridge, I'll with his ale be re-acquainted and then mayhap I'll drink t' change."

"You may have some difficulty there, Sir Francis," Julian tried to explain. "Not much chance of any of your old haunts still standing - they've all gone, been replaced with all this."

"But how is a man t' tarry in London if there be no taverns? Thou wilt spake that the bear pits be gone next."

"Well, there are loads of pubs," said Rhys trying to soften the blow, "funky bars and clubs. But they might be a bit different from what you remember, lots of bright lights and loud music."

"Minstrels?"

"Minstrels, yes," Rhys nodded with a smile as Max looked on jealously. "Of a kind."

"Hampton Court is still standing," said Brendan in compromise, "though the Queen doesn't live there. Oh, and the Globe, they've totally reconstructed it - you'll feel at home there."

Drake returned Brendan's enthusiasm with a mournful and dispirited look

"The Globe, what fortune that? Canst they construct one building of mine age an' build they a theatre, what wasted chance!"

"There won't be any time for sightseeing," said Julian firmly as the train pulled to a stop. "Now you all have to follow me, stick together like glue and don't let anyone get lost."

He led the way off the train and demonstrated to them how to insert their tickets to pass through the barrier. In a few moments they stood together, having left the platform for the hustle and bustle of the main station. Julian led the way to the underground platform, a journey he did daily and could have done with his eyes shut were it not for the crowds, which even for a weekend were heavy. He bought tickets from the machine, glanced at the board, which indicated all trains were running to time, and having again demonstrated how to negotiate the barriers, he led his party onwards and downwards towards the tube line.

King Arthur backed away from the escalator at first, shuffling his feet like a mistrusting child as he tottered at the top of the menacing yet fascinating moving staircase. Again, he suspected sorcery. The stairs themselves moved, without having to walk it took people down as an adjacent one brought people up, and the stairs themselves disappeared into the floor as they reached the top. He was initially uncertain, but as Julian stepped boldly onto the stairs to be born down into the depths, he too followed, with Rhys at his side, eager to face each new phenomena without being seen to hesitate lest Drake mistake thoughtful judgement for cowardice.

"Exciting, isn't it?" Rhys spoke to him in Welsh. "Ever thought you'd be on a moving stair?"

"It's like descending into hell," Arthur spoke plainly. "Like Hades, the Underworld."

"Well, in a way we are. You see, we have to go underground to move around, it's so much easier in a place like this."

"The air is foul and the heat rises," Arthur muttered quietly, "but if we must go to the bowels of hell to take the battle to the enemy, then so be it."

"Well you're right, it certainly stinks, but you wouldn't be so hot if you didn't have so many clothes on."

"Aharrr!" yelled Drake from behind them in excitement. No sooner had he got on the escalator and begun to experience the strange sensation of being carried downward, than he had turned round to see the top of the stairs disappearing behind him, and had begun to climb the stairs in reverse. Amazed by the thrill of remaining in one place by climbing as the escalator fought against him, he let out whoops of delight and had to be manhandled by the twins into facing the correct way and letting the stairs convey him steadily to the bottom. "Again, again must we ride it," he demanded in protest.

"You're drawing too much attention to yourself," Jess rebuked him, irritated and embarrassed by his childish behaviour. "Have you any idea how ridiculous you look in your suit and behaving like a naughty child? If we don't hurry we'll miss the train."

But it was the expressionless throng of people in the confined space and claustrophobic, heavy atmosphere of the underground platform which made the experience so different, so much more oppressive than the clothes-shopping crowds they had mixed with earlier in the day. Arthur told Rhys that he felt like an ant, one of many in their labyrinth of tunnels, and Rhys had to agree this was not a bad comparison.

The distant thunder-like rumble of an approaching train announced that it was drawing near, and almost as one the mass of people on the platform shuffled forward, creating a near-impenetrable phalanx right on the edge. As the noisy, smelly tube train drew up with a squealing of wheels, and wafted hot, stuffy, oily air over all of them and the doors clunked open, Drake stepped forward to try and board it. He found his way barred by an exiting mass of zombie-like people, eyes fixed and starring ahead, who seemed to break free from the internal crush like water from a leaking pipe.

Jess tried to tell him to stand back and let people off, but Drake was being pushed from behind and fought the flow like a salmon desperately trying to break through a waterfall. It angered her that everyone seemed so impersonal, that manners seemed to go straight out of the window and that courtesy was abandoned when people came down into these depths. No one seemed the remotest bit aware of anyone else; they just pushed, stared ahead, and walked with purpose as if they were the only one in the City, as if they were frightened to look anyone else in the eye. She didn't know how her father could manage this journey every working day.

Eventually they all squeezed aboard, Brendan only just in time. The doors, sensing his presence between them mid-shut, hissed open to ensure he could get in before clunking shut behind him. They stood crushed together in the almost-silent, crowded carriage as people all around focused ahead, at newspapers, at the floor or ceiling, ignoring all around them and saying nothing. Suddenly, and with an unanticipated violence, the train lurched forward causing several of them to bash into each other as they tried to recover their balance, and Rhiannon got rather squashed by Max and Arthur as they desperately grasped at handrails for support.

"She pitches and rolls," Drake declared in excitement, but even he, sensing the sombre and subdued atmosphere that the carriage created, voiced his enjoyment in a, by Drake's standards, quiet voice as the train rattled and clattered along to an unfamiliar high pitched buzzing.

Arthur found himself feeling sick almost immediately and tried to distract himself by looking around the carriage. The people he saw amazed him. All around were people of radically different appearance, size, shape and colour, and many wearing very different clothing. He'd noticed such strange-looking folk earlier when first they had entered the station, and there had been others too in the centre of Bath, but so preoccupied had he been with the buildings and the need to follow Julian without getting lost in the crowds that he hadn't taken proper note of the crowds themselves.

Look he now did, and he continued to take note as they switched trains further down the line and finally emerged from the artificially lit bowels of London into the heart of Whitehall. There had been many like the Finch's, but also white people with features and a colouring most unlike that of his host family. There had been black people whose skin was to him like the cloak of night, brown people, yellow people, thickset people, thin people, very tall and very short people. People who covered their heads, and others who appeared to cover their entire bodies, whilst others still seemed to be barely wearing anything at all. Others had shaved their heads while others still appeared to be wearing tapestries or wore their coloured hair in elaborate curls or spiked up. There were people with wide flat noses and others with freckly skin, and he overheard many different tongues being spoken, all very different in pitch and sound to the modern language spoken by Julian Finch and his family.

It was a lot for the King to take in. He'd experienced ethnic differences for himself, of course, for he had traded with the Iberians, campaigned in Brittany and travelled in Gaul. His own people were a mixture of Celtic descendants and those of Roman settlers, and even those who were the result of inter-racial union looked completely different again from the Saxon enemies they'd fought. There had been a handful of black people in his kingdom too, the descendants of unfortunate North Africans who had been enslaved by the Romans and dumped at the frontier of the empire to work themselves ragged in earning their masters a fortune, and the crew of trading ships often numbered people from all over the Mediterranean. So it was not the appearance of the people so much as their number which most surprised him, for here like a basket of fruits, fruits of every season gathered together, was a total mixture. People of every shape and colour, their skin ranging from jet black to pasty white and every shade in between, and there were thousands of them.

"Who are all these?" he asked Rhys in Welsh, and in tones of confusion, as they ascended the steps out of the tube station and into the London evening.

"All what?"

"All these different peoples, how came they here? Are they slaves?"

"No, no," Rhys sounded amused, "the days of slavery in this country are long gone."

"But each looks so different from the other and yet each walks as free as if in his own village."

"Well that's how it should be, the city is home to them all."

"Well, don't they all fight each other? Don't they raid each other and carry each other's goats and cattle away?"

"Of course not, no-one's doing anyone else any harm. Most of these people were probably born here, they have as much right to be here as I do. Wherever their ancestors might have come from they're all British now, same as we are."

The king frowned, for whilst his own people had been a mix of those who had gone before, his life had been to champion their preservation from the invading foe.

"These people aren't trying to drive us out," Rhys read his mind and tried to explain, "they aren't a Saxon horde, they aren't going to kill us and take our farms. They want to join in peacefully, integrate, contribute to the economy, to settle down. Sure, there are some cultural differences, but people can live the way they want, just so long as it doesn't cause anyone else harm."

"Clash of culture brings war," Arthur reflected, "especially when food is scarce. There must have been many invasions, many bloody battles to leave so many peoples behind."

"But food isn't scarce, not here anyway," Rhys explained, "though the chance of a better quality of life might explain a lot of the immigration."

"Immigration?" Arthur didn't understand. "You mean like the Vandals or the Huns, migrating tribes who pillage and slaughter everything in their way?"

"No, not at all, I'm talking about individuals who have simply chosen to make a new life for themselves. People want to come here, and though there will always be some who don't like it, it will make us stronger in the long run."

"Well if they come in peace I can see some benefit, we will be all the wiser a nation if knowledge and understanding is shared. Rome yoked the people of this land, and though they tried to shake it off and bellowed in their bondage they ploughed all the better for it in time. Even when Rome abandoned us to stand alone she left us united, some of us literate, and with the legacy of the empire and all it brought with it."

"See, I always thought integration was a good thing. We wouldn't have anywhere near as many different restaurants to eat in if the ancient Britons had been left to themselves."

"You shouldn't joke, Rhys, for mixing strengths brings a powerful combination. You combine Roman discipline and tactics with the raw bravery and fierce warrior spirit of the Celts, and you get a force to be reckoned with. Each of my men is worth two of the Saxon axe-swingers in a field of battle; it's only a shame they came on in many times our number. You mix Celtic farming with Roman irrigation, or the skill of the Celt in horse and hound breeding with Roman administration. How else could I have properly assembled my war band suitably equipped, and drilled as a unit?"

"Well, there you have it then. So think how much more improved the country might be with influences from all over the world."

"Not all influences are good."

"You're right, of course, but that's where the skill of the leaders comes in. Britain is a nation of many peoples now, and I guess that makes you King of them all."

"I guess it does," Arthur smiled. "And if they can live together without making war on each other then they have surpassed already what the ancient Celts could manage when it was just them."

(i)   What act of the Devil is this? Be seen I defy thee.
(ii)   There is no sorcery, everything is fine.

(a)   The ground is moving.

Chapter Fourteen – Security

They stood by the banks of the Thames in a gentle breeze and studied the skyline, so unfamiliar to the King and the Tudor Sea Captain.

"It be so transformed," Drake declared. "Can it be said I stand now 'pon the banks o' that very same river?" The murky brown water was much as he remembered it but the parliament buildings, the office blocks and grand institutional buildings along the banks of the Thames were a far cry from the timbered London he remembered, and everything was so much taller. "Ah, there be the Globe." He noticed the reconstructed Elizabethan theatre on the opposite bank. "Accurse it, a pox 'pon the swine therein. All heads a-full o' player's lines, turn they the stout men o' England from the sea an' all useful purpose."

No-one answered Drake, and Arthur just stood in amazement trying to take it all in. What had once been a small garrison town was now a thriving metropolis, and he confided in Rhys his utter bemusement.

"Never have I seen such a place, nor from my distant birthing at Tintagel to my return have I ever conceived of such a place as this."

Rhys patted him gently on the back. "You've been away a long time, but we've come a long way without you, haven't we mate."

"Here it is, gentlemen," Julian announced as Big Ben clanged nine times in the background, "the big city. Tower Bridge, the London Eye, even that monstrous glass Gherkin," he pointed out each in turn, "all symbols of modern England. If you can't get inspiration from a skyline like that, there's little hope for us."

"Are we going anywhere near Trafalgar Square, Dad?"

But no sooner had Max asked the question than his sister elbowed him in the ribs and whispered in his ear, "Don't mention Nelson's column, Max - if Drake realises there isn't a statue like that to him he'll never shut up about it."

After one last look Julian led them all off on the short trek to his place of work. The Commissioners occupied a rather grand Georgian fronted building a stone's throw from the houses of Parliament.

Drake walked between Brendan and Jess and remarked on the lack of evident thieves, cut-throats and beggars. "For scoundrels a many didst prowl the alleys when last I trod this town, an' rats an' filth didst clog the roads t' blockage. Aye, she be more ship-shape an' o' a fashion like t' Bristol than whence last were we acquainted. For gong wouldst the townsfolk throw, 'pon a cheer, from the windows. Most oft wouldst they look not, an' for thy pains wouldst thou below receive a covering o' night soil 'pon thy unprotected head."

"That's disgusting," Brendan grimaced. "To think that people really used to just sling their poo into the street. It's no wonder there was so much squalor and disease back then."

"I speak true, Master Brendan," Drake continued, "for oft whence afoot, an' havin' toiled an' trudged passed beggar an' widow, child an' sellers o' wares most foul an' fair, wouldst I behold mine hose an' shoes, an' groan I at their state."

"Dirty?"

"Aye dirty, dirty be aright." The memories alone seemed to frustrate him beyond consolation. "From knee t' toe be mine stockings soiled an' muddied, an' mine buckled shoes be not known t' me from the mire o' the gutter itself."

"Gutted," said Max butting in, "you should have worn wellingtons."

"They didn't have them then," Jess rebuked him impatiently, and Max, who was beginning to feel that everyone had it in for him today, was pleased to hear Drake enquire further as to what these were, even after Jess had explained them to be 'rubber boots that my silly brother thinks you should have worn even though they hadn't been invented.'

"They're waterproof, Sir Francis, and they come up to your knee," he stuck his tongue out at Jess mid-explanation. "When you've got where you're going you just take them off."

"Not really needed in this smart part of London," Rhys added unhelpfully, "but it's not all this clean. People flock here thinking the streets are paved with gold, what they don't realises is they're cluttered with chewing gum, bus tickets and kebab wrappers."

"Kebab...?"

And plenty of lazy people's cigarette butts too, Rhys," Jess berated him. "Honestly, if people only used bins for their rubbish."

"Ah, stand she has since centuries past, an' God willing wilt she stand for many t' come." Drake breathed deep, as if revelling in his return to this incredible city.

"Yeah, so long as it isn't all blown up with an atomic bomb," Rhys winked at Rhiannon. "I'm still looking forward to seeing how you two are going to stop that happening."

"It doesn't need to be anything that drastic," said Brendan slowly. "If the polar ice caps keep melting at the same rate as they are now the whole city will be under water in a hundred years. Global warming will be the death of this place, the death of the whole human race eventually."

"You'll need more than Wellingtons then Sir Francis," Rhys joked.

"Yeah waders, and an aqualung," Rhiannon added.

"It's a serious matter, I wish more people would take it seriously,"

Jess shook her head and glanced at Brendan, who gave her a look as if to say that although the others didn't understand, he at least agreed with her totally.

In sight of the office, Julian briefed the party quickly. "Right - here's the plan. Max, Jess, Brendan and Rhiannon will come with me and we'll all go in first. Rhys, you wait here with Arthur and Sir Francis, it'll look really suspicious if I try to get you all in together. Once we're in I'll signal you from my office window, it's the third from the left, two floors up. When you see the signal go to the front desk and ask for..."

"What will the signal be?" Rhys interrupted.

"Oh, um, I'll turn the light on and off twice," suggested Julian distractedly. "When you see the signal, Rhys, walk with Arthur and Sir Francis to the front desk and tell the security chap that Drake and Arthur are aides to the Italian Commissioners and have come to collect some papers from me. Tell them you're their interpreter and get Arthur and Drake to rattle on in Latin if you want, the Security bloke won't understand and it will seem more authentic. He'll probably just tell you to wait and he'll call me down from my office to welcome you."

"No dramas, Jules, you can rely on me," Rhys assured him, glad of the responsibility.

"Rhys, just don't let them wander off or do anything stupid, there are security cameras everywhere around here you know."

"Oh right," Rhys replied, though this time he felt the burden of responsibility a little more heavily.

"And good luck," Julian added as he led the rest of the group off towards the front door. His heart was pounding in his chest, and the enormity of what he was about to do struck him once again. His throat felt tight and he felt a bit sick as the sweat pricked at his skin; this was really it. He felt like he'd been crawling slowly up to the top of a roller-coaster, and now he was tottering at the top about to plunge down the other side. It was exciting - to break into the Commissioner's office to try and steal a confidential document was the stuff of spy stories - but it was also nerve-racking. For although he knew he would almost certainly get the sack when they found out, and although he had tried to put this to the back of his mind, this wasn't just theft, this wasn't just the end of his career; this was a breach of his position of trust. It might get him branded a traitor, he could go to prison for what he was about to do, and what good would he be to his family then?

Julian tried to focus, but instead he conjured to his mind's eye the sneering face of Sir Morgan Dredmor. "Protocol Fifteen is none of your business, Finch," Sir Morgan repeated again, and he and the Duke of Man tapped glasses in toast once more of the document in Julian's memory. The disembodied heads of Trevor Rindburn and Nigel Sludboil suddenly joined them and in the forefront of Julian's mind they confidently chorused together,"Drafted and agreed on," before, (for some reason Julian didn't dwell on,) their bodies suddenly appeared and they began to dance in a circle, holding hands and flicking their heels in the air.

Julian blinked twice to clear his head, and he slapped himself as he desperately sought clarity. This was really it, he told himself again as he ascended the steps and the automatic doors slid open. He couldn't hesitate, and he tried to boost his confidence by reminding himself that The European Environmental Act was to be a public document and as such he was entitled to read it, all be it a day or two early, he simply had to satisfy his hunch. In any case he told himself, he was resigned to it now, they might say he was mad when he appeared in Court but he might as well try to enjoy the moment. His work was dull and his life had been fairly uneventful up until now, but here he was, actually involved, actually doing something. He tried to visualise himself as James Bond, calm, cool, in control; and although he knew he was far from this and felt a most unlikely protagonist he reasoned that surely half the necessity of being a successful spy was being inconspicuous.

Julian's pulse quickened further as he entered the lobby and approached the security desk, and as the others filed in silently behind him Julian was sure the Pakistani security guard would be able to hear his heart beating.

"Good evening, George," he greeted him, trying desperately to keep his voice even, not to give anything away.

George was in his forties with slick black hair and a thick moustache. He wore black trousers and a white shirt with blue epaulettes at the shoulders, and he looked rather bored.

"Mr Finch," he looked up in surprise from the portable television set he had positioned on top of the desk, "what brings you here on a Saturday? And so late?"

George rose slightly and Max noted a security badge which bore his picture hanging from a chain around his neck, but the tone of his voice implied that the questions were more in the line of friendly small talk than a challenge.

"Um, er, a show," Julian lied, and hoped the tension in his voice wouldn't register with the security man. "Brought the kids into town to see a show, thought I'd show them round the office while we're here, you know - they're always on at me wanting to know where daddy works."

"A show, how nice," George replied, and he certainly didn't seem to have noticed anything suspicious.

Julian also noted that the National Security level (assessed daily and published on the whiteboard behind the security desk in blue marker pen) announced itself to be 'amber,' and was therefore quite low. He wasn't sure what to read into this considering Drake and Arthur's presence in the capital, but reasoned that this could be entirely meaningless. It merely confirmed that the intelligence agencies knew nothing of their return and that they were none the wiser about any potential threat than anyone else.

"And these are all your children, Julian?" George asked, breaking his chain of thought.

"Oh no, Max and Jess are mine, Brendan and Rhiannon are friends of the family," he indicated each in turn and was relieved that he could at least tell a few truths.

"Ah," George replied in a kindly voice. "Well it's nice to meet you guys, your father goes on and on about you, you know." Jess and Max both looked a little embarrassed, but George, unintentionally, only made the group more uncomfortable as he pressed further. "So you brought your boyfriend and girlfriend, eh?"

Jess blushed while Brendan shuffled his feet, and as Max smirked to himself Rhiannon, at his side, grimaced at the thought of going out with a boy several years her junior.

George, satisfied that the visit was entirely genuine, retook his seat and waved the whole group through. "Oh, what show did you see?" he asked casually as they passed him.

"Grease."

"Oliver," Max and Jess replied at the same time. Both winced when they realised their mistake, but the security man just raised his eyebrows and looked at Julian Finch.

"What can I say?" Julian shrugged awkwardly, he didn't consider himself much of an actor. "Two shows in one day, I must be spoiling them."

George emitted a slow whistle. "Expensive," he said shaking his head, "very pricey. But you have to spoil them once in a while, Julian, you have to spoil them."

"Oh George, there is a possibility that someone might come in to see me this evening, some aides to the Italian Commissioners. They wanted to come in and pick up some papers at some point, and when I knew I was coming in I let them know I'd be here briefly." Julian desperately tried to sound cool, as matter-of-factly as he could.

"Yeah well if they do I'll give you a buzz," George replied dismissively, but his eyes had reverted to the television.

"Yeah, well, I'm not sure they will, it's just if they do..."

"Well if they do, you won't be the only ones working late tonight." George turned the volume up a notch; they were free to go.

"No indeed," said Julian as he led the others quickly across the lobby to the security door which clicked open as he activated it with his fob, "I couldn't do the hours you work." But it didn't cross his mind that anyone else might actually be present in the office.

Phew, they were through, and halfway up the stairs to Julian's department on the second floor.

"That was easy," said Max in an unnecessarily loud voice, "a real siltch."

"Well we're not all in yet my boy," Julian hushed him, and he experienced a moment of guilt amongst all the excitement. He liked George, the security man had always been friendly towards him, and had once confided in him that a lot of the staff were not. This had always baffled Julian slightly; after all, everyone in the building passed George at least once a day, and how hard was it to say hello? He just hoped that George's faith in him wouldn't be the security man's undoing. He hoped that letting the thief, the spy, the traitor in, wouldn't cost George his own job too.

They passed through the double doors and onto Julian's floor. A big open plan office with lots of work stations for the junior secretaries all kitted out with shiny wide desks and computers on stand-by. Off to the side were several small offices, of which Julian had one, and at the far end a narrow corridor led to a thick wooden door, the Commissioner's office itself. All was in darkness, as just the fire escape signs were illuminated, and it was eerily quiet.

"Can we talk?" Rhiannon whispered.

"Yes, I think so. Go and signal Rhys and the others Max, my office is the third on the right. Flick the light on twice; we shan't put the main lights on until they're in, otherwise they might not see the signal."

Outside, Rhys let out a sigh of relief, they'd only been left alone a few minutes but the flicking light signalled the end of a nightmare. He hadn't found it easy to keep Drake and Arthur under control and things had almost gone horribly wrong.

He lamented his charge's stupidity, for as if they hadn't looked suspicious enough lingering on the corner of a building opposite the Commissioner's office and within spitting distance of Parliament, Arthur had sighted a small group of pigeons on the grass just a few yards in front of them, grazing greedily before flighting to roost. He had gruffly suggested to Drake in Latin that they try and catch them, a meat source to bolster their supplies, and Drake had agreed in principle to the plan, though he had pointed out that the birds would be unlikely to cooperate and might not be easily trapped.

"What are you two jabbering about?" Rhys had asked, only for Drake to reply, "The King hast intent t' trap yon birds, yet for want o' a falcon I seest not how canst be done."

"A falcon?" Rhys hadn't followed.

"Aye, for t' catch..." But in a flash Arthur had grabbed Drake's paper wrapped sword and swung it left and right amongst the flapping, panicked birds.

Rhys had tried desperately to stop him, trying to explain in Welsh that these were city pigeons and weren't edible, but the King was rather carried away and was swinging the long parcel above his head as the last of the untouched pigeons made it's bid for freedom.

It had then been Rhys' turn to panic, for approaching at a purposeful walk were two uniformed police officers clearly intent on requiring the parcel-swinging lunatic to account for his behaviour.

"Arthur, Arthur," Rhys had managed at last to calm the King down, and handed the sword back to its owner. "We must wait quietly, we can't create a scene."

"Who be these liveried fellows?" Drake had enquired, oblivious to the potential consequences of being found in possession of an offensive weapon in so public a place. "Be they of the militia?"

"Sort of," Rhys had replied, "they're policemen."

"Police..."

"Police constables," Rhys had explained.

"Ah, constables," Drake had registered a little understanding, "o' the guard? For seest I helm an' tunic, but bear they no arms upon them."

"Well, let's just hope they don't decide they want to search us, I think your undergarments might arouse a little suspicion." Rhys had been stretched to improvise quickly, but as the Officers had drawn nearer he had urged Arthur to sit on the ground and both his companions to say nothing. He greeted them with a friendly "Evening, Officers," and before they could enquire as to what the threesome were up to Rhys quickly pre-empted the question with an explanation. "We've been to a party and I'm afraid my friend here has had a bit much to drink, but don't worry, we'll look after him, we'll see that he doesn't cause any trouble."

"Well see that he doesn't," one of the Constables had replied, "and keep him off the grass, there are signs up you know."

"Oh yes, sorry," Rhys had responded, trying his best to look super-apologetic.

"What are your names?" the other officer had demanded, but before Rhys could reply Drake had answered for them all.

"Sir Francis Drake, Stout Yeoman, at thy service," he'd announced himself with a flourish and a bow. "This here be thy servant, Master Rhys Jenkins o' Newport, an' pon his haunches, an' pon mine oath, King Arthur o' distant Albion makest us three." Drake had indicated the King with a gesture of his arm, but as Rhys hid his head in his hands and desperately tried to work out how he could save the situation, the first Officer had responded with none of the awe nor recognition that Drake had rather rashly anticipated.

"I see, a joker are we? King Arthur and Sir Francis Drake, eh? Been smoking something exciting have we, gents? I think you'd best turn out your pockets, don't you? And what's that you've been waving about?" He gestured to the brown paper-wrapped tube.

"Oh, um, it's only a poster, Officer, it's all wrapped up as you can see, a present for a friend, I'd really rather not open it up," Rhys had replied nervously. He had been cursing Drake in the back of his mind for his foolishness, for the man was about as reliable a secret-keeper as an excited toddler.

"Where camest thou by they helm, Constable?" he'd enquired, "An' who be thy Lord an' Master at arms?" But neither Officer was listening; both had been preoccupied with radio traffic and it had quickly become apparent that they were being called urgently away.

As one had sent a stream of codes into his radio the other had turned quickly to the subdued three and had advised them sternly: "It's your lucky day, we have to go," and as they'd turned to leave he'd called back over his shoulder "I don't want to see you lot hanging about when we come back," and "You get him off home, you hear."

"Oh, I will," Rhys had called after them as they jogged urgently away, and, wiping his brow, he'd let out a long sigh. "That was close," he'd said under his breath, "Sir Francis, you are a total..."

"There be the signal," Drake had interrupted, and under strict instruction to leave the talking to him this time, Drake and Arthur followed Rhys into the Commissioner's building.

Rather uncertainly, Rhys approached the security desk, and the other two halted a few steps behind him. George took his tired eyes from the television screen and faced Rhys in greeting. "Good evening, Sir, how can I help?"

"Um hello," Rhys began hesitantly, "these two Gentlemen are staff from the Italian embassy... That is to say they are, um, aides to the Italian Commissioners rather." He reverted quickly to the prepared line and did his best to sound polite and formal. "I'm their interpreter, Mr Jenkins. They have an appointment with a Mr Finch; would you please let him know they've arrived."

George studied them quickly. The speaker seemed somewhat young to be engaged in such a role, but then again the political world seldom surprised him. A lot of the Civil Servants hand-picked from universities did seem to be getting younger and younger, and the lad was after all only announcing himself as an assistant to an assistant. What concerned him more were the two rather odd-looking fellows in the background, both were suited formally as he would expect, but neither quite had the typical bearing of one in such a position.

George was no style guru but the man in the pinstripe was clearly no Versace; he carried a brown paper tube with him and his clothing seemed to hang oddly on him, very flabby in the thighs and crotch and tight in the chest. As he strutted across the room he spouted arrogance, an asset George more commonly associated with more senior Civil Servants, but he rather contradicted it by demonstrating a childlike fascination with the cold drink and snack vending machines on the other side of the lobby. The Italian stood bent over with the point of his beard brushing the glass, as he tapped impatiently on the brightly-coloured buttons with his index finger.

The other man, short and very stocky in his tight grey suit, had no real human shape to him at all and appeared almost completely cylindrical. He looked rather on edge, his hard, cold eyes flitting un-resting around the room while his hands hung tensely at his hips like those of a Wild West gun-slinger. His tie was not done up properly and the tangle of medium-length greying hair on his head looked windswept and untidy. He looked most uncomfortable in his attire, not quite the smooth, slick, businesslike appearance typical of one who worked in the office of a Mediterranean politician. As he studied them the shorter man uttered some words of command in a language he couldn't understand at the other, who, looking rather hurt, straightened up and paced over to his companion's side.

George straightened, Mr Finch himself had only been gone a few minutes but that was no coincidence. Staff at the building were often in and out in the nick of time for scheduled appointments. What was more odd was Mr Finch having a meeting on a Saturday, let alone him being here at all, but Mr Finch had at least pre-warned him, so there was clearly nothing to worry about. It was the self importance of the taller of the two men which decided George eventually. He gave the security man such a look of irritated impatience at being made to wait, as he ran his eyes over them, that George took Rhys at his word and decided to put any doubts aside.

"Of course, Mr Jenkins, I shall put a call in to Mr Finch," he said politely as he lifted the desk phone. "Who am I to say has arrived?"

Blast it, thought Rhys. He hadn't for a moment considered the necessity of making up false names, and thought he'd already ridden his luck enough where making things up on the spot was concerned.

The phone rang in Julian Finch's office and he took a steady couple of breaths before answering it, letting it ring at least twice more than he needed to just to support the impression of coolness which he was so desperately trying to give off.

"Julian Finch," he announced himself.

"It's security at reception, Mr Finch," George's voice came down the line. "A Mr Arthurelli and a Mr Drakeotti have just arrived to see you."

"Oh yes, thank you George," Julian winced at the ridiculous pseudonyms, "I'll come down now and show them through." He replaced the handset, and leaving the others in the office, set off downstairs to meet his expected guests. He passed through the security door into the lobby, and for show approached each with a warm "Welcome," and extended his hand.

"You must be Mr Drakeotti," Julian greeted Sir Francis, who enjoying the act, shook his hand warmly and gave a slight bow. Julian took it a little further hoping a little authenticity would help to convince George that both visitors were entirely genuine, and so, as would be expected when greeting a Mediterranean guest, he grasped Drake by the elbows and kissed him quickly on both cheeks.

"What be thy game?" Drake quizzed in aggressive surprise, but giving him no answer Julian quickly approached Arthur in order to greet him too.

"And that would make you Mr Arthurelli," Arthur shook his hand, but as Julian came forward to greet him similarly Arthur stepped violently backwards out of reach and extended an arm to keep Julian at a distance.

Realising that he could blow the whole thing, Arthur quickly clenched the extended fist, proffering the gold signet ring for Julian, who hoped he had salvaged the situation by kissing this instead. But it was all wasted drama, for George's attention had completely reverted to the television set once more.

Rhys and Julian shook hands, introduced themselves formally, and

Julian apologised that his children were also in the Office with him, but the security man registered no interest; he'd long ago made up his mind that these Civil Servants were odd folk and that their quirky ways were best ignored. Julian thanked him as he led his new guests through the security door, but George happily dismissed them with an inattentive wave, his eyes fixed on the little screen.

Chapter Fifteen – Behind the Wooden Door

Back on his own floor, Julian Finch turned on all the lights and led the way across the office, with Drake and Arthur following in his wake, and casting curious glances to right and left. At the end of the narrow corridor they reached the imposing wooden door which divided the office of Britain's two European Commissioners from their underlings.

'Sir Morgan Dredmor and Sir Dennis Hitoadie, Duke of Man' announced the inscription on the shiny brass plate displayed on the outside of the very heavy, very shut, polished oak door. Julian took a breath and tried the handle, it turned but no joy, as he pushed it the firmly locked door wouldn't budge a millimetre. Julian cursed his luck; he should have anticipated this but hadn't planned on any means to overcome it.

Silently, Arthur tapped Drake on the arm and led him to the work desk in the next office down.

"Oh aye," Drake declared, "a battering ram."

"Mind the…" Crash - it was too late. "Computer…" Julian finished, as between them the King and the Admiral tipped the contents of the workstation over, and bore the table, one each side of it, out of the room and into the corridor.

"I think we'd best stand back," Rhiannon advised as Drake and Arthur together eyed up the door, a short run up in front of them.

On the Latin count of 'Unus, duos, three,' they ran at it and really let fly, swinging the table, itself no lightweight piece, at the heavy door in unison and with great force, causing it to emit a mighty crash. The door visibly shook on its lock and hinges but didn't open first time, and as they moved back for a second attempt all could see that the shiny name plate was badly dented.

Arthur and Drake hit it again, just as hard but nearer the lock this time, and the table they were using splintered badly as the door again jolted and shuddered, but it remained shut.

With a heavy breath each they once again prepared their run-up, though Drake suggested they try from a little further back this time, and with fixed expressions of determination on their foreheads and the count of 'three' on their lips, they once again charged at the door.

As on cue, and with near-perfect comic timing, the door suddenly swung wide open just as Drake and Arthur approached it, which caused them to run straight through and collapse in the room beyond, their battering ram colliding heavily with the Duke of Man's expensive desk, throwing up splinters and black feathers amid squawks of terror.

As Julian Finch looked on from the corridor, a bald, bucktoothed face protruded round the door bearing an expression of great annoyance which turned to one of surprise when he recognised his caller. "Good Lord, Finch," he exclaimed.

"Good Lord, Rindburn," Julian replied. "What the Devil are you doing in here?"

"Um, well Finch, we were just, er, that is to say..." Rindburn tailed off, as Julian Finch was now able to glance round the door and into the room.

Directly in front of him in a heap of splinters on the floor, and at the foot of the Duke's desk, were the prostrate Drake and Arthur. Sitting in one of the Commissioner's heavy leather arm chairs drawn up to the coffee table, and wrapped in a blanket with his sock-less feet in a basin of steaming hot water, was Nigel Sludboil looking very sorry for himself, and scattered around the room, flapping, and looking rather alarmed, were six large, black, birds.

The state of the place was horrendous. There were droppings everywhere and food; bits of bread and sliced-up ham were strewn all over the surfaces. The two human occupants had clearly been putting newspaper down in response to the birds' bowel movements, but the birds evidently hadn't stayed still, and it having been rather hard to pre-empt their next deposit, the pink pages of the crumpled Financial Times were now strewn almost wantonly around the room, giving off the impression that the whole office had been deliberately trashed.

Jess joined her father in the door way to take in the once-extravagant interior. Big bay windows at the back of the room gave an inspiring view over London, while the furnishings were nothing short of luxurious; the huge wooden desks, sets of draws and filing cabinets all matched and had a finely polished finish, and the executive chairs were of padded leather. Glancing up, she took in a gaudy clock hanging on the wall and a tray of drinks on the sideboard, and looking across, her eyes came to rest on those of the Duke of Man as he beamed out of his heavy framed picture, set in pride of place on the left hand wall.

"You only had to knock, Finch," Rindburn mocked him in a sarcastic tone.

"And would you have answered the door?" Julian asked coolly.

"Well, obviously not," Rindburn replied angrily. "And just what do you think you are doing?"

"I could ask you the same question."

"Get out of here at once, Finch, do you hear? I'm calling security."

"B-yes, bo abway," Sludboil added, and sneezed noisily through his sizeable blocked nose.

"It's the ravens," Max declared urgently as he pointed at the birds, "I recognise them, it's the missing ravens, Dad."

"What are you doing with them?" Brendan waded in.

"Yes, what are they doing here?" Jess demanded.

"Er, um... We found them," Rindburn replied uncertainly, "now get out, I'm calling security. Security, security," he shouted.

"You shall do no such thing," Julian advised them as he ushered his party through into the Commissioner's office, and having shut the heavy door he locked it behind them.

"Oh you've really done it now, Finch," Rindburn sneered at him, "wait until Sir Morgan hears of this. Your life won't be worth living."

"Nob that ib was worb libing anywabe," Sludboil jeered from his seat in the chair.

"Yeah, good one, Sludboil," Rindburn cheered his friend. "You're useless Finch, useless. Need your children to do your dirty work, do you? What is it, bring your kids to work day or something?"

"Something like that, but I think you'll find we mean business." And Julian indicated to the two suited gentlemen who were picking themselves up off the floor.

"Oh, of course," Rindburn sneered to extend his teeth even further out of his mouth. "Who are the two heavies?"

"Never you mind, Rindburn," Julian replied. "Now answer the question, what are these ravens doing here? Do the Commissioners know you're using their office as a zoo?"

"R, rabens," Sludboil stood in his water basin, "bees are blab birds," he declared pathetically, and emitted a massive sneeze which sprayed all of his immediate surroundings with snot. He wiped at his nose with a soggy handkerchief, but no sooner had he sponged it clean than another huge drop formed on the end of it.

"Oh, pull the other one," said Jess impatiently, "they are ravens," and with a swing of her arm she sent one off the Duke's desk, and over the ducking Max, to flap onto a coat stand behind the door. Her brother, rather anxious of the large birds, looked nervously over his shoulder at it as it squawked at him from its new perch.

Arthur approached Sludboil from behind and placed one thick hand on each of the tall man's shoulders. He had to stand on tiptoe to reach, but he brought the Commissioner's Private Secretary back down heavily into his chair with apparent ease.

"These be the missing sovereign ravens lately o' the Tower," Drake announced angrily, and he ripped the paper from his sword as he spoke. He came now in front of the cowering Sludboil and kicked the water basin over with purpose, coming to stand on the Civil Servant's bare toes, and leaning forward over the seated man his beard came to within just an inch of his face. "Speak now, thou churl," he ordered; but Sludboil sneezed again, and Drake, in fury, leant back, his own face covered in the snot of the other.

Drake wiped his face with a suited forearm, and thrust his long sword at Sludboil's throat, forcing him to sit right back in his chair and arch his back as the point of the weapon pressed hard against his lumpy Adam's apple.

"How, knave, didst thou come by them?" Drake continued, "Loosen thou thy tongue or by thunder I'll away an' wilt I find a barber surgeon who shalt bleed thee, an' with lance an probe shalt thy tongue be loosened aright."

"Ibs by nobse," Sludboil replied in terror, his eyes wide open and his head pressed back against the chair as he desperately edged away from the weapon. He wanted to swallow, but couldn't due to the pressure of the sword point at his throat, and as he winced at the pain in his toes a huge droplet fell from his nose and onto the sword blade. "I'b gob a cold."

"Ah, wi' a few turns on the rack shalt thy nose be forgot," Drake berated him. "Speak thee thy wrongs, or shalt I smite them from thee."

"A cold shall be the least of your worries," Julian tried to speak as menacingly as he could; it was not a role he felt remotely comfortable with but the effect appeared to work. "Don't worry, I won't let my friend here torture you, I'll just order a quick and painless death, well, as painless as it can be," he indicated the sword. "But you answer my question right now, Sludboil, we know the ravens have been stolen from the Tower of London, it's been all over the news... Oh, but it was you two, wasn't it? Of course it was, I should have recognised you from the CCTV pictures." Julian shook his head slowly and could see from Rindburn's fixed goofy expression that he was right. "I want to know, I demand to know why you have taken them," he snapped impatiently.

"All in good time, Finch." Rindburn tried to remain cool, and he backed gently away towards Sir Morgan Dredmor's desk. "In time all your impertinent questions will be answered," he spoke evenly. "Just ask your man over there to relax a little," - he indicated towards Drake and his sword arm - "my colleague, Sludboil, has difficulty enough breathing at the moment."

"Yeah, okay," Julian conceded. "Ease off, Sir Francis," he requested gently.

"Better, that's better, that's much more calm," Rindburn continued, and as Drake took his sword from Sludboil's neck he sensed he was exerting a little more control. "Much more amiable, Finch," he continued. "Now the truth is we saw there was a reward for the return of the Tower's ravens, so we thought we'd try and pretend we found them," he grinned impishly. "We trapped these birds earlier in the evening and we were planning on taking them down to collect the reward first thing in the morning. Bit dishonest I know, but..."

"Liar," yelled Max.

"Traitor," Brendan added, and Jess, who was getting fed up with this stream of lies, now began to demand answers.

"We all know the country will fall if the ravens leave the Tower. Now tell us why you took them - is this your plot, or are you working for someone else?"

"All in good time," Rindburn protested, himself playing for time, and now backed up to Sir Morgan's desk he fumbled behind himself with his right hand on the desktop.

King Arthur had lost patience with the whole charade, and seized Rindburn by his clothing with a mind to manhandle him back into the other heavy leather chair, just as he had seated Sludboil. But as he seized him, Rindburn brought his hand round from behind himself, clasping a sharp wooden letter opener shaped like a knife, and dug it as hard as he could into the King's ribs.

To his amazement the wooden blade just snapped like a matchstick on impact as it collided with the concealed chain mail singlet beneath Arthur's clothing.

There was a moment of silence in which both men glanced down at the splintered wood, and Rindburn let out a simple 'Oh.' But in response to the cowardly murder attempt the King head butted the shocked Rindburn violently, and the Civil Servant hit the ground like a sack of potatoes, out cold.

"Oooh," Rhiannon winced.

"That's gotta hurt," Rhys added, and Julian Finch turned his attentions to the quivering Sludboil.

"Not your plot, I fear. You'll be doing your Master's dirty work for them, you haven't the nous to pull off a stunt like this off your own bat." Sludboil made no reply but sniffed noisily and rubbed at his throat to reassure himself that it was un-punctured. "And of course your Masters are in Brussels with their precious European Environmental Act," Julian suddenly changed his tone to snap at the seated man. "Where's Protocol Fifteen, Sludboil? There has to be a copy document of the whole Act here somewhere, where is it?"

"Ib don'bt bow," Sludboil pleaded.

"Then we'll just have to look for it, won't we. We may not have much time," Julian turned to his assembled team, "we're going to have to turn this place upside down. We're looking for a specific document, and I'm sure it's got to be here somewhere." He paused thoughtfully. "But before we start searching we had best get these two idiots tied up and restrained so they can't try pulling any other stunts like that. Arthur," he called to the King and addressed him in Latin. "Can you find something to bind them with?"

Arthur winked, and having delved into his trouser leg at the ankle for his dagger, he quickly departed the room to return to the main office floor.

When Rindburn regained consciousness he and Sludboil were back to back and bound tightly with computer cable to two lightweight secretarial chairs. Julian Finch dreaded to think how many machines had been damaged, but there was no doubting the ancient king's ingenuity in sourcing appropriate restraints.

The office had become even more of a tip. Rhys and Max were slowly dismantling the desk drawers, and as Brendan and Rhiannon went through the filing cabinets systematically a raven perched on top of the unit and squawked at them with impatience.

"Byou'll neber find ib Fimbch," Sludboil was goading them. "Eben ib we dib knowb where ib was we'bd neber say."

"Well one thing I no longer doubt is that you two don't know where it's hidden," Julian agreed, "the Commissioners are far too sensible to make the mistake of giving you two that much responsibility. Your job was just to pinch the birds for them at the time they said."

"Oh, bear gibbing us rebsponsibilibty all right," Sludboil snapped back carelessly rising to the bait and almost giving the game away. "Arhb," he exclaimed, as the waken Rindburn back healed his left foot to strike Sludboil in the right heel and usher him to silence.

"What responsibility?" Julian questioned him.

"Ob, nubbing, nubbing," Sludboil shook his head in denial.

"You just said they're giving you responsibilities," Jess wasn't giving up, "that means you're in on the plot. What responsibilities are they giving you? What's in it for you two?" she pressed.

"I'm nob spaying anything," Sludboil shook his head again, "I'mb nob belling you whab rebsponsibilibties bay are gibbing bus."

"So you admit it, then," Jess declared, a pile of documents heaped at her feet. "There is something in it for you, you are in on it."

"Shush," Rindburn hushed his friend to silence, but announced his consciousness to the rest of the room in doing so.

"Oh, Mr Rindburn, you're back with us, that's good." Brendan thought he'd try and trick Rindburn by leading him to think that

274

Sludboil had revealed all while he had been out for the count. "Mr Sludboil here has just spilt the beans on the two Commissioners; he's just told us everything, how they're trying to bump off the Queen, everything... The game's over, you might as well just talk."

"Think yourself very clever, don't you, little boy?" Rindburn rebuked him, "You really are a fat little twerp aren't you? Do you think I was born yesterday, podgy?" Brendan's face reddened. "If you know everything, why are you still searching the office? You haven't a clue, not the faintest iota of an inkling. None of you can live with the genius of the Commissioners." He grinned wickedly to himself and his jagged teeth protruded in a vile leer.

"Nice try, Brendan," Max patted his deflated classmate on the back, "but I still think we should torture them into telling us all they know. Dad, can't I put a raven down his trousers?"

"Ah, let us dispense wi' such frippery," Drake agreed. "King Arthur an' mineself wilt tarry a while wi' these scoundrels alone." He seized Rindburn's wrist and squeezed it so hard that he forced the clenched fingers to open out. "Each digit that the dagger cleaves off shalt loosen the liar's tongue."

"Oh, I'll help you, Sir Francis," Max volunteered, pulling Rindburn's sleeve to the elbow.

"No, no, Finch," Rindburn pleaded, "you can't allow it."

"Leave him be," Julian ordered as he persisted rummaging through Sir Morgan Dredmor's desk drawers. "We can't use your old techniques in this day and age, Sir Francis. Now I just know it has to be somewhere here. That European Environmental Act has to have something to do with it."

"Cold," Rindburn mocked him from the chair. "Still cold, Finch."

"Don't push your luck, Rindburn, I could always change my mind, you know."

"Is this it, Jules?" Rhys asked for the dozenth time as he handed Julian a weighty document which he'd found in a filing cabinet.

"No," Julian replied slowly, "that's the dossier on air pollutants they commissioned from the Environmental Study Group last year."

"Colder still," Rindburn mocked them, "oh that's freezing."

"Freebing, byeah. Bood bun Bindburn," Sludboil cheered on his colleague, whose back was against his own, and he sneezed loudly so that snot dribbled from his nose, ran down his chin and dripped onto his lap.

"Now that's just revolting," Rhiannon winced at the soggy mess that covered the prisoner's lower face.

"Bwell Ib canb't wibe ib, can I?" the Civil Servant defended himself, and wriggle though he did, he couldn't free his arms from their bindings.

"Look, Dad," Max protested, "if he's saying cold he knows we're no where near it, so he must know where it really is, - go on, let Sir Francis slice off a few fingers."

"He doesn't, Son," Julian responded casually. "He's just trying to wind us up. It's like I said, the Commissioners wouldn't risk their whole plan being blown out by these two morons. They know the plot and that's obvious, and they've done their bit, as the presence of these regal birds in this office confirms. They're traitors alright, but they won't know where the document is. The Commissioners would never actually entrust these two cretins to look after the evidence."

"Evidence, Finch," Rindburn continued to mock him, "let's see if you can find any evidence. Right lot of idiots you'll look trying to prove a plot without any evidence; evidentially that should be evident."

"Yes, thank you Trevor - now you just keep quiet, and we'll just keep looking."

"Just explain to us again why we are actually looking for this document," Rhiannon asked of Julian. She was getting rather tired of searching, and felt like giving up.

"The document we are looking for is a commitment to change European environmental policy and will become law if passed. So you can be pretty sure that as our Commissioners have the directorate on the environment most of the ideas have probably come out of this office."

"It would be logical, Finch," Rindburn slated him cruelly. "Not that your contribution to the research was worth a bean."

"Byeah, bean buseless," Sludboil snorted, and a bubble of snot billowed and bubbled at his nostrils.

"Bean useless! Good one, Sludboil," Rindburn congratulated his suffering companion on his feeble taunt.

Drake, who had been feeding a piece of bread to one of the ravens perched on the Duke's desk, yelled "Thou shalt keep silence," and flung a heavy stapler across the room at the shackled traitor who was seated in the middle of it.

Rindburn saw it coming and managed to move his balding head aside, but his fellow captive, facing the other way, couldn't see the missile and had no idea it was coming. The stapler crashed into the back of his head, causing a yelp of pain and an: "Ib say, bear's bo neeb for bat."

"As I was saying," Julian continued, "it's a step by step process. For it to be made law the elected European Parliament get to discuss the draft document in debate, and the European Council, which is basically the leaders of each country, the Prime Minister of the United Kingdom, the President of France etc... or their representatives, have to sign up to it for it to actually be made law."

"For an Act to be passed," Brendan voiced his understanding.

"Indeed so, Brendan. The idea is that the Parliament are there as a kind of quality control to make sure that in principle they approve of it. They can raise questions, objections really, and if they do the whole draft goes back to the Commission again."

"Before the Council get to see it?" Rhiannon asked.

"Exactly - it's still not law at this stage. The document goes back to the Commission for further work, basically to resolve any issues the Parliament might have had with it, and then, once the Commissioners are all happy with it and have signed up to it, they pass it to the European Council, and if they sign up to it too it's law."

"So the European Parliament don't get a chance to approve any alterations?" Brendan asked.

"No Brendan, the Parliament only get one look at it, it goes straight to the Council who either endorse it and pass it, or vote against it. The Parliament has a fairly minor role in the process really, considering they are the elected element. The Council will normally look at any points raised by the Parliament to check that the second draft has addressed them, but they can overrule the Parliament anyway if they choose, and can revert back to the first draft if they so wish."

"And then?" Jess urged him.

"Well then the onus is back on the Commission again. You see, once the Act is passed they have the responsibility to think up secondary legislation. That's additional more minor laws which might be needed to put the principles of the Act into practice."

"This is boring." Max yawned and put a hand to his mouth.

"Boring it may be, Max, but this could be important. You see the Commission have virtually a free hand in creating and enacting the secondary legislation, subject to Comitology of course, and they can make all sorts of new laws to ensure that the laws created by the Act will work in practice."

"So no one can question them." Jess couldn't believe it. "They could come up with anything."

"Well, the Comitology is there as a kind of watchdog, it's a body to ensure they act fairly, and the European Judicial system is also there as a safeguard, and that's also independent of the Commission - but you're right, Jess, that's why the Commissioners are so important and the Commission is so powerful, and the reason, Rhiannon, that we are looking for the Commissioner's copy of the European Environmental

Act in this office right now is that there is something about it that stinks."

"Like you'd know, Finch," Rindburn goaded him.

"I do know, Rindburn," Julian assured him. "And when I find the document I hope to sniff out exactly what it is that stinks about it. This Act has been through the Parliament and the Commission signed up to it yesterday. On Monday the Council get a chance to vote on it, and if they do it will be made law. The Commission haven't indicated just how they plan to clear the continent up, it may be a noble proposal in principle, but it's clear that if this Act is passed the Commission will have a lot of scope to bring in whatever secondary legislation they deem fit to bring about these ambiguous objectives, and the problem is, I think they've already agreed on what they plan to do."

"Well the Council will notice - surely they won't sign up to it, will they?" Brendan looked anxious, but Max was almost completely lost and stared out of the window with a totally vacant look.

"They probably will sign up to it," Julian explained, "and I don't doubt his Grace and Sir Morgan are counting on them doing just that. Only last night on the news they said they knew the Prime Minister had confidence in it, basically in them. In any case, the Environment is such an emotive issue I think the Council will be desperate to sign up to it just to be seen to be doing something about it, and as you said yourself in my office just down the corridor, Rindburn, Politicians don't actually tend to read the legislation."

Rindburn continued to sneer in defiance, but he gulped and it was enough for Julian to see that he was on the right track.

"Well, can't the European Parliament stop them...?"

"The Parliament have had their chance, Rhys," Julian tried to explain. "When they got to debate it months ago they objected to proposed offshore wind farms on the Spanish mainland and requested clarification on the scale of recycling, and they don't get another reading."

"Scale of recycling," Brendan echoed.

"Yes, the Act proposed to cease mainland European landfill and at the same time stated it would cease in expensive and polluting chemical recycling of waste. The Parliament couldn't understand it, as if we stopped recycling there would be even more waste to throw into landfill, and they sought clarification on where all the waste would go."

"And where will it go?" Brendan asked.

"I've no idea - it would be up to the Commission to address the issue with their secondary legislation. The Act simply says measures will be brought in to deal with it. Quite possibly the Commissioners know exactly how they will deal with the waste, but they aren't sharing their plan with the rest of us. The point is, the Parliament have had their chance, Rhys, and they won't get another."

"So what makes you say the Act stinks, Dad?"

"Yeah, what's so unusual about it?" Brendan seconded Jessica's question.

"Well, a number of things really. For one, the speed at which they have rushed this legislation through - I mean, the Council will barely get a chance to look at it, let alone discuss it. Then there are all the secret meetings the Toad and Sir Morgan have been having here in the office, they've had all the other Commissioners in for cosy little discussions in ones and twos, and it's clear some deals have been made. And last but not least, if there is nothing suspicious going on, what are the ravens doing in this office?"

"Well, it would certainly smell better without them," Rindburn jeered.

"And the presence of these two gentlemen likewise indicates treachery."

"Well, they certainly smell too."

"Bell too, ha bah. Bood bun Bindburn," Sludboil, rocking with laughter, joined Rindburn in likewise failing to register the significance of the as yet un-introduced Drake and Arthur.

"Quite the spy, aren't you Finch?" Rindburn mocked. "You haven't a clue about the content of any secret meetings which have gone on in here."

"A-ha - so there have been secret meetings," Julian wagged a finger at his captive. "You admit it."

"I said nothing of the sort. You haven't been privy to the meetings, Finch, so how can you speculate as to their content?"

"You're quite right, my dear Rindburn, I haven't been. But I think I can make a few educated guesses. In light of the little bits yourself and Sludboil have carelessly dropped for me I think the Commissioners should have been a little more careful choosing those they took into their confidence, don't you?"

"Bwhat bo you beam?" Sludboil challenged him.

"Oh well, isn't it obvious, Sludboil?" Julian paced round to face the other man tied to the chair. "Great men you called them, geniuses blessed with a vision of the future." Sludboil's face fell but he made no reply. "Did they confide this vision of the future in you, Sludboil? In you, Rindburn?"

"Of course not, the Commissioner's business is the Commissioner's business," Rindburn protested.

"Drafted and agreed on," Julian quoted them, "that's what you said. You said the secondary legislation was drafted and agreed on, and you said it yesterday in my office. It's obvious what all the secret meetings have been about. They've been doing dodgy deals behind closed doors. You may well have sat in on some of them, but all I want to do is find the document so we can see exactly what it is that they've pre-arranged."

"Liar," Rindburn raged at him, "you can't prove any of this."

"Oh no. Does the phrase 'there are going to be some changes around here shortly' mean anything to you?"

"Bwe bon't bnow anything about ib," Sludboil protested.

"Real changes, you said, and you even hinted at yourselves getting promoted," Julian continued. "Honestly, the price of loyalty. Of course you know they are up to something. Exactly how much you know is another matter, but you know the secondary legislation has been well and truly planned and that the Commissioners have all privately agreed to the EEA prior to signing that too, and I know you know because you two idiots have as good as told me."

Rindburn made no reply, but in frustration he kicked his heel back into Sludboil's calf again, as if punishing his colleague for his slips of the tongue would make him feel better about his own.

Max was impressed. He still didn't really understand what was going on but he was so proud of his father, who clearly did, and Julian Finch, feeling somewhat elated to be airing his theory, began pacing the room as he dared his prisoners to challenge his words.

"I know you took those ravens," he continued. "You may not be aware of their significance, but I don't doubt it was you two who took them from the Tower, and that this was the 'little task' given to you by your Masters before they left for Brussels." Both men looked blank but Julian could see that they were at breaking point.

"Oh come now, you were bragging only yesterday about how important you were and how you'd been given a special task to do, and as we can see, this was it. To snatch the ravens from the Tower, to betray your country. You may not know it, you may be too stupid, too ignorant to know it, but the legend is plain. If the ravens leave the Tower the country falls, and you two idiots had been tasked with the job of stealing them." Julian could see them cracking and thought one more little twist might tease the truth out of them. "That in itself was probably the biggest risk the Commissioners have run, actually having to rely on you two complete and utter cretins not to mess it up - but hey, you managed it."

"Byes bwe dib," Sludboil defied him, fury in his eyes, "howb bear byou subgest we bwould bess ub."

As Sludboil received a further kick in his calf from his reversed colleague, Julian came round to face him. "Thank you, Nigel, for confirming all our fears. You are traitors and there is clearly a plot centred around our dear Commissioners and their precious Act."

"Byou'll neber stob them Finbch, neber," Sludboil ranted, and his running nose dripped onto an ever increasing puddle of snot on his lap.

"Oh, I think we owe it to the nation to try. Clearly the Commissioners are rather counting on the Council signing up to the Act on Monday, the good old EEA as his Grace would call it, and we'll just have to do our very best to stop them."

Julian paced back around the room, and caught Arthur's eye. The King, who had understood little of the conversation, stood in silence, but it was clear to him that Julian was in control and that bit by bit the captives had given ground to him. His host had been proved right, torture hadn't been necessary, and he gave Julian a reassuring nod to let him know that he was fully approving of the actions he had taken.

Drake, however, did not mirror Arthur's patient demeanour.

"All this talk o' politics, o' documents. Shouldst not we light the beacon fires an' call all England to arms? Ought not we to away an' bring Queen Bess our warning?"

"Not just yet, Sir Francis," Julian urged for calm. "We just need to find a copy of the Act, the proof should be in the pudding itself."

"Oh really, Poirot, or is it Clouseau?" Rindburn sneered. "You are a proofreader, Finch, if it hasn't escaped your notice. You must have read it through a hundred times already, if anyone knows what's in it you should, and if you haven't found any proof up until now, well..."

"I haven't found any proof in the document, Rindburn," Julian agreed.

"Well there you are then, Finch, let us go. You can't prove anything."

"Because I haven't found Protocol Fifteen."

"Ah..."

"Ah, indeed, my dear Trevor."

"Um, Protocol Fifteen?" Jess urged her father to explain.

"I'm so sorry, Jess, I should have made it more clear. It's Protocol Fifteen to the Act which we really need to find."

"Right, so what's a protocol?" Max rubbed at his pounding head in frustration.

"A protocol, Maxwell, is a kind of additional little bit, a small pamphlet in this case which has been added, sort of tacked on to the Act

281

itself."

"So…"

"Quite often protocols are added to address any issues raised with it so far, for example Protocol Thirteen was added after the Parliament objected to wind farms on the Spanish mainland. It suggests an alternative location be found, though I must say it wasn't specific as to where that would be.

"Now, Protocol Fifteen has been written up by Sir Morgan and his Grace personally; they've been really secretive about it and I never got to proofread it. It appears that Sir Morgan and the Toad, and almost certainly the rest of the Commission as well, are rather hoping that the Council won't bother to read it either."

"Sign up to it without reading it," Jess spoke slowly.

"And make it law," Brendan finished the sentence for her.

"Exactly," Julian confirmed in ominous tones.

"You didn't get to read it as it's none of your business," Rindburn snarled.

"If it reveals the substance of a plot so malicious as to charge you two with stealing the ravens, I think it could be all of our business. Damn you, Rindburn, I know there's something not right with it - I've even heard the Commissioners toasting it, for goodness's sake."

"You're just guessing, you haven't a clue what's in it."

"Precisely why I intend to find it. Now come on, everyone, keep looking."

"I still don't get it," declared Max, who still didn't.

"Well, Max," his father continued as he resumed rummaging through Sir Morgan Dredmor's desk, "let me put it like this. When you cuddle Benji you also cuddle his fleas don't you?"

"No I don't, he doesn't have any."

"Of course he does, all dogs have fleas from time to time and all kinds of bugs and dirt and little mites, you just don't notice them."

"Thou wouldst seest them if thou had a care t' seek 'em out." Drake confirmed.

"Exactly," Julian continued, "but usually, Max, you just cuddle the dog, you don't look for fleas first, and when he runs at you in a hurry you wouldn't even get a chance to look, even if you wanted to."

"But I wouldn't want to."

"Exactly, and the Commission are likewise no doubt hoping that the Council won't examine the Act for protocols."

"Oh," Max nodded.

"You see, if they pass the Act they will also pass whatever is in that mysterious secret protocol, and it too will also become law. There is clearly a plot a foot and that protocol may go some way to explaining it, it might just reveal who this unidentified enemy is, who it is that's trying to take over the country and how. Now if I know anything about our two illustrious, self-interested Commissioners, they will be seeking to gain personally from whatever mischief they have engineered."

"Thou art as stout a fellow as any I hath sailed with," Drake declared, and clapped Julian on the back so hard he nearly fell over. "I thought 'twas but a fool's errand t' run hot foot to yon office, but here be the ravens o' the Tower, here be proof that those traitors who challenge the sovereignty o' our isle be close at quarter."

"Oh these two muppets are just puppets, like Julian said," Rhys observed, "they've just done their Master's dirty work for them. It's exposing the Commissioners, that's what we're going to have to do."

"Ah, thou speakst true, Master Jenkins, poppets they be," Drake mocked them, and patted Rindburn on his bald head, the wild movements of his arm causing several of the ravens to panic once again and flutter around the room.

"And who be you? I mean who are you?" Rindburn reacted in annoyance, "And why are you speaking in that ridiculous way? You sound like a total retard."

"Byeah, betard, goob one Bindbu..."

"Oh, how rude of me," Julian interrupted the snot covered Sludboil mid-flow, "I never did introduce my friends, did I. Well it's very simple, really, and it all ties together rather well, Rindburn. You see, just as the ravens being here is evidence that your masters are involved in a plot to overthrow the country, so likewise their very presence here confirms that the country is in trouble, and that someone is trying to overthrow it. Though I must say we thought initially some invading army might be the danger, not treacherous Politicians and their pathetic Civil Service lapdogs."

"Damn you, Finch, who are they?"

"Well the man you tried to murder is King Arthur, and you've just had the privilege of Sir Francis Drake slapping your bald head," Jess revealed coolly.

"Bahhaaaa," Rindburn laughed, and Sludboil, behind him, snorted so heavily he nearly drowned in his own snot.

"Byour habbing a laughbh, Ah hab hab," he mocked as he desperately tried to recover his breathing. "Bing Barthber and Bancis Bake, bahch, hab, hab," he sneezed loudly through his laughter.

"Shalt I, thou churl, reacquaint thy wretched neck wi' the point o' my sword?" Drake challenged him, for he was rather hurt by this response. "An 'pon my troth this time shalt I run thee through for thy disbelieving." This silenced Sludboil, for whoever the lunatic in the pinstripe with the pointed beard and the pearl earring was, the sword was of genuine steel and he could vouch for that.

"Finch, it's you who's living in a dream world," Rindburn chortled. "Whoever heard such nonsense?"

"You don't have to believe it, Rindburn, it makes no difference to us at all," Julian replied casually. "But it's very simple - you can't deny you've heard the legends. Drake and Arthur are both meant to return when the nation is in trouble."

"Think you're clever, don't you, Finch? But no-one believes in ghosts."

"Yeah, but ghosts don't tend to go round delivering knock-out head butts, do they?" Jess grinned.

"Yeah, good one, Sis," Max mocked the captives.

Rindburn was absolutely furious. All he could think to do was to try and keep Julian and his cronies in the office as long as he could, he had to try and distract them from finding any documents, and to buy the Commissioners as much time as he could.

"Prove it, Finch," was the best he could do.

"I don't have to," Julian replied, for he had no intention of playing games, "but if he hadn't had his chain mail under his suit, you might be under arrest for murder right now."

"Murder!"

"You heard, and that's evidence of a plot if ever we needed any more. You were prepared to kill for this conspiracy, Rindburn - shame on you."

"Yeah, you're a coward," Max goaded him. "In combat Arthur would make mincemeat of you, you wouldn't stand a chance. It's only because Dad's here that we haven't let them kill you both."

"Ah," Rindburn shouted, "security!" at the top of his voice. The yells unsettled the ravens, who took off and flapped round the room once more.

"Shut up," Brendan ordered, "or we'll just gag you."

One of the birds came to land on the bound man's bald head, and despite Rindburn trying to shake it off, it held firm to its perch.

"Look, if you know where this protocol is, where the Act or any of the documents are, why don't you just tell us?" Brendan implored Rindburn one last time in the hopes he might speak, given one more chance.

"I tell you, I don't... Confound this bird!" It was pacing over his head, digging its claws into his scalp for grip. "I don't know where it is."

"He doesn't," Julian confirmed, "he might know more than he's letting on but he won't have been told where the documents are. It was worth another try, Brendan, but we'll just have to find them on our own."

"See, fatty," Rindburn leered at Brendan, and his teeth protruded an astonishing distance from his lips, "listen to Finchy and shut your flabby cake hole you lardy, pie-munching, piggy wig."

Brendan was obviously rather hurt by this comment and as Sludboil launched into a "Bake bowl, bood bun Bindburn," the raven dished out swift justice on the teenager's behalf. Leaning forward, and almost looking into Rindburn's eyes, the big black bird defecated twice, once on the angle, firing a wet turd straight down the back of Sludboil's neck; and then in quick succession it loosed another, straight downward to splat on the bald head directly beneath its bottom.

Rindburn paused a second as he registered what had happened, and once it became obvious where the warm deposit, even now slipping down around his ears, had come from, he let out an enormous shout.

"Argh, security!"

The bird was startled, totally shocked. It left its perch at speed and flapped straight off his head, and beak-first into the gaudy framed picture of the smiling Duke of Man on the wall. The glass smashed, the bird recovered itself and flapped away unhurt, and the picture, frame and all, fell from the wall with a crash.

With the picture gone the wall revealed its secret, and Rindburn immediately fell silent as he and Julian simultaneously registered the dull, grey metal block in the wall which had been concealed behind the picture to be a safe, pin code combination lock and all. Nothing else needed to be said, for it was immediately obvious to everyone in the room - bar the sobbing Sludboil who faced the wrong way - that if there was a copy of the document anywhere in the room it would be securely contained behind the sturdy metal door.

Rhys tried the door on the off chance, but it wouldn't budge.

"We could try forcing it, but I think we'll be lucky. As for the pin code," he reported as he looked at the combination key pad, "it could be any combination of the numbers one to nine, and we don't even know how many numbers we need to key in."

"Let us defy reason," Drake declared, and he and Arthur spent several minuets trying to prize open the sturdy little door with the points of the dagger and sword, their laboured grunts accompanied by the heckling sneers of Rindburn and Sludboil. "T'will never give," Drake eventually announced in defeat, and Arthur punched the door in frustration before reeling away, clasping his sore hand with the other.

"It's no good," Julian told them. "We're just going to have to guess at the code."

"They might know the code," Max suggested. "Go on, Dad, just let Sir Francis torture them a little bit."

"No, no, you can't let them torture us, Finch - if I knew the code, I'd tell," Rindburn pleaded pathetically.

"If Sir Francis started lobbing your fingers off you would."

"No Max, no," Julian frowned. "I won't allow it, and anyway he was as surprised as we all were to see the safe, he didn't know it was there, he's not going to know the code."

"I bnow ib," Sludboil ventured, hoping that if he fed them a string of false codes it would slow them down. "Ibs bree, bive, heckchoo, bnine." Rhys tried the code three, five, nine, but the door didn't open. "Oh bno ibs nobt, billy bee," Sludboil made up another one. "Ibs bine, bive, bun, seben." Rhys gave this combination a try, but again no joy. "Ibs abcually..."

"Oh shut up, Sludboil." Jess had taken enough of being made a fool of. "Find something to gag them with, won't you Rhys. Cut their trouser legs off if you have to."

"Bub I bon't be able to breatbe," Sludboil protested, "by bnose is blobcked."

"Then keep silent," Julian ordered. Now how hard could it be? he thought, as he considered the code. It was the Duke of Man's safe, or he assumed it was as it was behind his picture, and therefore it seemed reasonable that the code might have some significance to his Grace. "Try 1951, Rhys, I think the Toad was born in 1951. One, nine, five, one, it may be worth a shot." Rhys shook his head slowly as he tried the code, and the door remained shut. "Right, well, he's quite superstitious by all accounts, um... magpies! Now what's the rhyme? One for sorrow, two for joy, three for um..."

"Three for a girl, four for a boy, five for silver, six for gold, seven for a story never to be told."

"Excellent, Brendan," Julian smiled. "Well he's got no children, but silver and gold make him happy, and the code is a big secret so try, um..."

"Two, five, six, seven," Jess shouted the numbers out. "Good thinking, Dad."

But again, Rhys couldn't persuade the lock to move. "It's no good, Jules, can't we get our hands on some dynamite or something?"

"We'll just have to try and work it... Er, wait a minute, battles!" Julian clicked his fingers. "Famous battles. Hitoadie likes his history -

think of some famous battle dates."

"Try 1815, Waterloo, Rhys," Brendan suggested, "one, eight, one five."

"No."

"1805 then, Trafalgar."

"Nope."

"Um, Agincourt, Crecy... Now what year was..."

"1588," Drake interrupted. "T'was in the year o' our Lord 1588 the Don armada was put t' flight - there be no more significant a year Master Rhys."

"No, sorry Sir Francis," he announced after trying it.

"1066 Rhys," Julian suggested in desperation, "the battle of Hastings, the Norman conquest."

"Useless."

"I'm hungry," Max announced impatiently to the room, "it must be time to start the picnic by now."

"That's it," Julian laughed. "Well, it's worth a try anyway."

"What is?" Rhys didn't follow.

"Lunch time. Try thirteen hundred, Rhys, one o'clock, lunch time. It's Hitoadie's favourite hour of the day; the Toad plans everything around lunch."

Rhys tapped in the code, and with a sharp little 'click' the safe was open. Whoops of delight filled the room and Julian Finch delved in to retrieve not one, but two documents.

"Here it is, the European Environmental Act," Julian held it in the air in victory, "and what's this one? The New Environmental Solution Act!" He read the cover of the second document out loud and his heart began to thump again and his pulse quickened like never before. "I knew it. This is it, this is really it, their pre-arranged secondary legislation. My proof, Rindburn," he taunted his prisoner, and, plonking the second document down on the coffee table, he began to flick quickly through Sir Denis Hitoadie's private copy of 'the good old EEA.'

"Now, where is it?" Julian urged himself on in a whispering voice, passing one familiar section of the document through his fingers after another, until at last he found a little unassuming, understated section, with which he had not previously been acquainted. "Here it is," he announced again in excitement. "Protocol Fifteen, slipped in towards the back amongst all the appendixes where no one is likely to notice it, and it's only very short."

"Well, what does it say, Dad?" Jess came to almost perch on his shoulder.

"Give me a moment, I'll need a chance to read it through. Um, Rhys, can you and Sir Francis get those ravens bagged up, we'll need to take them with us when we go."

"Use this," Max suggested as he shook out a sack marked 'confidential waste', to make it available to the taller men whose job it would be to catch the birds. "I'll hold it open for you if you like." His initial wariness of the birds in the confined space had given way to more casual familiarity.

Julian Finch settled in one of the heavy, leather padded chairs and began to read, and as he scanned his eyes over the document they widened in amazement. His heart was beating in his ears and he felt faint; he just couldn't believe what he'd just seen. He sat up and simply starred silently at the ceiling as if in shock, while all around him birds flapped and squawked as Rhys, Arthur and Drake all tried to catch them.

"Well, what does it say?" Max demanded impatiently.

"Yeah, what's in it Dad? Tell us," Jess shook her father, and it seemed to snap him out of himself and back to the rest of the room.

"Wow!" he exclaimed. "This is big, I think I need to sit down."

"Dad, you are sitting down."

"I am? Oh yes. I just, I simply don't believe it."

"You're sitting down, Dad." Max gave him a very suspicious look. "Are you alright?"

"No I mean I can't believe this," Julian waved the document at them.

"What?" Max and Jess shouted at him in unison. "What does it say?"

"Well, all the safeguards. The protocol does away with all the safeguards to the legislative process, it just bins them all." He breathed hard, looked away and blinked and then scanned his eyes over it again. "It does - look, it scraps article 202."

"Article 202, Dad," Jess knelt down beside him and patted his leg reassuringly. "We don't understand any of this, you're going to have to explain it to us."

"Yes, sorry Jess, you're right, I've got to pull myself together. You know I told you about the Comitology, a body set up by the Council to check that the Commission are behaving correctly and that the secondary legislation they bring in is in the spirit of the Acts they follow?"

"What about it?" Brendan asked, as Arthur dropped a struggling raven into the confidential waste sack and Max closed the bag together after it to stop it escaping.

"Well, it'll be scrapped," Julian explained, "done away with as soon as the Council sign this Act."

"I still don't get it," Max declared, and he still didn't.

"It means once the Council have been tricked into signing the Act, the Commission will have no one to check up on them," Brendan explained. "They will have done away with the overseeing body by stealth."

"Oh right," said Max uncertainly, thinking he would at least try to give the impression he understood.

"And that's not all, that's just the beginning," Julian continued. "They've also included commitment to dismiss the European Parliament as well, to withdraw their power to veto the Commission by majority and deprive them of all their powers and functions..."

"So that's the elected element gone," Brendan considered.

"And they've included a commitment to prevent the European Courts from examining the legality of the Commission's actions as well..."

"And there goes the legal element."

"So no one will be able to question the Commission once this gets signed?" The enormity of the plot had hit Jess now and she uttered her next words slowly. "There won't be anyone able to check up on them, no one will be able to over-rule them?"

"That's right Jess," her father continued, "even the right of derogation is taken away, there's a commitment here to repeal the member state's individual rights to derogate from European Legislation. It's all but the last straw; any rules made from now on will bind them all, no country will be able to opt out of them." Julian paused. He could sense that other than Brendan and Jess the others didn't really understand the significance of what he was telling them.

"It's just one blow after another to make the Commission more powerful," he explained, "don't you see? As it stands at the moment, when the Council make European laws each individual country still has the right to opt out of it if they don't agree."

"Like us and the Euro," Brendan explained.

"Exactly, we opted out of it - but that right of veto, like everything else, will be taken away. Each and every means of constraining the Commission is to be signed away, they'll make the laws, no one will be able to challenge the laws, and once they've brought them in all the Member States will be totally bound by them whether they agree with them or not. All the safe guards will be gone."

"'Tis but the plotting o' a rogue, that wouldst they trick yon Council

289

t' sign away their powers wi' the sweep o' a quill."

"That's politics for you, Sir Francis," Rhys reflected. "What are we going to..?"

"But surely when the Council realise what the Commission are up to they'll just repeal this Act, you know, scrap it, or at least they'll never give the Commission a chance to bring in any more secondary legislation after this? Not once they realise what they're up to," Brendan interrupted.

"If that was the limit of their plot you might be right, Brendan," Julian advised, "but as I said, that was just the beginning, removing the safeguards is just preparatory. Up until now they've just been drifting around the fringes of what they are trying to achieve, just removing any challenges to this, this filthy underhand deception that they've hidden away at the back of this little protocol, at the back of this very big, very waffly document."

"You mean there's more?"

"Oh yes, Jess - listen to this. It's this single line which matters most, section three A, sub section three." Julian read the line out loud. "The National Commissioners to become independent Heads of State in each of their respective Member States, assuming power with immediate effect."

A hush fell over the room, and Arthur, who could only pick up on the vibe, could see that all was not good.

"So there it is, plain and simple," Julian continued. "By signing this document the oblivious Council won't just be signing away their authority, but their very nation's sovereignty. The Council sign this on Monday and they'll make themselves obsolete, they will have effectively resigned unknowingly, and every Member State in Europe will have a tyrant on its throne. Each country's Commissioner will take control of that country, and there will be nothing that the European system or the independent National Governments can do about it."

"Nothing?" Max looked dismayed.

"Nothing, son. The countries won't be able to veto it, it'll bind them all. No Court in Europe will be able to question the legality of it, and no elected or appointed body will be able to challenge or investigate it. They'll be accountable to no one, they'll have supreme power and authority, and they'll be able to bring in any new laws they wish. Here we were thinking our little island was going to be invaded, and all along the freedom of all Europe's citizens has been hanging by a thread."

"But they can't," Jess objected, "surely not? I mean, that's just silly."

"It's a brilliant coup," her father sighed gently. "The Council will bring it in themselves, they will cede the power to the Commissioners, it won't even be a power seizure in real terms because the Council will sign Europe over to them by their own hands."

"But it's ridiculous," Rhiannon agreed with Jess. "Everyone will be able to see that they didn't mean to."

"Of course they will, Rhiannon, but by then it'll be too late. There will be no going back on it, once this EEA is signed the whole system will fall victim to its own silly rules. As heads of state, a new Council if you like, only the Commissioners will have the power to change their minds and repeal it, but it's hardly likely is it? They will take supreme power and no one will be able to stop them."

"And any other laws they choose to bring in will be unopposed," Brendan observed quietly. "They'll be able to do exactly what they want."

"In a nutshell, Brendan, you've got it." And Julian, switching to Latin, explained quickly for Arthur's benefit the extent of the plot they had uncovered.

"Oh heck," Max punched the Duke of Man's computer in anger so that it fell off the desk and the monitor screen smashed on the floor. "That means Dredmor and the Toad will be Kings of England."

"Of Great Britain," Brendan corrected him, "the whole of the UK."

"They must be stopped," Arthur shouted in Latin, and slammed his hand on the desktop. "Cannot we just tear out the bit we don't want them to sign?"

"From this one, yes," Julian explained, "but this is only a copy. The document the Council will sign will be with Hitoadie and Dredmor in Brussels."

"Then must we take the fight to them," Drake looked animated, "shalt we strike the traitors down and seize yon writ afore the Council have a mind t' put their seal upon it."

"I think we are all in agreement," Julian looked round the room at the determined faces. "There's nothing for it - we have to stop the Council signing it. I think we'll need to take a trip over the Channel."

"Scum," Max was furious, "what total scumbags." He dropped the sack and hurled Sir Morgan Dredmor's computer to the floor beside that of the Duke's. "How could they betray us like this?"

"Geniuses." Having kept silent, Rindburn, couldn't resist the gloat now the truth was finally out and his own small part in the plot seemed forgotten in light of the discovery; he just felt compelled, so in awe was he of his Master's brilliance that he couldn't help but express it.

"Traitor," yelled Max, for the taunt had been like a red rag to a bull, and, letting go of the sack, Max charged across the room, fully intent on knocking Rindburn's goofy teeth out.

"No, no, Max," his father tried to stop him, but Max pushed past him in his fury, and as Rindburn flinched in anticipation of the blow that could only be milliseconds away, King Arthur leapt silently forward to hold Max and stop him dead in his tracks. Max puffed and struggled but the King was far too strong, and when he looked up into his eyes Max immediately calmed. He could see a hardness and yet a coolness to them which could only bring confidence in one who emitted control, and when Arthur winked at him Max nodded back in understanding, and, feeling almost foolish, he strode gently away.

"They may be vile little worms, Max," Julian explained, "but they can do no more harm while they're tied up like this, and though they deserve more than the worst hiding you could dish out, it wouldn't help our cause, son. Just let them alone."

"Oh blast it," Rhys exclaimed as several of the ravens struggled out of the discarded sack and flew up onto the surfaces once more. "We'll have to catch them all again now, Max."

"Always the gentleman, aren't you, Finch?" Rindburn grinned back at Julian. "You wouldn't let any harm come to your old mates, eh? Your old muckers Rindburn and Sludboil, eh, comrade Finchy?"

"Responsibilities," Julian replied simply, refusing to humour the pathetic creature in front of him. "You were to be given new responsibilities once the Act was signed. What are they?" he asked them again.

"Oh, can't say, don't know, Finchy, there weren't any responsibilities. Can't you just let us go now you've found out about it all? We'll just go home and keep our mouths shut eh, you know we will. We'll be good little boys, won't say a word, promise."

"Secondary legislation." Brendan pointed at the second document from the safe, which Julian had left on the coffee table.

"Of course, and here it is. The New Environmental Solution Act," Julian picked it up. "NESA." He recalled the Commissioners toasting the unknown abbreviation those long days ago. "The secondary legislation that will come in on the back of the EEA. Let's see what the first act of Europe's new masters will be, let's see what they've 'already drafted and agreed on,' let's see what answers we find inside it, shall we?" He grinned back at the defenceless Rindburn, and with his back to Julian, Nigel Sludboil emitted a massive, snot-wrenching sneeze.

Chapter Sixteen – NESA

The last reluctant bird had been penned in a corner by Rhys and Arthur with nowhere to go, and though it crowed defiantly at them, it cowered suddenly as Sir Francis Drake, in what had become a rather grubby pinstriped suit, leapt from the Duke of Man's desk to field it off the filing cabinet and palm it, two-handed, into the waiting sack. Maxwell Finch shut the raven quickly inside with its fellows and Arthur searched the room, dagger in hand, as he sourced a tie to seal the bag with.

The king quickly sliced the power lead from Hitoadie's own personal computer at both the plug and terminal ends, and handed the cord to Rhiannon, who tied up the confidential waste sack so the birds would not be able to escape again.

The two prisoners 'Mmmmed' and 'Nnneered,' behind the makeshift gags which now bound their poisonous mouths to prevent them making any significant comprehensive sounds, and they looked quite ridiculous, as with their trouser legs cut to make the gags, each now had his right leg exposed to the knee.

With the ravens finally away, and in the knowledge that they would at last be free of any further interruptions, they all now turned their attention to Julian as, almost with reverence, he prepared to give the New Environmental Solution Act its first public scrutinising.

"So this is it," he said slowly. "With all the safeguards gone and with themselves sovereigns of Europe, this will be the first thing the Commission plan to bring in. Let's see what our would-be masters have in store for us."

Julian took a deep breath and began to read aloud.

"Purpose of this legislation: It has been agreed that Europe is in the grip of an environmental crisis and that all Member States must commit to a common stance on the relevant issues... Blah, blah, blah," he skipped a bit. "The issues are listed in Section Two, blah, blah, blah... Commitment to the premise that greater European society be able to continue functioning as at present with as little disruption as possible being caused by the proposed measures as set out in Section Three. Blah, blah... It's all a load of jargon really," Julian observed, "let's get to the point."

"Yes, come on Dad," Jess agreed.

"Relevant issues," he turned to Section 2 and let his eyes skim on ahead. "Oh, all the usual stuff, really: increase in pollution, the greenhouse effect, the use of fossil fuels, carbon emissions, etc... Domestic waste management for existing and ever-increasing refuse -

excessive packaging and all the trappings of a consumerist society - waste management for the by-products of commercial and industrial waste, chemical waste, nuclear waste and human waste, that's sewerage etc... Blah, blah, blah. It goes on: meeting the cost of recycling, the effects of landfill on Europe's topography and the loss of arable and building land to accommodate the increasing landfill requirement. Addressing issues presented by the difficulties of nuclear waste disposal, and meeting the cost of existing inefficient processing of biodegradable waste products, etc... It's all guff, it really is. They're just acknowledging the existence of all the problems we all know we've got already.

"Section Three - here we are. Proposed measures. Measures will be introduced to deal with domestic refuse, chemical and industrial waste, human and bio-degradable waste, blah, blah, blah..." Julian skimmed through it, "Sorry guys," he looked up, "like all these waffly documents, they do tend to repeat themselves. Section Two laid out all the relevant issues and Section Three, in repetition, lists all the relevant issues again as those the Act proposes to address.... Oh here we are, Section 3 (b) - Purpose of Itemised Schedule of Measures Proposed - here's their mission statement, so to speak:

"To reduce mainland European landfill and increase the efficiency of disposing with bio-degradable and non-biodegradable refuse. To minimise the burden of recycling and minimise the cost of processing human, chemical and nuclear waste, and the risks therein. To reduce greenhouse gasses and carbon emissions generated by the recycling process, and to increase significantly Europe's capacity to generate power from stainable means... That sounds like a green policy, but what's this? To reduce labour force migration by ensuring a cost-effective, that's cheap, Europe-wide labour force is made available to employers in industry! I think they've gone off the point a bit here, gone a bit beyond their brief..."

"Yes, but how are they proposing to do all this?" Rhiannon asked. "It's all very well listing the problems, then the problems they intend to deal with and then their goals in dealing with them, but how are they going to actually tackle them?"

"Aye, Finch, get t' the rub," Drake echoed her sentiment, "shalt we tarry herein till Doomsday else."

"Hang on, hang on, have patience, we're getting there. All legislation is lengthy and drawn-out," Julian tried to assure them, "it makes it sound unnecessarily complicated and intelligent when it's often far from that. The Duke of Man will have dragged this out over numerous lunches with or without Sir Morgan's approval, but we'll get there eventually... Ah, here we are. Section Three (c), Schedule of Measures. This is it, this is how they are going to solve the Environmental crisis. But don't forget, these aren't actually proposed measures at all. They're pre-drafted, pre-agreed on, the Commission have secretly approved them all and they'll make this all law as soon as that damned EEA and its filthy Protocol Fifteen are signed by the Council..."

"Yes we know, Dad." Jess was getting frustrated. "we understand that much, just read it out."

"Alright, alright. Schedule of measures," he began again as the others leaned in over his shoulder to see the document themselves. "To utilise unwanted European offshore land as designated landfill for all types of waste. To put an end to recycling and avoid expensive processing of waste, and to cleanse Mainland Europe of these problems. To construct massive offshore wind farms to run as giant batteries providing Mainland Europe with power from a renewable and sustainable means... It's an interesting concept, let's see the details...

"Section Three (c) subsection (i) Great Britain and its islands identified as suitable unwanted offshore European land... What?" Julian just couldn't believe it.

"Subsection (ii,)" he continued. "Within Britain suitable derelict mineshafts, caverns and underground cave networks to be identified and utilised for the disposal of nuclear and chemical waste."

"Subsection (iii): Valleys in Britain's highland areas to be identified and utilised for the disposal of bio-degradable and non-bio-degradable waste until such time as these areas are levelled. The lowland areas to then be gradually backfilled with refuse. There is a note here: inland waterways will help break down the waste and rainfall likewise, there will be no need to cover the waste as it will over time break down naturally. The rest of the world could be persuaded to pay Europe to likewise dump their waste on these isles... This is outrageous," Julian ranted, "but there's more... Subsection (iv) - A pipeline to be set up Europe-wide to transport all unprocessed human waste to Great Britain, where it will be deposited on top of the mounds of surface rubbish... they can't do that!"

"It'd stink." Jess couldn't believe it either. "All that rubbish and unprocessed poo being dumped all over our countryside."

"There goes our green and pleasant land," said Brendan, aghast.

"I'll take not umbridge," Drake declared, "t'will be like to mine own age whence gong scourers wouldst haul night soil unto the fields."

"I don't think this is any time for nostalgia, Sir Francis," Rhys tried to explain, "even slightly gross nostalgia. Don't you see? They're planning to just turn our country into Europe's dustbin."

"Subsection (v)," Julian continued. "Appropriate chemicals to be sprinkled to assist in the breaking down of waste in order that further quantities can be deposited on top. The process to be completed until the whole of Britain is covered, and to then be repeated as appropriate and in accordance with need in perpetuity..... They'll just keep dumping," Julian was reddening with rage. "They'll dump and dump, throwing rubbish on top of rubbish forever, and our whole country will just disappear. In a few years' time it'll just be a massive, smelly heap of waste, a filthy toxic soup."

"This can't be happening," Max was shaking his head. "I mean, this has to be some kind of joke, doesn't it? I mean, they can't just cover the country in rubbish, we all live in it."

"Subsection (vi) doesn't appear to be a joke, Max." His father continued reading. "The population of Britain to be relocated to Mainland Europe to provide an unskilled labour base and prevent a hitherto unprecedented migration to Britain of Europe's skilled labourers from their home states. All persons to be evacuated with the exception of an appointed task force of waste disposal and waste re-distribution operatives employed to manage the process. Two waste disposal Executive Managers to be appointed as overseers of the process; they will be answerable only to the Commission. Once the land has been completely covered by the first layer the operatives will leave the country via the channel tunnel, which will be backfilled behind them. Pipelines for the dispersal of all types of rubbish from mainland Europe will then be established and will be controlled by remote mechanical means. A small fleet of helicopters to be employed to regulate appropriate areas in which to deposit further waste and to drop further chemical deposits as required."

"So there'll be no-one left at all?" Brendan was astonished. "All our houses, covered in rubbish."

Jess was in a state of shock. She was imagining Bath, her home city and the valley the old Roman town nestled in, being slowly and deliberately filled up with refuse and debris. The rubbish climbing up the valley and hiding all the Georgian streets, filling the Royal Crescent and the Circus, and covering all the historic buildings; her entire city being lost under an ever-increasing mound of European waste, layer upon layer would be piled on, filling the valley up until it was flush with the surrounding hilltops. Then the hills too would disappear as layer upon layer of putrid blankets of waste covered the whole country. It wouldn't just be her city that would be lost, there would be so many others - Edinburgh, York, London, Manchester, the whole of England,

Scotland and Wales - millions of homes. A whole national homeland was to sink like Atlantis, only under filth and be lost for all time.

"So these are the sacrifices your boss was talking about on the news then, Dad," she said simply. "When the Toad and Sir Morgan spoke at that press conference they said there would be sacrifices, and they were right. They want us to sacrifice our homes, our country, our culture and ourselves."

"That's right," Julian remembered, "they said it was to build a better Europe."

"I take it that's it." Max turned to his father and tapped the document. "It might as well be."

"Oh that's rich," an enraged Rhys shouted, "they'll sell us out and then have us enslaved as well. We can't allow it, we'll have to fight."

"Subsection Three (c) (viii)," Julian read on. "Wind farms to be set up in the Channel and the North Sea, in former British waters, to generate sufficient sustainable energy for the whole of Europe from renewable means, thus reducing emissions of carbon and so-called greenhouse gases, and their harm on our environment... That's about it." Julian Finch flung the New Environmental Solution Act onto the floor in disgust. "There are some appendixes, a UK survey covering the specifics of how the whole thing will be managed, but that's about the size of it..."

"Well, it's bloody outrageous," Max stomped round the room. "We can't let them get away with this."

"A pox on the treacherous dogs," Drake cursed the Commission as a whole, and Julian, noticing the enquiring expression on the unenlightened face of King Arthur, apologised to the King for his neglect and explained in Latin how the Nation's sovereignty was to be signed away by an unbeknowing Council, only for the country's new leaders to sell the nation into slavery so the land could be laid to waste.

"Laid waste," the king sought clarification, "by whom?"

"No, covered in waste," Julian explained, "the whole country will be buried in rubbish. It'll take many years, but it will all be gone."

"I think I understand," Arthur spoke thoughtfully, "but I'm a soldier, Julian - a warlord, not a politician. Merlin tutored me to be a speaker, a judge, but I know nothing of this law, and though it cannot go unchallenged I know not how we can best fight it."

"Methinks the means be plain," Drake spoke up, and as he did so he raised his sword in the air in a meaningful gesture, which only backfired when he pierced the lampshade with it. "Thou spake, Finch, that 'tis of import that the Council be not enabled t' place their seal 'pon said document."

"Well yes, we'll have to stop the Council signing the EEA. If we do, we'll halt the Commission in their tracks."

"As play to a child it be," Drake grinned. "Thou and I, Arthur, shalt put to the sword all members o' the Council in the chamber assembled."

"Um, I like your thinking," Julian pondered, "but the Council aren't really the enemy, are they? It's the Commission who are up to no good."

"No matter. Then shalt we go about our business wi' the Commission, an' spill their treacherous blood afore they seize all power from the Princes o' Europe."

"Again, ten out of ten for constructive thinking, Sir Francis, but it would be impossible. The Commissioners will be scattered all over Europe right now waiting to make their own individual power seizures as soon as the Council have signed the Act."

"Then shalt we take to us a palfrey an' ride 'em down. Shalt we, by the will o' God an' our Queen, bring justice unto 'em."

"We simply don't have time, Sir Francis, we've missed our chance. They were all assembled yesterday, but they'll be well-dispersed by now and they'll be well-protected too."

"Hitoadie and Dredmor," said Brendan simply, "we'll have to nobble Hitoadie and Dredmor."

Arthur recognised the names and rallied to Brendan's call.

"For this then have I returned. We kill the two traitors before they present the writ to the Council, and its over."

"We can't kill them." Julian wouldn't be swayed. "They'll have to answer for their plot in a court of law, we need to expose them... But how?"

"Easy, go to the papers."

"We can't go to the press, Max, they'll never believe us, and even if we took them these documents we've found, all the Commissioners will have to do is rip Protocol Fifteen out of the copy they've got and deny all knowledge of it. They'd just say it never existed, and we'd look like a load of anti-European... um..."

"Muppets."

"Yes if you like, thank you Rhys. The problem is, Max, that this NESA doesn't formally exist, remember? Even if we managed to make the Commission cut out Protocol Fifteen for now, it would be as if NESA had never been written. No one would ever know, again no one would believe us, and the Commissioners would just make up credible secondary legislation in its place. They'd just make sure we were out of the way and they'd slip their plot through on the back of the next Act they propose to the Council.

"No, I think I've got a better way. We want the Commission to think they've got away with it, and then we'll be able to expose them when they try a power seizure and they haven't the authority to back it up, I think I may have an idea. As you said earlier, Sir Francis, we cannot allow the Council to sign this document." Julian held up the EEA.

"But as you said earlier, Dad," his daughter reminded him, "that's only a copy."

"Precisely, so we must get our hands on the original version," said Julian slowly, "and swap them over."

"With what?" asked Rhys.

"With what I am about to write," Julian continued in excitement. "I'm a proofreader, aren't I, so I'll become a proof writer for a change. All I need do is take this copy, script up a bogus Protocol Fifteen which in essence looks similar but has a few double negatives slipped in and suggests the Commission be dismissed en-mass rather than they be crowned Kings of Europe, and at a glimpse they won't notice. When they try and declare themselves it will all backfire, they might even condemn themselves by their own actions. Think about it - an extra 'not' here, and 'won't' there and all the safeguards they're trying to do away with can be preserved. With the plot averted the pressure will be off, and we'll have more time to work out how to expose them properly. That is, if they don't expose themselves in a failed attempt."

"It might well work," Brendan considered the suggestion, "but the hard bit will be swapping it."

"Well we need to get to Belgium and try and track down the Toad and Sir Morgan, we can be pretty darn certain they won't leave anything as important as the master copy lying about. So far as pinching it is concerned, well, we'll have to cross that bridge when we come to it... I'll take the laptop from my office when we leave here and I'll get our new Protocol Fifteen scripted up while we're travelling."

"To Belgium!" Max sounded excited at the prospect. "Let's get going."

"Well, some of us will be going to Belgium, Max," Julian thought carefully. "But there's something else which needs to be done, something else which is every bit as crucial to our success and to causing their failure."

"What, Dad?"

"It's really important, Max, and I want you, Rhys and Rhiannon to do it."

"So we can't come to Belgium with you?" He looked devastated.

"I need you to do this, Max," his father implored him, "all three of you. It's a huge responsibility but I know you three are up to it."

"Well, what?" Max looked blank.

"You want us to take the ravens back, don't you Jules?" Rhys guessed correctly.

"Yes, I do, they have to be returned. The Commissioners clearly considered it important that they be stolen and absent from the Tower when the document was signed, so it's got to be just a crucial to get them safely returned before the Council prepare to sign the EEA. Perhaps with the ravens back at the Tower the country won't be able to fall."

"But I want to come with you, with Arthur and Drake," Max protested.

"This be as important, Master Maxwell, as any charge we be undertakin,'" Drake explained. "Your task, Master Mariner, be at the very heart o' our errand, an be of such import as be the hull o' a ship to her Captain."

"You've been there, Max," Julian reasoned with his son. "You have a good idea of the layout, how to get in, where the ravens roost, it makes you the best man for the job."

"We'll do it, Jules," Rhys offered.

"You can trust us," Rhiannon added, "and you can rely on us to look after Max too."

"I don't need looking after."

"You may not, Max, but the ravens will," Julian smiled at him. "You've got to get them safely back to the Tower, and most importantly you mustn't let yourselves get caught. Don't forget, the Police think it's a student prank, and if they catch you three with the birds they'll probably think you stole them in the first place."

Rhys explained his task to Arthur in his native Welsh, and as Max continued to appeal to his father, asking why Brendan or Jess couldn't go instead of him, the King stepped forward and took Max by the shoulders. The words he spoke were alien to the boy, but Rhys translated, and as he did so Max could feel his bottom lip tremble and his heart swell with pride.

"Many of my Knights have I dispatched on errands," Arthur told him, "yet none of such importance. You need not prove yourself to me, Maxwell Finch; your heart is pure, your spirit worthy and your mission just. The land of your birth now calls you, the Nation depends on you though it doesn't even know it. This is your hour, Max, your chance to be a hero. I Arthur, your King, send you on this mission in confidence that you will achieve it. Wear this mantle of champion well, and if you play your part in this and make your father and your King proud, you shall be a Knight of my new round table, and I shall count myself honoured to sit beside you."

A tear rolled down Max's cheek, and when Arthur held out his signet ring to the boy once more, he kissed it gently in a sign of submission, and said in a hushed voice "I'll do it Dad, you can all rely on me."

"I see then that I need not beseech thee also," Drake shook the teenager's hand. "For I knowst thou art a stout fellow wi' a heart for adventure o' a like t' mine own. Ah, an' now seest I mine folly in appointing Master Rhys quartermaster, for all provisions shalt sail wi' you valiant adventurers three," he joked.

"Well now that's all settled we'd better get a move on," Jess suggested, "we're racing the clock really, aren't we?"

"You're right Jess, we haven't much time." Julian prepared to launch himself into action.

"Mmmmh! Ummmhhhh!"

"Oh, Rindburn and Sludboil," Brendan remembered, as the two bound and gagged men announced themselves once more. "What are we going to do with them?"

"Leave them," said Max dismissively, "lock them up, throw away the key."

"It's an idea," Julian agreed. "The Commissioners won't be returning in a hurry, they aren't going anywhere, and I wouldn't have thought anyone else will be coming in until we get back and the whole business is finished with."

"That's providing we don't forget to come back," Rhiannon teased the two incapacitated traitors.

"Mmmuhh." Rindburn and Sludboil thrashed at their bindings.

"I think they want to say something," Jess observed casually, and Drake slipped off their trouser leg gags.

"You'll never get away with it, Finch," Rindburn challenged.

"Neber, neber, neber," Sludboil chanted, relieved to be free of his snot-drenched gag. "Bhe Bommissionbers arenb bar boo cleber forb you... Heckchoo..." He sneezed.

"Treachery o' the like most foul," Drake chastised them, "an' still, thou dogs, wilt not relent nor repent thy folly. Thou shouldst be keel-hauled an' scourged t' thine ribs for thy unrelenting."

"And what was in it for you two?" Jess enquired coolly. "What were your thirty pieces of silver?"

"There's no point asking them, Jess." Brendan already knew the answer. "Two waste disposal Executive Managers were to be appointed to oversee the landfill, weren't they? Got to hand it to you really, Mr

Rindburn, Mr Sludboil, landfill without even having to dig a hole first - now that's easy peasy, isn't it? Lazy even."

"Oh yes, how right you are Brendan," Julian smiled at the sneering face of the restrained Rindburn before him. "That'll be the promotion you were boasting about, won't it? Lords of the dung heap, very high and mighty I'm sure."

"Well they'd have fitted in well," Max mocked them, "two more turds on top of the pile. Be seeing you, we have to go."

"You can't leave us like this, Finch, we're senior Civil Servants... And anyway, I need a pee."

"Well you'll just have to hold on won't you?" Max joked. "Only for a few days or so."

"When this is over, Finch, I'm going to see to it that you and your precious party find themselves at the bottom of a very deep, very dark mine shaft." Rindburn's teeth were biting at him in his fury and a malicious frown covered his high forehead. As Julian watched he could see that the raven poo on his head had dried and hardened, and it now cracked as he ranted at them. "You'll be sorry when the slurry starts pouring out of the pipeline, I'll see to it that we fill your mine shaft in first, you shall all be mine, mine," he shouted almost manically.

"Byeah, bine. Bood bun Bindburn," the snivelling Sludboil joined him in laughter. "Byou'll bee slorry albright, cubbered in slubby. Harb har ha... A bine shafbt, beh, he bee..."

"You'll be in it up to... Well up to above where I could raise my arms, if I could raise my arms."

"Be silent, Rindburn, you total waste of space." Julian Finch had taken enough. "Gag them again, Sir Francis, they clearly have nothing wholesome to say."

"I hope you rot in hell, Finch, in my putrid hell." Rindburn's final challenge echoed around the room as his gag was replaced, and his eyes almost popped out of his head as he continued to mumble incoherent muted obscenities at them through the trouser leg which bound his mouth.

"I hope someone finds you, Rindburn," Julian replied once silence had finally been restored, "just not too quickly."

"You be good little boys now," Rhiannon blew them a kiss as the group left the room. "Don't get too excited, Mr Sludboil, you'd better control your breathing with a cold like that. Oh, and Mr Rindburn, I'd cross my legs if I were you."

The heavy door slammed shut on the two UK European Commissioner's two Private Secretaries, and as they sat in the dark, tied back to back, the last they heard of Julian Finch and his party was the key turning in the lock.

They crept back through the main office and Julian cringed at the sight of so many computers missing their cables, it would certainly baffle the returning staff on Monday morning. But still, he thought, the cost of the damage was nothing compared to the cost of failure from here on. He grabbed his laptop and portable printer from his own office, and carried them out in their smart carrier case, which he slung over his shoulder.

"Good evening, George," he bid the security man on the front desk farewell as they returned to the lobby. "I'll show Mr Drakeotti and Mr Arthurelli out myself. It's been a pleasure, Mr Jenkins." He turned to Rhys and made a big show of saying goodbye to the supposed dignitaries whilst covering George's view of Max, who ran round behind them all with the bulging sack of confidential waste, and disappeared through the front doors. Once again Julian needn't have bothered with the distraction dramatics, for George was a picture of unconcern as he sat entirely engrossed with his portable television.

The real farewells had been saved for later. After a meal and the purchase of train tickets, and after Rhys, Max and Rhiannon had been booked into a bed and breakfast and the ravens were safely hidden under Max's bed, all had wished each other good luck.

Max had even shaken Brendan's hand, and to his surprise found himself asking his classmate to look after his sister, Jess had of course kissed him, much to his embarrassment, and his father had taken him quietly aside and told him how proud he was of him. But Arthur had seized Max by the elbows, and through his cousin's interpretation had once more charged him to complete his mission with words of inspiration.

"Defend these noble birds as a she bear would her cubs, Maxwell son of Julian. Do well your deeds and the bards will sing long of them, the people and your King shall forever be in your debt." As they parted, Arthur shook his hand more formally, and in an up-to-date fashion, and spoke in his laboured English: "My friend Max - go Max, my friend."

Jessica Finch settled into her Eurostar seat in anticipation of what was to come. She'd never been through the Channel Tunnel before, but this was no holiday and the excitement she felt was all nervous anticipation as the train began to roll out of the station.

All were weary and spoke little. Brendan Johnson gazed out of the window at the passing lights of the London night, the shrill sound of his mother's voice still ringing in his ears. She'd been far from happy when he'd told her over the phone that he'd spontaneously gone off with friends on a camping trip and wouldn't be back for a few days. She'd argued, of course, but he'd been brave and insistent. 'But you haven't got any clean underpants with you,' she'd yelled down the line as he'd finally put the phone down. If she went looking for him in Cornwall, she certainly wouldn't find him there.

Sir Francis Drake, his sword re-wrapped and stowed away under his seat, played an improvised game of draughts with King Arthur, using a packet of mints and a handful of coins as the pieces, and an old handkerchief of Julian's, which was sporting rather squiggly lines all over it crudely etched on in biro, was serving as the board. The King was ahead once more and Drake was doing his best to cheat.

Julian Finch tapped away on his laptop with surprising energy, occasionally letting out a contented sigh, a "tut" or a "very good" to himself as he read his altered version of Protocol Fifteen back in his head.

As he did so, his daughter flicked through the New Environmental Solution Act, and in idle curiosity turned to the UK survey contained within the appendixes. The detail of the plan amazed her. It was really so specific; it listed the depth of the valleys, the volume of the cavern networks and the capacity of every low-lying region to accommodate rubbish. They clearly intended to make the most of every inch of space, from the Scottish highlands to tranquil Kent. It was no surprise to see both Cheddar Gorge and Wookey hole listed on the 'inventory of resources,' and Jess could only imagine the caverns being filled in to bury nuclear and radioactive waste deep under ground, and the gorge spilling over with refuse as it joined Snowdonia, the Lake District and countless Scottish lochs in humiliating degradation.

Jess felt such anger at the Commissioner's betrayal. Had she known what the surveyors were doing at the top of Cheddar Gorge when she'd pointed them out to Abbey Saunders on the school trip, she would have given Sir Morgan Dredmor what for when he forced her to pose with him before the cameras at Wookey hole.

It had only been a few days ago, and though it felt like an age away she could sense him now, she could picture the narrow eyes, the sneer which had made her feel so cold, so mistrusting of him at the time, so clearly in her memory. Yet on reflection she had judged the Commissioner well, for there he'd been asking the doddering manager all sorts of questions about the capacity and volume of the caverns, and he'd never suspected he was trying to secretly calculate how much sewage he could store below the earth. Jess doubted the surveyors even knew why they had been required to make their calculations.

"Humph," Brendan sniggered to himself, bringing Jess out of her daydreams.

"What's up with you?" She elbowed him gently.

"I was just thinking about Rindburn and Sludboil being found in a few days' time, by the Police, hopefully. What a sight they'll be, tied together, covered in snot, and with their trousers missing from the knee down. They'll probably think some strange cult got hold of them."

"Yeah, I bet Rindburn is still trying to hold his bladder. That'll teach him, he deserves no less for saying such horrible things to you."

"Oh it's alright, Jess," Brendan reddened and scratched his head nervously with a tubby finger. "When you're my size you get teased quite a lot, I'm used to it. That Abi Saunders..."

"Yeah, I know. I'm sorry Brendan, I'll try and stand up to bullying a bit more when all this is over."

"If only we had our own raven to plop on every bullies head, eh! I think that would put a stop to it."

"Yeah, I think it would," Jess laughed.

Drake and Arthur had been muttering in quiet discussion, and now Drake opened their conversation to the floor.

"The King saith that astride a horse wouldst entry t' yon City be most fitting, yet methinks 'tis a most ignoble passage t' skulk beneath the very ground hither, beneath the very waves, for 'tis like to a mole t' flit about in secret, not a manner t' befit a King an' most noble Admiral o' our isle."

"I know travelling under the sea must seem so wrong to you, Sir Francis," Julian defended his decision, "but I assure you it will be much quicker, and it'll take us right into Brussels."

"Ah, but that thou had a mind t' sail the Channel, Finch," Drake lamented missed opportunity and pointed to the blackness above. "In any craft couldst I sail o'er these waters, they be known unto me like to the curls o' mine beard - oh, to ride them again."

"I'm sure you'll get a chance to..."

"The craft in yon book, Mistress Jessica. Wouldst I give all the spice o' the Orient t' sail a ship o' a like unto it."

"Craft in my book?" Jess didn't follow.

"Aye, thou, Brendan, spake that she be sat even now i' Portsmouth Harbour. I beheld her awhile in thy book, Jess, as Master Brendan and thyself brought the past unto the present. Oh t' sail her wi' her bristling guns an' webs o' rigging...."

"Oh the Victory, he means HMS Victory," Brendan remembered, "he saw it in the History book. What a thought, eh, Francis Drake in

Nelson's Victory. I wonder what Nelson would say."

"T'would be a match none could better." Drake licked his lips at the prospect. "The greatest sailor who ever graced the surf, an' the finest vessel e'r hewn o' English oak for t' match him."

"Greatest Sailor! Nelson might have something to say about that," Jess muttered under her breath, and then more loudly she pointed out "It's in dry dock, Sir Francis, you'd never be able to sail it. As soon as it hit the water it'd sink."

"There are boats which can go under water these days, you know, Sir Francis." Brendan tried to change the subject.

"Belly rot," Drake replied, "thou speakst as wi' flux o' the mouth."

"No there are, they're called submari…"

"I'll hear none o' it." Drake waved him to silence.

"Well, if we did sail the Victory over we'd certainly arrive in style," Julian humoured his guest, "and quite an experience it would be I'm sure. But quite apart from Jess being entirely right and the old girl sinking straight to the bottom, even if she did stay afloat, I think our arrival in the Victory might arouse a little more suspicion and draw a little more attention to ourselves than we need to be inviting at this stage of our adventure."

"Portsmouth is also miles out of our way," Jess added, and as she watched the crestfallen Admiral sink disheartened back into his seat she was sure she could actually see the legendary hero sulking.

Chapter Seventeen – Sunday

Sunday was both the longest and shortest day that Rhiannon and the cousins Max and Rhys could remember. It was the longest as it dragged and dragged, but the shortest in that they knew they had so little time, and every moment that went by was one less in which to complete their task.

As the dusk fell on a warm London they sat frustrated on a bench along the Thames and ate sandwiches as they looked up at the Tower in front of them. They'd expected it to be easy, but the steep red and grey walls now loomed over them like their personal Everest. Their target, which lay just a short distance away on the other side of the wall, seemed almost unattainable. For whilst all they had to do was enter and return the ravens to the lush green grass of Tower Green without getting caught, they now realised they faced extreme difficulty in actually gaining entry without being found in possession of the missing birds.

The day had started well as, full of eggs and bacon from their bed and breakfast, they'd set out to buy rucksacks in which to carry the birds concealed to the Tower. This first stage of the plan had been a success, and on return to the guest house they'd rounded up the birds from Max's bathroom (where they'd fed and watered them overnight to prevent them causing too much mess), and had distributed them evenly amongst the newly-purchased carriers. They had walked the short distance to the Tower with confidence and had joined the queue with high expectations, having aroused little if any suspicion, for just as Rhiannon had suggested they just looked like three excited young tourists visiting the London landmark.

The problem had presented itself in the shape of a large, silver-whiskered Yeoman Warder of the Tower, who had approached them, partisan in hand, as they'd neared the front of the queue.

"Good mornin' Madam, mornin' Gen'lemen," Joe Banks had greeted the three of them. "I hopes none of you fine people will mind if I has a quick look in your rucksacks, only we has to be security-minded now if you gets my meaning."

"Ah," Max and Rhys had exchanged glances. "Why do you need to do that?" Max had challenged him.

It had been a clumsy response likely to arouse suspicion, but Rhys had ventured a less confrontational, "We're just tourists, you know, all we've got in there is our lunch and cameras."

"Even so, sirs," Banks had persisted, "I has me orders, no one comes in 'less I has searched their bags. If its cameras an' what not I don't see as how that's goin' to cause a problem, now hand 'em over."

He'd lunged towards Max, who'd been nearest to him, but the elderly Yeoman, despite his pedigree as a former RSM, lacked the speed of the teenager, and Max had twisted away from him easily.

"I have my orders too," Max had responded combatively; he'd taken Arthur's words about protecting the birds seriously and he hadn't been about to let his King down at the first hurdle. Imposing though the armed war veteran was with his uniform, medal ribbons, flowing whiskers and parade ground voice and posture, Maxwell Finch had been determined not to let himself get intimidated.

"Come on now, lad, I can't let you in wi'out searchin your bag." The queue had moved forward a bit, and though Max had been able to see past Banks to the green grass of his raven drop zone beyond the colossus clearly had no intention of making it easy.

"What are you looking for then?" Rhys had asked, trying to distract Bank's attention from his younger cousin to himself.

"Eh, don't know really, lots of things. Can't be too careful in this day an' age."

"Well, like what?" Rhys had persisted.

"Well we can't be too careful, you could have a bomb or something in there, country's in a high state of alert, you three could be terrorists for all I know."

"Do we look like terrorists?" Rhiannon had scoffed at him, thinking she'd made a valid point.

"Well erm... I don't rightly know. No one knows what terrorists might choose to look like does they?" Banks had responded uncomfortably. "For all I know you could have anything in there."

"Could be a raven even," Rhys had replied with a nervous laugh.

"Ah, it could indeed." Banks had taken this last remark a little too personally, and Rhys had sensed how uncomfortable the comment had made the Tower's guardian, and he twisted the knife into this little chink in their obstacle's armour.

"You should look out, you know, just about anyone could be trying to take over the country now you've let those birds get carried off. Perhaps you should tighten security."

Banks had wanted to point out that his very desire to search them was in response to the humiliation the Tower's staff had suffered, but he resisted the urge and remained professional. Instead, with straight back and straight face he'd replied sternly, "You shouldn't joke about such things, young man."

"He's not joking," Max had parried strongly.

"Now you look here," Banks' front had capitulated, "since that unfortunate episode security's been stepped up, see. There's extra Security men all night and extra Yeoman Warders in the day time. We've got CCTV covering every inch of the grounds and them battlements, we've got brand new alarm systems in operation and we've got guard dogs patrolling all round the compound after dark. Just now a fly couldn't get in without being spotted, see, but just in case it can, I'm here to check people's bags on the way in."

"What, all day long?" Rhiannon had asked him.

"It's me duty, Mam, it's me orders. Now you look like students an' I wants to check yer bags."

"Oh right, so terrorists look like students do they? I've told you we're tourists," Rhys had responded angrily.

"Tourists, students, terrorists or not, I've gotta look in them bags," Banks had insisted, and he'd reached towards Rhiannon, who'd then been nearest to him.

It had then been her turn to twist out of his frustrated reach, and she'd then taken a turn at trying to persuade him otherwise.

"Excuse you, but it's really intrusive to look in a girls' bag. Honestly, I could have all sorts of lady's things in there," she'd responded flirtatiously.

"Ooh, sorry Madam, but you see orders is...."

"I do like a man in uniform," she'd interrupted, fluttering her eyelashes, and taken completely off his guard the Yeoman Warder had coughed uncomfortably.

"I'm old enough to be your Grandfather."

"Oooh look at all those medal ribbons, you must be very brave to be a Beefeater," she'd continued divisively, sensing a potential way in. "I bet you've got loads of stories you could tell us."

"Well, as it happens," Banks' had swelled with self-importance, "I does have a few tales to tell."

"Ooh, I thought so." Rhiannon had retained her front of enthusiasm and stepped towards him. "Let us in quick, I'd love to hear them."

"Yeah, do you think I could hold your pike?" Max had likewise advanced, showing mock-excitement.

"Well yes, but it's not a pike it's a ..."

"Where did you get that one?" Rhiannon had pointed wide-eyed at Banks' DSO medal ribbon nearest to his buttons on the left hand side; it was his most important decoration, and though she hadn't known it, that which he wore with the most pride. He was always delighted to be asked to recount his heroic exploits and had so nearly fallen for it. Flattery had almost got them inside but they'd pushed their luck just a little too far, and as Rhiannon had pressed him with a demanding "Go on then, tell us," Banks had closed ranks once more and had refocused on his duties.

"Now look here, this is the Queen's castle and I be her guard, you don't come in without my searchin' yer bags."

"Look we don't mean to be funny," Rhys had appealed one final time, "but we really don't understand what gives you the right to..."

"What's that?" Something had caught the Yeoman's eye and he turned his attention to Max's rucksack with alert curiosity.

"What's what?" the other had replied defensively.

"That there. Yer bag moved, something in your bag is movin' on its own."

"Look, we told you there's nothing in..."

"There it goes again I tell yer, the bag's movin,' there's somethin' in there." Max had had tried to protest, but a muffled squawk from inside the bag had almost given the game away completely.

"I heard somethin' then," Banks persisted, "you've got somethin' in that bag and I intends to locate it." He'd stepped forward authoritatively, trying to dominate the teenagers with his uniformed presence. "Come on now, condition of entry. I will see inside that bag, young man."

"Oh, condition of entry is it?" Rhys had thought quickly. "Well we haven't entered yet have we? I mean we haven't actually bought any tickets yet so you've no right to search us."

"Ah... But..."

"Don't think we'll be buying any tickets now either," Rhys had taken Rhiannon and Max by the arms and had begun to lead them away quickly. "Come on you two, let's get out of here."

They'd run back passed the rest of the queue and out of sight round the corner at a brisk jog, leaving Yeoman Warder and ex-Regimental Sergeant Major Joseph Banks rather bewildered and scratching his head.

"I don' knows what they had in them rucksacks," he'd congratulated himself in ignorance, "but we don't wants it in here."

Rhys, Rhiannon and Max had spent the rest of the day strolling backwards and forwards around the Tower's castle walls trying to find a way in, and as the day had dragged and they'd become exhausted they'd bought their sandwiches and now sat on the bench, trying to talk through their next move.

"That was quick thinking, you know," Max congratulated his cousin. "With all that noise from flappy here, the cat, or should I say the raven, was nearly out of the bag. If you hadn't pointed out that we hadn't actually bought a ticket at that point, he would've caught us red-handed."

"Oh, I learnt a few things from your dad in that office, Max," Rhys brushed it off. "If the EEA needs a signature to make it binding then likewise that old boy can't enforce his silly rules on us if we haven't bought a ticket."

"And I didn't think you were listening to all that waffle of Julian's." Rhiannon squeezed Rhys' knee. "What a clever boyfriend I've got."

"Yeah, well, clever or not, we've still got to find some way of getting these birds back in there, and we're running out of time."

"You heard him though," Max spoke ominously, "extra security, more cameras, alarms everywhere. We aren't getting in in daylight."

"Yeah," Rhiannon echoed. "I heard him say dog patrols as well, I don't think I fancy breaking in at night either."

"But if those idiots Rindburn and Sludboil can do it we must be able to get in somehow."

"You're right, Max," Rhys sounded excited. "They went over the wall, didn't they. All we need is a rope, a ..."

"Rhys, you're not going to get me climbing those walls, they're far too steep," Rhiannon protested.

"Well maybe not in those shoes, babes, but Max and I could..."

"No, not in any shoes, and you and Max aren't trying it either, its far too dangerous. If you don't break your necks getting up there the dogs will bite your feet off on the other side. You don't even know how to get down once you're up, we never got to see the inside, and anyway with all the cameras and..."

"Yeah, yeah, okay. It was just a thought."

"Traitor's gate, we could swim in." Max suggested.

"Nice try little cousin, but how are we going to teach the ravens to hold their breath underwater?... In a bag?"

"Yeah ok, I didn't think of that," Max conceded.

"Hang on though, you might have something there. Who said they had to be alive? I mean even if we return them dead they'd be back, we could just throw them over and...."

"Arthur told me to defend these ravens, to protect them," Max wouldn't hear of it.

"Of course they have to be alive, Rhys Jenkins, you idiot," Rhiannon also rebuked him, "what good is a dead raven to anybody? Honestly, the very idea."

"Well it was just a thought, I..."

"We don't want any more thoughts like that."

"Right," Max interrupted, sensing a slight rift in his companion's relationship, "we can't go over the wall and we can't get under it. We've been all the way around and we can't find a way in.... Wait a minute, delivery vehicles, they must get in somehow, and probably by a back entrance."

"Yeah," Rhys considered it, "but there are unlikely to be any more deliveries now, we'll have to wait till tomorrow."

"Well I don't know how you two are planning to conceal a load full of ravens in a delivery vehicle," Rhiannon reflected, "but those birds need feeding. However we're going to manage it it's going to have to wait for the morning. Come on then," she stood and beckoned the other two, "at least we've got all night to think it over."

"We'll bring a change of clothes in our bags tomorrow," Max suggested as they began the walk back to the guest house. "It may come in handy."

To Julian Finch, his daughter Jessica and their companions Brendan, Francis Drake and King Arthur, Sunday had also been the longest and shortest day they could remember. Tired and dishevelled from their late night journey, the day had for them also dragged and dragged, and they, like their fellows in London, were also conscious that every minute that passed was a minute lost.

"The hours slip through our fingers like t' the fine grains o' a sand timer," Drake was growing impatient. "Wherefore must our company wait on their very move? Canst not we seek them out, Finch, an' bring 'em unto heel?"

"For the thousandth time," Jess began in answer, "it would be like looking for a needle in a haystack. Taking the Commissioners by surprise is a great idea, Sir Francis, I would like nothing better, but you can't play hide and seek with people in a City the size of Brussels."

Drake grunted in Latin, inviting Arthur to share his grumble in their common language, but when he did so Arthur too impressed on him in no uncertain terms the importance of sitting tight.

"We must wait as Julian suggested," he counselled. "If this is the place to mount a trap, this is the place to sit and mind it."

"Quite so, Sire," Julian Finch confirmed, "this is the place they'll come. I know we've been waiting ages but I just know the Commissioners have to be staying in one of these hotels. The Toad can't resist but stay in the grandest, you see, and when dinner is over they're sure to make their way back to it. That's when we'll pounce, when we know where they're staying."

"I can think of worse places to sit and wait," Brendan remarked as he sipped his cool drink in the failing light, "though I'm sure these café owners will miss us once we're gone, we must have spent a fortune sitting around all day."

"We certainly have," Julian replied dryly, "though this really is the best spot, we can see the whole square from here."

"Yeah, just look at it, it's really impressive," Brendan gestured as he waved his arm in an arc at the beautifully intricate fifteenth century facades of the 'Grand Place.' "You can't deny it, Sir Francis," he swept his eyes round the whole of the Belgian capital's grandest old market square, "these are pretty amazing buildings. Why, it's like sitting in an art gallery when you think about it."

"Thou speakst true, Master Brendan, that each frontage reflects grandeur, though methinks them more to the look o' a ship than t' paintings an' sculpture."

"Yeah, I can see that," Jess agreed. "It does look like the backs of a load of old ships packed in tight together."

"Oh, that we lack the endeavour o' the dock yard," Drake lamented. "The wind in the sails, the salt in the air, the shrieks o' the gulls an' clamour o' men loading the fleet. Oh, for the bustle o' the harbour an' the shouts o' the Harbour Master. I like not this waiting, Finch," he continued restlessly. "This far have we come, our voyage complete, an' all for t' sit in a foreign square an' keep our feet an' blades idle." He shook his head in demonstration of his frustration. "'Tis not the battle we sought."

"Ooh!" Jess put her head in her hands to demonstrate her own.

"It's alright, Jessica," her father began to explain. "Look, Sir Francis, it's only a matter of time. Now I wish I'd tried to find out from Rindburn and Sludboil exactly where the Commissioners are staying, but they're bound to be staying in one of these hotels in the Square, it's just a matter of patiently waiting for them. And so far as the battle's concerned, we'll see. The main thing is to get into their briefcase and swap the documents over." He tapped his own little bag which contained his new draft of Protocol Fifteen, which he hoped would put right all that the Commissioners sought to change. "This will stop the immediate threat, and then we can expose their would-be coup."

"And how will we do the swap, exactly?" Brendan sought clarification.

"Well we'll just have to take our chance, shadow them inside, work out which room they're staying in and then go from there. We'll have to cross that bridge when we come to it."

"Sneak in when they're sleeping, perhaps," Jess suggested.

"Yes, that might work. We'll catch them at anchor, eh, Sir Francis?"

313

"Yet we still await them to take anchor," Drake grumbled.

"Look, I know we've been waiting all day, I know we're all tired," Julian appealed to them all again. "But, well for you two, you've been waiting for this moment for centuries, what's a few more minutes?"

"I says't again, Finch, the traitors be worthy o' death."

"I won't let you murder them," he snapped back, then sighed deeply. "Look, I told you, times have changed."

"Then shouldst we take them unto the Queen as prisoners an' make known the plot - wi' her seal on their warrants their heads shalt be on Tower bridge by the morrow eve."

"There just isn't time, and who'd believe us anyway? We just have to swap the documents so they can't succeed, and then tomorrow we'll try and petition the Council and show them the work of the plotters. We'll ensure they are dealt with, but slow time."

"Once the Council have signed your re-edited one, Dad," Jess confirmed.

"Yeah, once the Council have signed this the Commission will be surprised to find themselves sacked rather than Lords of Europe."

"Excellent," Brendan grinned.

"Yet who would not believe a hero such as I...?" Drake began, only to be interrupted by Brendan, who spoke in urgency and pointed at two figures who were crossing the square a little distance from them.

"There they are!"

Arthur, who was feeling rather hot under the collar where his tie was bound round his torc, followed the line of the teenager's arm and could see for the first time Britain's two European Commissioners, his countries two enemies, in the flesh.

Sir Denis Hitoadie the Duke of Man waddled along in a smart, food-spattered dinner suit, a briefcase in one hand and a fat cigar in the other. He puffed on it greedily as he crossed the square at a leisurely speed, while his companion, the slick Sir Morgan Dredmor, also in smart attire and with his narrow eyes flitting uneasily around the 'Grand Place,' scurried along beside him trying to force the pace.

"Just as I thought," Julian Finch sounded more relieved than jubilant, for the truth was that even he had begun to doubt that they would ever turn up.

"Up an' at 'em," Drake rose quickly. "Let havoc fly."

"Wow, Sir Francis, this is no fox hunt," Julian tried to calm him. "We must follow at a safe distance, we can't let them see us."

"It's you they mustn't see, Dad," Jess reminded him, "the rest of us are strangers to them - you must hide at the back."

Just as Julian Finch had predicted, the two Commissioners headed straight into the lobby of one of the 'Grand Place's' very finest hotels. Julian's party anxiously followed at a discreet distance, Arthur and Drake in front, Brendan and Jess behind, and Julian himself at the rear.

As they entered the lobby, Jess could see Sir Morgan Dredmor cast a scathing look at the concierge on the reception desk as he retrieved his room key without a word of thanks.

"A fine meal, Sir Morgan," Jess heard the Duke addressing his fellow Commissioner. "We should dine out in Brussels more often - plenty of fine wine and rich sauces, what!"

"Indeed, Dennis, it was most pleasant, though a little filling."

"Gotta say one thing for the Belgies," Hitaodie continued in a loud and slightly slurred voice, "they don't skimp on the portions, not like these fancy Frog chefs. Its French food in Dutch quantities, simply glorious... Problem is, it don't half bloat a chap, eh?" His grace let out a huge blast of flatulence which caused the unfortunate concierge to twitch his upper lip in disgust and quickly busy himself with other tasks some distance from his farting guest.

"I trust the Mediterranean will treat us more kindly," Sir Morgan sneered, "and that trips to boring old Belgium may soon be a thing of the past."

"Oh how right you are, Morgan, how right you are. The sun on our faces, and as many olives, grapes and carafes of wine as we can slip away. This old horse is well overdue being put out to pasture." He patted his enormous stomach and smiled contentedly. "So nearly delivered, Morgan, so nearly signed and sealed eh! Triumph is in the air, what! Bring on the morrow... Ooh, indigestion." He let rip once more. "Um, to the bar I think."

"I think I'll sleep on it, Dennis, one last sweet dream of glory before it becomes reality."

"Nonsense, man!" The Duke protested. "Yer must have time for a cognac before you retire."

"Before I retire..." Sir Morgan sneered. "Yes, perhaps I should drink to that."

"Ah, good fellow," The Duke slapped his companion on the back, and as Jess looked on, the two Commissioners, Hitoadie still clutching his briefcase, entered the hotel bar.

They made to follow them through but the concierge sprang out at them as if from nowhere. "Do you have a reservation, Monsieur-Dam?" He asked them respectfully.

"Um, no," Julian replied quickly, "but some friends of ours are staying here tonight and they have arranged for us to meet them in your excellent bar."

"Ah, you are of course most welcome," the concierge gestured with a gloved hand to point after the Duke and Sir Morgan. "The bar is a doit, um, how you say... on your right."

"Most kind." Julian led his party into the bar, and quickly behind the backs of the two Commissioners, as they ordered cognacs from the barman, to a table behind a pillar in a discreet corner of the room from which he hoped the group would be able to watch the Commissioners without being noticed.

"Shouldn't we get a drink, Dad?" Jess suggested. "We're going to look a little sus up here in the corner if we don't have one."

"I suppose you're right," her father agreed, though reluctantly, as funds were already running low. "The problem is, you two are too young and I can't go up to the bar while they're standing there."

The Commissioners were handed their glasses by the barman and clinked them together with a simultaneous 'cheers' which could be heard across the almost empty room.

"Sir Francis could go up to the bar," Brendan suggested, "so long as he promises not to stab the Commissioners."

"No, there's no need after all." Julian had sat long enough to eye up the venue and it looked expensive, "I expect there'll be a waiter over in a minute to take our order." The thought of Drake trying not to arouse suspicion whilst trying to get his head round modern metric currency was more than Julian Finch was prepared to risk. "What are they doing now?" he asked Jess, hardly daring to glance round the pillar.

"Oh, they're just chatting."

"Has he still got the case?" Julian poked his head out slightly to see if he could sight them.

"Quick Dad, hide your face, they're coming over," and they were. Julian ducked back behind the pillar as the gigantic Duke of Man, with a cigar stub in his mouth and a large glass of cognac in his hand, led the oily, slimy Sir Morgan Dredmor to the table right next to Julian and his party, and separated from them only by the presence of the wide pillar.

The Duke parked himself heavily on a chair, his fat legs billowing over it, and placed the briefcase down on the ground beside him, and within just a couple of feet of where Jessica Finch sat. He tipped cognac down his neck, undid his bow tie to leave it draped and dangling undone around his neck, and drew heavily on his cigar stub.

"Ah, bliss," he exclaimed as he lounged back in his chair and rested his hand that held the cognac glass on his huge gut.

His companion seated himself almost silently, seeming to just slither onto the edge of his seat, and he placed both his glass and his room key down on the table top before looking around the room through his narrow eyes with a sarcastic sneer on his face. "Very nice spot, Dennis," he announced but his tone did not suggest genuine sincerity. "One of your usual haunts?"

"Well it ain't quite me club, Morgan, but it ain't bad for Brussels, what!"

Brendan peered round the pillar and over Sir Morgan's shoulder. "His keys are on the table," he whispered to Julian.

"Can you see a room number?" Julian whispered back.

"Elegance and ambiance yer can create, Morgan, I've always said so," the Duke continued loudly, "but yer can't buy class."

"Quite so, Dennis, quite so, but there are other things in life that most certainly are for sale," Sir Morgan replied, oblivious to the teenage boy peering round the pillar and over his shoulder once again.

"The number tag is upside down," Brendan reported back, half mouthing the words lest the Commissioners should overhear him.

"Damn it!" Julian cursed their luck.

"Pssst, Dad." Jess caught his attention and pointed down to the briefcase sat tantalisingly close to her and within her reach.

"Seize it," Drake demanded a little too loudly. "Place thy hand upon it, Jess, and bring it unto us at table."

"Shhh," Arthur hushed him, but the Commissioners continued chatting as if they hadn't heard him, so engrossed were they in their own conversation.

"A better life, for example," Sir Morgan continued, "and at such a meagre cost."

"Oh a trifle Morgan old boy, a trifle merely," the Duke agreed. "None will miss old Blighty, not one. Indeed, Morgan, I fear we have found a use for Britannia at last, eh? What!"

"Yes, I think our European cousins will agree that Britain will soon be fulfilling her destiny," he joked.

"Oh she'll be full alright." The Duke let out a mighty belch. "Damn shame though really, damned shame; the nation that brought Port wine and Stilton to the table to be sacrificed for a better world."

"Well I'm sure we can arrange for plenty of Stilton to be put aside for you, your Grace. You can take it with you to warmer climes when the dump trucks move in."

Brendan couldn't believe his ears, that two such celebrated statesmen could turn their backs on the land of their birth so easily, and that they could discuss the imminent betrayal of their country in such an unconcerned and off-the-cuff fashion. He had to clench his fists together with all his might to contain his rage. It was as if the Duke was discussing the sweetness of a pudding - there wasn't even a hint of genuine mourning for the passing of a nation.

"And so easily done, Morgan old boy, so easily done. Not quite through the woods yet, eh, but near as damn it... Genius idea, that Protocol Fifteen."

"Oh, you're too kind. But the solution to the Environment Dennis, that was the deal breaker, that was the carrot to lead them on. Mere power our associates would jump at, but NESA will give them security, the solution to ensure their popularity with their people and that their usurpation of power will be easily accepted. The Environment is the single most contentious issue in our modern constricted world, my friend, and when their people see that their new leaders have solved it they shall place them each on a pedestal... It is also the solution, of course which will guarantee yourself and I a very comfortable existence from here on in."

"Amen to that." The Duke drained his cognac glass and stubbed out his cigar.

"Mine ears canst take no more," Drake rose in his seat and spoke far too loudly. "Now must I run the traitors through or shalt madness take me in mine fury."

King Arthur leapt up, and in a moment cupped his hand over the Admiral's mouth as he dragged him back into his chair. "Shhh!" He whispered in Drake's ear.

"What was that?" Sir Morgan sat bolt upright and surveyed the room uneasily once more.

"Oh don't fret, Morgan, these Flems and Walloons have rather heated debates sometimes," the Duke reassured him. "We'll give 'em something to talk about tomorrow, eh!"

"Get the case," Julian whispered to Jess; he just felt they had to do something, the resolve of his group was breaking fast.

"And amen to Rindburn and Sludboil," the Duke continued, "a fine man that Sludboil, got potential, always said so."

Jess leaned round the pillar and stretched her hand out towards the briefcase ever so slowly, inch by agonising inch, desperate not to make any sudden movements. She could feel her heart beating in her throat as she stretched for it, so conscious that if Sir Morgan were to spot her delving at the Duke's feet the game would be up.

"Fools both," Dredmor disagreed, "unutterably useless in every way. I shall be glad to be rid of them Dennis."

"Ah, but they fulfilled their task with honours," the Duke defended his charges.

"A simple task, Dennis, as simple a task as we could have entrusted to them. I doubt they made easy work of it, but a baboon could have bagged those birds for us so I see no honours in gifting them plaudits. Come now, Dennis, by this time tomorrow the course of European history will be changed for good, the old order swept away, and I shall not have our efforts attributed to those blundering imbeciles Rindburn and Sludboil."

Jess held her breath. Her hand was almost on the briefcase handle and she braced herself to take its weight; she knew she'd have to lift it, for if she scraped it along the floor the noise would surely alert its owners.

"Touch wood," the Duke replied, doing just that to the table-top.

"Oh I do wish you would dispense with all that superstitious clap-trap," Sir Morgan berated him. "Your insistence on taking the ravens, for example - an unneeded nonsense!"

"A necessary step, I assure you. The forces must be on our side, Morgan," the Duke replied uncomfortably.

"Well, let's hope they are."

"Indeed so," Hitoadie dropped his right arm down and grabbed up his briefcase to the safety of the table top with a grunt of exertion. "If it is to be done it must be done properly - we cannot afford to leave the t's un-crossed and the i's un-dotted."

Jess had withdrawn her arm just in time, narrowly avoiding contact with the Duke's fat fingers, and brought her hand helplessly back to her lap. She gave Brendan a despairing glance as the Duke continued his rhetoric.

"With a few strokes of the pen, Morgan old boy," he tapped the top of the case lovingly, "our baby is born. The pen is, as they say, about to be proved mightier than the sword after all."

"I'm not sure the citizens of the Volga will agree with you there, Dennis," Morgan Dredmor grinned impishly. "After all, Herr Hitler got up to rather more mischief invading Russia than he ever did writing Mein Kampf."

"Ah, how right you are Morgan." The Duke allowed himself a belly laugh at the joke. "But the beauty of all this, as we have always said, is that through stealth will sovereignty be passed. And not one life lost, eh!"

"You are, as ever, the consummate philanthropist, your Grace," Morgan Dredmor replied sarcastically.

"And this is only the beginning, remember," the Duke continued. "With a free hand, just think what else we can make happen."

"Why Dennis, our every whim shall become reality," Sir Morgan smiled. "I think I might suggest a ban on football in the first year; it's such a loutish activity, is it not?"

"Ah! Yer can taste it, can yer not, Sir Morgan? Can yer relish it? No more red tape, no more bureaucracy, nothing to stop us, nothing to get in our way, what!"

"Indeed Dennis, it's as wonderful as it is masterful. Yet I'm afraid I must leave you now, there is one thing in the way of my enjoying the end of this evening."

"Ah, a call of nature eh! Can't handle the affluent fayre, eh, Morgan?" The Duke tapped his own belly as if it were itself an achievement worthy of accolades.

"I regret, but I lack the capacity of your Grace to enjoy myself more fully. Yet, think on this; as of tomorrow the flush of these lavatories will signal the start of an epic journey for deposits like the one I am about to make."

"Ha har, a homing turd," Hitoadie laughed. "Send it with regards t' me maiden aunt Mabel in Ludlow."

With a sneer Sir Morgan Dredmor left his virtually-untouched cognac on the table, snatched up his room key, and made his way to the toilets.

Julian Finch and his party could only sit in silence as Sir Dennis Hitoadie the Duke of Man, sat alone just inches from them, yet with his copy of the European Environmental Act, Protocol Fifteen and all, safely secured within his briefcase and on the table top in front of him, right under his big red nose.

The Duke tapped the top of the table and breathed heavily as he "Pom-pom-pommed" to himself under his breath. He held off for a moment or two, but unable to resist the temptation he snatched up Sir Morgan's unattended glass and tipped the contents down his open gullet... A little more tapping, but he clearly felt uncomfortable sat alone, and without a drink.

"I'll not sit idle," he grunted to himself, and with some effort he took to his feet. Leaving the briefcase on the table he waddled over to the bar across the otherwise almost empty room, shouting "Garçon, more cognac." He snapped his fingers rudely at the bar man as he drew nearer the service counter. "More cognac, Garçon, and be quick about it."

Jess couldn't believe their luck, this chance that had been gifted to them - and she jumped forward to the Duke's table where she leant over the case.

"Thou hast little time," Drake stated the obvious, and Arthur, wanting to give Jess some cover, quickly rose and stood between her and the bar. He seized the leather-backed 'carte du vin' from a nearby table and tried his best to look casual - as casual as an uncomfortably suited man pretending to read a wine list in an unfamiliar language could look - but his position was what mattered, and where he stood he shielded Jess from Hitoadie's view.

In effect it mattered not, for the Duke stood with his back to them and made no effort to turn around. He produced a fresh cigar from a silver case within his dinner jacket and requested the bar man cut it for him, but they all knew he wouldn't be distracted for long.

"Will it open, Jess?" Julian hurried her from behind the pillar.

"It's a combination lock, Dad, it won't budge."

"We're going to have to keep him distracted," Brendan suggested, "he'll be back any second."

"Yeah, you're right," Julian agreed. "Sir Francis, you've got to go up to the bar and talk to the Duke."

"At last, Finch, an' so I shalt. Now wilt I share mine own mind with him and speakst aloud mine thoughts on his plot."

"No, no Sir Francis, you just have to engage him in conversation, hold his attention, keep him distracted."

"Hold his attention," Drake repeated the instruction. "So be it."

"Yeah, just stall him, that's all. Now go on," Julian urged him forward.

"I can't get into it, Dad," Jess whispered again in angry frustration as Drake approached the Duke.

"Well, try thirteen hundred again," Julian suggested, "most people can't be bothered to remember more than one code."

Jess fumbled with the combination lock, trying not to hurry too much in case she spun the little brass wheels round too far. With two little metallic 'clicks' the case was open.

"Be I even now disposed in the presence o' a Duke?" Drake asked as he joined Hitoadie at the bar.

"Indeed yer be, eh, what!" But as Hitoadie turned to address him he was rather taken aback by the speaker's rather odd, crumpled, pin-striped appearance and ragged pointed beard. "Erm... Recognise me, no doubt? Autograph hunter I s'pose, eh?"

"From thy very disposition canst I see that thou art a man o' noble birth, for as thou standeth betwixt the common men, these walls within, thy bearing heralds thee as one o' lofty countenance."

"Ah, indeed," the Duke replied, succumbing easily to flattery. "The Duke of Man," he introduced himself, "delighted to make yer acquaintance I'm sure, what...! And you are, erm...?"

"I too, my Lord, bear rank, a Knighthood bestowed 'pon me by the

Queen," Drake pushed out his chest proudly, "yet from thy attire wouldst I judge thou canst be not as favoured as I, for thy little tie Sir be dour blue and plain, like to a pauper's drape."

"Knighted eh... good show." the Duke did not quite follow. He racked his brains but couldn't place the stranger.

"Aye, thou doest perchance recognise me, honoured as I am for exploits o' discovery? Mine deeds o' endeavour an' mine true an' loyal service to our sovereign Lady, her crown an' her people."

"Eh... No, no I don't think I've had the pleasure," Hitoadie responded awkwardly as he scratched his head with a fat finger. "So who am I addressing?"

Across the room Julian Finch handed his daughter the replacement document, and in a flurry the switch was made, and the briefcase shut and abandoned on the table as Julian's party made haste to the door.

"Thou must now hear me, Sirrah," Drake's tone raised in anger, he just couldn't help himself, "an' heed thee well mine words, for now wilt I counsel and ask not thy pardon. Thou, my Lord of Man, art but a churl, a nave o' fly blown honour. For wi' rank an' privilege, so too comest duty t' thy vassals an' homage t' thy sovereign."

"Ah, noblesse oblige," the Duke replied light-heartedly, but Drake prodded Hitoadie in his flabby chest with an extended finger to make his point all the better.

"Your Lordship must reverence the..."

"Your Grace!" Hitoadie shouted back at him, now equally angry to be spoken to so cheekily; he demanded he be accredited his proper title by this upstart who had ambushed him.

"Ah, your Lordship is too kind," Drake smiled, and mistakenly believing the title a credit to himself, he gave a little bow of his head in courtly acknowledgement which tipped the furious Duke of Man over the edge.

"Yer speak of rank, Sir, yet conduct yerself with the manners of a serf," the Duke fumed, spittle flying out of his mouth as his face reddened. "Your name, Sir. Speak now your name," he demanded.

"As thou wilt," Drake spouted fury back, and both men raised themselves to their full height and squared up to each other toe to toe. "Be it known, thou bloated sea cow, that even now thou standeth in the presence o' Sir..." And in one movement Drake was gone, swept away by a stocky, dark haired, bestubbled figure in a grubby grey suit.

"Come, Sir Francis, we must fly," Arthur advised his colleague in rough Latin as he led him out through the lobby and into the 'Grand Place' once more.

They sped after Jess, Julian and Brendan, who'd jogged on ahead, and Arthur re-united Drake with his paper-wrapped sword as he tried to calm him.

"I had him even then within mine grasp," Drake protested, "wi' our blades, my Liege, shouldst we alone finish this sorry business."

"Do you not remember your undertaking on the train, Sir Francis?" Arthur spoke firmly. "We trust now in Finch and his tactics; he will give us the word, he better had when the time is right."

"An' if he doest not?"

"Then we shall strike, I promise you. But the time just now be right for flight."

Out of the square, and in the safety of a quiet Brussels street, Julian Finch congratulated his troops. "Well done all of you," he panted as he caught his breath. "It was very well done. That was quite some stalling, Sir Francis."

"Yes," Brendan wheezed. "I'm glad you didn't stall him a moment longer."

"It's done," Jess grinned from ear to ear. "It's done, that's the main thing, and now we need to rest so we can be fresh for tomorrow."

As Drake and Arthur had disappeared from the room, Sir Morgan Dredmor had returned from the toilet to meet Hitoadie at the bar.

"You seem a little rattled, Dennis." He noted the pained expression on his fellow Commissioner's face. "Don't tell me you've just discovered they don't do pork scratchings!"

"Indeed Morgan, indeed," the Duke replied, "I am most perplexed, and this is no time for banter. I fear I have a most strange occurrence to report." He took a long drag on his fresh cigar as if for comfort. "Really most strange, I shall be needing... Brandy!" he shouted at the unfortunate barman impatiently.

"I trust the case is still with us?" Sir Morgan looked around the room in concern, for the foolish Duke did not appear to have kept it with him as they had agreed.

"Oh, er, it's on the table," the Duke responded in a tone of bewildered distraction.

A glance confirmed that this was indeed correct.

"Then everything's alright, I'm sure," said Sir Morgan thoughtfully.

Chapter Eighteen - The Council Chamber

It was Monday morning and, Arthur, son of Uthyr Pendragon, the scourge of the Saxons, bludgeoner of the Picts, vanquisher of the Scots and King of the Britons, rose with the sun.

The dawn of battle found him calm in body but anxious in mind. It was all very well having a destiny, he told himself, but one still had to fulfil it. More so, he couldn't help thinking that in many ways his destiny to save the British people once more in their hour of need, was both very much still in the balance and very much still out of his hands.

This was indeed a very different calling, a kind of combat completely unfamiliar to Arthur. True, the princes of his age had engaged in petty squabbles as they made and broke brittle alliances with each other, and in this way he'd been no stranger to politics and diplomacy. But this had almost always been through word of mouth not through reams of documents.

Diplomacy, to Arthur, meant words of challenge and defiance exchanged immediately before battle, one warlord to another, macho banter designed to intimidate and gain the moral high ground by offering your opponent a dishonourable way out which you knew they could never accept.

"Leave this field at once and yield it to me and I shall not strike down your sons in front of you."

"There is no honour in yielding this field, but there is honour in falling upon it. I shall yield you nothing but wood enough for your funeral pyre, and for all those of your followers who choose to fall with you."

"If you will not submit now, by dusk this field will be littered with your men, and I shall geld any who are not man enough to fall upon it and choose instead to surrender themselves or flee in disorder."

"At dawn will the crows pluck the eyes from your limbless corpse. You shall have no grave, no burial cairn, and none shall be left to mourn you. The buzzards and kites will carry your innards away and their young shall grow fat upon them...' etc, etc. But this was different.

This was not the backs-to-the-wall stuff, the siege mentality that Arthur was used to where all his people were all too aware of the threat. This was a war of stealth and trickery, and the British people were completely unaware that within hours they could be sold into slavery, their very land pulled from under them like a bearskin from under a sleeping hound.

It was Julian Finch who led them, he who understood the situation, and whilst the king had to admit that it was a strong hand of fate indeed which had brought him from his rest to Julian Finch's own house, it was Julian Finch, and not himself, who thus far had carried the destiny of them all on his narrow shoulders. Arthur was a man of action, action with consideration certainly, but he knew all to well it was ultimately through deeds that foes were defeated and legends were created, and whilst he'd been happy to trust Julian's judgement so far, he felt that it would take more than words alone, spoken and written, to see the day out successfully.

What Arthur craved was the chance to make that move, and make it at the appointed time. He felt the overwhelming desire for action building up inside him, and his greatest fear was that this chance would be denied him as statesmen of powerful word moved bits of paper about and declared technicalities.

Morgan Dredmor and Dennis Hitoadie had been allowed to live, and though he understood that cutting a man down in public was not as accepted now as it had once been, as he lay awake in bed he had to concede that the flamboyant and arrogant Drake may have been right; letting them go when they had been in their grasp may have been a mistake. The document had been switched, but the Commissioners should not be underestimated. Arthur felt that leaving them in possession of the switched document on the presumption that they wouldn't check it was a bit like handing them the dice for the final throw. He did not want to stand helplessly by as the dice was cast with no control over them - he wanted to strike at the hand which held them.

Whilst the King wrestled with his thoughts the others slept, tired and wearied by all their efforts, and with no alarm to wake them. They slept on and on in their downtown guesthouse, and it was only when Brendan was roused by the king reciting in Welsh verse the lyrics of his favourite bards, that the rest of the group were alerted by the tubby teenager to the lateness of the hour.

They left in a rush, missing out on breakfast and the chance to wash, and all were hungry and felt dirty and scruffy as they ran hotfoot to the Council meeting. They still wore the same clothes they had travelled in, and Julian, Drake and Arthur had none of them the time, nor the articles required to have shaved. As such they made a strange sight, suited but grubby, and all three of them, even Julian, who carried the stolen copies of the European Environmental Act and the New Environmental Solution Act under his arm, looked rather rugged.

Although the bored-looking Security guards did give them a cursory pat down on arrival, they declined to use the metal detector which would surely have alerted them to raise questions about Drake's wrapped sword and the dagger which Arthur had concealed upon him, let alone the chain mail singlet which the King still wore beneath his now-tatty grey suit.

They climbed the stairs to the public gallery two at a time, and although the grandness of the Council chamber struck them all, Drake and Arthur had been subjected to so much change already since their return that they were unfazed by the huge room with its gaudy chandeliers, hanging tapestries and renaissance paintings.

The gallery wound round the room to each side, and as they moved round to the left wing they could see on the floor beneath them, on a raised stage, a huge crescent-shaped table with all the European Council members splayed out around it. Each Head of State had their own space with their country's name written on a card in front of them. The identifying cards were flanked by both their national flag and that of the European Union in miniature, and each politician had an earpiece in place which was simultaneously translating the alien words of their colleagues.

To the front of the room, and nearest the door through which they had entered, Europe's press were assembled. Journalists, cameramen and film crews from every Member State, all packed in tight and trying to get the best 'take' of the historic moment when their own countries, through the signatures of their Councillors, endorsed the momentous European Environmental Act. It was felt by all present that the threat to the environment was huge, the cause, the need to do something about it, was just, and that this commitment to it was as moral a decision for the good of mankind as it was a political one. It mattered not to those assembled to witness it that the specific method for tackling the environmental conundrum had not been revealed in any great detail; what mattered was commitment to the aims as laid down by the Act. Public opinion seemed united. Europe would lead the world on climate change and environmental reform, for once the press were not here to hound their leaders but to praise them, and it was their job to generate the same feeling of pride amongst their public that they all felt for their representatives today.

Between the press and the Council table, in the middle of the room, Sir Morgan Dredmor paced the polished wood floor like a prowling tiger. Were it possible for his ears to prick up they would have been, and though his eyes were narrowed and he had an arrogant sneer on his face, his shoulders were loose and he looked relaxed.

The speeches were over - Julian Finch cursed himself for missing them - and now one by one the Council members, the most powerful men in Europe, the Presidents and Prime Ministers, the Premiers of each country, rose from their seats and made their way to a single desk on a raised stage behind the crescent and towards the back of the room. Here they signed the document, each pausing for the press to catch the moment in pictures and on film as they each put their personal signature to the European Environmental Act. In a barrage of flash photography they each made their way from the left side of the crescent in order, and having signed they did not return to their seats but stood instead to the right of the chamber together as if to demonstrate united purpose. The manner was orderly, none rising to leave his seat until invited to do so by Sir Morgan once the previous Councillor had joined the rest of the standing, clapping group.

As each signed, Sir Dennis Hitoadie the Duke of Man, one of Britain's two Commissioners with the directorate on the environment, one of the men whose office had been instrumental in the creation of the bill, stood over them. He looked over their shoulders like an authoritarian schoolmaster, salivating in approval as name after name was added to the document. The background babble and the clicks and flashes of cameras echoed round the roomy chamber, creating a somewhat surreal atmosphere.

From their position on the left wing of the galley high above them, our heroes surveyed the scene.

"I don't like it, Dad," Jessica Finch spoke in a stage-whisper, and many crushed in on the public gallery could hear it. "They look far too relaxed, the Toad and Sir Morgan, you'd think they'd look more nervous. Look, the Toad is even rubbing his hands together now - he must think it's in the bag."

"Yeah, but we know it's not don't we?" her father replied. "Look, there's Hitoadie's briefcase down by the desk, the document that was left in it last night will be the copy they're signing."

"See now, behold as the Don leader puts his Dago seal upon it."

"You're right, Sir Francis," Brendan confirmed, "that's the Spanish Prime Minister alright."

"Aye, by his ensign be he known."

"Yeah, and as they're going from this side it looks like the Dutch Councillor is next, then the British one - yeah, we're after the Netherlands, look, it's the Prime Minister." He pointed down to the one truly familiar face at the table. "Our Prime Minister... Hey, they must be nearly halfway through." He counted up the empty seats quickly, and then those still occupied. "They are," he confirmed. "Once the Dutchman's signed, that'll be half of them done."

"I like not this standing by," Drake spoke in Julian's hearing but addressed Arthur in Latin,. "'Tis most ignobly done that men such as we who have returned t' spill our blood ere Albion fall, shouldst like humble groundlings be not players but witnesses only t' her plight as't unfolds afore us."

"Ah, that such different men as we can be one in mind," Arthur replied sullenly, "for below us our enemies walk the field unhindered and we trust only in our traps of last night... Our traps which go unchecked."

"I sayst again, my Liege, that hath we struck them down last night we wouldst not now be in the hands o' the winds."

"That's the Spanish Prime Minister done," Brendan continued his un-requested commentary. "Look at him pausing on the steps for the TV cameras, he can't get enough of it."

"TV cameras, of what doest he speak?" Drake asked the question in Latin, inviting the reply in the same tongue, and Julian obliged, answering the question on Brendan's behalf.

"Television cameras," he explained, "they are recording these images, sending them simultaneously and transferring them into every home in the country. Why every household in Europe, the world, could be watching this right now. You know, like the little box we have, the screen we watched the Commissioners on on Friday night."

"So be this stage now to all the world in view? Be we now upon it before the whole world displayed?" Drake licked his lips.

"Potentially, and that's what we need, because once they've got this signing out of the way we'll need to try and organise some kind of press conference. We'll need to reveal this plot sensitively once we're sure it's been averted...."

"So now is the battlefield widened," Arthur spoke up and interrupted Julian, completely ignoring his last comment. "Now, Sir Francis, can our people see first hand the works of these traitors."

"Now canst our public behold again, and in the flesh, Sir Francis Drake, El Draque - he who singed the Don King's beard, the terror o' the Spanish main," Drake's voice filled with excitement and heads in the gallery turned as his vanity threatened to spill over. "In glory couldst I be now revealed, shalt now I drum them again as I drummed 'em afore... Um," he paused as he registered Arthur's stern expression. "Thy pardon, my Liege, if thou warrant, yet thou an' I both, King and Knight, Soldier and Sailor together stand now on the jetty ready t' launch ourselves out on the sea o' fate..."

"The field of dreams..."

"T' be resurrected."

"In good time." Julian was getting impatient. "We can't overstate announcing your return, we'll never be believed."

But Arthur's head was full of sounds and images. Shield walls closing on each other, the impact of the hacking crush, the shouts of men and the crashes of weapons on helms and shields. His pulse now was quickening and a glance at Drake told him he felt it too.

"Feel thee now, Arthur, that same pull which makest thee raise sail, an un-be-knowing wherefore thy spirits dragged thee, set a course for home?"

"If you speak of the desire, the instinct indescribable which hauled me from my rest to the homestead of our host in pursuit of my enemies and in the hope of raising my standard again, then yes, Francis, I feel that force now, and stronger than ever."

"The Dutch leader is signing now." Brendan, oblivious to the content of the Latin exchange, continued his commentary. "That's exactly half of them who've signed it - by my reckoning one more signature, and they pass the Act."

"One more, and the Commissioners will think they've got it passed," Julian corrected.

"And it's the British Prime Minister next."

"Dad, I really don't like this," Jess persisted, "I've got a chill going up my spine - don't you think we should do something now?"

"Pon my troth, Finch," Drake spoke for both Arthur and himself. "Master Brendan spake that be one more seal placed upon it this charter wilt be law, an' thou sayst that yon traitors wilt believe it so an' their plot complete. Sayst now the King an' I, an' heed thee our counsel, that be this signed, whatsoever be it's content, so shalt it be endorsed."

"You're right, of course," Julian replied, "whatever they sign will be made law. But we know what's in that document, it's the document we switch..."

"No. Not so," Drake rebuked him in English, and Arthur too, sensing for once, indeed for the first time with his heart and soul and not just with his head, that it was now right to deviate from Julian's plan, said plainly in Latin, "We cannot be sure what they sign, for the document has been in our enemy's hands overnight. They play at tricks, Julian, and whilst you remain a righteous man you will not be able to out-cheat them. We have handed them the dice, and if they have loaded those dice they will turn as they will them to."

"Our PM making his way to the podium," Brendan observed nervously.

"A good warrior checks that his weapons are in good order before the battle, Julian," Arthur explained, "and whether they have checked

329

that document or not, a great warrior never takes anything for granted. He never anticipates a mistake, he merely reacts to one... We simply cannot afford to take a chance on it, we cannot trust in the word of law, we need to act."

"Look, let's just think about this..." Julian protested. He knew Drake and Arthur spoke sense, but he just didn't know how the meeting could be successfully intervened, and had hoped he'd done enough to stall the Commissioners until he could work out an appropriate way to publicly disgrace them.

Jess had not understood all of the conversation but the gist of it was clear and apparent to her. "Dad, we're running out of time!"

"You are a courageous man, Finch," Arthur assured him, "and you have led us this far. It is not that you lack courage, but knowledge of when to strike. For action have we two returned, you have shown us the way. You have led us this far and we have followed, and we sense, we know that now is the time."

As the astonished occupants of the public gallery looked on, the two suited gentlemen who had been turning heads through their noisy and heated conversation, now very quickly began to unclothe. The man in the pinstripe shed his outer skin to reveal the ornate doublet and hose beneath, and with a shout of "To arms!" made in ancient Welsh the short burly man with the wild, wiry hair ripped off his suit and shirt like an unlikely superhero. He now stood before them in a shirt of chain mail with a thick belt around his waist, and woollen trews strapped with leather thongs to the knee.

On the stage, the British Prime Minister took the pen, gave a fixed smile to the European press, and amid a storm of camera flashes brought the pen onto the paper.

"Here we are at last, Sir," the Duke of Man almost drooled in his ear as the Politician posed, ready to sign. "Make your mark if you please," he joked.

Those in the gallery had gone silent, but now took an audibly sharp intake of breath as the man in the doublet ripped the paper from a tube he carried, and in a second held a long-bladed sword in his hand.

The other man, in the mail, produced a wickedly sharp-looking dagger, and promptly cut the cable to one of the large lighting rigs above the public gallery which illuminated the Council chamber below. He re-sheathed the dagger in the strapping at his calf and handed the cable to the other, who had climbed onto the balcony rail specifically designed to prevent those in the gallery from falling down into the chamber.

330

With a shout of, "For good Queen Bess an' merrie England!" the man held the sword in his teeth, took the cable with both hands, and swung down from the gallery like a circus performer to land in the middle of the crescent-shaped space between the press and the Council table. Drake made it look effortless, swinging with his legs in front of himself like the master of rigging he was; he kept his balance, and landed perfectly on his feet.

Sir Morgan Dredmor had little time to react, and had only half-heard the shout from above before Drake was almost upon him. As the cameras fixed on the new entrant, and before the Commissioner could speak, Drake took a pace up to him, and with a shout of "Aha!" punched him hard to the face. Sir Morgan fell to the floor instantly.

The press could not believe their luck; this was news, live and breaking, and just as they focused on this new drama there was a second shout from the gallery to grab their attention - "Artos Rex!" - and a second intruder, this time less gracefully and clad in chain mail, also descended the same, yet now slack, plastic-coated cable by simply sliding down it (and perhaps a little faster than he had hoped and anticipated).

As he hit the floor heavily two members of the Security staff tried to impede him and stood in his way, but the barrel-shaped man just dipped the shoulder and burst through them like a rugby player on his way to the try line. The would-be tacklers fell off him as he surged on, and it was clear to the whole room that he was heading straight for the Duke of Man. Before the big-bellied aristocrat had time or space to make a move the ancient King had closed the gap and was climbing the steps to the raised stage.

The Duke, panicking like a toddler afraid of a bee, squealed in terror and tried to get away from Arthur by edging round the table, doing his best to use the seated Prime Minister and the table top as cover to keep the madman from him.

He edged right around so that his broad back now faced the press, and the King, who had approached from the same spot, now followed him round, edging after him and trying to get hold of him, so that they now stood at opposite sides of the table, Arthur directly behind the astonished Prime Minister.

Arthur levered himself onto the table top by utilising the unsuspecting politician's shoulder as a step, and the Duke backed away from him in utter panic. In a bound Drake was up and over the crescent-shaped Council desk and had a sword point depressed firmly between Dennis Hitoadie's fat shoulder blades.

"The chase be up methinks," he shouted in a jubilant tone which could hardly contain his glee at the sport he'd just enjoyed, and the Duke turned his head round slowly to catch a glimpse of the second of his captors.

"You!" He said in disbelief as he recognised the pointed beard and pearl earring of the man who had so rudely accosted him in the hotel bar the night before. "And still, Sir, do I not know yer name."

"That shall be revealed," came a further shout from the public balcony, "and very shortly." The cameras again turned to the gallery amid gasps from those watching, but Julian Finch thought it best to ignore the cable and make his way to the chamber on foot. He made quick progress down the stairs - everyone was too astonished to stop him - and in just a few seconds Julian, Jess and the wheezing Brendan, (who wished he'd remembered his inhaler) pushed through the press to reach the chamber floor.

Shocked silence rang around the high ceilinged room, but the world's press were hooked. The cameras still rolled the live footage, and from dozens of studios the anchormen and commentators informed their gripped audiences that "We have a hostage situation developing!"

A huge feeling of relief surged through Julian Finch. He felt as if the vast weight of responsibility and uncertainty had been lifted from his shoulders in the one fell swoop of Drake's, and the barrelling run of Arthur's, which had seized control of the floor. Rightly or wrongly they had made their move, they'd taken the decision to act and in so doing had taken the pressure from him. He no longer had to agonise over what he was to do next, they had won him the stage. Now he had to react to the sudden change in circumstances, he had to grasp the limelight and use his limited time well.

As the adrenaline pumped Julian felt confident, ready to confront his nation's enemies and to reveal their plot in front of the harshest of scrutinisers, the Heads of States and the World's press. He had a strange feeling of elation and felt his heart might explode as he stepped up to face Sir Morgan Dredmor, the man who was still officially his boss, the stolen copies of NESA and the EEA, complete with Protocol Fifteen, still tucked under his arm. The moment was here, and even if the showdown had been manufactured for him it suddenly felt right. Julian felt invincible, he was relishing the prospect, and wondered if this was the same feeling that Arthur and Drake had themselves felt at the commencement of battle.

Back in Weston-Bissett the living room was silent and the television set made no noise at all. The commentators in the broadcasting studio joined the watching Patricia Finch in being glued to their seats in open-mouthed horror and bewilderment as Sir Morgan Dredmor, one of the most respected statesmen of the age, picked himself up off the floor and dabbed at his bleeding nose with a handful of tissues.

"You join us at last, Finch," he said with a sneer, and ran a hand through his oily hair as he tried to regain a little composure. "I wondered when you were going to turn up."

"The game's over, Sir Morgan." Julian spoke loud and clear in a firm and un-quavering voice. "The gloves are off. I've got the document here, NESA, your so-called New Environmental Solution Act, your Private Secretaries Rindburn and Sludboil are currently incapacitated, and even now the stolen ravens are being returned to the Tower." Julian turned to the Prime Minister, who sat in astonishment. "I ask you, Sir, not to put your name on that document until I have checked it. We have, of course, taken a precaution, but my friends here were anxious to ensure it was sound." He then turned to the press and said loudly, "Needless to say, as my colleague has the Duke of Man on the point of his sword, everyone should stay exactly where they are. I ask for your patience; all will very shortly be revealed."

"Bravo!" Sir Morgan clapped his hands slowly together in mockery. "Yet you remain indeed a most unremarkable man, Finch, you may have pinned your hopes of fame on this little outburst of exhibitionism, but your big moment has not come. You are, as I say, a most unremarkable individual, a sorry and pitiful creature who has shown little, if any, promise." Dredmor turned to the cameras, enjoying the opportunity to react to the intruders' entrance. "This buffoon who gatecrashes important European Council meetings works for me," he explained crudely, "and his career is a dead-end one. Perhaps he's jealous of the achievements of others, perhaps he's just seeking attention by bursting in like this. Your career, needless to say, is over."

"Shut up, Sir Morgan," Julian ordered, but with a wicked grin the Commissioner continued unabated.

"You may have seen yourself as held back, Finch, you may believe your time has come, that this is your great opportunity to make something of yourself, but it is not. You're a fool to yourself, you'll get nowhere, indeed you'll never get anywhere, no one in their right mind will listen to you. Look at you, madmen in front of you and children behind... Why, look at the state of you, you're a disgrace Finch, a no hoper, useless, boring... Julian Finch... Even your name is square."

"Shut up, Sir Morgan," Julian demanded again.

"Aye, be silent, thou treacherous dog, or sure as black powder burns shalt I run thy fellow conspirator through an' twist him like to bread 'pon a toasting fork."

333

"Quiet, Sir Morgan," The Duke of Man shook with fear like a leaf in the breeze as Drake prodded him impatiently with the point of his blade.

"That's better," Julian felt in control once more as all eyes in the room passed back to him. "Now let it be known that... Hang on. What did you mean you wondered when we were going to turn up?"

"I received a telephone call from Mr Trevor Rindburn earlier this morning," Sir Morgan replied coolly, trying to come across a little aloof. "He seemed somewhat eager to make me aware that you had broken into our office and had stolen various private documents. He also brought it to my attention that you had taken the birds away with you."

"Morons!" Hitoadie had gone red with rage. "Why, Morgan, did we entrust those fools? Why did we involve them in our business?"

"Come, come, your Grace, be fair, why only yesterday you said that Nigel Sludboil was a fine man of high potential," Sir Morgan mimicked his colleague sarcastically.

"This is no time ter mince words, Morgan." The Duke was sweating. "Yer don't have a swordpoint in yer back, damn it."

"No, indeed. Had you let me finish, I should add that Mr Rindburn fully appraised me of all your little exploits, Finch." He paused and grinned to himself.

"In addition to kidnapping the Duke and assault on my person in here, have we at home suffered burglary, and our loyal servants Sludboil and Rindburn suffered assault and false imprisonment... He saw to it that I was fully up to speed with your plan, so you can rest assured that your spoof Protocol Fifteen, very cleverly worded though it was, found its way into the shredder before we arrived here today.

"I don't doubt the distress caused last night to the Duke was your doing, a distraction tactic no doubt to lure him away from his case whilst you swiftly made the switch, but I too take precautions my dear Julian. I carried another copy with me and can assure you that we have reverted to the original text." Sir Morgan paused for the impact of his dispiriting words to take effect.

"Yer mentioned none of this ter me, Morgan, confound you!" The Duke of Man was puffing red. "What the Devil is going on here?"

"Finch thought he'd swapped the document, your Grace," Sir Morgan sounded informally casual, "indeed he had, but disaster is averted, I swapped it back."

"Ah, good."

Julian was crestfallen. "But how did...?"

"The cleaning staff arrived in the office this morning," Sir Morgan explained, "and by all accounts you'd left it in rather a mess. They suspected burglars, did a full check, and located Messrs Rindburn and Sludboil in our office, and as you say, incapacitated.

"I understand your major mistake to have been discussing your plan in their presence. You see, blundering oafs they may be, but they are, unlike yourself, not entirely disloyal. I think trusting in teenagers to return the birds was a little foolish, wasn't it? They're probably still in bed." The familiar sneer spread over his face - evidently Sir Morgan was rather enjoying the showdown now. "I suppose you haven't had a progress report," he smirked. "You're not actually sure if the ravens are back, are you? Come now, Finch, you're far too late..."

"Max will return them," Jessica Finch spoke up, daring to challenge the sneering Commissioner. "My brother will make sure the ravens are back where they belong."

"Oh really, little girl?" Sir Morgan turned his attention to his new adversary. "It's so moving when infants have hope," he patronised her. "I rang the Tower this morning to enquire, and can inform you now, Finch, that not a feather has flown back to roost."

"Mind now the serpent's tongue," Drake warned.

"Yeah, don't listen to him, he lies," Brendan agreed. "None of you can trust a word he says."

Julian Finch's mobile phone rang, and as he awkwardly took it out to answer it Sir Morgan grinned from ear to ear.

"Ah, an update," he smirked sarcastically, and then kept an amused expression on his face as all present turned to watch Julian try to hold a muted conversation with his son without giving too much away.

"Dad, we can't get in, security's too tight - we haven't been able to return the ravens." Max's tiny voice explained privately in his ear, and though no other could hear him, Sir Morgan's facial expression all too readily reflected the news for all to see.

"Where are you now?" Julian asked, the room hanging on his every word.

"Outside the Tower again, we've got them in backpacks, it's just..."

"Get them home, Max, at all costs get them home," his father pleaded, for he couldn't explain to his son the circumstances nor predicament they were currently in over the phone. He hung up to face the complacent mockery of the Commissioners once more.

"Lie, do I, little boy?" Sir Morgan turned his wrath to Brendan. "Why it's clear to all here that you've failed, and failed miserably."

"Failed in what?" The Prime Minister asked impatiently from his seat at the desk.

"Ah, by Jove, but any attempts yer make now are academic, Finch, purely academic, what!" It was now the Duke of Man who sought to spread doubt amongst the intruders. "The legend is dependent on the birds leaving, is it not? Well they left didn't they? It matters not whether you try to, God forbid even manage ter return 'em now. Fact is, they've flapped off, eh! Too late, Finch - might as well just scurry off home, old boy."

"Too late for what? What is all this talk of swapped documents and ravens?" The British Prime Minister, the European Environmental Act open in front of him, demanded answers.

"It's quite simple Sir," Sir Morgan responded in a slimy tone. "This imbecile who is even now wasting the Council's valuable time, and who is causing my colleague, the Duke of Man, acute discomfort, has tried to swap the Act in front of you with a document of his own in the hopes that the Council will mistakenly endorse it. But fear not, he has failed in his attempt, which was superbly pre-empted, and believe you me he will be dealt with appropriately."

"Prithee, but methinks thou art best suited t' tarry as gong farmer, Master Weasel, for there ist nought but gong an' filth thou speakst," Drake too was growing impatient. "Make known the treachery, Finch, for 'tis treason o' the foulest kind. Would that they be strung from a yard arm an' their bodies lashed t' stakes at low tide all for the sea t' pass o'er 'em on the morn, for their corpses t' be tarred an' left for the gulls, 'twould be a fate too kind."

"What is this cabaret you bring with you, Finch?" The Duke of Man was gaining confidence. "Two children wet behind the ears, a caveman with breath like a heated cesspit, and this pompous widow Twanky. It's like carnival time - have yer raided pantomime for support, eh? What!"

"No, Hitoadie, I have not," Julian spoke forcibly and refused to address the Duke with the formalities of his title, for he could feel his confidence returning. "I have raided history instead..."

"Oh, have we not heard enough?" Morgan Dredmor yawned in mock boredom.

"I will hear him speak," the Prime Minister demanded.

"Thank you, Sir," Julian continued. "As I was explaining, history has returned to us. Indeed, from the pages of history and legend come heroes long thought dead whose very presence here, Prime Minister, will give credence to my words and authority to the truth I will bring before you.

"Of both these great men the legends tell that they will return in our nation's hour of need, when the country is on the brink of falling they will return to defend it, and so they have, for here they are for all to see.

"Sir Morgan spoke a half-truth, but a half-truth only. Attempts have been made to trick you and the other Council Members within this chamber into signing the Act in front of you in the hopes that you would, as he put it, mistakenly endorse its contents. The full truth is that it is these traitors before you, Sir Morgan Dredmor and the Duke of Man, in harness with their fellow Commissioners, who have through their own contemptible deceit attempted this coup."

Gasps from the assembled Council and press resounded round the room, and after a pause, and as a clamour of voices broke out in the room, Julian raised his hand for silence and continued in explanation.

"If that Act is passed the very sovereignty of our Isle will pass to them. Their plans for our land..." he paused for effect. "They'll throw it to the dogs." Julian felt more and more in control now as he built the drama. He felt powerful, even commanding; the spotlight was on him, and all were listening.

"I shall explain further. They have even seen to it to steal the ravens from the Tower of London in the hopes that a legend will act in their favour and that the country would fall meekly and easily to them, such was their superstition, yet it is legends who have returned to stall them... Here before you, Sir, before you all, are two great defenders of our Isle, Sir Francis Drake, and... King Arthur."

As each was announced audible gasps again filled the chamber, and the camera flashes lit the room in a frenzy. Julian Finch once again held up his hand for silence as he demanded order, for the press and Councillors within the chamber, and the throng in the public gallery above, had broken out in a clamour at the incredible revelation. In every language shouts of disbelief had broken out, yet also gasps of awe and astonishment.

"This was a plot which could so nearly have succeeded, such was their cowardly stealth and abuse of position," Julian continued as he shouted over the background murmurs. "Yet it has been for this moment that King Arthur, the once and future King, has been resting all these years, and now he has come back to fulfil his legend. For this moment that Sir Francis Drake, who once helped vanquish an invasion fleet, has returned to vanquish this new threat to our freedom just as he saw off that threat of our enemies of old. Oh, it's true that neither acted alone in their heroics, but both epitomise the spirit of our Island Nation and they shall not be moved. I don't know how you thought you'd get away with it." He turned to the Commissioners. "I don't know how you can hope to stand against them."

"Preposterous," Sir Morgan laughed, and he looked somewhat unfazed, for with Rindburn's tip-off he'd expected Julian to arrive with such ludicrous claimants and he didn't expect belittling them to be overly difficult. "What utter nonsense, whoever heard of such total, fanciful rot? This man is completely mad, totally and utterly bonkers-barking! See how he discredits himself? Play time is over, children - come now, it's time to return to reality," he snapped.

Again noises of confusion broke out amongst those in the chamber, though this time there were chortles of amusement and ridicule mixed in with the clamour.

Julian feared that he was fast losing his audience, but a glance at the Duke of Man reassured him that his Grace was not so dismissive. Beads of sweat were running from his brow, and now that his adversaries to his front and rear had finally been made known to him the superstitious Duke looked white as a sheet, as if he had seen a ghost and was trapped in a nightmare.

"Bod a rafa,"(i) King Arthur jumped on the desk, practically on top of the document itself, and waved his arms for quiet. "Archa ddistaw,"(ii) he continued in his native tongue, and then in the Latin language he appealed more politely for calm and order to be restored. "Per silentium mos verum exsisto ostendo sum."(a) In mail singlet, and with the gleaming torc at his neck, the wild-looking man seemed to embody authority, and be it due to his demands, or just out of curiosity to establish the truth of all these claims, the room did indeed fall silent once more.

"Will you explain yourself, Mr Finch?" the Prime Minister rubbed at his temples. He seemed dumbfounded and deeply frustrated, yet like all the others in the room he was also deeply intrigued.

"Certainly Sir," Julian continued, "but first, you, as a Council Member, must explain to me what that Act you are in the process of signing is all about."

"It is an Act committing to take better care of the environment by tackling the issues threatening and harming it, Mr Finch, everyone knows that."

"And so it may be, yet on whose advice are you signing it?"

"On the advice and recommendation of the Commission. We have debated the legislation within this Council and we have been fully briefed by the Commission as to the…"

"But have you?"

"Of course."

"Are you fully aware of the contents of that document?" Julian asked it as a straight question, but like all Politicians the Prime Minister would not respond with a straight-answered reply.

"I have been briefed as to the contents and I've been made aware of…"

"But you haven't actually made yourself aware!" Julian pointed a finger at the open Act and almost barked at him in urgency. "Have you actually read that document in full, Sir? It's really important you answer truthfully."

"Not in full." The Prime Minister conceded in tones of deep regret.

"Then had you signed it you would have made the cardinal error, Prime Minister, the huge and ignorant mistake of signing something, signing an Act on behalf of and to bind the British people, without first having read it. You sign that document and you hand power over to them. You sign that document and their first act will be to sign our very country away... This is what they have in store for us." Julian carried his stolen copy of the NESA across the room and placed it down on the desk top in front of his National Premier. "I urge you to read that now - Section Three is of particular interest. I've highlighted the important bits, I expect that's what you're used to."

"What is this, Mr Finch?" the Prime Minister began.

"That is the New Environmental Solution Act," Jessica Finch explained. "Secondary legislation, pre-drafted, pre-arranged and already agreed on by the European Commission. This is their solution, this is how they will deliver the aims as set out in the Act you were about to sign."

"Secondary legislation already pre-arranged!" The Prime Minister was shocked. "You mean they've already approved it?" Julian nodded. "But this is really most irregular - you mean arranged before the EEA itself was even passed?"

"Sign the EEA," Brendan confirmed, "and the plan as laid out in this NESA will become a reality. They will bring this in straight away. Read it, Sir, please."

The room retained a quiet library-like decorum as the British Prime Minister ran his eyes over the document. As he did so his jaw dropped open and he starred ahead into nothingness with a look of complete bewilderment on his face. In response, the babble of voices rose once more.

"So there it is," Julian Finch announced. "There before you in black and white is their plan, the plan of all the Commission, which will be their first act once the EEA is passed."

"You will appreciate," Sir Morgan Dredmor smiled to himself dryly as he broke his long silence. "That the rest of the people in this room are on tenterhooks Finch. They are not privy to the document the Prime Minister has just read. I think perhaps you should satisfy their curiosity."

"I think I should," Julian replied, "though it is rather strange that you now ask to be so publicly exposed."

"Oh," Sir Morgan shrugged as he feigned disinterest. "So the surprise has come a day early."

Jess too, felt uneasy that Sir Morgan seemed so happy for her father to reveal the contents of the NESA now that he was himself on the back foot, but Julian believed he had to keep the momentum going. The world's press hung on his every word and the Commissioners were caught before the cameras.

"As the Prime Minister has just discovered," Julian began, "the Commissioners plan was in essence a simple one. To identify a significant European land space and to utilise it for the disposal of all European rubbish and waste, everything from nuclear radioactive waste to human sewage. This would put an end to expensive recycling, prevent the bi-products of breaking the waste down chemically, the release of gasses etc... and the costs of the process. As the land is to be given up eco-friendly landfill was not to be an issue - too labour intensive, too expensive. The rubbish was simply to have lain piled, using the natural contours of the land initially, and then layering it once level.

"In short, the designated land was to become a smelly rubbish dump for the whole of the European community, its industrial waste products and its people's effluent. This is not a realisation of a commitment to deal with climate change and environmental problems. This is merely shirking responsibility, selecting one area to dump on so everyone else will be able to carry on as normal at the expense of those who lived in it... The Commission had chosen Britain!"

The clamour of noise in the chamber rose to a crescendo as the plan was revealed, and Julian had to shout to be heard over it.

"The whole of Britain was to be sacrificed by these traitors," he yelled as he pointed an accusing finger at the Commissioners, "and the British Prime Minister has just read it for himself."

"Very good, Finch," Sir Morgan Dredmor was grinning with confidence. "I really couldn't have put it better myself."

"The depths of their treachery do not end there," Julian was shouting over the continuing noise and raised his arm for silence. "What of the people of Britain? I'll tell you. The occupants were to be displaced, relocated to mainland Europe as cheap support labour to European industry. The British were to be sold out by these traitors and enslaved by the other nation's Commissioners."

The bellowing noise of outraged voices spilled over in the room once more, and Drake amongst them called for action.

"Shouldst not we rig up a gibbet within this chamber an' be rid o' the swine ere the bell sounds the watch?" But Arthur motioned him to calm. He could not comprehend all the dialogue, but he could sense that this scene had to play itself out.

"Is it not customary, Finch," Sir Morgan asked, "to allow one to speak in one's defence before judgement is passed?"

"Speak you should, Sir Morgan," the Prime Minister demanded. "Explain yourselves this instant."

"Well, far be it for me to speak for the whole Commission," Sir Morgan began smugly, and gradually the noise subsided, for all were intrigued to discover what he had to say. "Yet after all, this has been passed by the whole Commission unanimously, so perhaps with the power vested in me I should act as the Commission's representative and enlighten you all.

"You see, you have it really in a nutshell, Finch, you really are a clever boy. Land has been identified for use by Europe as a rubbish dump, and where better I ask than Britain?" A murmur rang out around the room again, but this time it was Sir Morgan who raised his hand for quiet. "The land mass identified will be more than able to cope with Europe's waste for over a million years, why, as waste breaks down and is layered up the land could be used in perpetuity, it's the perfect answer to the waste disposal crisis which affects the whole of Europe today. Britain is an island separated from mainland Europe, yet close enough for waste disposal pipelines to reach it."

"How can you turn your back on the land of your birth?" Brendan blurted. "How can you sacrifice your country? Your people?"

"Look, you little creep," Sir Morgan responded, "can't you see the age of patriotism is passed? There is no Great British empire, the Brits have been living in a dream land reflecting on past glories, thinking themselves in some way superior due to the conquests of their forefathers, but the rest of the continent has moved on. This is no time for sentimentality, we are citizens of Europe now, and there are places enough even for prats like you in useful jobs on the mainland.

"The suitability of the land is not in doubt, and it makes sense for the future of Europe - why else would the whole Commission have signed up to it? Why I see even now that the rest of the Council - surprise, surprise, Britain excluded - can all see the logic in the plan."

"It's a total breach of human rights," Brendan persisted.

"Human rights?" Drake questioned, for it was a concept neither he nor Arthur were likely to understand. "What be they?"

"Exactly, what are they?" Sir Morgan retorted. "They are not intrinsic, they were not God-given, and they did not pre-exist the hand

341

which penned them. They were nothing before they were prescribed by law, and as law they can simply, and just as easily, be repealed. In any case the proposal is a brilliant one, the liberties of a few may be compromised, but the lives of the whole will be bettered for ever."

"Makes perfect utilitarian sense," Sir Dennis Hitoadie added to Sir Morgan's momentum. "The overwhelming majority of Europeans will benefit from it." The Duke sounded incredibly pompous as he spoke with as much Churchillian gusto as he could muster with Drake's sword still at his back. "The time has come for the people of Britain to make their sacrifice stoically and to join their cousins in the sunnier climes of the continent. A better life awaits us all."

"Oh, I'm sure a better life awaits you two." Jess stood arms folded in defiance.

"Yeah, and I'm not convinced the members of the Council will be mad keen on the prospect of millions of Britains flooding into their countries in search of work, swelling their towns, overstretching their resources, over..."

"My dear Finch, I think the prospect of manual labourers coming in to boost their economies will strike a cord with a lot of the Council Members here." Sir Morgan grinned. "For years the cream of their own States have migrated, now they will stay, and with humble British immigrants working hard for a pittance, the boot will be on the other foot for a change. Each country shall get an even share, new settlements will be built, new..."

"How dare you suggest that Britain be allowed to disappear, that Britain, Great Britain be so humiliated, that she be lost for the good or not of the rest of Europe!" The Prime Minister was on his feet and raged at his Commissioners.

"In case you have forgotten, Prime Minister, we live in a democracy," Sir Morgan responded dryly. "Were this plan not a good one, would our fellow Commissioners have signed up to it? Would your fellow Councillors, Sir, be even now nodding their heads in contemplation? The people lose their homes, not their lives, and we shall build new ones. Cheap ones, admittedly, but brand new..."

"Do you think your stubbornness, your typical British arrogance will endear you to your Council colleagues any more than it has endeared the British to the rest of Europe over the centuries? Stop looking down your nose at the rest of the world and embrace the future."

"I, I, humph." The British Prime Minister sat down in his chair red in the face and in total disbelief. He just didn't know what to do, and he didn't know what to say. The rest of the Council, the revelations being simultaneously translated through their earpieces, turned to each other with interested and enquiring looks.

"And what of our commitment to cost-effective renewable energy Finch?" The Duke of Man felt a little more comfortable, as even though he was still under guard, the sympathy of the European audience appeared to be shifting somewhat. "You have managed to omit that part of the plan I notice. Is such a commitment not also included in the New Environmental Solution Act? Speak the bits that suit eh, Finch, leave out the bits that don't, what!"

"Wind farms," said Sir Morgan slowly, once again catching the attention of the whole room. "Sustainable wind power, a huge green battery for the whole of Europe. As Britain will no longer be inhabited, the whole of the Channel, the North and Irish seas, will be filled with wind turbines which will generate between them enough electricity to power the whole of the continent. A long-term goal, I know, but proximate and very desirable..."

"Would have been, I think. Not now," said Julian combatively. "Not now we have exposed your plan." But there was a babble of interest amongst the assembled Council at the slimy Commissioner's suggestion.

"It would look awful," said Jess defiantly. "Filling up the channel with wind turbines - why, even the French would have to admit it will look bad off their coast."

"Mmm, won't look great," Sir Morgan conceded with a disinterested yawn. "But the French will have control of it, won't they? And it's a good use of the empty sea. After all, when it all gets underway the only traffic to the UK will be rubbish on a designated route through the wind farm... Oh, and it will be functional too," he continued with mock absent-mindedness. "We shall turn the turbines to face Britain," he explained with a sneer, "and it'll blow the nasty smell of all that rubbish away from the continent and over the Atlantic towards Canada."

"The French Commissioner, Monsieur Crouton and his chums weren't too happy to start with at the thought of all that rubbish piled at their doorstep," the Duke chipped in. "But once he was assured that the smell won't get up his nostrils he seemed especially keen on the idea."

"What about the Irish Commissioner," asked Brendan quickly, "Won't the smell get blown over Ireland from time to time?"

"Well I have to admit, Mr O'Hooligan was rather anti," Sir Morgan conceded humbly.

"Well there we are, then, so the Commission didn't approve it unanimously," Jess looked jubilant. "You were lying all along."

"Oh he signed up to it alright," Sir Morgan grinned.

"Democracy, as I said," the Duke beamed back in triumph, "simply met up with him fer a spot of lunch, and over a few quiet bottles I simply explained to him that he'd be..."

"Outvoted." Sir Morgan shook his head in mock despair.

"So you pressurised him, told him he might as well go along with it."

"Oh, I do so dislike the word pressurised, little girl, it sounds most crass, what!" The Duke chortled to himself.

"He was persuaded," Sir Morgan explained. "His Grace and I employed a little light persuasion, and..."

"You bribed him." Jess was disgusted.

"Now there you go again," the Duke objected, "you make it sound so coarse. He was offered a little enhancement to ensure his support, if one must put a light political spin on the process."

"You bribed him," Jess repeated her accusation.

"Naturally," Sir Morgan seemed unrepentant. "He was offered his pick of the Balearics, and..."

"Plumped for Mallorca," The Duke sounded his approval, "a very wise choice. He'll be swapping Galway for Palma imminently."

"The Commission was so keen to present a united front." Sir Morgan sneered.

"Such is politics," his colleague sounded bored now, and the Duke's enormous belly let out an audible rumble. "Wrap this up, Sir Morgan; the room is won, and it must be nearly lunchtime."

"The room is not won." The Prime Minister was on his feet once more. "Now that I fully understand what you are trying to do I will ensure that you are stopped. The UK will simply derogate from this NESA. We will opt out of it, then you won't be able to use our Islands as you plan."

"Not if you sign that EEA," Julian Finch explained, "you won't be able to. Turn to Section Three (a) to Protocol Fifteen of the European Environmental Act Prime Minister - it's right at the back, hidden amongst the appendixes. The ends as set out in NESA contain only half their vile plot."

Julian crossed the room to stand behind the desk, and himself turned through to the relevant page. He could see that, just as Sir Morgan had claimed, the original document had been reinstated once more, and running a finger down the page he quickly identified the vital lines amongst the paragraphs of Protocol Fifteen.

"You see. If you sign this document your right to derogation, as is suggested here, will be taken away."

"What?"

"Read it for yourself, Sir, it will be gone," Julian explained. "So too the European Parliaments right of veto, so too the European Parliament. Sign that Act," he turned to face the assembled Council, "pass this Act, and you dismiss the European Parliament."

"It can't be," the Prime Minister was furious. "The Comitology will have something to say about that... The European Courts will never allow it!"

"The European Courts and the Comitology will also both be scrapped," said Julian slowly. "There it is, in black and white. It's a trap, don't you see? If the Council sign this, you make it law. You've all been tricked by the Commissioners. None of you have read this EEA in full, none of you had even noticed Protocol Fifteen until now, and by passing this Act you will be signing away all the safeguards of the European process. By signing this you will make it law and will allow the Commission to bring in their NESA; you would allow them to sacrifice Britain."

As the room fell into commotion again Julian felt the Council members were again rallying to him. However they felt about Britain becoming a rubbish dump they would all be angry that the Commission had tried to deceive them, and he felt sure that now was the time to drop his bombshell.

"Furthermore, Prime Minister, would you be kind enough to read from Section Three (a) subsection (iii) of Protocol Fifteen? I think your fellow Council members will be suitably swayed by its content." Julian stood back as the Prime Minister read aloud.

"The National Commissioners to become independent Heads of State in each of their respective Member States, assuming power with immediate effect..." The Prime Minister could not believe what he'd just read.

The noise in the room rose with shouts and jeers, and the rest of the Council became infuriated as the significance of these words was translated via earpiece to each of them. They ranted and raged and several of them seemed intent on rushing Sir Morgan and the Duke in the absence of their own Commissioners, but Julian implored them to calm once more.

"There you have it," he shouted, and he had to climb on the crescent-shaped desk and wave his arms for quiet. "There you have it," he repeated as he addressed the Council members, "the Commission have betrayed you all. Not just Britain but each and every one of your Nation's sovereignties will be forfeit to your own representatives within the Commission if you sign this Act. All of you will loose your jobs, all of you will be replaced by your country's Commissioners, and as you have seen, this Protocol Fifteen, this pamphlet hidden in the appendixes of the Act you are here to endorse, will remove all the safe guards to stopping the Commissioners having absolute power.

"The NESA is just the start - they would be able to bring in anything they want, and there would be no way of challenging it. The Commissioners would be masters of Europe, and if you sign this Act, Prime Minister, if you pass it, you hand power over to them."

"How right you are, Finch." Sir Morgan allowed himself a sneer, and he and the Duke of Man exchanged delighted and confident glances.

"It's a Trojan horse," Julian continued; he was actually enjoying his moment now. "It appears noble and attractive as a commitment to challenge European environmental change, yet this was only a front to trick you into admitting it. Let this pass through your gates, approve this Act, and you approve Protocol Fifteen."

There was a huge shout of defiance from the Council now as they roared in anger at the two representatives of the Commission within the chamber.

"Only two of the traitors stand here," Julian believed himself invincible once more. His heart was pounding within him as he went with the flow and let the adrenaline take him. "The whole Commission are at fault, they are all concerned in this together, and they all stand to benefit from this deception as your loss is their individual gain. The enemy in all this is not the European process but those who through their own greed have tried to destroy it. We must stand united against this corrupt Commission; they are the common enemy, and it is they who threaten us all.

"Whilst there can be no doubt that Sir Morgan Dredmor and the Duke here have been instrumental in this attempted coup, I suspect that you will find that even now, in each of your nation's capitals your own individual National Commissioners are poised to seize power. They too must be stopped."

Julian turned to Sir Morgan in the absence of the rest of the Commission and spoke to him as if he embodied them all. "You were the guardians of the treatise, and you traitors have betrayed it."

There was again total uproar as various Council members shook their fists at Sir Morgan and the Duke as they demanded they be brought to justice.

Julian felt elated. He'd won, he'd turned it around, and motioned again for quiet as he tried to continue with what he hoped would become a unifying speech.

"For had we not stopped the Prime Minister from signing the..."

"Not so!" The Duke of Man barked at him, and Julian could see that it was Sir Dennis Hitoadie who now looked invincible. "You have our thanks for explaining everything, Finch." The Duke laughed at him. "But, as we told you when you first gate-crashed the democratic process, you are too late!"

"Too late?" But Julian needn't have spoken; the Prime Minister's posture said it all. A broken man, he sat with his head in his hands, and rocked.

"He's already signed it," the Duke grinned widely. "God preserve us, Finch, but yer could've saved yer voice all along. He signed it as you idiots were first barging in here. See the document, see the signature in neat, dry ink. Yer should've read yer document, old boy, before yer started rattling on about it, eh, what!" The room fell silent as the balance of power shifted once more. "We have our majority, Morgan; the Act is passed."

"Right you are, Dennis." Sir Morgan sneered at Julian and the others each in turn.

"You and I now preside over Britain, Sir Francis Drake and King Arthur or no Sir Francis Drake and King Arthur. The Commissioners are now - as yer put it yerself, Finch - masters of Europe."

Julian looked, but he didn't have to. The Prime Minister's mark was upon the Act after all, and his sullen, agonised face confirmed it. The Council chamber went silent and a sense of foreboding doom filled the room.

"I think me first act as British Premier will be ter break for lunch." A huge toad-like grin engulfed the Duke's fat face.

(i)   Be quiet.
(ii)   I demand silence.

(a)   Through silence will the truth be revealed.

Chapter Nineteen – The Bloody Tower

"What did he say?" Rhys asked Max as his cousin put his mobile phone away.

"Yes, how are they getting on?" Rhiannon questioned.

"I don't know," Max replied. "He didn't say, but it didn't sound too good."

"Well, you told him we couldn't get in," Rhys spoke again, "I heard you say that. What did he say in reply?"

"He said to get them home at all costs."

"Sounds desperate then," Rhiannon reflected, "sounds like the pressure's on."

"Well, here we are again," Max looked up at the cold, uninviting walls of the Tower of London, "and with no more of an idea of how to get in than we had last night." They'd waited hours for a delivery vehicle, but hadn't worked out how they were going to intercept one or how they were going to get inside it.

"We could just revert to plan A," Rhys suggested logically, "so long as it's not that grey-whiskered old fella on the gate again we might get through this time. Could just have been bad luck yesterday."

"It'll be double bad luck if it is him again," Maxwell Finch was low on confidence. "He'll recognise us straight away."

"Well, we've got the change of clothes like you suggested," Rhiannon tried to sound upbeat. "Perhaps if we change now…"

"No, if it is him he'll recognise our faces soon as we look at him, the change of clothes might come in useful later," Max explained. "Drake and Arthur needed a change of clothes so they'd blend in and wouldn't be recognised - we might be able to do the same."

"Smart thinking, Cous," Rhys congratulated him.

Max, though, bore a look of grim determination. The beginnings of an idea were forming in his mind, the stakes had been raised and his father had made that clear through his tone alone, and Max now felt he could allow himself a little recklessness, so desperate was the need for success.

"We may have to chance it," he said simply. "Run a few risks."

"Chance being caught?" Rhiannon's tone did not indicate full support of his suggestion.

"He said at all costs," Max reasoned. "We'll just have to chance it, try and run through Security, get the ravens home and take our chances from there. Getting them back home is what matters."

"Plan A with a twist, then," Rhys agreed. "You're right - there's nothing for it but to try."

The three backpacked teenagers approached the Tower's main entrance for the second time in two days. As before, each rucksack contained an even distribution of the precious birds, (though this time Max had hooded them all with odd socks in the hopes that they'd keep calm and wouldn't draw attention to their carriers.)

"Oh, it is him." Rhiannon's voice was heavy with disappointment. "It is that old duffer again."

"Well keep your head down girl," Rhys tried to encourage her, "we'll get as close as we can, then bolt through."

Joseph Banks, on sentry and on red alert following the preceding day's encounter with the three students, was taking extra care to scrutinise each and every visitor today. Indeed, most found it rather flattering that the smart Yeoman Warder in his fine regalia greeted every one of them personally. They enjoyed the interest he was taking in their attire as he looked them up and down saying how nice this was or how smart that looked, and the consummate professional was politeness personified as he carried out searches of bags, camera cases and the like in the name of security.

He bantered with the visitors, he made it a novelty. 'Not every day you get searched by a Beefeater,' they said to each other as he went about his work. But Banks was not to be distracted, and he kept his old eyes open for anything remotely suspicious.

He noticed three youngsters approaching, having clocked them from a distance, and as Max, Rhys and Rhiannon walked passed the queue for tickets and proceeded towards the entrance, he strode out to meet them.

"Beggin' your pardons but you has to join the back o' the... You three again!" He recognised them as soon as they got closer. "Are yer going to let me peek in yer bags today?" he asked the question as he dropped onto the defensive, bringing the mean-looking partizan across his body to cover them. As before his bulky figure barred the gateway, and today he would not be messed with. Max couldn't even see round the Yeoman; there was no way he'd be able to run round him.

"Not again," he said in a tired voice, trying to think of a way of distracting the Warder into enabling at least one of them to pass. He just had to try and catch him off-guard - perhaps if he could be persuaded to step away from the gate Rhys might be able to get through. "You can try and catch me if you like."

"I'll not be drawn from me post."

"Can't you just let us in?" Rhiannon pleaded.

"Indeed I can. So long as you pays up at the booth and lets me search them bags. Condition of entry, I told yers yesterday."

"But what's the need to search us?"

"Oh no, not again. We went over all this yesterday, did we not?" The former parade ground Sergeant Major was growing impatient of the teenager's bleatings. "For security Miss, like I told yer. You could have anything in there for all I knows, a weapon, a bomb..."

"That's it." Max leapt forward, he knew exactly what he had to do and shouted, "Bomb!" in the maddest voice he could muster. "I've got a bomb!"

Banks jumped back in surprise, so sudden was the outburst, and the rest of the queue melted away from Max in a split second of terror. As shouts of "Get down," and "He's got a bomb," were passed along the panicked queue, Max seized his chance and bolted passed Banks, through the arch, and into the Castle courtyard.

Joe Banks didn't know what to do. His first instinct was to his duty, to stay and guard the entrance, to stop the other two teenagers likewise bursting through, and to offer reassurance to the petrified, screaming crowd outside. But Joe Banks was a proud man and the boy had made him look silly. He just hadn't expected a sudden move like that, he'd been taken by surprise, and he was as embarrassed as he was angry. For the second time in just a few days Banks left his post in pursuit of an intruder, so desperate was he to catch them.

"Stop that boy!" he yelled at anyone who would listen as he ran after Max.

But Max shouted, "Out of the way, it's a bomb," and was understandably able to run on without being impeded.

Rhys and Rhiannon took one look at each other. The Yeoman Warder was gone and the entrance was clear. Without a word they too sprinted through and into the courtyard.

Banks was no youngster, and though for his age he was fit, his uniform and the studded partizan were heavy and slowed his progress. Rhiannon and Rhys, despite their own avian cargoes, were much quicker on their feet and passed him easily. They caught up with Max as he arrived at the far end of Tower Green, leaving the puffing Warder in their wake.

"Now," Max shouted, given the safety of a thirty-yard gap from their pursuer, "let them go."

"Quick, quick," Rhys hurried Rhiannon as she undid the backpack which remained fastened to his shoulders, and they formed an odd-looking circle, each undoing the backpack of the person in front. In a rushed fumble, the bewildered big black ravens were unceremoniously returned to their beloved Tower Green, and the odd socks were snatched off their heads.

As the last bird hit the grass, Max gave a shout of "Run for it," and the teenagers took off again as Banks had closed the gap and was almost upon them, wielding his partisan as if to strike.

The visitors in the Courtyard could hardly believe their eyes. Most were aware that the ravens had been missing and to see them returned should have been special. Instead they saw the youngsters fleeing with a crazed Yeoman Warder in hot pursuit. His white whiskers stuck out in stark comparison to his red face as he bellowed after them, "Ruddy students. Had yer fun with 'em have yer? Think yer can just leave 'em and run? I'll skin yer alive when I gets me hands on you!"

"Over there," Max led the way, and they opened up the gap from Banks again as they scampered for the nearest tower. They ran in, up the steps, turned a corner or two and found themselves on a landing off the spiral staircase.

"We could be safe in here," Rhiannon panted, as she tried to catch her breath.

"Not for long," Rhys winced; he'd brought on a stitch. "There'll be loads more of them out looking for us in a minute, the old boy will sound the alarm. You heard what he said yesterday, CCTV cameras everywhere, we don't stand a chance. We might as well give ourselves up and save ourselves getting decapitated. We got the birds back, that's the main thing. Well done, Max."

"Yeah, well done Max," Rhiannon gave him a quick kiss on the cheek. "That was quick thinking."

Max blushed, but there was more quick thinking to be done and he wasn't for giving up yet. "Where are we, anyway?" he gasped. The chase had passed in a flash and he'd lost his bearings.

"Well, it said 'Bloody Tower' on a plaque by the door," Rhys informed him, "whatever that means."

"The Bloody Tower," Max recalled from his previous visit. "That's where Sir Walter Raleigh was imprisoned. Hey, we might see Raleigh's ghost."

"Well if we do," Rhiannon began as she prepared to climb the stairs once more, "we'll just tell him his old mate Francis Drake sent us."

As suddenly as she said it an almost transparent, floating figure in green and yellow doublet and hose, and deathly white, emerged before them on the spiral stairs. Like Drake he had a pointy beard and moustache, though his was a little better kept, even longer, and somewhat darker in colour, and he wore a fluffy lace ruff at his neck.

351

"Follow," he said simply, and floated on up the stairs in front of them.

The three exchanged uncertain glances, but they could suddenly hear a clattering at the foot of the stairs beneath them and Banks' voice saying, "They be up there, after 'em," which quickly decided the matter, and needing no second bidding they did so.

They followed on, one after the other in silence, as the effortless, lifeless figure wound round the twisted stairs, over landings, through doors and along corridors, and never passing another tourist. He led them down through narrow ways and over squeaky floorboards seldom trod, to within a few feet of another exit back out into the courtyard.

"'Twill suit, methinks," he said cheerily, and then spoke simple words of advice. "Now, shouldst thou exchange thy garments. 'Twas well thought out, Master Maxwell."

"But how did you know we'd....? And how do you know my...?"

Max was baffled, but rather than answer him the other bid them "Godspeed, friends, an' remember me unto Sir Francis," and was gone.

"Was that...?" Rhiannon was in shock; she felt she'd just been trapped in a day dream.

"No time to think about it now," Max urged them. "Like he said, we need to change our clothes now, leave our bags here and we walk away. We won't look the same as we did when we came in, the cameras won't realise who we are, and if we see that old duffer again hopefully he won't recognise us either."

"Genius, Max." Rhys was impressed. "I think you've learned a few things from Arthur and Drake."

"From my dad, perhaps," Max conceded. "He changed their appearance to get them into the office, we change ours and we can get out of here."

Transformed into their spare clothes, and leaving their rucksacks in a heap just inside the door, they walked out into the courtyard one at a time and at a casual pace and separated. Max passed the happily scratching and pecking ravens as he crossed Tower Green on his way back to the exit, and within just a couple of minutes he was out and felt as free as they did.

When they met up again outside the Castle shortly afterwards, and while the internal hunt for them was still in full swing, Max sent a quick text message to his father's mobile phone: 'They're back!"

As they passed the same bench at which they'd sat disheartened the previous day they were now in jubilant mood, and in unified disbelief they questioned the identity of the floating, dreamlike figure who'd led them through the back ways of the Tower to safety.

Chapter Twenty – The Balance of Power

Patricia Finch was having heart palpitations as the live footage from the Council chamber continued to roll into her living room. Like one of millions of others throughout the Continent, she was glued to the set as the tension mounted.

"Before we break for lunch, my dear Dennis, I think we should have these upstarts arrested, don't you?" Sir Morgan Dredmor sneered as he paced the room, tiger like and domineering once more.

"Need I remind you that we are the ones with the hostage?" Julian Finch would not be intimidated, and Drake prodded his sword point just a little harder into the Duke of Man's back to leave him in no doubt as to the brutal reality of this fact.

"Damn yer Morgan, do something man," he sweated. And in his fury the Duke turned to his captors once more and shouted at Drake, "Unhand me now, Sir, can't yer see you've lost? We are the victors, we have the majority vote and there's nought yer can do about it, what! Might even have a little job fer you boys." He calmed slightly. "Could use a legend or two in me new Britain, eh," he joked.

"He lives in a Britain of the past," a defiant Jessica Finch explained. "He can't understand a word you're saying to him, but even if he did I don't thing valiant King Arthur would ever succumb to bribery, Hitoadie."

The Council, subdued, had gone quiet. They believed the day lost, and Sir Morgan Dredmor made a point of telling them so.

"Fair and square. Come now, you're outvoted, you've outvoted yourselves, you know how the system works. You are Heads of State no longer, you're all sacked... Now get out."

"Wait." Brendan Johnson stood in the middle of the room and counted up the empty seats and then those still occupied more carefully. "It's all square," he announced excitedly, "I miscounted earlier, Mr Finch, Julian - I was in such a hurry - but look, it's even. The Prime Minister's signature makes it an even split - they need one more."

"We do not, it's over I tell you." Sir Morgan shook his head, but spoke calmly; he would not be swayed by the boy's enthusiasm.

"Rubbish, there are as many left to sign as have signed already," Brendan challenged. "It's fifty-fifty, everyone can see that. Poo to your majority."

"I assure you, we've won," Sir Morgan sneered with confidence and spoke so casually it was almost eerie, but Brendan wasn't listening.

"I think we can take it as read the rest of the Council will not be signing it now," he appealed to the rest of the seated Members, and as they clapped him and jeered Sir Morgan. Brendan declared the Council meeting closed. "Your attempt has failed. This Act has not been passed."

Julian's mobile phone alerted him to Max's message and he joined in the chorus with shouts of: "They're back, the ravens are back! Your plans are foiled, Commissioners. My son has returned the ravens to the Tower of London - Britain cannot fall."

Applause thundered round the chamber, and even the banks of journalists and cameramen cheered. But while all around him seemed to explode in relief, and while all in the chamber bayed for his blood, Sir Morgan Dredmor, his face a picture of unconcern, just smirked to himself silently.

It was only when the noise subsided slightly and Arthur walked forward to lay hands on him that he made his move. A sharp intake of breath resounded around the room as the slick-looking, oily-haired, sneering Commissioner pulled out a shiny pistol from the inside pocket of his snazzy suit.

"That's better," he said gently as complete silence was restored, and Arthur, sensing that something was wrong, stopped in his tracks. "You could hear a pin drop now, couldn't you? I mean, I was so reluctant to have to resort to this sort of thing, but you know, needs must."

"When you've lost," Brendan challenged.

"Little boy, I've told you we haven't lost. This is just a matter of using a little authority to establish decorum when I'm talking... And now I think the phrase is: nobody move or I'll fill you full of lead. Shut the main door," he shouted the order. "No one comes in and no one goes out." Sir Morgan grinned slyly to himself. "Now tell him, Finch," he pointed the gun at Arthur, "tell him to get back. His antiquated chain mail won't stop bullets."

"Retire, my Liege," Julian explained in Latin. "He has a weapon which can throw a small but deadly dart."

"Fear not Finch, for he be lacking in match - 'twill not take fire lest he hath one concealed."

Drake's cocky tone left Sir Morgan little alternative. He had to demonstrate he was serious, and did so by firing a round off in the air.

The loud, echoing noise of the pistol in the chamber, and the sound of smashing glass as the chandelier above was first struck by the bullet, and then sent a shower of broken glass ricocheting to shatter on the floor, had a sobering effect on the whole room. The Councillors present fell instantly silent and not a murmur could be heard, whilst on

354

television screens across Europe the commentators once more had a development in the hostage scenario to report. In Weston-Bissett Patricia Finch, with one hand over her mouth, watched in horror.

"The Belgian police should intervene," one such studio commentator urged over the air, "but they had probably best wait until we establish whose side they need to take in all this. I mean, we still can't be sure of who's won, we don't know who's in charge."

King Arthur stepped back as Julian Finch urged him, but he broke the silence in an authoritative tone, and in a language known only by a few.

"What did he say?" Sir Morgan demanded. "What did he..."

"He said you can wait," Sir Dennis Hitoadie translated for his fellow Commissioner. "He said the tide of battle changes fast and frequently, that he fought through wind, fog and rain at the battle of Dyrham. That the valley was won and lost many times in the day as the battle raged on for twenty hours. He says he can wait a little longer before he takes his chance to kill you."

"Very good, Dennis, I'm sure, and where did you...?"

"Classical Latin, Morgan old boy, you don't mean ter tell me that..."

"Not all of us are so privileged, your Grace, as to have benefited from the kind of schooling where Classical Latin was taught." Sir Morgan looked slightly hurt by his linguistic inadequacy, and with pride he pumped out his shoulders in determination to big up his working-class roots. "Some of us had to work our way up you know..."

"Morgan..." The Duke interrupted.

"Some of us had nothing but misery and hardship handed to us on a plate..."

"Morgan..."

"No silver spoon for my infant mouth, I can tell you, it was...."

"Sir Morgan, damn yer," the Duke barked impatiently, "will yer not order this pantomime dame ter take his sword from me back. Let's have a little order please, now the balance of power swings our way."

"Oh, of course Dennis, I do apologise, really I do. I was forgetting my manners." Sir Morgan sneered and pointed the pistol at Sir Francis Drake, aiming right for the centre of his chest. "Now you have seen the effectiveness of my firearm. Drop your spike and scurry over there, oddball, or I'll blast you back to your uncomfortable past."

"Rather wouldst I die now wi' all honour..."

"Sir Francis," Jess begged with great urgency, "that gun has many more bullets in it. Come and stand with us. There's no point throwing your life away, no point tempting him."

355

"No indeed," Sir Morgan mocked, "though I must say you're all tempting my trigger finger at the moment."

"As thou wilt, Mistress Jess." Drake reluctantly dropped his sword and crossed the room to stand with his hosts, Arthur and Brendan. All of them were now covered by Sir Morgan Dredmor's pistol, which flicked restlessly to cover each in turn. "Blade canst not stand 'gainst fowling piece. Yet 'tis ignoble for a hero such as I t'..."

"A hero, poppycock!" Dennis Hitoadie blurted at the man who until seconds ago had been his captor.

The Duke's relief to be free was immense. He'd been made to quiver and sweat at the end of Drake's sword, and in his superstitious mind he'd genuinely feared he was in serious trouble. But now, as he rubbed at his sore back as best he could with the back of a podgy hand and felt a tear in the back of his expensive suit, he fired a broadside of his own, hoping to sink the pride of the man the Spanish had once acclaimed 'El Draque.'

The Duke knew his history, and he now knew his foe. He was filled with anger and hate from the way Drake had treated him, and he considered this an apt time to finish the unfinished business of the confrontational night before.

"This man calls himself a hero. Maybe in his own mind he is, eh! Ask the Irish he slaughtered, what! Ask the Spanish he raided. Ask the Africans this man enslaved and shipped to the Americas. The British may love him, but to the rest of the world he's hated, a despised figure. Everyone else can see straight through you, it's just damn typical of the British sense of..."

"Stand I here betwixt God, parliaments and peoples," Drake challenged, "an' no treachery be found within me. Thou, bulbous boar, art all filled up on thine own arrogance. Thy black heart thirsts for power, and thou wouldst see thine own nation perish. Shalt thou feel the lash o' justice whence thy fat head be struck from thy bloated corpse 'pon the block, for t' be mounted 'pon Tower Bridge as befits thee, in disgrace."

"Oh, how nobly said," Sir Morgan Dredmor mocked sarcastically. Yet as Drake bowed his head theatrically to the polite applause of a handful of brave Councillors, the furious Duke of Man let rip at him once more, shouting red-faced just as he had done the previous evening in his hotel bar.

"Justice - you, sir, know nothing of justice. Ye Gods, yer filled with hypocrisy - famously gave Thomas Doughty a fair trial, didn't you? Eh! This man's no hero, he's a vagabond, a common pirate, what! I shall turn yer over to me Spanish colleague when this nonsense is all done.

356

He'll string you up, Sir, you'll hang for yer thieving, I'll show you how justice can catch up with history, what!"

"Oh shut up, Toad," Jess Finch blurted back at the Commissioner, and Hitoadie, somewhat shocked to be berated so by such a young female, was rather taken aback. He just stood still, stuck to the spot, opening and shutting his mouth, but with no words coming as he gawped in speechless fury.

"Fear not, Mistress Jessica," Drake winked at her. "There be no saw-bones barber surgeon alive who has skill enough t' mend the wounds that shalt on his carcass be inflicted. No apothecary who canst in all wisdom find out a remedy such as wilt be able even t' relieve a little o' his suffering. The King speaks true, the tide will turn, an' shalt I also wait on a fair wind."

"Blast him, I d-demand s-silence," the Duke stammered. "Morgan, will yer not just shoot the fancy-dressed fuddy duddy."

"Rest assured, Dennis, I have every intention of doing so," Sir Morgan calmed him, and he yawned as if the whole thing was unnecessarily tiring. "It's just a matter of deciding which one of the delinquents to shoot first. Life is full of difficult choices," he mused.

"Oh, just shoot him," the Duke demanded. "Despatch Sir Francis, shoot Finch, gun down the hippy. Just get on with it, Morgan, its way past lunchtime."

"Oh I do wish you'd calm down, Dennis, I really do, there's no need to over-dramatise everything." Sir Morgan spoke coldly now and paused a moment to ensure he had the full attention of the room. "But once again we seem to have forgotten our manners, for though the day is won I don't think the full formalities are over. Do you not think we should give the rest of the Council the opportunity to sign the beautiful EEA as they fully intended to prior to Mr Finch's rather rude intrusion?" Sir Morgan grinned slyly and swung round to cover the remaining seated Councillors at the crescent shaped desk with the barrel of his pistol.

"They'll never sign, Morgan." Julian Finch defied him. "You forget these are the leaders of nations, they have honour and will not cast it aside as easily as you have, not with their own peoples watching. The unforgiving European public will never allow it."

The background babble rose once more as the uncomfortable burden of pressure was passed to the national Premiers, but Sir Morgan Dredmor, constantly shifting his pistol from one unfortunate to another, just smiled to himself.

"I think you are forgetting who has the gun here, Finch. You will speak only when spoken to, got it?" Try as he might to look cool on the outside, Sir Morgan's patience had been pushed to the limit and the pressure was really getting to him.

"Now be silent, Finch, you little has-been. You've had your five minutes of fame, now its someone else's turn to step into the spotlight. This is your last warning."

"You can fix the result all you want," Julian shouted in defiance, "it'll never be binding under duress."

Sir Morgan had really had enough. Without flinching and without a second's hesitation, he pointed the gun straight at Julian and fired. There were gasps, and then a deathly hush fell over the whole chamber once more.

"Dad," Jess cried as she fell to the side of her collapsed father. "Oh Dad!" She put her hand to her mouth and tears filled her eyes.

"Need I be pushed so far?" Sir Morgan Dredmor appealed to the room, his eyes icy cold. "Need I have to prove I'm serious?" He looked down at Julian Finch, who lay sprawled on the floor. Julian clasped his left hand to his wounded right shoulder as he tried to control his breathing and fight the all-embracing pain.

"I'm a good shot, Finch, I practise. One more peep out of you and next time you'll get it right between the eyes. Now stop whimpering and be silent. Don't interfere again, there's a good fellow."

"Ah, a fine shot." The Duke of Man licked his lips. "Well hit, Sir Morgan. If only I could knock grouse out of the air like that, what!"

Arthur knelt to examine the wound, and tore back Julian's shirt with his stubby fingers to reveal a small, neat hole in his shoulder. He could see how the body had offered no resistance to the missile, and imagining the consequences of it having struck him in the chest, he could only consider it a devastating weapon.

As Julian tried shuffling his feet in an attempt to prop himself on his left elbow Arthur busied himself fashioning a sling from Julian's tie, and as he crouched beside him he whispered in his ear urgent words of Latin.

"Julian, remember my counsel on the train. United they are strong, divided they will fall. Tell the boy, Julian. I need just one chance."

"At least grouse move," Jess screamed back at the Duke, and then at Sir Morgan: "You can't just go round shooting people."

"I think you will find, little girl, that his Grace and I are European Premiers now, and we can do just whatever we choose. You can mount no legal challenge, you can quote no law, the buck stops with us. These muppets have given us our majority. Call us autocrats if you like, dictators, but the fact is we're in charge now, so get used to it."

"It's equal," Brendan blurted.

"Oh, I do wish you'd listen," Sir Morgan yawned. "I've made it very clear that it is not. I see no one in here who disagrees." He spun round the room very quickly, pointing the gun at each member of the Council in turn, and not surprisingly none of them dared say a word.

At home Patricia Finch was beside herself. She'd just seen her husband get shot, and now the lunatic who'd gunned him down had her daughter in his sights. Worst of all, there was nothing she could do but sit by and watch.

"Help me sit up," Julian beckoned to Brendan, and as the teenager leant down to steady him, Julian whispered Arthur's words in his ear.

"Sir Morgan." Jess raised her hand politely. She had tears in her eyes still but was over the initial shock, her father wasn't dead as she'd first feared when he fell to the ground, and so long as the Commissioners didn't make good their earlier threats his wound did not look lif- threatening. "I have just one question, can I ask just one thing?"

"Fire away," the Duke of Man joked. "I'll humour the child, Morgan, old boy."

"It's just, well, I'm curious to know - what do you two stand to gain from all this? I mean, all the other Commissioners get to take over their own countries, but you two plan on giving yours up to become a rubbish dump. What's the point of all this effort to seize power, just to throw it all away?"

"A fair question." The enormous Duke of Man stood bloated by his sneering colleague. "In a word, child, retirement."

"Retirement?" Jess didn't understand.

"You have it," the Duke grinned. "Sir Morgan and I are tired of working for a living, tired of Britain, tired of her climate. Have you ever been to the Isle of Man? Good Lord, but its wet. Windy, wet and cold, a bleak place for a great statesman of the age to contemplate seeing out his days. Our European cousins wanted to show us a little gratitude for all our hard work in helping them seize power. Swap, do yer see? I'm not Duke of Man any longer, I'm King of Sicily now, eh! Ain't that true, Sir Morgan?"

"Indeed yes, Dennis, a most wise choice," his colleague congratulated him, "and I shall be taking up residence in Sardinia soon, the whole of Sardinia."

"Oh, we'll winter alternate years in Monaco, what!" the Duke added casually.

"Important to have a holiday home," Sir Morgan smirked.

"Very nice for you," Brendan had walked the few steps to where the British Prime Minister sat in silence at his solitary desk, and glanced down at the EEA over his shoulder. "Must be a great feeling to have pulled off a stunt like this. Must be great to be able to trust each other so completely when the whole plan requires such total unremitting dishonesty."

"Who told you to speak, boy?" Sir Morgan interrupted.

"But you can't, can you?" Brendan persevered bravely as the Commissioner's pistol turned on him. "I mean, the Duke can't trust you, can he?"

"Quiet," Sir Morgan ordered, but the little seeds of doubt had been sown in the Duke's head.

"What do yer mean, boy?" he enquired.

"Well he didn't trust you, your Grace, did he?" Brendan responded cleverly. "He didn't trust you not to loose the copy of the EEA with Protocol Fifteen inside. That's why he brought another copy along himself."

"Humph!" The truth hurt the Duke.

"He didn't trust you with it, did he?" Brendan twisted the knife. "It was as if he expected you to lose it."

"He didn't tell you my Dad had switched the documents, either." Jess realised what Brendan was doing, and having picked up on it quickly she sought to capitalise on the damage which had already been done. "Didn't trust you not to panic, did he? Didn't trust you not to give the game away."

"Silence," Morgan Dredmor fumed at this impertinence, but the Duke was hooked.

"Go on," he said in his anger, and he was visibly shaking slightly as he tried to keep his composure.

"He didn't tell you Rindburn had rung him and told him everything," Jess continued boldly. "He didn't want you to know we'd seized the ravens and taken the documents, he was probably worried about how you might react."

"Bet he didn't even tell you he had a gun," Brendan added as the Duke's face reddened with rage. "Made you sweat waiting to produce it, didn't he? He could have got Sir Francis off your back ages ago."

"Silence, be silent. I shall not hesitate to gun you down, even though you are children." Sir Morgan was furious and moved the gun constantly to point at one teenager, then the other.

"He's not denying it," said Brendan simply.

"Can you trust Sir Morgan?" Jess asked the Duke. "He clearly never trusted you."

"Can you vouch for everything within this copy of the EEA?" Brendan peered down at the document before him. "This is Sir Morgan's copy, isn't it? Can you be sure of everything within it? How can you be sure he hasn't made any extra additions of his own?"

"Morgan...?" the Duke began.

"Don't listen to them, Dennis, it's all lies."

"It's a destructive force, greed," Brendan went on.

"Morgan..." The Duke turned on his colleague again, he wanted answers, clarification.

"Have you seen this? It says here, subsection three (viii), that you are to be keeper of the dung heap, your Grace. You are to be confined to the Isle of Man as 'Rubbish Master General.' No kingdom in the sun for you, Sir Morgan, is to have Sicily as well as Sardinia. You will be stuck at home as 'Lord of the Flies', instead. Perhaps he resents you because you're an aristocrat, maybe he's gone back to his socialist roots. Yes, I thought I detected a note of bitterness earlier..."

"Morgan, is this true?" The Duke turned on his fellow Commissioner.

"Don't listen to them, Dennis, it's a trap. Keep silent, little boy, it's your last warning now," Sir Morgan snapped at Brendan.

"So treacherous, so deceitful, so many lies." Brendan knew he was pushing his luck, but he had almost achieved his objective. "Must be so hard. After a while I bet you start believing the lies yourself, eh, Sir Morgan?"

"Now look, I told you..." Sir Morgan took aim.

"The truth will out..." Brendan Johnson cast the dice for the last desperate time, and looked casually down at the document on the desk in front of him, trying to look calm and convincing outwardly, as inwardly he braced himself for the bullet which would surely shatter his skull and spatter his brains all over the seated Prime Minister in front of him.

"Morgan, I demand an answer." The Duke had hold of his fellow Commissioner by the lapels of his jacket now and spun him round to face him, shaking in his red-faced rage.

For the first time since the gun was produced the barrel had been turned away from a potential target as the two Commissioners stood face on and toe to toe. King Arthur, delighted by the heroic exploits of Brendan and Jess, prepared to seize his chance.

"Look, you fat fool, I've told you, it's a trap," Sir Morgan snapped back at the Duke, his own temper stretched to the limit. "Can't you see, you stupid toad..."

"Carnwennau," Arthur shouted the name of his trusty dagger, and

361

having brought it stealthily from concealment he hurled it across the room at the neatly-presented area of Sir Morgan Dredmor's back. His target was turned neatly to him and was held secure at the elbows by the untrusting Duke of Man, and as the dagger struck home Sir Morgan lurched forward, discharging the pistol as he dropped it, and both Commissioners hit the ground together, almost in an embrace, as the echo of the shot rang round the chamber just as the first had done.

They lay tangled on the ground for a second in almost total disbelief, but quickly rolled apart - Sir Morgan fighting for breath, the dagger deep in his back, and the Duke of Man clutching both chubby hands to his podgy left thigh, which was bleeding profusely from where the bullet had struck.

In a bound Sir Francis Drake had crossed the floor and was diving for the fallen gun. Hitoadie lunged pathetically in an attempt to retrieve it but Drake stamped on his fat fingers as he stretched for it, and having snatched it up, he stood covering the traitors with the firearm, to the rapturous applause of the Council Members and assembled press alike.

Arthur strode forward to collect his dagger, and as he passed Brendan he clapped him on the shoulder. The King spoke a few sincere words of Latin and Julian Finch, now on his feet but sweating as he held his wounded shoulder tight with his good hand, translated for him.

"He says that was well done indeed, that you showed great courage and that he is very proud of you." Brendan blushed. "He says you are worthy to be numbered amongst his war band, Brendan; he values skill of tongue as well as skill at arms."

With a jerk and a squeal King Arthur withdrew his dagger from Morgan Dredmor's back, and unceremoniously he wiped the blade clean on the traitor's shoulder.

"R'n goch ddraig ewyllysia ca 'i ddiwrnod,"Arthur bellowed in triumph, and Jess flung her arms around him as he repeated the words again in Latin. "Rutilus extraho mos have suus dics."

"And so it has," Drake translated. "The red dragon, so spake the King, hath had its day," he smiled as he turned to the teenagers. "'Twas skilfully played out, Master Brendan, an' thou makest a fine pair, for 'twas pon a groat didst thee an' Mistress Jessica turn our fortunes to the wind. Shouldst thou crew together hereafter, for canst I see thou couldst weather any storm through wedlock."

"That was brilliant, Brendan," Jess spoke quietly in her classmate's ear. "You're my hero."

"Oh Jess," he turned to her modestly, "it never would have worked if you hadn't..." But he never got to finish the sentence. As she kissed him he blushed again, and then they embraced.

"Indeed, it was well done, Mr Finch." The Prime Minister shook Julian's good hand to a standing ovation. "I think not just Britain but the whole of Europe owes you a huge debt of gratitude, and your daughter and her friends too."

Julian winced, but smiled through the pain. He was losing blood and felt weak, but the sense of relief overwhelmed him and numbed the injury in his shoulder.

"You, you idiot!" Sir Morgan Dredmor, clammy, deathly pale, and gasping for breath, looked up from where he lay at his sweating, puffing colleague who sat gripping his leg less than a yard from him.

"Me, an idiot!" the Duke protested. "Yer shot me, Morgan, you of all people, I thought I could trust..."

"Ah!" Sir Morgan thumped the ground in rage. "Trust...!"

"Well, what now?" The Prime Minister turned to Julian. "What next? I mean, obviously they've been disarmed and everything, but did we pass the Act or didn't we? Who holds the power?"

"Why, Finch, did yer not listen to us?" Hitoadie interrupted from the floor. "I tell yer the Council passed the Act damn yer. The power is ours, the Act legally binding," he bellowed. "You shall pay for this, yer shall all..."

"They didn't pass it," Brendan persisted. "Only half of them signed."

"Ah," a wide grin of victory spread across the face of the bulky Commissioner. Blood pumped from his thigh but victory twinkled in his eye, and looking buoyed by certainty he straightened himself up as he declared, triumphantly, "It's really perfectly simple, old bean, what! Qualified Majority, do yer see?"

A groan of horror rose as all the Councillors present realised the truth of his words.

"Of course," Julian slapped his forehead with his good hand, "how could I be so stupid? How could I have forgotten...? Qualified majority," he spoke almost under his breath, "but, of course, you knew all along that the Act was passed."

"We told you," Sir Morgan lifted himself onto his elbows and gritted his teeth as he spoke through his own agony. "We told you right at the start that you were too late."

There were a sudden series of mighty crashes from the rear of the chamber, and through the assembled press, which parted for him, strode a large and imposing man with a huge red beard.

He carried a sword in his hand and wore chain mail and a shiny battle helmet, and behind him came two other equally strange looking intruders moving together. Both, likewise, wore chain mail. One was taller still than the first male with a shock of fair hair and paced loftily, as the other, short and stocky, scurried alongside him trying to keep up. Bearded like the first man, he wore a Norse-style battle helmet and gripped a heavy battle-axe with both hands. He breathed heavily after the exertion of using it to smash through the heavy chamber doors.

Behind the trio filed a number of others, most in Dark Age and medieval attire, and once the red haired man had positioned himself towards the centre of the chamber and the background noise subsided for order to be restored, he started to rant in a guttural tongue which Jess could neither understand nor place. She could see that his beard ended abruptly about halfway down his chest, square-cut rather than tapering to a point, and that all the new arrivals had the bearing of heroes as all seemed almost larger than life.

"Ask him if he speaks Latin, Sir Francis," Jess suggested, and Drake did so.

The newcomer confirmed that he did, and having established communication and identified the usefulness of the old language once more, Drake was able to translate to the room as the dominating new arrival spoke.

"Spake he that he be Fredrick Barbarossa, late o' the Kyffhauser mountains. That there be now no ravens t' circle o'er his place o' rest, an' that for fear that his people be now in peril hast he arisen."

The German Chancellor stood wide-eyed as the Elizabethan sea captain translated the announcement, and he in turn heard the revelation translated via his own earpiece; for whilst over the centuries Arthur's legend had lived on in the minds of the British people, so too had this man before him slept in the psyche of the German volk.

"Sayst he that 'twas in haste didst he arise an' 'twas on account o' his beard that he were not here yet a while sooner," Drake continued.

"His beard?" Jess didn't understand, but once the broad-shouldered, red-haired newcomer had conversed with Drake a little longer, all was revealed.

"Quoth he that hast he lain in sleep at table for many an age, an' that o'er that time hast his beard an' table joined as one. So inter-twined, couldst not he make wi' all speed, an' like to a horse who must be free o' his cart t' make up time, didst he cleave his beard free wi' the edge o' his sword. An' here stands he now t' defy those who wouldst threaten his people."

The members of the Council turned to each other again and the murmurs rose to excitable levels, as through Drake, Barbarossa introduced his companions.

"This here be none other than the Frankish King Charlemagne, 'the Quint', vanquisher o' Saracen an' Saxon alike." The tall fair-haired man bowed in recognition, as to gasps his presence was announced to the room. "Now be he bound in friendship wi' Barbarossa, an' were they well met 'pon the road unto this chamber.

"Hence stands Holger Danske, who wi' strong arm an' stout axe didst cleave for these passage through yon doors." Drake identified the short, stocky man in the Norse helmet. "Be he now reunited for battle wi' Charlemagne an' seekst he now vengeance 'pon those who wouldst betray his lands."

"And who are these others with them?" The Prime Minister could make little sense of what was going on, as one by one the new arrivals stepped forward.

In answer, Barbarossa, acting as spokesman, pointed out each in turn and through Drake, each was introduced.

"Tell, Master William o' the Alps." A man in light armour and carrying a crossbow on his shoulder raised his hat to the Council.

"Matthias Corvinus o' the Magyar plains." A heavily-armoured knight raised his visor to survey the room.

"Olaf Tryggvason, Viking o' Norway, an' King Sebastian o' Portugal." The Norwegian King of the dark ages and the Portuguese hero, who wore clothes similar to those of Drake himself, both stepped forward to be acknowledged. "An' these twelve clad in radiant armour be knights o' Allaberg." The Swedish knights stood together in a powerful phalanx, their gold and silver armour sparkling under the light.

"An' this be the Welsh traitor, Owain Glyndwyr, who wouldst wreak havoc pon the merrie folk o' middle England," Drake announced a neatly presented light-armoured squire less fondly. "Thou, Sirrah, hath been in flight o' justice too long, hast though not been in sleep but in hiding from thy rightful Masters."

But the latest newcomer, ignoring the Elizabethan, was imploring Arthur in the King's own native language.

"They say you are Arthur, and now, Arthur, can we two be rid of our foes at last, united can we drive the cursed English from our lands. You may know nothing of our plight, but we, your ancient people, were enslaved by the English and groaned in our bondage. We took the fight to them, but the flux and famine destroyed us, now together can we…"

"No," Arthur replied, "Britain is a land of united people's now. All this have I seen, and we are stronger for it…"

"Justice shouldst be done unto these for wrongs past, as to these Commissioners whose wrongs Finch hath righted," Drake interrupted them in Latin.

"No Sir Francis," Arthur reverted to Latin himself. "We must stand united against those who would threaten our future, not engage in squabbles of the past.

"We are all warriors and sought in our time to settle grievances of our own age, most brought on our generations by those who preceded us. Likewise, how many of us will not have been blamed by our foes' descendents for the hardships we wrought on their forefathers? As one tribe smite another, so will the other seek vengeance for the shame of defeat which their bards cannot bare. Victory lives long in song but defeat festers longer in the mind."

"Arthur speaks wisely, Sir Francis," Julian Finch interrupted, and both Glyndwyr and Drake hung on every Latin word. "Reconciliation for the past is the first step to peace. He would make a great statesman in any age, I'm sure Nelson Mandela would agree..."

"Nelson Man...?"

"Oh I'm sorry, you won't understand such contempory politics, but the point is the same, Arthur speaks true. He really is a ruler of sound judgment, the ruler of legend."

"The good of the whole of Europe is at stake," Arthur continued. "We must leave the past behind and think to the future. No doubt we could all be blamed for one wrong or another in the present which in the past seemed right, yet we have a chance now to unite and secure that future from the Commission who would seize the sovereignty from every one of us. Trust me, I have seen it, we are a nation of many peoples now, we must have peace and we must act in the interests of them all... I realised that on the train."

"What's a train?" Glyndwyr, who had also had a command of Latin and now also reverted to it, looked confused.

"Oh it's a wonder indeed, I'll explain later..."

"So sorry to interrupt your little mother's meeting," the Duke of Man attempted, mocking laughter, but it was unconvincing. "What is this circus you parade before us, eh? You'll produce Fionn McCool next, or giants ter tell me there are yet men left on the Isle of Man! It's preposterous, what!"

"You know full well who these are and why they're here," Julian Finch rebuked the Duke. "They're all heroes of history, every one a legend destined to return. They've slept long, but have returned each in their own people's hour of need to be rid of those who would rob their descendants of freedom. They may not understand the world they find themselves in nor the road their people have travelled through history while they have lain asleep, but they are here to prevent this coup so they can return to sleep once more."

"Spake Barbarossa," Drake continued, "that their road hast been both long an' windy, yet were they drawn, united i' this purpose unto this very chamber. Every one o' this merrie band hast a tale o' endeavour t' tell."

"No doubt," Sir Morgan heaved on the ground in his agonised impatience, "but we do not have time to hear them all now, you idiot."

"This it then, I s'pose?" Hitoadie scoffed. "Not waiting for anyone else to arrive? No one else wanting ter kill us? Eh!"

"Pon the word o' Barbarossa, this building be now besieged by King Wenceslaus an' his knights o' Bohemia," Drake assured him. "They be so encamped wi' knights o' Giewont an' number many hundred strong. Spake Barbarossa, were but this chamber a little larger, so too wouldst they even now be upon this treacherous pair an' smiting them wi' weapons which hath too long lain in restless peace."

"Why should you be so surprised to see so many of these heroes of Europe?" Julian asked them. "All are subject to legends that they will return when needed, and you and your fellow Commissioners are threatening to take power Europe-wide. It's only a shame their own nation's Commissioners are not also here to answer to them as you are to us. I can see from the assembled Council that they too wish their own Commissioners were here..."

"If you are quite finished," Sir Morgan interrupted, through gasps of breath. He had manoeuvred himself onto his left side, propping his head up on his elbow to support himself sufficiently to take in the entire scene, and from the look in his eye all could see his agony was marred with victorious ecstasy. "If your publicity stunt is quite finished, Finch, can we now return to the question of Qualified Majority...?

"As we have told you, the day is won. Through Qualified Majority we have taken power, it matters not who you bring against us, we are in charge now... Take control, Dennis," he turned to the Duke. "I'm losing blood, I'm growing weak."

"You heard the man." The Duke took up the fight, clenching his teeth against the pain in his own leg. "We are the victors, sufficient votes were cast, the ballot may be incomplete but the Act is passed... Now, as your leaders we order you to disarm, all of you, and..." he paused trying to find the right words. "And, and, push orff," he blurted in frustration.

"He's right," Julian Finch conceded. "Damn it, but he's right."

"Course we're right." The Duke grew more and more impatient. "We told you that from the start, we told yer that yer were too late when yer first barged in here, what!" He turned to the room. "Now, as

367

your leaders, we order Doctors, Paramedics, an ambulance each... Oh, and a sandwich."

"How can you think of food," Sir Morgan began, "at a time like...?"

"In an Autocracy a flatulent tyrant like myself can think of anything I darn well choose, Morgan; now, will yer stop bleeding on me shoes."

"What is Qualified Majority, Dad?" Jessica Finch asked her father, and as Julian replied it was King Arthur's turn to ask Drake to translate for him.

"Well, Jess, when it comes to European Council voting some countries get more votes than others."

"Well, that's not fair."

"It's meant to be more fair, Jess. That's the whole point. It comes down to all sorts of factors; economic strength, population density, the major players if you like. The Council members who represent a significant proportion of those who will be affected by the legislation, get more say than the more minor nations who only get one vote each because they have smaller populations and contribute less."

"So the bigger the country, the more votes it gets?"

"Basically, yes. The countries with the smallest populations, if you like the smallest nations in the European Union, get one vote, others two, and the largest, the biggest industrial founding powers, get four votes each."

"So, yer see, it's a simple matter of mathematics, eh!" Huffing and puffing, the Duke of Man pulled himself to his feet, and limped painfully over to the desk at which the EEA had been signed.

He leaned against it as conqueror, though his breathing was heavy as he winced at the wound in his thigh.

"Yer may have half the Council who have signed it, young man, and half who have not," he spoke down at Brendan, "but counting people will get yer nowhere. What yer must do is work out how many votes yer have standing over there," he pointed to the standing group of Council Members who had already signed, "and take away the potential votes of those who still remain seated, eh! It don't make pleasant calculations ter you, what!"

"So we should have counted votes, not Council Members," Jess was stunned. "But there must be several with more than one vote left to sign. The French President hasn't signed yet, nor the Greek or Italian Councillors; they're all still sitting, and I bet they've all got more than one vote."

"Indeed they may," the Duke conceded, "but alas, too many of the big hitters have signed." He grinned like the toad he was, gloating to the whole room. "All about the seating plan, me dear, very important ter get yer batting order organised right, eh! The British... sorry, I'll correct myself," - he was enjoying the moment - "ex-British Prime Minister's votes were the crucial ones, his four votes carried the motion, what!"

"And you knew from before they even started signing that once he had signed you would have your majority." Julian looked disgusted.

"Of course," the Duke beamed, "Morgan and I wanted ter be pinpoint sure of when our victory had come, makes victory all the sweeter when yer can literally watch it coming, count down to it so ter speak, what! A nice touch that, Morgan old boy, making sure it was our own PM in the hot seat, having him be the one to hand over the European reins an..."

"You really are the most insufferable pig." The British Prime Minister was on his feet now, and stood toe to toe with the fat Commissioner, "I don't know how you dare speak of your devious and despicable methods so proudly - there must be some way to..."

"Oh I prefer the word cunning, if you don't mind," the now pale-faced Sir Morgan interrupted from the floor. "We did tell you from the start it was all academic, Finch," he leered at Julian as he spoke in tones of the deepest sarcasm. "But thank you for breaking the news of our little coup so dramatically, thank you for explaining it all so well."

"Wait a moment." The Prime Minister's eyes widened as thoughts of a challenge came into his head. "You've left a loophole in all this, a gaping great loophole." And the rest of the Council hung on his words in the hopes that he was right.

The cameras of the massed European Press and Media turned on the British Premier; could the man whose pen strokes had lost Europe now win it back?

"All the safeguards have been dispensed with, save one," he continued excitedly. "You have forgotten, you fat fool, that the Council retains the right to dismiss the Commission." He turned to appeal to his fellows. "All we need do is dismiss the Commission as a whole and these two traitors and their friends will be sacked into obscurity... All those in favour," he shouted, and the whole chamber erupted with cheers once again as the Council Members, believing their jobs and their countries safe and secure once more, slapped each other on the back and shook hands with relieved smiles.

The Duke of Man, looking utterly unflustered, raised his hand slowly for quiet and gradually the elation subsided.

"A brilliant thought," he conceded, "quite, quite brilliant Prime

Minister, I commend you for it," he began generously, "but I'm afraid it's brilliantly flawed.

"Yer see, when yer signed this document yer handed power over to us. This document is in effect yer resignations, and as we have at last established, the Commissioners are now their countries' leaders.

"From the time the Act was passed you all lost yer privileges as Heads of State, yer can no longer represent yer nations in this Council, and yer no longer have the power nor the authority ter dismiss us, eh, what!" Groans of despair rose around the chamber once more as the assembled Council realised that, too their horror, he was indeed correct.

"God bless bureaucracy," the Duke concluded, "it's so wonderfully, ambiguously, confusing."

"Now hath I stood to hear enough," Sir Francis Drake shouted the room to silence. "Mine human heart canst withstand no more, must we be rid o' these treacherous scheming dogs." He aimed the pistol at the Duke's forehead. "A pox upon thy heaving gut in hell."

"No, Sir Francis," King Arthur bid him stop in broken English, and the whole chamber now harkened to him as the ancient King began to speak.

His tone was regal, his voice steady. The language he spoke was Latin, and although many of the other, seemingly resurrected legends, could understand the speech, Julian Finch translated as he spoke into modern English so the whole room, through the wonders of the earpiece translation, could share in Arthur's words.

"The King says that though he believed he had returned to fight a war of swords he sees now that he must fight a battle with words, one last furious battle to save his people. The King says this is a battle he is well capable of fighting; Merlin trained him well, and he will acquit himself with honour. The King says he is privileged to stand amongst the leaders of nations, past and present, that he has heard all the arguments, and now will he speak his judgement as he did of old."

"Bah!" The Duke of Man heckled dismissively. "I think politics have advanced a little since..."

"The King says he is the true King of Britain," Julian continued to translate, and as Arthur spoke he raised his left hand for all to see the ring, and with his right indicated the twisted golden band at his neck. "So he calls you all to witness his marks of Kingship, the signet ring of the Governor of Britain on which the seal of Rome is mounted as a sign of authority, and the torc at his throat, the ancient crown of his people, the mark of a chieftain."

The pride in Arthur's voice was tangible as he spoke, yet he spoke humble words for Julian to translate to the eager audience.

"He says these great things are entrusted to him by the British people, and that likewise he is pledged to them as both their protector and their Lord; thus does he count himself honoured in service to his folk. The King says he speaks for all his people as this is his privilege, and that yet is he privileged to be their speaker."

"Will yer stop waffling on?" The Duke of Man was getting nervous. "Load of old clap-trap, what does he know of democracy, he who lived by the sword?"

"No one understands democracy better than Arthur," Jess Finch shouted back at him. "The whole concept of the round table is that everyone is equal, everyone gets a say and no one sits higher than another."

"The King says," Julian continued his translation in a raised voice undeterred, "that he has never given up his throne but has merely lain in rest. He says he reigns still and that he has not cast his vote, that he, as King, as ruler and representative of his people, has not signed this document, that his seal of Britain has not been added to it, nor will it be.

The King reminds you all that he was present in this room as the Prime Minister signed, yet that as he was present it was not the Prime Minister's place but his own to speak and act for the Britons. He says that as he has not placed his mark upon this Act it cannot be considered passed, it cannot be considered law and it cannot bind his people."

A huge cheer rang out, first from amongst the other heroes of legend present who understood the Latin of Arthur's original, and then from the Council Members as their translation of Julian's words caught up; for they all knew that if the British were not bound by the EEA it was not passed and that their own nations were, likewise, freed.

Drake and Barbarossa took up the shout, and very quickly chants of "Artos Rex," echoed around the chamber, drowning the protests of the desperate Commissioners as King Arthur, looking tired but every bit his country's champion, picked up the European Environmental Act in two stocky palms. He shouted his last words with passion, yet waited for Julian's reliable translation before he finished the matter with action.

"The Kings says, the King declares, that it is for this that he has rested all these years." Julian shouted Arthur's words with all the vigour that Arthur himself had shouted them, and Julian could feel the pressure of his beating heart within his chest as King Arthur simply tore the EEA in half, demonstrating through this basic act of defiance the total finality of his argument.

The cheers rose to the rafters, and Arthur threw the torn document to the floor, where heroes past and Councillors present set about it ripping its pages out and to pieces, all seizing for scraps which they might reduce further in their desperation to have a part in its total destruction as a physical artefact, a concept, and a threat to freedom.

"Carry them away," Julian Finch directed attending police and paramedics who had moved in to deal with the two fallen Commissioners, as the television stations announced the end of the stand-off. "Treat them well and heal their wounds; they must be fit to stand trial for treason."

As Drake and Arthur embraced her family on the screen in front of her, and as they, Julian, Brendan and Jess were hoisted onto the shoulders of Charlemagne, Barbarossa and a host of national leaders, Patricia Finch danced round her empty sitting room, her hand clenched in the air victorious, as she too joined those in the chamber in their chant of "Artos Rex."

"Woo-hoo! Get in there," she shouted at the sleeping Benji in such total relief. Unsure how one should properly join in the celebration of millions she really let herself go, and in what was almost a parody of her son watching the football, she bounced off the sofa with whoops of delight.

The enormity of what she had witnessed might take a little time to sink in, but she knew that none of it would have been possible were it not for her husband, son and daughter, and while the rest of Europe cheered the return of legends, she yearned for her own hero's safe homecoming.

As the telephone rang, impatiently displaying Mrs Johnson's home number, Patricia Finch tried to compose herself, and in the Great Hall at Buckland Abbey an old drum rumbled out a jubilant victory roll.

Chapter Twenty One – Fond Farewells

The remaining weeks of Maxwell and Jessica Finch's summer holiday were like no other. They had been hectic, a roller-coaster ride of press conferences, talk shows and celebrity appearances at numerous functions.

From a Downing Street reception, where their recovering father had been offered one of the newly vacant European Commissioner's posts by a grateful Prime Minister, the family, King Arthur and Sir Francis Drake, Brendan, Rhys and Rhiannon had been conveyed by limousine to Buckingham Palace to meet the Queen, so that she too could offer her personal thanks for all they had done.

Her Majesty had greeted them warmly, and to the delight of Sir Francis, once more within the Royal Court, she had no hesitation in bestowing knighthoods on them all. King Arthur, in a display of mutual respect and generosity, had risen, taken the sword with which the Queen had knighted him, and had immediately knighted the reigning monarch himself in return. He'd then removed the ancient chieftain's torc of twisted gold from around his neck and presented it to her with all the reverence of a crown. It had sat a little more loosely on her shoulders once he'd placed it upon her, and as he had done so he'd announced that this act bound all Britons past and present to the monarch, and the Queen and her descendants to her people for ever.

The old warrior and the reigning monarch had sat in each other's presence as equals, and with a somewhat overwhelmed Rhys Jenkins acting as interpreter, they'd spoken long into the night of their country's future.

Yet, while the nation had been grateful, their school friends had become irrepressible as the weeks went by, all seeking a piece of them and a chance to share in their newfound notoriety. It seemed to the twins that they had an endless stream of teenaged visitors fighting their way through the hordes of photographers and newspaper reporters that camped outside their house day and night, waiting to erupt in a storm of camera flashes and questions every time one of them so much as appeared at the window. Abi Saunders clung to Max like a bad smell; she followed him around and giggled in a completely over the top way whenever he said anything, whether it was remotely funny or not, much to the annoyance of his sister. The boys hassled Max too, all hoping for a chance to meet Drake and Arthur, and even Brendan Johnson, the unlikeliest of heroes, found himself the subject of most of his female classmates admiration, if not adoration.

King Arthur did his best to avoid the journalists, for he quickly became tired of the fickleness of his modern public and the hysteria which determined he couldn't even take Benji for a walk without being surrounded by autograph hunters. Unhappily, he found himself spending most of his time holed up inside, and tried to use it purposefully by getting Jess to teach him modern English.

Even Sir Francis, who on his return to Britain had longed to recapture the fame he had once enjoyed, now found the demands of modern celebrity status truly exhausting. He often grumbled to Julian that people weren't interested in important things and instead seemed fixated on the trivial. What he wore seemed to excite them more than what he said, and deep down in his heart he felt unsettled. His old drum had been returned to him, and though his work was done, in his bones he longed for adventure.

The rest of the Commissioners were rounded up one by one across Europe, and though some had gone to great lengths to try and escape, they were all eventually imprisoned. The remaining question was whether they should stand trial in their own individual countries or all together before the European Courts which they had tried to de-power. Julian Finch, who'd thought long and hard before refusing the Commissioners job offered him, felt enormously wearied by the whole business and the new pressures on his family.

As the last weekend of the children's summer holiday approached and the comparative normality of a new term at school beckoned, Julian booked a cottage in the remoteness of Pembrokeshire down on the West Wales coast, which was big enough to accommodate all those who'd taken part in the adventure. He hoped that together they might be able to find a little peace and quiet, and that perhaps they might be able to discuss, without outside influence, what was next for Drake, Arthur and the Finch family.

They talked, they walked together on the beach, and tried to forget the media hype which now threatened to drive them all insane. They joked together, Drake giving Rhys his pearl earring as a gift to the friend who'd brought him into the adventure in the first place, and Rhys, who had once declined it as payment for a lift from an eccentric hitchhiker, was delighted, this time, to accept.

Patricia Finch's face was a picture of horror as Drake placed it straight into Rhys' ear lobe, as, much to the amusement of all the others, she was the only one who hadn't realised her nephew's ear was already pierced, and almost fainted in the belief that the Admiral had driven the antique piece of jewellery straight through his ear by brute force.

Max, Jess and Rhiannon too, had laughed long and loud at Rhys' own pained expression in turn when Drake asked him for a cigarette in front of his disapproving aunt.

"I don't smoke, Sir Francis," he'd lied, but had then gone beetroot red under Patricia's accusative stare as Drake replied, "Aye, but thou doest, Sir Rhys, for thou hast 'em even now in concealment 'pon thy person lest thy aunt, Lady Finch, rebuke thee."

That night they ate fish and chips, a newfound Arthurian favourite, in the solitude of the cottage, and as the dusk fell and the sun began to disappear over the sea Julian and Patricia shared a bottle of wine with Rhys and Rhiannon as they sat playing cards.

The King led them down to the deserted beach where the Elizabethan Admiral was waiting. Drake was busying himself making the final preparations to a small sailing boat, and declining to shout and draw attention to himself as they approached, he instead held up an arm in silent greeting.

"What's going on?" Max asked, noticing Drake's drum packed in at the front of the little craft. "You're not leaving, you can't."

"We must, Max," Arthur replied sombrely, showing his new command of the modern English language.

"We hath fulfilled our quest an' must now return unto legend," Drake smiled from the boat.

"B-but, you can't," Max protested. "Your place is here with us, there is so much left to do, so many..."

"Our time has been and gone." Arthur laid a calming hand on his shoulder. "This Britain is ours no longer."

"The King an' I hath sat long in counsel," Drake spoke quietly, "an' in this be we two decided. We canst not sit idle an' speakst o' deeds, nor canst we sit for ever in splendour as prisoners t' praise o' glories past.

"Spake I, whilst still the spirit o' adventure beats within mine breast an' mine feet tire wi' rest, wilt I seek t' tame mineself wi' endeavour.

"Spake the King unto me, that he too doeth thirst for action, adventure, be it to lead t' a gateway unto the past or unto a new quest in a land far off. For, spake he, shall he else rot in the present, an' grow fat on the indulgence o' this prosperous an' peaceful time."

"I see that you must go," said Brendan sadly, "though none of us want you to. It's right that you just go quietly, just as you arrived."

"Thou speakst wi' wisdom, Sir Brendan." Drake stepped from the boat and shook his hand. "Mind now, Mistress Jessica, for she and thou be well-matched." He kissed Jess on the hand and bowed low before her.

"Thy Servant, my Lady," he declared, "and it shalt fall on thee, who drummed me homeward, to impart mine thanks an' farewells upon thy kinsfolk. Thy father, Sir Julian, is a man o' steel, an' hath he within his bosom a heart o' gold. To thy mother there is none fairer, an' by her hearth didst we find welcome. Her memory shalt dwell wi' us, an' for this didst the King name our craft Patricia."

"I'll miss you." Jess felt choked, she could feel the tears welling in her eyes. For all her resentment of his impertinent arrogance, she had really warmed to Sir Francis.

"Fare thee well, Master Mariner," Drake shook Max by the hand, "thou hast mine blessings for all the seas thou hast to sail ahead o' thee. Yet by the bard's beard, Sir Maxwell, I knowst, an' quoth true, thou art well prepared t' sail 'em."

"Wait, I'll come with you." Max stepped forward, hoping to follow Drake into the boat.

But Arthur stepped in front of him, and with a steady, stocky hand he held him back.

"We belong in the past, Max; where we go, you cannot follow. This country is ours no longer, but its future belongs to you." With a smile he handed Max his dagger, and Max felt the full pain of the King's parting as he grasped it by the handle.

"I entrust Carnwennau to you; bear him well in my memory. My friend, Max," the King exclaimed as Max embraced him, tears in his eyes. "I regret I ever frightened you."

"I shall make you proud, my King, my friend." Max blew his nose noisily and tried to be strong.

"The ring of Britain," the King announced to Jess and Brendan, and as both began to kneel in preparation to kiss it one last time, he bid them stop.

"No, no one has done more to preserve the sovereignty of this Isle. You should never bow to kiss it, nor to pay homage to the wearer. You have done me great honour, and in turn I honour you," he said, slipping the heavy gold signet ring off his finger. "I give it into your keeping." Brendan and Jess exchanged confused glances as Arthur placed the ring in Jess' palm, and having closed her fist, he wrapped Brendan's hand around hers. "Never speak of it, but keep it safe - it represents the freedom of this people."

"But surely..." Jess began to protest, but the King silenced her.

"Keep it for me," Arthur smiled, "I may have need of it again. Keep it for me until next I return."

"You will come back?" Jess spoke as much in hope as in disbelief.

376

"Maybe, if God wills it and the nation has need again of my old bones. I am now the twice and future King, then, am I not!" He hugged them both, and having splashed and heaved as he pushed the craft into the surf, he nearly tipped it up as he joined Drake in the boat.

"Be thee King or no, thou hast no sea legs and wilt know that I be Captain 'pon this ship, Patricia Fair," Drake spoke sternly to his new crew mate.

"It should be plain sailing then, so long as you sail as well as you talk of sailing," Arthur grinned back at the teenagers on the beach. "Be it otherwise, there will be mutiny."

Drake had produced an oar, which he'd held like a punting pole to hold the boat from being washed back to shore in the surf as Arthur jumped aboard, and now he was safely inside, Drake quickly dug the other from the bottom of the boat. Having seated himself, he cradled them, and with skill and speed he rowed hard and steady, bringing the boat over the gentle breakers and out onto the deeper water beyond.

"Where will you go?" Brendan called after them.

"The new world, the Indies," Drake replied, holding the boat steady just beyond the waves about fifteen yards from the shore, "for t' seekst out the lost colony o' Raleigh."

"America!" Brendan laughed. "You're going to America in search of a quiet life, to get away from all this attention!"

"'Tis a land much uncharted," Drake called back, "all but unsettled. It be mostly forested, uncultivated, there may be found natives o' so savage a disposition that only Admiral Drake wilt be able t' harness em'."

"You may be right there," Brendan joked, and he whispered aside to Jess, "They're mad, totally doolally, and they're also in for a shock."

"Shalt we on arrival be not Drake an' Arthur, but Don Alfredo an' Master Richard o' Lancaster who shalt put 'emselves ashore."

"A new life in America," Brendan waved after them as Jess took his hand. "I don't think anyone's ever thought of that, Sir Francis."

"I still say we'll fall off the edge of the world," Arthur waved to them, but his words caused Drake great annoyance.

"Thou hast forgotten, o' King, that thou sailst wi' one who hast circled the globe." He puffed out his chest with arrogant pride, but the thrill of the sea beneath his feet filled him with excitement and he couldn't keep still. "Sound thee my drum," he ordered, "for we must away."

As King Arthur tapped out a slow rhythm on the old Elizabethan drum, Drake pulled on the oars once more and took them slowly out to sea.

377

"Where did you get the boat, Sir Francis?" Jess called after them.

"'Tis but small matter o' thanks," Drake shouted back, "but thinkst I the people o' Britain shalt not begrudge mineself an' their King this humble vessel."

"You stole it, then."

"In a manner o' speaking."

"You are a pirate still," she shouted back, and as she and Brendan, hand in hand, waved them off, her brother Max yelled out to the rower and his mate.

"God speed you, from the present to the past."

"'Tis to the past we return wi' the help o' the present," Drake bellowed from a distance, and satisfied that he was now in deep enough water, and far enough from the shore, he grinned impishly to himself, leaned down into the boat, and produced an outboard motor.

He licked his lips in anticipation, and with a glint in his eye he pulled the cord. The engine roared to life, deafening the sound of the old drum, and immediately began pulling them out to sea, towards the west and into the setting sun.

In just a few moments they were a speck on the horizon in the shimmering red distance, and in under two minutes they were out of sight completely, lost in the gathering gloom.

In silence, Brendan, Jess and Max filed back to the cottage to give the others the news. Sad as they were to see the heroes go, they felt a sense of relief and a warm feeling inside.

And did Don Alfredo and Master Richard of Lancaster ever reach the distant land they sought? We'll never know, but 'Patricia Fair,' the boat in which King Arthur and Sir Francis Drake sailed towards America, was caught in a violent storm, was blown off-course, and entered the Bermuda triangle about tea-time on a Wednesday.

.

Lightning Source UK Ltd.
Milton Keynes UK
UKOW041926071212

203344UK00003B/414/P